The Echo Chamber

The Echo Chamber

LUKE WILLIAMS

VIKING

VIKING
Published by the Penguin Group
Penguin Group (USA) Inc., 375 Hudson Street,
New York, New York 10014, U.S.A.
Penguin Group (Canada), 90 Eglinton Avenue East, Suite 700,
Toronto, Ontario, Canada M4P 2Y3
(a division of Pearson Penguin Canada Inc.)
Penguin Books Ltd, 80 Strand, London WC2R 0RL, England
Penguin Ireland, 25 St. Stephen's Green, Dublin 2, Ireland
(a division of Penguin Books Ltd)
Penguin Books Australia Ltd, 250 Camberwell Road, Camberwell,
Victoria 3124, Australia
(a division of Pearson Australia Group Pty Ltd)
Penguin Books India Pvt Ltd, 11 Community Centre, Panchsheel Park,
New Delhi – 110 017, India
Penguin Group (NZ), 67 Apollo Drive, Rosedale, Auckland 0632,
New Zealand (a division of Pearson New Zealand Ltd)
Penguin Books (South Africa) (Pty) Ltd, 24 Sturdee Avenue,
Rosebank, Johannesburg 2196, South Africa

Penguin Books Ltd, Registered Offices:
80 Strand, London WC2R 0RL, England

First American edition
Published in 2011 by Viking Penguin,
a member of Penguin Group (USA) Inc.

1   3   5   7   9   10   8   6   4   2

Copyright © Luke Williams, 2011
All rights reserved

Publisher's Note
This is a work of fiction. Names, characters, places, and incidents either are the product of the author's imagination or are used fictitiously, and any resemblance to actual persons, living or dead, business establishments, events, or locales is entirely coincidental.

LIBRARY OF CONGRESS CATALOGING IN PUBLICATION DATA

Williams, Luke.
The echo chamber : a novel / Luke Williams.
p. cm.
ISBN 978-0-670-02283-0
1. Exceptional children—Fiction. 2. Hearing—Fiction. 3. Nigeria—Fiction. 4. Psychological fiction. I. Title.
PR6123.I55255E35 2011
823'.92—dc22
2011004125

Printed in the United States of America

For Natasha

Contents

Contents

PART ONE

I

First Questions

Who are you?
  My name is Evie Steppman.

Where were you born?
  Children's Hospital, Lagos.

When?
  2 August 1946.

In any special circumstance?
  I was late.

How late?
  Two months.

Go on.
  I was not ready to emerge after the allotted time. Happy in the womb, free from worldly concerns and the rules of men, I felt no impulse to move on. I possessed the foetal licence – indeed, the prerogative – to gambol. Trembles met with, 'Do you feel him kick, dear?' or, 'Certainly a strong one.' Hands, ears and lips were pressed to my mother's stomach. 'It's like a factory in there,' joked my father, 'I can hear clattering machinery, a baby-construction works.' I delighted in my formlessness. Half-fish, half-girl – a mermaid – I rolled as if free from gravity. I luxuriated in the confusion. Such licensed disorder.

[*Pause.*]

How did your belated arrival affect your life?
  It killed my mother.

Yes?
  It caused my father to lose his faith in Progress.

Yes?
  It gave me the power of listening.

How so?
  In the evening, when each day's duty as District Officer was complete, my father crouched beside my mother and chattered to her swollen belly. Kneeling awkwardly on the hardwood veranda floor, his hands gripping the reclining chair upon which Mother lay, he read me Dickens and Darwin, the fairy tales of Oscar Wilde, *Typhoon* and *Treasure Island*. He recited Housman and the Lord's Prayer. I learned how the elephant got his trunk, the principles of Indirect Rule. We entered with El-Edrisi into distant lands where fantastic races lived. We accompanied Mungo Park north towards Timbuktu and, with Sir Frederick Lugard, sojourned at Lokaja. He discoursed on zoos and craniology. He talked of masks, of goblins, turning from myth to biology to Christmas. One evening, bent over Mother's stomach, as he attended to the names of the seven seas, in between the Indian and the Aegean, I punched him on the nose. Undeterred, he opened the Bible and recited the seven deadly sins. Then he told me of the colour-filled nights of Bruno Schulz. While I turned somersaults and figures-of-eight, Father worked through the volumes that informed his inconstant mind.

And perhaps it was the monotony of this persistent address (accompanied by the tick-tock of Father's pocket watch, which invariably slipped from its niche to rest – an inverse stethoscope – on Mother's belly) that bred in me the will to listen. He spoke in the most formal and stilted manner – as if I were a schoolboy – his voice loud and always earnest. Each history, novel, treatise sounded similar, and I found it hard to distinguish H. Rider Haggard from Aunt Phoene's letters, the Great Chain of Being from the Nocturama at Edinburgh Zoo.

Week after week he persisted with this schooling. I felt the discomfort of one who is compelled to sit through a long and awkward joke. Setting out to tell a story, which may have been a fine one, Father invariably failed. The world he brought me via my mother's stomach was vibrant, but devoid of nuance, a world in which every legend and report, every plot and character sounded alike.

How strange it was, then, to find, in the outside world contrast, division, *difference*. I knew that outside my mother a large territory existed. Six months into my gestation, my ears started to pick out sounds from the amorphous hum of Lagos. I recognized, for instance, the murmur of the sea. This was easy, since I grew in moon cycles. I perceived the sharp salute of gunfire and the chimes of Lagos clock, sounds I feared. Yet these scattered tones were engulfed in the coursing hum of blood, soothing to my ear, and by my father's nightly readings. It was much later that I perfected my art of listening.

[*Pause.*]

You dallied in the womb because you were afraid of the outside?
    I was comfy.

5

You were hungry for your father's knowledge?

I never wholly understood what he was talking about. Father was pedantic but erratic. A whim might catch him and take us on an alternate inquiry. He would abandon his station beside Mother and go cycling, returning days later only to begin elsewhere. Quite simply: my father rarely finished a single lesson. Just as he was reaching the high point of his recitation, his mind failed, and he wandered from the current theme, anxious to pursue the next.

Did you enjoy your father's readings?

They wearied me. He gave me lessons, and I wanted stories. But I listened. With frustration I listened. And as I did my ears began to develop. The more I heard, the greater my knowledge, and the keener my powers of listening became. My other senses had no time to refine themselves, for what can you see inside that dark chamber? The amniotic fluid – salty, viscous and vile – is the only flavour. And what to smell?

[*Pause.*]

Tell me about your powers of listening.

I am losing them. The sounds I once so clearly perceived are starting to merge; no longer can I distinguish, order and remember each noise. It is true, my hearing is still uncommonly acute. With effort I can pick out echoes of my childhood in Lagos: seated uncomfortably in my wicker swinging-basket, suspended above our immaculate lawn, which sloped towards the Lagoon, I hear the calls of Jankara market women, broadcasting the succulence of their goods with words I do not understand, so that amidst the commonality of staple foods – palm oil, tilapia, yams, groundnuts and spices – I fancy I hear entreaties to enter card games, river cruises, witch-hunts. The elephant grass at the edge of our garden obscures my view of Ade, our servant-boy, but I can hear him; he is making telephones from empty cans and lengths of string. In the distance the thud of leather striking wood tells me that Riley has scored another four. I hear teacups rattling, the sound of Father playing solitaire, clocks, footsteps, the bulb-horn of a goods lorry; listening harder, I hear the sound of the driver's forehead pressed against the windscreen, vibrating in time to the engine idling. In the harbour, below the mastheads, there is the clamour of men and derricks unloading soap, pots and pans, mail, saddles, a jukebox, an umbrella, tea, sugar, gin, boxes of cigars, rifles, tuxedos, steel, fireworks, brine, chocolate, camp-chairs and an elegant high-sprung dogcart made in Manchester. I hear the cries of merchant seamen and they commingle in my mind with older, less familiar voices; those of the first English explorers, the unfortunate men who not two hundred years ago sang the most sinister of sea shanties as they neared the Niger coast:

Beware and take care of the Bight of Benin
There's one comes out for forty goes in,

and those of the slaving ships, their silent crewmen, and the barely audible dirge of their living cargo.

Yet there are disturbing lapses in my audition. I find for instance I cannot play my favourite childhood game. During the hot hours after lunch, with Iffe at the market, I would slip from the onion stand to the streets of Lagos. I recall the brightness. The smell of sweating bodies, drying fish and open sewers. I would close my eyes. The street-sounds, I found, were intelligible – by my eighth year I could distinguish between the pitch of the Governor's Austin 12 Tourer and Oba Adeniji Adele's Mercedes – yet I detected other noises, new to my ears; noises that disturbed and delighted; noises that appeared to a maturing girl at once violent and inspired. Back home I would play out the drama of these stolen moments with my dolls. I had Red Riding Hood kiss Rupert Bear, my Victorian china doll grope with the Nigger Minstrel from America.

Still worse: I find I can no longer listen to others; as if now, in my middle years, I am turning into the vacant, fidgety child I never was. Where once I possessed the power to listen, I now squirm, empathize and feel compelled to interject. How different it was before I grew, developed like any child. I began to see, to touch, to smell and taste. But before it all I learned to listen. This, together with my gift for rapt attention, was a combination irresistible to the men and women of British Africa. The servants of Empire were a muddled bunch: second sons, bored wives, athletes, soldiers, clergy. They each had something to prove, to boast about . . . to confess. 'Why did you come to Africa?' – none knew precisely, but everyone had a story – 'How I got here? Well . . .' 'Those pesky clerks!' 'I love to shoot monkeys.'

And I, Evie Steppman, heard all their stories. I am the (until now silent) repository of the dreamers of Empire.

Why did you put up with it?
I found in these confessions the stories that were absent from my father's lessons.

[*Pause. A scurrying among the rafters.*]

It is these same stories that I am now forgetting.

What are you going to do?

I must write. Set down on paper. Faithfully record my past before it becomes tinnitus and is lost. But how dreary. How dim and unnatural words are! How distanced from the live thing, the unknown generous gentlemanly thing, the cutting and distorting yet strangely exact pitch of my child's hearing, are words. There are no words that can transcribe the vibrancy of my audition.

Reluctantly I write.

[*Pause. Silence. From which open quiet sea-sounds, dully, distantly, echoes of sea wrecks, surfpurl, tin-can music. Silence. Through which rasps a shrill whistle, a dog's bark. Silence. And now wakings of battles, seagulls, sirens.*]

Where are you?
  Gullane, East Scotland.

From where, exactly, are you writing?
  From the house that we – Father and I – moved to in 1961, after Nigeria became independent from British rule.

Tell me about this house.
  It is a two-storey house on the sea-front. I have confined myself to the ground floor, although lately I have made frequent trips to the attic, which I am attempting to clear out.

What is there to throw away?
  A machete, a Lord's lamp, railway timetables, a matchbox containing not a single match. There is a tin marked 'unica', a radio, piles of audio cassettes, pocket change, keys, mirrors, a rifle, a silver pocket watch with an absent minute hand. There is a cricket bat, a phonograph with its great horn, a family

9

photograph album, an elephant tusk, files, tacks, pencils, cigarette ash, paperclips, rubber bands, a bronze pendant from
Benin, several pairs of shoes, unanswered letters, an old purple
dressing-gown. Hanging by a single hook is a map of the world,
with gaps bitten from it. Books line the west-facing wall: histories,
novels, treatises, a set of *Encyclopaedia Britannica*, 1911. Domin-
ating the room are piles of papers, most my father's, some my
own. At one point, during his final months, my father bundled
them up, ready for burning. It was also at this time he became
infected with a debilitating lethargy, a sickness which seeded
from his having left Lagos, but which only now came to fruition.

Go on.

Back in Britain Father sank deeper and impenetrably into his
past. Spending more and more hours in the attic, listless with
false memories of a glorious career, he receded into the incon-
gruous corridors of history. During his top-floor retreat (he
descended only to pass water, and, latterly, not at all, making
use of a metal pail, which I would have to empty), he com-
plained of scratching noises – mice. Even now, writing these
words from my own place in the attic, I can follow the sound
of tiny feet up beyond the ceiling, and across, left, right, to the
oak-wood walls; yes, the scratching is all about me, the mice
are in the attic, making homes among the discarded items.

But I tell too much.

Go on.

Let me tell you a story. When Sagoe was aged eight he saw
a sheep hanging in a butcher's window. Sagoe told his father
about it, because he was hungry and had not eaten meat in
months.

'Go, buy me the head of the sheep!' his father commanded.

Sagoe went to the butcher and bought the head. On the way home he ate the meat and returned with a skull.

'What have you brought me?' his father cried.

'It's a sheep's head,' Sagoe said.

'Where are the eyes?'

'The sheep was blind.'

'And where is the tongue?'

'The sheep was dumb.'

'And where are the ears?'

'The sheep was deaf.'

'Sagoe,' cried his father. But Sagoe had already run to the forest, leaving scorch marks on the dirt road.

Go on.

[Pause.]

Tell me more.

[Silence.]

You can't stop there.

[Pause. Silence. A winged insect thunders against the skylight.]

Listen: A woman, not young, sits at her makeshift desk; ponderously, with shaking hands – it is cold – she surveys the room; her eyes first rest on the keyboard of her computer, then rise to the skylight, taking in the darkening sky. She hears the noise of the traffic; slowly, eschewing the city-sounds below, she turns from the skylight, rubbing her palms together for warmth, and begins – where to begin? – to recount her history – which is really the history of herself and Ade and Iffe and Nikolas and Mr Rafferty and Babatundi the idiot boy and Riley's pointer and Mr and Mrs Honeyman and Damaris and Taiwo and her own father, as well as the impossibility of a mother who died in childbirth – and what to tell? – what is true, what was once true, what has been, might have been, what is? – and how to go about it? She asks herself a question – Who are you? – and another – Where were you born? – because this is what she knows best – at the outset, in the middle, she always asked questions; and here come the words, bit by bit; bit by bit the words form upon the page.

2

Pocket Watch or My Father Meets
a Stranger on a Train

A winged insect, possibly a crane fly, or a moth, thunders against the skylight. Now and then the beating stops and the creature spirals to the floor. In the renewed silence I return to my computer, ready to get started with these stories. But without warning the drumming starts up again, and I am aware of what was present all along. The attic is filled with noise: the buzz of streetlamps, the scratching of mice, fat drops of water running from the treetops and striking the roof. I hear the tick-tock of Father's pocket watch, car tyres on the street below indistinguishable from the surging of the sea.

Inspired by the din in the attic, the sounds of my past begin to rise to a clamour. The remnants of all I have heard, once clear but now shrill and indecipherable, are screeching in my ears, as though I have walked into an aviary. Father's lectures merge with the sustained babble of his dying days. My own history combines with legends of sailors and witches that were read out to me from books. City sounds – Lagos, Oxford, Edinburgh – are alike, so what I thought might be a childhood memory is really only a memory of last week.

How can I write amid this commotion? I have to find a way of controlling these voices no longer guided by the clock. When one's history is not governed by past, present or future, when every sound mimics another, one must order it by another principle.

Something closed must contain my memory. I will, then, enclose these stories within the tent-shaped margins of the attic; and the little I do let out – tales, lives, cities, monsters – will come by way of the attic; for all that will live, will live in the attic. The attic serves no function but to hoard all kinds of objects – not forgotten but buried, hidden at the top of the house; objects that are each decaying in their own way; objects that are still, meaningless and silent.

The only object that emits a sound is Father's pocket watch. It sits upon a pile of maps in the south-east corner of the attic. It has lain there since Father, in a fit of madness, snatched it from his breast pocket and threw it to the attic floor, only later placing it on the topmost map in the pile.

The watch has been well handled. The silver casing is tarnished black. A deep scratch on its underside, an even curve about one inch in length, obscures three words of an inscription, which reads:

> Could not our tempers move like this machine,
> Not _____ by passion nor delayed by spleen.
> And true to Nature's _____ power,
> By virtuous acts distinguish every _____

Embossed on the inner casing, below the Roman numeral VI, is the signature *Breguet et Fils*. The watch winds at the centre of the dial. The bezels and bow are gold. Originally a pair of tiny diamonds decorated the hands of the watch, although now both the minute hand and its jewel are missing. If I have made a special point of describing the pocket watch, leaving no doubt, I hope, that the minute hand is absent; if indeed I have gone so far as to call the whole chapter *Pocket Watch*, it is because I know how much I owe to it. After all, it was because of that decrepit piece of clockwork that my parents came together. Listen!

. . .

There was once a stranger, formerly a watchmaker, who would become a grandfather. He had an address but was never home. He spent his days in second-class compartments, his nights in sleeper cars or station-side hotels. And yet if you looked in the registers of these hotels, the Turnberry, the Great Eastern, the Laharna, the Caledonian, the Liverpool Adelphi or the Yarborough New Holland, you would not find his name but a hundred different names.

There was once a student who would become a father. He was travelling to Balliol College, Oxford, to train for the overseas civil service. His name was Rex Steppman, he had a scar on his chin, and he carried a pocket watch in his left breast pocket.

There was once a stranger, formerly a watchmaker, now a murderer, who would become a grandfather. He had a house in Oxford, where his daughter lived, but he himself was never there. He spent his days in second-class compartments, evading the law, and in one of these compartments, on the London and North Eastern line, he met a student with a scar on his chin, who would become a father, and who carried a pocket watch in his left breast pocket.

Once there was a second-class compartment on the London and North Eastern line. It had twin banks of seats, upholstered in umber. Looking in from the corridor, through the glass-panelled door, one would see it had a window with a pomelle frame, four lamps and marquetry depicting antelopes leaping between palm trees. Beneath the window was a radiator which filled the compartment with an infernal heat. On one particular day, an October morning in 1938, there was a single passenger in the compartment. It was the student. As the 10 o'clock to London Kings Cross heaved itself out of Edinburgh Waverley, he was reading an article entitled 'An Elephant's Sagacity' – the animal had been proceeding along a narrow road in the Punjab, towards a water pump, when she found her way blocked by an unconscious child. Seeing cars approaching, she swept the child up in her trunk, stepped to the roadside as the cavalcade passed, then gently laid the child on the verge and resumed her journey to the pump.

Suddenly, there was a commotion in the corridor. A squat man, dressed in a black suit, brogues, sable tie, with a Bombay Bowler pressed low over his brow, hurried through the corridor, banging his suitcases against the side of the carriage.

'I'm terribly sorry for the inconvenience!' the stranger said in an exaggerated English accent. He shouldered open the door and surveyed the compartment.

'May I . . .?' he said. 'You don't mind if . . .?' Without waiting for an answer he entered the compartment. The stranger had a round face, crow eyes and a thin-waxed moustache that seemed to point to ten-past-ten.

The train rolled slowly through the outskirts of the city. Restalrig ambled by, then the green hump of Duddingston Mains. The track curved left, and Leith Strand came into view, with the Firth of Forth beyond. The sky was vast and cloudless and the sunlight came and went.

'Let me introduce myself,' the stranger said, holding out his hand. 'My name is Julien Le Roy.'

'Rex Steppman,' said the student, shaking hands without standing up.

'A pleasure.' The stranger glanced suspiciously around the carriage then brought his lips to Rex's ear. 'What are you reading?'

'The newspaper.'

'. . . which is the very reason I intend to sit beside you! One *ought* to read the paper on the train. At least this is preferable to taking a window seat, since there's always the danger of looking at the scenery.'

The student said nothing.

'Don't you think?'

The train was gathering speed. Gardens and allotments rushed by, rubbish dumps, radio masts, and, at Joppa, a cluster of houses whose windows threw back a blistering, fragmented reflection of the sun. The line of buildings soon dispersed, and there were green fields and, beyond, the North Sea, broken here and there by tiny white crests.

The student removed his jacket and placed it across his legs. He twisted himself towards the window, hunched his shoulders and buried his head in the newspaper – now the elephant was performing pirouettes, creating a rumpus among crowds of British Indians; now she was fountaining water from her trunk; now producing ice-creams, as if from nowhere, and passing them to small children in the crowd –

The train followed the contours of the cliff top; the sea, indistinguishable from the horizon, was quivering, as if a thousand fish were turning on the surface. Blades of sunlight streamed mercilessly through the window – refracted, splintered – and crept towards the travellers. The stranger began to sing.

My heart is warm with the friends I make,
And better friends I'll not be knowing,
Yet there isn't a train I wouldn't take
No matter where it's going.

'A pretty tune, don't you think?' he said. 'But where was I . . . ah . . . one should never stare out of the window because the scenery – right at this moment there is a copse – don't look! – about a mile's worth passing by. It can make one's head spin.'

'But –'

'Better stick to your *Scotsman*.'

'That's what I am trying to do! But you are distracting me. Please, leave me in peace.'

'No need to raise your voice. I haven't introduced myself properly. My name is Sylvain Mairet –'

'That is the second name I have heard you use! First you introduced yourself as Julien Le Roy and now you say your name is Mairet.'

'I have more than one hundred names,' the stranger said. 'And what about you? I see you're studying at Oxford. Balliol – I'd recognize that crest anywhere.'

The student was taken aback.

'What are you studying?'

'I'm training for the civil service – overseas,' he said after a short time.

'And that is why you keep a pocket watch in your left breast pocket.'

The student placed his hand over the bulge in his jacket, then took the pocket watch out.

'Where did you get it?' asked the stranger.

'From my parents. On my twenty-first.'

'It's a pretty one.' The stranger took the watch and turned it in his hands. 'You are in company with one of the most illustrious travellers. Phileas Fogg made his journey keeping time with a Breguet.'

'Breguet?'

'Abraham-Louis. What was it that French fellow said? *Breguet makes a watch that never goes wrong for twenty years, and yet this wretched machine, the body we live with, goes wrong and brings aches and pains at least once a week.*' The stranger broke off the conversation and turned towards the window. A shadow fell over his face, as if the train had entered a tunnel. He gave the impression that he wanted to be alone. He stretched his arms out towards the ceiling in a curious way.

'Where are we?' he asked.

The sun had not yet reached its zenith when the 10 o'clock to Kings Cross approached Berwick. It was quiet in the compartment. But as the train curved past the town and over the Royal Border Bridge, with its high arches of black and earth-coloured brick, a soft whimpering could be heard. Berwick receded out of sight, and the train resumed its passage through the countryside. Sun-bleached fields stretched as far as the horizon.

When the stranger spoke again the shadow had lifted from his face.

'Let me tell you about Breguet. He was the greatest of all the eighteenth-century watchmakers! He cut a striking figure – tall, round face, scar under his left eye, bald as an egg-timer. From the age of fifteen Breguet studied with the famous watchmakers Berthoud and Lépine. But perhaps you know this already? No? I'll go on.

'By the time the French Revolution had begun, he had made his name with a number of important horological advances. He'd also joined the Jacobins. Following the beheading of Louis XVI, he was forced to escape from France. When he returned in 1795, he found that the Revolutionaries had started time all over again . . .'

'That's impossible,' interrupted the student.

'Not at all. The Revolutionaries threw out the Gregorian system and replaced it with the *calendrier républicain*. They proclaimed 1792 as year one of the new calendar. Weeks were ten days long, with three weeks per month. Days were divided into ten hours, each of a hundred minutes, and every minute contained a hundred seconds.'

'Time,' interrupted the student, pompously, 'is one straight line extending without end.'

'Don't believe that blockhead Locke. Where was I? . . . ah . . . the Revolution. French watchmakers produced clocks with ten hours. Not Breguet. He continued to make clocks according to the Gregorian system, which was re-established in 1806. He went on to invent the first carriage clock, the *montre à tacte*, which made it possible to tell the time by touch, the *tourbillon* regulator, and the finest military pedometers. Although he continued to labour into his antique years, Breguet lost the power of hearing. But he was never morose, which is the usual result of this malady.

'Your pocket watch is in good condition,' the stranger said, scrutinizing its face, 'although the minute hand is slightly rusty.'

The stranger took out a hip-flask and offered it to the student, who refused.

'I'm deviating. I realize I haven't answered your questions. When I entered the compartment I immediately noticed you were studying at Oxford. I knew I would have to speak to you about an important matter. You see, I have something for you . . . I have something that I wish for you to pass on. The person who should receive this article lives in Oxford. What is it? A letter!'

The train was belching clouds of black smoke. The wheels chattered unceasingly against the track. The stranger produced a packet of cigarettes, and the student accepted one.

'Before I entrust you with this letter, I ought to tell you about the situation in which I find myself. I've told no one before. I've had no reason to until now. But I need your help. You must promise on your honour that you won't tell a soul what I am about to say.' The stranger gave the student a searching look.

'That depends upon what you tell me. I can't promise when I know nothing about you.'

'I give my word,' said the stranger. 'Nothing of what I say will cause you harm or adversely affect you in any way.' The student hesitated. He took quick puffs from his cigarette. The train charged through a wooded incline, and light and shade fell on his face. The student folded his newspaper and placed it by his feet. And then the train emerged from the copse and sunlight bleached the compartment. The stranger offered the student another cigarette.

'I promise,' the student said, taking it and putting it between his lips.

The stranger opened a suitcase, from which he produced a folder in a dark grey binding. He pushed it towards the student. Inside were more than a dozen passports, issued in several countries. Each was marked with a different name: Thomas Mudge, George Graham, Joseph Winnerl, Taqî ad-Dîn, Julien Le Roy, Edward Prior, Ulysse Nardin and several more. The student, his head tilted in curiosity, looked at the stranger, who went on blowing smoke from his mouth for a while.

'As you have guessed, I'm trying to mask my true identity. I'm wanted for murder. The charge is false, of course. Nevertheless, should the law catch up with me, it is the hangman's noose, or the madhouse, I'm told. But they never will. Once the warrant for my arrest had been issued, you see, I decided to flee. Not only is this the surest way to evade capture – the police really are a dull bunch! – but if I were to go into hiding, cooped up in some attic or basement under the stair, I'd become wolf-mad. So, I decided that I would remain constantly on the move, under a hundred different guises, taking one train after another – the Orient Express, the Trans-Siberian railway, the Flying Scotsman, the Indian-Pacific. Oh, how I love to travel on the Iron Horse!' The stranger, beating out a rhythm on the seat, broke into song.

> *Faster than fairies, faster than witches,*
> *Bridges and houses, hedges and ditches;*
> *And charging along like troops in a battle,*
> *All through the meadows the houses and cattle.*

'By train I can run much faster than a fox or a hare and beat a carrier pigeon for a hundred miles. I feel as if the mountains and forests of all countries are advancing on me in the compartment. Even now, I can smell the German linden trees; the South Sea's breakers are rolling against my door!'

The stranger inched forward and gripped the edge of his seat.

'Travelling by train enables me to fend off the two great fears of my life – loneliness and crowds. I want either companionship or solitude. The train solves this problem because it permits one privacy, if one desires, or the company of strangers. The intimacy of travelling in a compartment allows me to strike up a conversation. Alternatively, when a mood of melancholy draws me in, I can retreat into the echoes of the train, which are very distinct, and whilst traversing the corridors one seems distant from all communication with the world.

'Consequently, I have disguises to suit these opposing moods. Today, for example, I have chosen to be an English gentleman. This is because I'm in a talkative mood. Other times I might put on a pinstripe and a Homburg and become an American industrialist burying his head in his papers. In the first suitcase, the round one, I pack my clothes, together with various travelling papers. The second holds a range of timing devices. The third holds my accessories – jewellery, moustaches, toupees, wigs, kohls, spectacles of all kinds, false eyelashes, padding, tweezers and so forth. Oh, the battles I have with railway porters to keep the luggage by my side. English and Indian officials cause the biggest fuss, you know.

'Enough! Let us go to the dining car. I'd be honoured if you would be my guest for lunch. I will tell you what I know about the events leading up to my being charged with murder. Nothing but the truth. And in what can one believe if not the truth?'

There was once a stranger, formerly a watchmaker, now a murderer, who would become a grandfather. He met a student with a scar on his chin, who would become a father. The stranger carried a letter, which he asked the student to deliver. First they went to the dining car. As they ate the stranger told his story.

'Ever since Julia fell sick I have been in a state of grief and agitation. But, you understand, I had my work to distract me. At the time of Julia's death I had almost solved the most pressing problem of my life. Julia had a weak heart. No, I should say, the most extraordinarily fragile heart and I knew she was not long for this world. Of course, I hoped she would survive . . . And as I hoped, I realized that the fact that she and I had met;

no, the happy fate of our meeting and marrying, was a sign that I could help to prolong her life. You see, I am, or, I ought to admit, was a watchmaker. Not only this, I also made automata – you know, those miniature dolls that look so lifelike and even move like humans, their hearts made of boxed clockwork. I was quite famous. Tsars and princes were commissioning my work. Perhaps you have read about the little Mozart whom I made for Sophia von Hohenberg, the Austrian princess. I sat him at a miniature Hammerklavier and he played the finale from the 1777 sonata in C major, and he played as well as the Austrian himself. But it was not just little people I made. My most lucrative venture was musical clocks. I managed to compress air through pipes in such a way as to produce devices that perfectly imitated the song of certain birds – the golden plover, the shearwater, the bluethroat, the nightingale, the curlew and countless others. It was this which gave me the idea to try to preserve Julia's failing heart. She had the heart of a bird; I can hear it now, quivering, flute-like, below her breast. I thought, if I can reproduce the song of the curlew, I might be able to reproduce a human heart in clockwork. I had tried everything else. I had read everything concerning the nature of time. I conducted research into the arcane science of anamnesis. If, as I believed, it were possible to stall time, that is divide it into such small portions that it were impossible to measure the present second – for this is the logical upshot of the watchmaker's art – then time just might stand still, and Julia would not be ravaged by its decaying effects. I can't tell you the trials I put poor Julia through, all in her best interest you understand, although she didn't see it that way at the time. There were instances – I admit – when I had to use force, against my conjugal duty, in order to realize these experiments. Oh how she would beg me to let her depart in peace. But I couldn't see my beloved leave me without feeling I had done everything in my power to try to prevent it. So when these experiments into the practical application of theories of time had run their course, failed that is, I turned to the aforementioned idea. I now attempted to build Julia a clockwork heart.'

As he spoke the stranger looked intently at the student. He had become increasingly agitated, taking quick sips of his wine, and glancing around the dining car. The student appeared at once horrified and intrigued. Both had neglected the food, and the dining attendants, in their umber-coloured livery, curved past the tables, unfazed by the motion of the train, clearing the plates, cutlery and glasses and producing the next course. Speaking hurriedly, the stranger continued his tale.

'If one reads the *Encyclopaedia Britannica*, it will tell you that the word watch derives from the old English *wæcce*, which suggests a keeping guard or watching. The word, by derivation, means "that which keeps wakeful observation over everything". This notion became my starting point – for the heart must remain ever watchful over the body. I focused my attention upon creating a mechanism that would connect in subtle ways to Julia's arteries. By means of research and through a series of terrible experiments I mapped the exact passage of the blood as it flows through the body. The human heart possesses two chambers – ventricles – which propel blood to the organs. I, in turn, made twin pumps, each with a disk-shaped mechanism. The action of my clockwork heart was similar to that of the human heart. There was, however, one difference – the heart is living muscle, while clockwork is nothing more than a series of mechanical components. Julia's new heart needed some internal source of life. Naturally, I couldn't see her wound up every so often like a regular clock. I had to find a way to keep her independently ticking, so to speak. It was then I came upon a magnificent invention. In 1780, Breguet invented the first self-winding watch. He called it the *perpétuelle*. Using two barrels, a carefully balanced weight reacting to the slightest movement and an additional train wheel to provide a going-period of sixty hours, he produced a watch that could be used by someone leading a relatively inactive life. The *perpétuelle* was capable of running for eight years without being over-hauled or going slow. With this technology I felt able to build Julia's clockwork heart.

'I won't go into details about the operation to fit the device. Rest assured, it was a messy business. When I'd completed the fitting, having set the clockwork in motion, I rebuilt Julia's rib-cage and stitched her skin. I waited for her to wake from her opium-induced stupor. But she never woke. Inside her other-wise lifeless chest I could hear the clockwork, ticking just as I had hoped. The heart appeared to be functioning perfectly – it even produced tiny tremors on her breast – and yet her chest failed to rise and fall, and I did not feel her breath when I wet my palm and pressed it to her lips.

'And now, through no more than husbandly devotion, I find myself wanted for murder! If uxoriousness is a crime, let me be damned!'

The stranger slumped in his seat. His limbs and shoulders dropped, and his whole body trembled. The student bent his head. He unwound his tie and placed it across his legs. He picked at the inside seam.

With a series of drawn-out whistles the train sped through York station, the platform filled with people standing to atten-tion. The engine roared; black smoke gushed from the funnel and plumed past the window. Inside, diners, having finished their luncheon, began to smoke. The student indicated that he himself wanted a cigarette, but the stranger was oblivious. The student wiped the palms of his hands against his trouser leg and helped himself to the packet.

'I must get off this train,' the stranger said. 'But first,' he said, rising from his seat, 'I will give you the letter.' He produced a crumpled but otherwise perfectly ordinary-looking envelope.

'Promise me you'll see it to its destination.'

'I promise,' said the student.

'I must get off the train! Should anyone ask, we never met.'

The student was alone in the dining car, clutching the letter. It was surprisingly heavy. He smoothed the wrinkles then scanned the address: Evelyn Rafferty, 16 Ingolstadt Place, Oxford. There was the first surprise – a woman! In his mind the addressee had assumed a theatre of forms – madman, accomplice, alibi, or target for the stranger's murderous imagination – but not a woman. He read the name again: Evelyn. Evie. Eve. (My name, of course, and my mother's too. But I was not named after her; I acquired my name by accident.) The student turned the letter – how gently the stranger had held it! – and lifted it to the window. He saw lines like tightly scrabbling ants beneath the envelope. He held it up to the sun. And those words, which he could not make out, stirred a desire in him.

Why did the student decide to deliver the letter? Why, when the stranger was unreliable, and his story improbable, was he prepared to embroil himself in an unknown fate? Perhaps because he had made a promise; perhaps for the sense of adventure it foretold; or maybe it was the stranger's own guarantee – 'Nothing of what I say will cause you harm or adversely affect you in any way.' In my opinion, there is a more immediate explanation. The student was simply curious.

3

How My Parents Met

There was silence, next day, as the student approached 16 Ingolstadt Place. Sunlight streamed through sycamores that lined
the edge of the pavement. The street was empty, the sky limpid
and still; and – why not? – a pair of moths circled a rose bush.
Number 16 was a watch shop. Inside, the air was cool. Corridors of dusty light sprang from shuttered windows, and high
glass cabinets displayed carriage clocks, nocturnals, music
boxes. There was a dynasty of grandfathers, chronometers,
mechanical dancing figurines. As the student approached the
counter, he saw a thousand faces staring at him. A thousand
hands formed the letter 'L' as he surveyed the room. There was
a clangour of gong-bells and chimes, melodies, a cuckoo's cry.
A thousand pendulums rocked back and forth. A thousand
ticks, a thousand tocks. The student spoke (amid the cacophony of three o'clock a young woman, dressed in an accordion-
pleated skirt with a cape over her shoulders, had appeared
behind the counter): 'Are you Evelyn? Yes? I have something for
you.' Then, 'My watch is broken.' Releasing watch and letter,
he stood, eyeing the floor.

'Where did you get the letter?' she asked.

'From a gentleman . . . he didn't tell me his name.'

'I know the handwriting.'

'I met him on the train to London.'

'I recognize his handwriting.'

'Whose?'

'Father.' Suddenly she collapsed into a fit of weeping. 'Your watch will be ready the day after next,' she said between sobs that shook her whole body.

Many years later, when Rex Steppman was no longer a student, and the stranger, whom I called Grandfather, lived in an institution with other fantasists, my father remembered the encounter. 'I was as helpless as she was.' Father, sitting at the edge of our veranda in Lagos; me, six years old, balancing on his knee. 'I didn't know what to do. I just stood there with your mother weeping and those clocks staring at me.' Suddenly changing mood, he looked into my eyes. 'Never underestimate the power of clockwork, Evie. Once you wind it up, it has a life of its own.' And I, timidly, 'But is clockwork *truly* alive?' Whereupon Father roared with laughter and reached for the pocket watch. 'I'll show you,' he said, sliding me to my feet. Crouching at the edge of the lawn, I watched as he flipped the body from its case . . . to reveal a tiny world of movement, a pinioned order such as every artist dreams of, a world of cogs and balances, each moving at different speeds and trajectories, but all, somehow, impossibly, in synchrony. Next he took a letter opener and wrenched the mainspring; it leaped from his hands thrashing and turning like a Catherine wheel; up it went, making a noise like the sharpening of knives, until it hit the roof and fell to the floor; where it continued to spin maliciously, without restraint, in ever-increasing circles, until finally, as I squirmed in fear and excitement, it died on the wood.

The following day, slightly embarrassed, winking at me and trying to turn the whole thing into a joke, Father gathered the parts and took them to the watch repairer. But that night I did not sleep. Father knew how to bring clockwork to life!

He also knew how to destroy it. And frequently, in the years we lived in Lagos, he succumbed to his appetite for stifling clockwork. This life-long struggle with clocks, however, began in the weeks after he delivered the letter. The pocket watch broke apart an extraordinary number of times, and on each occasion my father returned to the shop with the thousand faces and the corridors of dusty light. The watch's rusty hand was succeeded by a misaligned going-barrel, a broken arbor, an impulse which spun too slowly. My mother mended each disorder willingly and with patience. There was the matter of an over-eager escarpment, which she removed, filed and carefully replaced. The watch suffered from train-wheel convulsion, bevel seizure, a wonky chapter and, of course, the afflicted minute hand, which snapped and was placed in a drawer. Like many objects stored in drawers, however, it went missing, and my mother never got round to finding a replacement.

In between his visits to the shop, my father began his training for the colonial service. He was given a historical account of Empire, instruction in governorship by law, the basics of gunboat diplomacy. He learned that the instinct of sport played a great part in maintaining the British Empire. 'History,' he was told by a severe Oxonian in mufti, 'has demonstrated that the human race advances inexorably.' And, 'Strong, healthy and flourishing nations require a continual expansion of their frontiers.' He took out subscriptions with the *Royal Geographical Society*, the *Zoological Society*, the *Old Elephant* and the *Corona Club*. He learned that time marches ever forward, and yet he continued – unaware – to rebel against the sentiments of the age. Over the following weeks he proceeded to scratch and snap, to smash and unscrew . . . in short, to interrupt the otherwise steady progress of the pocket watch. By 1939, the pocket watch was falling sick roughly once a week. And gradually my parents were getting to know one another. Rex had begun to linger while Evelyn mended the watch; and, as she worked, she talked.

'When I was fourteen,' she told him, several months after their first meeting, 'my mother left home in mysterious circumstances. She was a singer and routinely toured. I rarely saw her. When she returned to Oxford in between tours we scarcely spoke. She regarded me with barely concealed boredom. I remember – I was nine years old – asking her, during an awful scene, why she was such a selfish mother. "I have a weak heart," she said.

'Father was devoted to my mother. Despite her ambivalence towards us, I cannot recall his saying a hurtful word about her. He tolerated her long absences from Oxford for many years, her distractedness at home, and even the infidelities; these last betrayals hurt him deeply, but it made him only more determined to keep us all together. When she left home shortly after my fourteenth birthday, however, departing with no explanation and taking half her wardrobe, Father knew that she wouldn't return. He made inquiries and discovered she was living with a cellist from the Berlin Philharmonic. It was then he began to spend long hours in his workshop, a little room at the bottom of the house, just below where we are standing. I don't know what obsession captured him in those months, because both he and his workshop were closed to me; he shut himself away for weeks at a stretch.

'One day,' Evelyn told Rex, 'some months after my mother's disappearance, Father emerged from his workshop. He told me he was going to Germany to reconcile the marriage. I didn't hear from him for several weeks. And then I received a telephone call; the reception was bad, but I understood that he was still searching for my mother. She had discovered that he was coming after her and was evading him, doing everything she could, laying false trails, decoys and simulations, dropping misleading clues and appearing on stage under various aliases. Father told me that he wouldn't rest until he found her and cured her weak heart.

'After that telephone call,' continued Evelyn, 'I heard nothing more. I told no one of Father's departure. My life was unusual for a child in her teenage years. I went to school. I cooked for myself, bought items of clothing when I needed them. When I was seventeen I left school and reopened the shop. I have since lived on the money from watch repairs, which, until now, has been meagre.'

'Will you see your father again?'

'In his letter he said that he is planning to return to Oxford sometime in the New Year . . . But tell me again. How was he when you met him? Did he look happy? What was he wearing?'

Soon Rex no longer needed a broken watch to visit Evelyn. Three times a week, in between his studies, he rode his bike to the shop, leaving it propped against a lamp-post.

But I tell too much. It is not easy, with my failing memory, to relate every detail of my parents' history. I keep a single picture of them in my mind. A simple scene, composed more of sound than image. They stand in the shop. Father's left hand cups the pocket watch, his right index finger points to the space where the minute hand ought to be. It is three o'clock in the afternoon. My mother's mouth is open as if to say something but all I can hear is the clangour of a thousand clock-calls.

· · ·

Today I travelled to Edinburgh to visit my maternal grandfather, Mr Rafferty. He was in bed, surrounded by enormous white pillows. I decided to take him for a walk. He can cause trouble outside the institution, but I needed some information, and he is more receptive to my questions in the open. Mr Rafferty is an important resource for these first stories, my pre-history. He is old and his mind half-cracked; nevertheless, he may provide me with certain details I cannot know. For instance, what happened after he returned to Oxford.

As we began to walk I held tightly to his arm because I feared he might run on to the street. It had been raining, and the pavements of Edinburgh are broken, so we could not take a step without treading in a puddle. I tried as far as possible to cross to the drier sections, but I saw at once that Mr Rafferty loved getting into the water. It took all my strength to force him to walk by my side. Nevertheless, he managed to step on to a section of pavement where one of the slabs had sunk in deeper than the rest. By the time I realized what he was doing he was wet through and covered in dead leaves.

Mr Rafferty is often gloomy and inclined to silence. His gestures are furtive; the tips of his moustache droop, and his eyes sink into the grey rash of his face. In this mood he spends whole days in bed, falling in and out of heavy sleep. At other times he is excited and talkative. Sometimes he gets quietly to his feet and runs to the corner of his room where a sink and shaving mirror stand; there he argues with himself, staring into his reflection. Or else he will sit up suddenly, knock on the side of the bed and answer, 'Come in,' in various tones for hours on end.

He was nervous and animated as we walked. His eyes gleamed, and everything that shone caught his attention. I knew that if I could get him to George Square, where we could watch the pigeons and drink hot chocolate, he would answer my questions. We walked to the corner of Warrender Park. As we were passing the windows of the swimming pool, full of green shadows and refracted light, he didn't want to carry on; he made himself heavier and heavier and, however hard

I pulled, I could scarcely move him. Finally I had to stop in front of the last window. For several minutes we watched the bathers moving smoothly between bars of broken light. I grabbed hold of Mr Rafferty and tried to walk naturally. But every step was an effort as in those dreams in which one's shoes are made of lead. In this way we proceeded down Warrender Park, through the Meadows until, finally, we reached George Square. He didn't want hot chocolate, so I bought him a packet of crisps and this seemed to make him happy. We sat on the brickwork surrounding the square. The edge of my skirt was damp, and scraps of leaves clung to the lining. I asked him about the days before the war. I asked what my mother was like when she was a child. Was she very beautiful? Did she wear long dresses? He didn't answer; he only stared up at the sky, placing crisps into his mouth every so often. But I could see that he was enjoying the day, the air which was sweet and unobtrusive.

'What was Mother's star sign?' I asked. He didn't seem to hear. All at once he turned his head towards me.

'Who are you?' he said.

'Evie Steppman,' I said.

'Where were you born?'

'Children's Hospital, Lagos.'

'Age?'

'Fifty-four.'

'Eyes?'

'Green.'

'Jew or Gentile?'

I didn't answer but sprung back a question: 'On what day did you return to Oxford before the war?'

'It was at night,' he replied.

'On what night did you return?'

'February 15th 1939.' I started to ask him questions about his return to Oxford, quickly, one after another, in case he lost interest.

Suddenly, he interrupted me.

'There's no cure for a broken heart. For a weak one, there is. I have found it. In fact, I am currently in the process of establishing a patent for this cure.'

'Yes?'

And he proceeded to tell me about the events after his return to Oxford.

Later, we walked without incident back to the institution, where we parted: he to his bed, I to Gullane. Now I am seated at my desk. Twilight is spreading through the attic, creeping into the corners, mouse holes and dusty spaces under the floor. Outside, leaves shiver in the gutter. The sea lets out a sigh, and at once everything turns sombre, lonely and late. In the relative quiet I will attempt to finish this third chapter, using what my grandfather told me earlier today, together with the stories I heard from Father in my childhood.

. . .

It was late evening on 15 February 1939 when Mr Rafferty returned to Oxford. Across Europe nations were building giant monsters of war. Engineers were dreaming dreams of destruction which those monsters could excrete and simultaneously raising defence lines against them. On my grandfather's return he and my mother began a different kind of blockade adumbrated by the build-up of arms. They sealed the upstairs entrance to the workshop, spread a rug over the trapdoor. They hung heavy curtains across the basement window, scattered sawdust on the rough boards. Blankets, books, towel and tea-set each found a place there, in that nocturnal bunker where Mr Rafferty installed himself.

Whether or not my mother believed the predicament in

which my grandfather claimed to be embroiled, whether she understood how deeply and inexorably he had retreated from practical affairs, she must have felt that he was in danger, because she made a great effort to hide him from the outside world. No one, she understood, was to know of his presence – not even Rex. In the waking hours Mr Rafferty was to remain silent, emerging from his hiding place at dusk for an hour or two, after which he would descend once again to the workshop, in whose dank light a strange, complicated and unnatural affair was taking shape.

It began with the reading of scientific treatises. Mr Rafferty concentrated on the writings of Jacques de Vaucanson, who in 1737 constructed a mechanism in the shape of a fawn, which could play the flute. Over the following weeks he consumed innumerable books and manuscripts. He noted particular sections on loose sheafs then pinned these fragments, to which he added illustrative diagrams, on to the walls. His reading matter became increasingly technical, including manuals on anatomy, alchemy and mechanics, the writings of the Italian Futurists and Pavlovian reflex theory. He ate infrequently, slept only for a few hours in the afternoon. His complexion acquired the tarnished hue of an old euphonium.

It was at this time that Mr Rafferty began to receive visitors (so he told me this afternoon in Edinburgh). Men wearing dark suits made their way to Ingolstadt Place, then vanished into the back entrance of the workshop. There they would remain throughout the night, drinking cocoa, conversing in hushed tones, observing demonstrations, remonstrating with one another, conducting their business with complicated handshakes. Later, when Mr Rafferty had ceased to appear above ground altogether, other darkly clad figures came to that fusty vault, human shadows conveying stiff and weighty packages.

And slowly, during the course of this midnight activity, this sinful undertaking brought to my grandfather the subtle, strange-smelling vapour of death; slowly – Evelyn did not notice the change – 16 Ingolstadt Place became enveloped in a blue haze. This strange mist originated from the small hearth Mr Rafferty had set into the wall and from which he drew brightly gleaming substances. By April, when Rex was nearing the end of his civil service training, the mist had started to creep up into the shop. Rex told Evelyn that he was to travel to Nigeria, his first posting abroad, but she hardly took in the news. She had too much to think about, keeping the shop by day, tending to her hideaway at all other times. What is more, she was harbouring a pair of secrets in the shape of my father and grandfather.

Secrets are like shadows; they transform the one who bears them, they flit and flicker behind the eyes, grow longer and more difficult to command by evening-time and disperse at night, only to appear with renewed authority during the day. Perhaps it was for this reason – the incorrigibility of secrets and shadows – that one afternoon my mother closed the shop early and invited Rex to supper. Perhaps it was good fortune that Mr Rafferty was working at the hearth. Maybe Evelyn really did feel faint and go to bed, telling Rex to show himself out. Whatever the truth, chance (chance yielding to my mother's will) led Rex towards the trapdoor. A great heat was emanating from beneath his feet as he stepped on to the rug. There was a sulphurous smell whose pungency grew stronger as he raised the rug, prised open the trapdoor and walked down the basement stairs.

He saw nothing at first, or nothing tangible, since the room was filled with smoke. As it dispersed, Rex made out a figure bent over a large wooden table, a broad, round-faced semblance of a man with unkempt hair and black shiny eyes under-arched with greying bags, eyes which, as they turned towards the stairs, Rex knew immediately. Basements, unlike attics, rarely accentuate sound; rather everything that stirs is muted, dampened by the inevitable moisture in the air, so that as Rex stood staring into the eyes of the stranger Mr Rafferty he felt strangely calm. Despite the muted though frankly appalling scene – a woman, or rather the likeness of a female form, white, bloodless, prostrate on the table, parts of her covered with a sheet, others simply missing – Rex spoke.

'Good evening,' he said. 'I didn't think we'd . . .'

'We have never formally introduced ourselves,' said Mr Rafferty.

'You already know my name. I know several of yours.'

'My name,' said Mr Rafferty, 'is Mr Rafferty.'

He held out his hand. Rex stepped back and lowered himself into the armchair, averting his eyes from the hideous form over which Mr Rafferty now drew a sheet. He spent a few minutes poking the fire, with his back to Rex, then joined him in a neighbouring armchair, and, settling, declared, 'Before you say anything more, please allow me to explain. Much has happened since that day on the train to London. If you recall, I was in a keen state of anticipation. I had conceived a plan that would enable me to return to Oxford, where, as you will hear, I could restore my former happiness.'

Mr Rafferty paused and gazed out into the distance. After some time he said, 'In the weeks following Julia's death, you see, I had been unable to forget one thing. The fact that my clockwork heart had functioned perfectly. I had managed to manufacture a human heart, one of the most complicated anatomical structures – why should I not repeat the feat for each of the vital organs? After all, what is a lung if not a sanguine bellow? And the eye – how faithfully it corresponds to a scientific instrument! Might I not forge each of the vital organs and clothe them in the likeness of my wife!

'I faced a major difficulty. I needed a base from which to begin my work, yet I was on the run. I had to get back to Oxford. For several months I considered this problem. It was not until, several days before our meeting on the train, I came across an article in *The Times*, that I saw my opportunity. In 1935, said the article, a group of scientists and engineers had developed a method for detecting flying objects by shooting invisible waves towards the sky. And the government had supported this absurd idea! They also, it was said, offered £1,000 to anyone who could demonstrate a ray that would kill a sheep at a range of 100 yards. How far the government errs! What desk-ridden imbecile supported this mad imagination? Still, I thought, I could use this governmental madness to my advantage. Such is the fear of conflict in Europe, so inadequate is our readiness for war, that Whitehall is willing to assist anyone who volunteers to help. So I contacted the Chiefs of Staff. After explaining my state of affairs, that is my enforced itinerancy, I proceeded to describe my skills as a maker of clockwork and automata. I put to their dreaming minds the image of a battalion of soldiers, each like the next, a defence force to which fear was as alien as hunger, an army of expendable automata whose glassy eyes would strike fear into the enemies of our little island. I arranged for the reply to be covertly announced in *The Times*. The reply came. I returned to Oxford and into the arms of my daughter.

'Of course, I concealed my true motive: to realize the plan to which, ever since Julia fell sick, I have dedicated my life. So, I first set about making each of the components necessary for life, all of which I have either built from clockwork or plucked from the corpses of criminals, which the War Office have brought me. You see, I cannot hope to forge every part of Julia from metal. There are certain structures, such as the organs of reproduction, not to mention the hair and skin that, through a strange alchemy, I plan to integrate with the manufactured articles. I do not expect Julia, upon waking, to function as before. I imagine her to be like one who enters into life for the first time. And just as the new-born learns to call his creator Mother, so Julia, with the right instruction, will learn to call me Husband. But there is more! I will not simply replicate Julia – that's the easy part – but improve on her! Just as our missionaries bring the torch of culture and progress to the dark people of the earth, so I, a Stanley in my own right, will mould Julia in my own image. Soon I will have a perfect simulacrum of my wife, the true likeness of myself in female form, Julia, my love!'

4

Map of the World, 1:
The Tale of El-Edrisi

I have prepared myself a writing table: a wardrobe door, unhinged from its body, laid horizontal and supported at each corner with pillars of books – yellowing volumes of the *Encyclopaedia Britannica*, 1911, whose pages come apart like pressed flowers in my hands. Upon the desk sits my laptop computer. Purring, it emits a bluish haze, faintly lighting the darkness. It is the brightest colour in the attic. Everything else is dulled by dust, moth-eaten, mildewed, encrusted with grime, carious, verdigris, flaking. The most decrepit item in the attic is also the largest. It hangs on the far wall via a single hook attached to its top left corner. It is an early example of cartographic dreaming. A mappa mundi.

Stolen from Waltham Abbey late in the fourteenth century, it was acquired by Sir Henry Wrecksham in 1448 for his collection of *unica*, later sold to an unknown German, who, during the Thirty Years' War, buried it then died; it lay four feet under earth for the next three hundred years, outlasting countless conflicts, including two World Wars, until it was discovered in 1948 by an American soldier in a field outside Nuremberg. Unsure of what it was, but perceiving its great age, the soldier brought it back with him to America. He showed it to an expert at the Metropolitan Museum, who verified its authenticity. This is the story my father chose to believe on purchasing the fake in 1963, not long after returning from Nigeria. He was suffering because the British had been ousted from the country.

Half crazed on account of the loss of his illusions, he spent almost two-thirds of his inheritance on another kind of fantasy. Since then the mappa mundi has hung in the attic.

Although it depicts continents and seas, nations and towers, it is not only a map but a decorative altarpiece, an object of desire among collectors and unscrupulous cheats. Painted on vellum, it measures three feet high and two feet six inches wide. The map itself is almost perfectly round. Asia occupies the upper half, Europe the bottom left-hand quarter, and Africa the lower right of the world disk. This scheme, the tripartite division of the earth, is based on the biblical story of Noah. After one hundred and fifty days at sea, Noah sent his three sons to repopulate the land, giving a continent to each. Japheth received Europe, Shem received Asia, and Ham Africa. The continents (only three are depicted on the map), are named accordingly. Diverse images embellish the mappa mundi. Christ is nailed to the cross. The Apocalypse is revealed to St John at Patmos. The Sphinx, the elephant and the pelican are portrayed inhabiting the western region of the African continent. Of these, it is the fearsome image of the pelican which my mind returns to most often: she is perched on the edge of her nest teeming with her offspring, who feed from a gaping wound in her side. Ragged gaps, where the moths have feasted, disfigure the map: an elliptical fissure in the Dead Sea, a growing tear enveloping Edinburgh, a hole east of Syria where the Garden of Eden formerly lay. The Mediterranean covers almost one-third of the work's surface. It is mottled with islands, notably Crete with its Labyrinth, and Sicily in flames. The rivers Don and Nile, which flow into the Mediterranean, mark the boundaries of Europe, Asia and Africa. Europe is dotted with cities and familiar landmarks. The greater parts of Africa and Asia are filled with pictures of fabulous cities and mythical beings. Africa, east of the Nile, is populated by a bestiary of monstrous races arranged in alphabetical order.

AMYCTYRAE·

I have a bottom lip that protrudes far from my face. It serves as an umbrella against the sun. I live on raw meat and am unsociable.

ANDROGINI·

I am a man-woman. My people make sacrifices to Osiris and the Moon.

ANTHROPOPHAGI·

I eat my parents when they are old, or anyone else I can find.

ASTOMI·

. . .

BLEMMYAE·

I am one whose head grows beneath the shoulders. I curse the sun and never dream.

CYCLOPS·

Round-eye, I am mistaken for treachery. Son of Cain.

DONESTRE·

I speak the language of any traveller I meet and claim to know his wife. Then I kill him and mourn over his head.

ETHIOPIAN·

I am named by Greeks. My face is burned black by the sun.

GORGADES·

I am a hairy woman. I will not tell you how I survived the Flood.

PANOTII·

My ears reach the ground and serve as blankets. Should I meet a traveller, I'll unfurl them and fly away.

PANPHAGI·

I devour anything and everything.

PYGMIE·

I am but two cubits tall, as are my cows.

SCIOPOD·

I am one-legged but uncommonly swift. In summer I lie on my back and shade myself with my giant foot.

SCIRITAE·

I am a noseless flat-faced man. I belong to the uninhabitable city.

TROGLODYTE·

Grrioeejubarbaraesdrthsjkslah.

WIFE-GIVER·

I honour travellers with wives.

Examining the mappa mundi in recent days, I have come to understand both its beauty and its menace, in a way that was not apparent to me when my fascination for the map was born.

The mappa mundi is like a travelogue, which reflects not the material world, but the fantasies of the traveller's mind; as if the mapmaker projected his desires on to vellum. It is a spatial imagining of the world, just as an encyclopaedia is an alphabetical imagining of the world, or a chronicle is an arrangement of common happenings in temporal order. But forgetting for the moment the mappa mundi – and turning to an earlier map – I skip back through centuries.

. . .

to another island in Europe, smaller than Britain and warmer, where the Norman King Roger II has lately established an uneasy empire, a merging of three religions, four cultures and diverse sensibilities, where splendid cathedrals vie for space in the skyline with palaces and mosques.

. . .

to an airy courtyard in Palermo, where scholars and cour-tesans gather beneath bronze cupolas and towering fountains, shaded by date palms, cooled by eunuchs wielding peacock-feather fans.

. . .

where one man, taller than the rest, strolls among his attend-ants, impatient, tugging at his beard, a man whose eyes bear the feral mark of storms – the sandstorms of the Sahara. A man for whom a crisis is approaching.

Who is this man, so tall and thin-lipped?

El-Edrisi – geographer, beekeeper, savant, lover, tyrant, philan-thropist, maker of maps.

Lean and sun-black, El-Edrisi is a man fashioned by weather. He has travelled in Europe, North Africa, Asia Minor and the Mediterranean. For twelve years Edrisi has been on the move. But now he is still, a city-dweller, residing in Palermo, where he is Chief Vizier to King Roger II.

I am getting ahead of myself, because this is not my story, or not entirely my own. I can tell it; punch the keys of my computer so as to arrange the letters on the screen. To record Edrisi's tale, however, is to distort it, because he cannot wholly be captured in words. He is, rather, a voice, a pursing of lips, the narrowing of eyes, sudden jerky hand movements – most of all a voice. Edrisi's story first came to me via Father, who would lecture Mother's belly, which was where I first heard the tale. Years later, sitting at the foot of my bed in Lagos, he would retell the story so that Edrisi became familiar again.

Here is Father. He is sitting in my bedroom after supper. Ben – our cook – is washing up in the kitchen. Ade – Ben's son, our servant-boy – is, I suspect, listening at the bedroom door. Mother is in the grave in Botley Cemetery, Oxford. Father begins, as he always begins, with a narrowing of his eyes, a half-grin and the single word: Well . . .

There was a young boy called El-Edrisi, who lived in the city of Ceuta on the North African coast. He was the son of a rich and prominent family of the Hammudid dynasty. When he was seven Edrisi found himself orphaned, and rich. He spent a wild and extravagant youth, eating and drinking freely, dressing flamboyantly, passing his days with friends. He believed this way of life would last for ever. But Edrisi woke, aged fourteen and a half, to find he'd lost almost everything. He'd spent his money on wine and women and bees.

Edrisi lay on his cool bed in the hot Moroccan summer. He was sad and listless, but all the time his cunning brain was at work. Eventually he thought of a plan. He sold all he had of clothes and property. Then this spoiled and ruined lad, this Moorish Sinbad, took himself to sea.

'Who's Sinbad?' I ask.

'I'll tell you tomorrow.'

Edrisi travelled in vain. Spending months at sea only increased his desire for his boyhood home. Or, second best, a city, any city. Arriving in Córdoba or Baghdad or Timbuktu, Edrisi saw – in the blue domes and pleasure-gardens, in the sandalwood ashes glowing in the braziers – only what differed from his native Ceuta. He noted these differences meticulously. He drew maps of his city, trying to recreate as much detail as he could muster. But the further he travelled the more obscure Ceuta became. He forgot details: the precise length of his garden, the location of that tiny door, always locked, on Meedan Street. He began to associate his native town with loss: the loss of his parents, his fortune, the city he hadn't seen for two, six, eleven, years. Edrisi attempted to fill this emptiness through movement.

He pictured the lands beyond as unmarked terrain. Suspended between a desire to keep moving and his fear of loss, Edrisi placed flags in cities and names on maps. In the North African desert he craved water so intensely he saw visions of paradise. Tall magnificent palm trees. A silver racetrack. Hordes of women. Beehives in perfect order. Edrisi babbled; ravaged, exhausted by thirst. He grabbed his goatskin flask and emptied the last drops of water. As he drank, feeling his thirst subside and the madness within him dying down, the dream-vista began to vanish. The water extended his life but took away his vision of paradise. In Ethiopia, during the rainy season, he saw a woman who became a man on her wedding-day. He learned that people struck by lightning when awake are found with their eyes closed, and, when asleep, with their eyes open. On the Sierra Nevada in Southern Spain, Edrisi was stupefied by snow. A miracle, he thought. How can something be at once so brilliant and cold?

. . .

There were details Father left out of the story, perhaps because he thought I was too young, perhaps because it changed with each telling. Sometimes, when it was late, the tale lasted five minutes. Other times Father talked for longer. The version I am relating now is, in a sense, a false rendering, since I am leaving nothing out. In fact, I realize that I am adding to the story even as I write.

Edrisi had a fearful temper. Yes, his temper was as changeable as the climates through which he had travelled. He was known among the courtiers of the Cappella Palatina – King Roger's palace and chapel – as, variously, Procella, Al-Çáúçõyé, Cheimazô, La Tempesta.

His desires were as vigorous and variable as his temper. Edrisi had fifty-three wives. He had fathered sixty-two sons and seventy-eight daughters. In and around his chamber dwelt slave-girls, eunuchs, handmaidens and concubines.

He loved none.

At this point in the story Father switches to the present tense. He edges closer and slowly straightens his back.

Today in Palermo a ship has arrived. The cargo began its journey in Nubia, moving in a train of two hundred camels northward, following the River Nile up through Egypt, and to the sea-town of Alexandria; where it swung left, hugging the North African coast until it reached Benghazi. The cargo was loaded on to the ship, which for two days sailed up through the Gulf of Sirte and into the Mediterranean. Sailing through the channel between Scylla and Charybdis, it rounded the coast of Sicily and arrived, right on time, at Port Vieveria.

Palermo celebrates. From the port to the Cappella Palatina crowds of revellers throng the streets. There are jugglers, vaudeville shows, acrobats and fire-eaters. Belly dancers swing and ripple to the sound of flutes, pausing only when coins fail to drop at their feet. Every five years it is the same. There are sounds of caged birds warbling in various voices and tongues, turtledoves, nightingales, thrushes and curlews. There are gambling dens, clairaudients, beggars competing for alms. As the train of camels, each supporting a curtained palanquin, passes with its hidden cargo, the crowds hush. They know what the curtains conceal: stolen virgins. Five hundred maidens from Nubia.

The camels walk unconcernedly on, through noise and perfume, passing La Ferria, beyond the blue domes of the Jami' Mosque, and now, climbing to the highest point in the city, draw near the gates of the Cappella Palatina. Outside, the carnival will continue long into the night. Inside, the courtiers of Roger's palace wait – emirs and viziers, ushers and giandars – in eager anticipation.

And here is Edrisi himself, impatient, tugging at his beard, standing by the side of his king.

Father leans forward, placing a hand on each knee. He fixes his eyes on a point above my head and, imitating Edrisi, speaks in a guttural voice.

'I tell you, Caliph, these maidens are fine. I gave instructions specially.'

'How were they chosen?'

'There is a province inhabited by infidels who are called Nubian, which is also the name of their city. They are a good-looking race with fair complexions. They are unlike other savages which inhabit that part of the earth. Their women are of a great beauty. I sent emissaries to Nubia to select their most beautiful maidens.'

Roger claps his hands, moving to embrace Edrisi . . .

But Roger is cut short. For now the bronze gates open; camel after camel lumbers into the courtyard, forming a wide circle around Roger and Edrisi and the courtiers. Roger beams. Edrisi feels faint; his eyes roll. Quickly he recovers his composure. The five hundred maidens from Nubia step, tentatively, blinkingly, into the courtyard. They are travel-weary. They are angry. They appear, to Edrisi, beautiful.

And among the throng, there is one whose indifference will provoke a crisis in Edrisi, one who will arouse in him a strange and disturbing emotion.

I'll call it by its proper name: Love.

Father stands up, opens the bedroom door, crosses the hallway and steps out on to the veranda. I hear his shoes like handclaps on the hardwood floor. It is dark outside. I do not feel tired. The insects sing. 'Go on,' I call out into the boisterous dark. There is no reply. 'Tell me more.' Father stops. I hear his footsteps growing louder as he approaches my room; they pause; the door swings open; and suddenly he is squatting beside my bed and we are looking directly at one another through the mosquito net. 'You can't stop there.'

There was a time when mapmakers named the places through which they travelled after their lovers; for Edrisi, it's the opposite. Each night, following the arrival of the Nubians, Edrisi calls a fresh concubine to his chamber. He looks her up and down, instructs her to turn around, then calls her by her new name.

There is Sala, so named because, like the peaceful province of Sala, a province rich in copper and seashells, she is, Edrisi thinks, calm, and her skin possesses the brilliance of copper.

There is Kaougha, a territory filled with mountain streams, from which prospectors sift gold dust, bit by bit, from the river bed; and Kaougha, named thus because Edrisi must tease from her silence her soft involvement.

Tonight, some five weeks since the celebration of the Five Hundred Maidens, Edrisi summons a new concubine. Inspecting her carefully, he is struck, not by her beauty, but by her gaze, which appears to him both serious and unyielding. He runs a gamut of names – cities, lands – through his mind, toying with each, trying to fit this bold maiden to a province. But he can't think of any. She has something of the sea about her, he thinks, something sleepless.

'I name you Abila,' Edrisi says.

Abila says nothing.

'Come, we'll drink some wine.'

Abila pours wine into a cup, drinks, fills another cup and gives it to Edrisi. He drains it and thanks her.

'You're welcome,' says Abila.

Edrisi fills his cup, drinks, pours wine into Abila's cup and kisses her hand. Abila takes the cup, empties it and sits beside the bed.

They go on passing cup after cup until Edrisi begins to feel tipsy and is aroused. He kisses her hand, toys with her hair, plays little jokes, all the time feeding her sweets. They continue drinking until the wine gets the better of Edrisi, who begins to praise her beauty.

'Abila, your forehead is like the new moon, your eyes like those of a deer or wild heifer, your eyebrows like the crescent in the month of Sha'ban; you have lips like carnelian, teeth like a row of pearls set in coral, breasts like a pair of pomegranates, and a navel like a cup that holds a pound of benzoin ointment.'

Abila says nothing.

'You are like a dome of gold, as the poets say, a Queen bee, an unveiled bride, a splendid fish swimming in a fountain.'

Edrisi, in a fit of arousal, and all at once, takes off his clothes. He stands naked on the bed. Abila laughs.

'Follow my example!'

Abila says nothing.

'Reveal yourself.'

'I won't.'

'You will pleasure me according to my desire.'

'I will not.'

'Undress and I shall take you.'

'No!'

Edrisi covers his nakedness.

'By god, you will!'

'No!'

Each night it's the same. Edrisi summons Abila to his chamber. They drink wine. He praises her beauty, then sheds his clothes. And, every night: 'Undress and I shall take you.'

'No!'

Edrisi doesn't know what to do. He paces his room, the courtyard, the palace chapel, tugging at his beard. In between entreaties to Abila, he takes ever more concubines into his chamber. They satisfy him less, and less often. Spending increasing hours with his bees, but forgetting to wear his face-net and gloves, he is stung thirteen times. He arranges sprinting contests with the courtiers and wins without fail. He attempts to copy out Book XI from Pliny's *Natural History*. Perhaps I am losing my charm, he thinks. It will be different tomorrow.

Night after night Abila remains indifferent. Edrisi's desire for her increases. Why? he thinks. She is only one among many beauties. It is true, she is able to bend her limbs extravagantly; but so can Sahart, Galla, Shari, Nufii, Zallah, Kawar and Alura. She is voluptuous and, I imagine, forgiving; though no more so than Ozala and O Abu'l-Bilma. Her legs rise from the round bulbs of her heels and stretch as far as Mount Etna. But Afno, Anbiya, Zayla and Sahart each have longer legs.

The nights of rejection continue. Edrisi begins to fear the day he might possess Abila almost as much as he longs for it. He doesn't know what his feelings will be on that day, forever deferred. He buys her presents, displays his skills on the race-track. Nothing works. Abila turns her back, laughs even. Edrisi, in a fit of ardour, decides to build her a silver map of the world. He reads the great works of cartography – Al-Mas'udi, Ibn Hauqal, Orosius, Ptolemy – combining his own experiences as a traveller with the universal scheme of the seven climes. He orders pure unalloyed silver from Germany, contracts metal smiths and an army of engravers.

'The world is a ball floating in the clouds of Heaven, like the yolk of an egg,' he tells the engravers. 'We'll produce a silver orb which will represent the world on a round surface. It will weigh forty thousand dirhams,' Edrisi instructs them, 'and when it is ready you'll engrave on it a map of the seven climes with their lands and regions, their shorelines and hinterlands, gulfs and seas, watercourses and rivers, their inhabited and uninhabited parts, their known harbours and the distances between each locality.'

This is done. Edrisi summons Abila to his chamber and unveils the planisphere.

'I present to you this silver globe.'

Abila says nothing.

'What do you think?'

'I think, sir, it's a plaything.'

'What do you mean?'

'It tells me nothing.'

'But here is Sicily,' implores Edrisi. 'And here the Mediterranean is charted. Look, here is Africa, Egypt, *Nubia*.'

'Where are the people?'

'They are too small to depict, even on a map such as this.'

'There are no stories.'

She leaves his chamber.

Edrisi despairs. Lying in his chamber by day, pacing the courtyard by night, he tugs ever harder at his beard.

Only when Milus, the travelling storyteller, arrives at court does Edrisi conceive his next plan. Abila wants stories, he thinks. By god, she'll have a story!

It was late afternoon when Edrisi approached Milus' chamber. The air was growing cold, pierced by the shiver-rustling of trees, catcalls, trumpets announcing sunset. He seized Milus, fixing his fist around his gaunt neck.

'Teach me your storyteller's art!'

Edrisi raised his eyes to the diminishing sky. Visible in the half-light were the masts of ships unhurriedly swaying to and fro, the cathedral spire, the barred windows of the leprosarium, railed parapets to which kites clung by their tails. Edrisi noticed none of the signs of the city. Instead he saw a crease in the sky, a faint and gauzy tear through which appeared a small though perfectly proportioned simulacrum of his Ceutan backyard. A shiver ran up from his toes, expanding in his chest to a tearing pain. He held the storyteller's neck.

'Teach me your storyteller's art,' he repeated without taking his eyes from the tear in the sky above Palermo, which now revealed the fascia of his favourite childhood sweetshop. He pictured the shopkeeper's hairy arms and his fat fingers which nevertheless yielded wonderful sugar-beaded sweets. Milus rocked back and forward, his mouth drawn wide, gums as pink as a kitten's. And Edrisi recalled the particular technique that as a child he had developed to eat sweetmeats, dropping one into his yawning mouth, then two, four, eight, sixteen if he could manage, until his tongue was forced against his palate and he spat the gummy sweetness on to the street, where one of the ragged dogs would gulp it down. The pain in his chest subsided, and Edrisi relaxed his hand. The storyteller collapsed on the ground. He was shaking violently and gasping for breath. Edrisi nudged him with his foot.

'Stand up!'

Milus got to his feet. Edrisi felt the pain in his chest return more insistently as he noticed for the first time the broken black teeth, the warty brow, the roomy smile for which Milus was renowned. Tendrils of spit trembled and fell from his bottom lip. Uncontrollably he heaved and shook. He cackled, wept, beat his chest; and then, unsteadily, with the tip of his big toe, sketched in the dust the words, *Get Lost.*

Calling vainly for a guard, Edrisi brought down an elbow on Milus' shoulder. As the poet's legs gave way once again, Edrisi spat, 'I'll come to your quarters tomorrow at three. Insult me again and you won't have a chance to get back to your feet.'

'Come in,' said a voice, next day, as Edrisi approached the doorless entrance. Milus lay on a hemp mat on the floor and instructed Edrisi to sit.

'Let me be frank,' he began. His grin was hideous but submissive. 'I could give you the fancy screed about storytelling, about the ancestors and heroes and the imparting of wisdom. I could tell you that one can learn the art of storytelling only from one's roots in the soil.

'But I see,' grinning and winking at Edrisi, 'you are not a man for whom a poet's trickery will work its charm. I'll speak plainly,' he said, moving closer. 'We rhymesters are liars. You hear? Liars and cheats. Give me a copper coin and I'll compose a lampoon that'll have your enemies writhing in their robes. A silver one and I'll make the earthworm in your pants grow into a snake. A gold coin will buy you a tale to seduce a princess. Tell me. Why do you want to learn to tell stories?'

Edrisi got to his feet and twice circled the room.

'I'm in love with a woman who is in love with stories.'

Once again Milus roared with delight. He struck his palms against his thighs.

'But will she love the storyteller as much as the story?'

'A fair point,' Edrisi conceded.

'You have two options.' Milus placed a knot of bark on to his tongue and began to chew. 'You could attempt to learn the storyteller's art, although this will be tricky. You are one who holds great authority, one who need not look over your shoulder. And that is the weakness of power.'

Edrisi said nothing.

'Tell me a story.'

'I can't.'

'Then come back tomorrow.'

And, next day, 'There are two types of story. Those that are distant in time and those that are distant in space. The first are ancient tales, tales of our past heroes. And the primary tellers of these are sedentary people. The second are told by travellers of one kind or another. Which are you?'

'Traveller,' Edrisi said enthusiastically.

'Tell me a story.'

After a long pause, Edrisi declared in a loud and breathy voice, 'One day . . .'

'A good start.'

'One day . . . there was . . . a boat owned by a king. The boat was full of soldiers dressed in garments of war. They were about to set sail for Alexandria . . . when . . . when a wave swept them to sea . . . and they all died.'

'Tell me another.'

'One day . . .'

'Not all stories start with *One day*. Try, for example, *There was once* . . .'

'There was once . . . there was . . . a small boy lost in a desert sandstorm. When he was more dead than alive, an old griot arrived with a skein of fresh water attached to his hip. The griot attacked him then ate him.'

The storyteller Milus closed his eyes. 'You will never charm your lady with storytelling.'

'You said there were two options,' Edrisi said after some time. 'Tell me the second.'

Milus spread his hands out before him. 'To write. Set down on paper. Woo your love with words on the page. No doubt, it's a base alternative. When I speak I draw the largest of crowds. A dense throng of listeners squat on the ground, and even the town idiot, to whom my words mean nothing, is captured and rooted to the spot. To write, however, is to substitute living words for empty scrawl. It is to filch and deceive. There is nothing natural in it – a parasitic, masturbatory art! But, my stubborn apprentice, my incompetent griot, it's all you've got. Steal from the writings of others in order to spin your tale. Pinch from a thousand sources, anything that fits. You don't know how to look but you're well versed in deceit. My proposal: Write it down!'

Edrisi took this advice. He embarked on his greatest attempt to woo Abila. As his starting point he took the silver globe. He decided to create a text illustrating in words each of the seven climes. He would call it the *Kitab Rujjar* or *Book of Entertainment for One Desirous to Go Round the World* and present it as an advancement of geographical knowledge. In addition to notes from his own travels, Edrisi began to collect information from written sources: the *Kitab surat al-ard* of Al-Khwarizmi, Al-Battani's *Astronomy*, works by al-Istakhri, al-Kashgari, and the *Periploi*. Then he contacted merchants, seamen, diplomats, itinerants of all kinds. He despatched envoys accompanied by draftsmen. The tone, he decided, would be narrated through the mode of curiosity. In addition to the mapping of the seven climes, he would describe the conditions of the lands and countries, their inhabitants, their customs, appearance, clothes and language, their seas, mountains and measurements, their crops and revenues and all sorts of buildings, the works they had produced, their economy and their merchandising. But at its heart, in addition to being a lexical map of the world, would be wonderful tales. The *Kitab Rujjar* would serve the primary purpose of telling stories.

Amid the description of the first climate, with its bitter fishes and coarse blue cloth, Edrisi wrote about the African princess who required her meals to be floated to her on a leaf. He mentioned that certain rich mandarins owned bathtubs made out of mollusc shells that measured over a yard in length. After cataloguing the races in the land of Mallel, with its strict though benevolent king, he inserted the legend of Gog and Magog. He narrated, by sleight of hand, as it were, including, as an objective summary of the land of Nubia, the story of the Mountains of the Moon, of the monstrous races that lined the banks of the Nile. He discoursed on the intelligence of elephants, on the city of Wangara, the source of all the gold in Africa. He wrote of the gardens in Tripoli whose plants, once sown, germinate to maturity in thirty minutes, of the Indian paper roses that open in water, and of the subterranean passages in the fifth climate from where an elderly woman, sitting at an unusual keyboard instrument, calls forth the sound of Japan at dawn, Christmas in Ethiopia, the Chinese selling tea, prayers in Medina.

As Edrisi worked on the *Kitab Rujjar*, he found that he no longer understood his feelings for Abila. She had acquired free rein of the palace, and every time he saw her, passing in one of the high-ceilinged corridors, or else viewing her from a distance as she walked in the gardens, he felt an unbearable sadness. He had his title changed from Chief Vizier to Geographer Royal. He no longer sprinted or took virgins into his chamber, although he remained loyal to his bees. And his desire for Abila became more complicated, less sure and insistent, confused with the emptiness in his chest, that void which was snaking its way through his inner organs. Still he laboured with his book, and, as more envoys returned to Palermo – bringing news of the Iberian peninsula, or a description of the city of Lemlem, or a hint or beginning of a story – he continued to add to what he had written, or else, when he had completed the description of a particular climate, a merchant would arrive to contradict the initial report. And so Edrisi came to understand that he would never finish annotating his map, because the world was always moving. It was at this point, having failed with Abila, Edrisi decided to travel back to his childhood city.

Edrisi recognized nothing of Ceuta. Walking through the square, he looked into a pauper's rheumy eyes, eyes that had once been young to the city, like his own, and he recognized neither eyes nor the sights upon which they had formerly gazed: the water clock, the tiny door on Meedan Street, the cemetery in which his father was entombed. Sickened, Edrisi began to draw maps of Ceuta, first on a scale of three inches to a mile, then six inches to a mile, and with ever-increasing ratios, until eventually he attempted to chart the city on a scale of a mile to a mile. He wished to create a life-sized map of Ceuta, so as to preserve its true form, as it was before time had engendered a second city that bore the same name. Point by point he retraced the pathways of his boyhood home. And because few places were large enough to house his map, and perhaps also to make the leap from life to death less abrupt, Edrisi brought it to the desert, that place where meanings and values are blown away, where nothing grows, and in which one is free to dream. There, in that void of endless sand, Edrisi put down his map and set about living the end of his life on Ceuta.

But what of Abila? This question never occurred to me as a child, since I was so caught up in Edrisi's fate. And once Edrisi left Palermo, Father, certainly, never gave her a second thought. With age and my waning powers of listening, however, with my struggle to follow the sounds which remain in my memory, silences have taken on new resonance. They are a kind of vacuum once occupied by sound, a story untold. What, then, of Abila? I would like to believe that, following her enchantment with Milus, the storyteller, she in turn enchanted him, enlisting his help to aid her escape from King Roger's court. As to where she escaped to, not even Milus, who waited for her, as arranged, by the pomegranate tree at the city gates, until the moon faded and the sun rose high in the sky, long past the hour she was due to appear, well, not even he knows that.

My Parents Marry – War Breaks Out –
I Am Conceived

Mother's trunk is made of iron and red-painted oakwood. Carved into the lid, in curlicued letters filled with dust, are her maiden initials – EHR. The wood is split and covered with a film of oily dust. The padlock and key are missing; nevertheless an iron hasp fastens the lid, the underside of which features three hand-painted miniatures. When my grandfather Mr Rafferty was still a watchmaker he collected these vignettes on his business trips to Asia, having planned to use them to decorate his export-bound watches. Instead he gave them to my mother. The first painting, the smallest and most finely detailed, depicts a littoral with the tide in full ebb; sand occupies the bottom third of the picture and the remaining area is filled by the sea; inscribed by the edge of the water is a little crab. The second scene is more typical of the period: a boat, armed with cannons and culverins, sets sail under a glowering sky; the port is thronged with well-wishers, and behind this multitude loom the dream-vistas of an Eastern city. The third shows the vizier's daughter Scheherazade kneeling beside King Shahrayar, who is wrapped in the bejewelled blankets of his divan. Dinarzad, Scheherazade's sister, peeps out from beneath the bed. All three are awake; the King's eyes are wet and amazed; Dinarzad smiles; Scheherazade looks commandingly towards the King, her arms raised, her whole person poised as if to say: 'Listen!'

Focusing my powers of listening, relaunching my history after that interloper Edrisi, and fixing my mind upon the sounds that flocked the air in the months after Rex and Mr Rafferty met in the basement of 16 Ingolstadt Place, I can reveal that my parents were married without pomp in June 1939. Reverberating around the cloisters I hear the sound of their dry-kissing lips.

There are other sounds that reach me from that day. I hear a chorus of well-wishers, admirers, advice-givers, but I can't detect the voice of Mr Rafferty. Years on the run had left him reluctant to appear in public, despite the legitimacy conferred upon him by his association with the War Office. He was unwilling to assume his duties as father-of-the-bride and, twenty minutes before the service began, approached the official photographer, an ungainly colossus who was lost when not peering through his viewfinder, and confiscated his apparatus, indicating that he – father-of-the-bride – would swap roles with him. The photographer, accustomed to life experienced in miniature, was led out of the church and into the arms of my mother, who, as always, indulged his paranoia.

Thus, it was not Mr Rafferty whom the guests observed accompanying Mother to the altar, but an awkward giant dressed in a grey suit. Had they looked over their shoulders, however, they would have seen an equally taciturn fellow in dark glasses, smiling like an open piano.

Mr Rafferty did not utter a word that day; instead he let his camera do the talking. (He was a shutterbug as well as a watchmaker, the clock and camera being kith and kin by virtue of their desire to measure, sort, and finally kill time.) His camera hung dormant during the ceremony, covered by his jacket, and awoke in the daylight of the churchyard. *Click* – Mother is captured in her accordion-pleated skirt with red roses in her hair.

Click – a portrait of the extended family with aching grins (Mr Rafferty waited too long before he tripped the shutter). *Click* – a dazzled-looking father-of-the-bride. *Click* – Father, his thick fair hair refusing to settle, despite the superabundance of hair wax, into a side parting, giving him a calamitous look. *Click* – the happy couple, their eyes bursting with hand-tinted colour; Mother's green and diaphanous; Father's the pale blue of a feeble dreamer.

The only evidence my grandfather left of his attendance at the ceremony were snapshots. As he was the photographer, and not the photographed, no trace of his presence survives. I could go on describing the photographs. But, although they are no doubt lodged in some cranny in the attic, and easily found, I shall leave them to the mice. Already, without setting eyes on them, my notion of the wedding has acquired a mawkish haze.

Shortly after the wedding, my father left Oxford, Lagos-bound, where he had been posted to work as an Assistant District Officer. My mother planned to join him some months later, but towards the end of July, as Europe prepared to unleash its martial hate, the government stopped non-essential sea-passages to Africa. And so Mother, who had packed her trunk in readiness, remained in Oxford during the war. She continued to look after the shop, since even during the war – perhaps especially because time takes on different properties, in particular for those who experience the rupture of death – people need to tell the time. During the onslaught, Mother refused to have me conceived. 'I will not birth my child into this firepit,' she told Rex in 1942, during his only leave. And so I, who, once introduced to the womb, chose to linger, was absented from the war. As I sit here at my desk, cold, my skylight framing the starless night, I ask myself questions. Would it have been different had I been born in the earlier decade? Would it have been me – Evie Steppman – no matter when Mother fell pregnant? Was I destined to matricide, or did circumstance make me a murderer?

. . .

I visited Mr Rafferty this afternoon. I found him in an excitable mood. As he swung open the door to his room, he said, 'Welcome, Herr Hoffmantel, you're already late for the performance.' He gestured me to sit. He busied himself in the white rectangle of his room, adjusting invisible knobs on the few pieces of furniture – iron bed, washstand, several moulded chairs, a low table; each white, seamless and unforgiving – doing little exercises with his fingers. Every so often he knocked on the side of the bed, scuttled to the door and flung it open. 'Come in, Mr Mudge,' he would say. Or, 'Monsieur Le Roy, it's wonderful to have you here.' He ushered each new arrival to their seat. After some time, during which more elaborate preparations were made, Mr Rafferty turned and faced his audience. He took out an ivory stick, which, pinched between thumb and forefinger, he brandished in an exaggerated arc. After appealing for calm, he went to the small perspex window at the far end of the room, flipped the latch, climbed onto one of the chairs and cocked his right ear as far as the white bars would allow. The throb of an Edinburgh afternoon drifted into the room. He snapped the window shut. *Silence.* 'Take your seats, ladies and gentlemen,' he said. 'The performance is about to begin.' He came down from the chair. He resembled a decrepit circus master. 'Signorina Marías, settle comfortably, I know how you like to fidget! And you, Mr Sinai, here's a handkerchief for your cucumber . . . to which we are all indebted, but whose noise we mustn't let spoil the performance. Regret-

64

tably, I must add, the Gräfin von Hahn-Hahn is unable to attend. She telephoned me this morning to say she has just invented electricity.

'Each of you is skilled in the art of listening,' he continued. 'You each received an aural training from childhood. This performance, then, is constituted by you. I am simply the conduit.'

Mr Rafferty once again opened the window. He stood facing the angled square of perspex, his back to me, both arms raised, in his left hand the ivory wand with which he conducted the silence. For, in spite of the open window, silence reigned over that padded room. Then he raised his arms, balled his hands and punched the air. At once, silence changed her name.

In swept the thrum of traffic, dully, distantly, vibrations of cars, buses, truck-thunder, the sudden shriek of a bicycle's brakes. Silence. From which opened quiet machine-noise, the Green Man's yelp. And now the flurry of footsteps, shouting voices, the collapsed hobble of the old. And there were seagulls, perched on roofs and everywhere circling; shifting, the sand at Portobello beach; shivering, the leaves of the old oak on Princes Street.

At length, when the city was sounding in an immense caterwauling, Mr Rafferty leaped to the window and snapped it shut. Delighted with his performance, I began to clap.

Later that evening, as I waited for a bus at York Place, the silence was immense. For the first time in many months the ringing in my ears had disappeared. And the few sounds I heard at that almost completely deserted hour were solitary and discontinuous, which only deepened the silence.

Why does that which makes the greatest noise breed silence?

Certainly, after the cruel disharmony of war, in the weeks and months following May 1945, and stretching into the New Year, a great silence prevailed.

Silent were the skies. Silent the soldiers, inched under the soil. Silent too the burned bodies, heaped in cinders. Unspeaking were my parents after the war. Silent the guns. Silent the wasted cavalcade of men, women and children as they journeyed, blind, towards their homes that were different to how they had left them. Without noise, heaped under blankets, my parents made love for the first time. Silent too the fires that had burned down cities. Silent the gas chambers, an echo of their quietening work. Silently the seed thrust towards the egg. Silent the monsters of war, spent of fuel. Silent the waves breaking against the bow of the mailboat as it pierced the seas towards Africa. Silence at the Captain's table, where Rex and Evelyn once dined on their way to Lagos. Silent, without tears, were the mothers whose children died for Progress. Silent the birds in Japan. Silent the rock. Without words, my parents crossed the bar of Lagos and motored towards Customs Wharf. Silent the yachts, rocking in the wake of their boat. Silent the lawns, with their muted underlife. Silently my parents sipped tea on the veranda. A season of silence.

And all the time I was growing inside Mother and listening.

6

I Gestate, Listen, and –
Finally – I Am Born

Listening, I gambolled in the womb. I turned somersaults and figures-of-eight. I saw nothing, felt only the warm stickiness of the amnion. No odours reached me in my chamber. Not the stink of gin or soap, spoiling meat or burned oil. A mermaid sings. I was not a mermaid. A grub in a preserving jar floats in an azoic age. I was not that grub. Without conscience, I took in every sound.

This is what I heard: the vicious spitting of feral cats, rug-beaters thwacking, traffic-bustle and crowds. Fat goats being led to market, their bleating disharmonious and afraid. Women pounding manioc. Hawkers singing shrill and repetitive love songs to vegetables, paeans to fish and fruit – *shrimps, prawns, smoked alive! Lovely oranges, lovely fresh oranges* – and tailors, their sewing machines chattering in bursts. Hiss and splutters were street food cooking in palm oil. I heard the punishing of boy-thieves. And at all times of the day and night the ringing of insects. The womb, helped by the resonance of the amniotic fluid, sounded with the buzz, the flutterings, the shrill almost musical droning. And in the rainy season, thunder and the wild mutiny of rain, the curtain cord striking the window. I noted the coursing hum of blood. The sea too was almost always present.

When I was twelve weeks in the womb my parents embarked on a tour of Nigeria. We – the three of us – travelled up from Lagos, past Ibadan and Illorin and, after crossing the Niger River, to the city of Zaria, where prayer-songs and cantillation echoed in my head, new sounds I took in hungrily. At Gusau I heard three bars of a chorus played on a piano, over and over again. My parents toured Nigeria, and the quiet but invasive whisper of the sea was replaced by the sucking-noise of car tyres on muddied roads, forest paths, long-drawn footfalls and aspirate conversation. I recall the unique echoing of public spaces, antechamber, church, mosque, state hall. The splitting crackle of a bush fire. Bird notes, one especially I remember, a flute-like call. And another, a kind of boom resembling the distant baying of a hound. I heard the slapping of limbs during wrestling matches. The agonies of a constipated child.

And if the sounds swept in any-which-way, I too was indiscriminate, so that amid the commonplace I also heard that which is normally held aloof, set aside for night or passed off with a quick intake of air, things which cannot be repeated easily: District Officers' dirty jokes, lovers' sighs, the death agonies of men. All of us, in the echo chamber of the womb, are able to receive the wildest spectrum of sounds; it's simply that we cannot retain them as we grow up. Who, in their maturity, can recall the special sound of sunlight? It rings in the ears as when one circles the top of a fine-wrought wine glass. And the tumescent heat of Nigeria, which sprawls and rumbles like a jet aeroplane. I heard the almost unbearable sorrow of an elephant's call, the sad music of the nightsoil workers at Five Cowrie Creek. I eavesdropped on smugglers' tales, and they reminded me of prey-birds swooping, bent on murder. I perceived three worlds in the rhythm a girl beat out on an aluminium barrel at the same time each evening: the one that surrounds us, the reality that one can sense; the world of those who are dead and buried but continue to exist and may participate in our lives; and the splendid realm of objects, which hold in their very matter, despite their incapacity, the sign of everyone who has held them, traded, buried, smitten, pocketed, hurled, sought knowledge from, tapped out a rhythm on or packed away. My ears were keenly alert. They were small, yet they captured every sound.

It was not always this way. In the beginning, when I resembled a transparent grub, there was silence. In truth there was none because silence needs its other; and since I had no ears to speak of I had no noise and thus no silence. Rather, in the beginning there was a great emptiness. The silence was in me. And the silence was me. It lasted eighty days.

Then the first stirrings of sound. Tiny to begin with, as if woken from hibernation. Next, on top of – or it seemed beneath – this animal crackle awoke a steady hiss that resembled gas escaping; which grew more insistent, filling out at the lower registers, becoming more complicated. And then the sounds really began to break through into the womb because every day now – one hundred days had passed – a new bark or caterwauling echoed in my head. I experienced this noise wholly and without names. The only modulation was by degree of volume – and steadily the sounds grew louder. There were too many at times, too many scratchings and thunderings to take account of, too great a roar as the world turned audibly – I could feel the shrill vibration of the heat on top of everything – all this abundance of noise, this wall of life turned into an exclusive sound, white noise perhaps, but more brilliant and penetrating, like a Victoria Falls made not of water but of seething flowing electricity and light. I took in the timbres all at once, the whole diapason of life, and also I heard, faintly but unmistakably, the slow-grinding fire machinery and toil of the shadows under the earth and within it.

It was then, at the point when my hearing became of this world and also of another, I understood that this cacophony was made of many different sounds. Just as, five months after my conception, I recognized that light and shade, and even shadow, played on the walls of the womb, it came to me that no single entity could make so much noise. I had discovered timbre, yet I had no way of differentiating what was an awesome Babel. One must understand that, womb-bound, the foetus is separated from the outside by layers of skin and muscle. She is surrounded by viscous liquid, and like the sounds one hears when swimming or lazing in the bath, they are deadened, but also amplified, so that her ability to discern different tones is distorted by this mutedness and echo. I must emphasize that the early sounds of my gestation had no name. It was only later, when I resembled a shelled prawn, that I was able to identify them. At the time it was one great tumult, a torrent of sound, and I was threatened with drowning. Soon, it is true, I began to perceive differences. For instance, I came to understand that inside me, although a pathetic parody of throb, was a heartbeat, when before I knew only my mother's thumping muscle. The murmur of my stomach was, I noticed, weaker and more aqueous than my mother's superior gut. And then, in the sixth month of my gestation, I began to distinguish between the sounds of my mother's internal workings and those from the outside. No longer did the sea match the flutter of blood though her veins and arteries. I next set apart the flurrying of the leaves, moved by the wind, from insect rustlings. And the rasping of lead on paper became marked in relation to the spiralling needle of a gramophone. All this is far from the final mastery I had over sound. Alien was any sort of classification system. This was to come later. My hearing was demotic and unprincipled.

It was, I understand now, the opposite of a photograph, which preserves only an image, divorcing, at the moment of the shutter's click, sound from vision. My hearing resembled more willingly a wholly different, though related, invention of the nineteenth century – the phonograph: a machine that for the first time captured sounds, isolated them from the object from which they came, and stored them, as if frozen, until they were ready to be replayed. Sounds in general are connected with action and utterance, tied to the mechanisms that produce them. I had no notion of the shape of an elephant, only its call and thunderous walk. To this day I take pleasure in thinking of such occasions: always vague and indefinite, encouraging movement, the essence of my freedom in the womb and, in part, the reason for my reluctance to be born. For instance, the sound of a ship's horn heard late at night so that the ship is obscured by darkness; or the sound of rain striking the roof of a house or tent, preferably at night; or birdsong in the trees when one cannot know if the bird is many-coloured or ugly spotted brown; or the sound of an orchestra tuning up in the pit which conveys an excitement, since not only are the musicians hidden but one cannot distinguish between their noise; or the many-levelled bell-peal on Sundays; who is tugging at the ropes, blind Captain? hunchbacked man?; or the soughing of the wind, heard beneath blankets so one cannot distinguish it from one's frenzied breathing; or any noise that is distorted by the echoes of tunnels and arches, such as when one whistles or shouts beneath a viaduct and one's voice returns undoubtedly one's own but changed, the reflection of one's voice; or, indeed, the diffusion of any recognizable sound into a space where it is distant, distorted, indeterminate and not easily made out.

It was, I think, for this same reason that my mother found my presence inside her difficult to understand. I was a fish swimming in her waters, tied to her and nourished by everything she drank down. But also not piscean, something that was taking on the form of her: two-legged, mostly hairless, with fingers and even fingerprints – undoubtedly like her – yet living inside her. Creation weighed down and confused my mother.

I delighted in my formlessness and incapacity to discern. What I heard I felt loath to interpret. Yet I understood I had to make something of this world that was pouring into me. If I did not I knew that the massiveness of it all, the abundance and disharmony would stifle my development. And then something changed. After seven months in the womb, a new sound arrived. Until that moment Father had been absent. I had not heard his voice, had spent my days alone with Mother in our mutual cave, which had been as large as the world. The sun, filtering through her dresses and pellucid skin, had filled the womb with diffused rust-colours, pinks, apricot, bistre. At night it was as if I had sunk to the bottom of the sea. The banks of darkness were occasionally disturbed by light, and I dreamed confusedly. But Father's voice changed everything; and with it the tick-tock of the pocket watch arrived, a new sound, like a heartbeat but more regular. And whenever I heard the clock I heard a voice. Let me describe that voice: slightly nasal, not deep and sonorous, but low all the same, monotonous, rarely altering its pedagogic drawl, sometimes sliding to the higher registers, abruptly cutting off, disappearing, always returning. It was not long before I began to pick out certain words. Where does the voice reside? I asked myself. And then I understood that my gurglings came from within and were the nascent forms of my father's superior lexicon. I perceived that it responded to Mother's higher, fluting voice, and that certain expressions produced laughter, others seriousness or consternation. Was it, the voice, attached to the body? And, if so, what relationship might it have to the mind or soul? I had no time to answer these questions because soon the words became sentences, and I knew syntax. I was at a disadvantage, of course, since I was growing under the sign of the phonograph. Yet there were moments of respite. For instance, when Father recited portions of *Gray's Anatomy* I was able to construct a crude map of my body. I felt my ear like a tiny conch. I came to think of tibia and fibula as sisters. I had only a partial idea of the shape of the human form; instead I gestured outward. I mapped the geography of Narium Minor, following in my mind the Intercostal Artery to the Costal Cartilages, where, across a thin and sanguine sea, Pectoralis Minor began. Here, so I imagined, stood the Pyramidalis Nasi built by the embondaged monsters Coccyx, Os Hyoides, Tarsus, Sacrum and Ischium, stolen from the Underworld. And there was Atlas holding the sky on his shoulders!

At first I revelled in this learning, for I perceived that I might be able to contain the sounds that threatened to engulf me. I discovered in everything Father said a certain way of compartmentalizing the world. Where once the sounds had segued together, now, with my father's teachings, I learned that each object and every sound had its opposite. I discovered that East and West repelled one another. I understood that Cat and Sparrow were coupled in mutual hate. And yet it struck me that, even as this conception of the world made it easy to know, name and thus understand, it also made the world unfree. And, of course, on all sides resounded the tick-tock of the pocket watch. I recoiled instinctively, since my inclination was to play. I found renewed joy in acrobatics. Night after night I was subject to my father's noisome words. It was then I decided to remain in the womb, quiet in my submerged cavern, where miracles daily occurred; there, amid the amnion, I was free to tumble and dream.

Meanwhile, on the outside, Mother lay supine on her

reclining chair. She sipped camomile tea. She ate limes. An ostrich-feather fan relieved momentarily the sticky fly-midden of heat. By the eighth month of her pregnancy, the weight of me was too great; fat-bellied, immobile, she would call for Ade – our servant-boy – to press wet cottons to her forehead and footsoles. In the day, when Father was at the Executive Board, Mother would clasp her arms tightly around her abdomen, crushing me into a half-portion of the womb. Sometimes she exposed me to the daylight, and I felt nearly poached and I twisted and sobbed. There were occasions when she would feather her stomach with lightly nerved fingers and call me her 'little hatchling', her 'bald dove', her 'stubborn splinter'. Her courage would suddenly leave her. She voiced fears: that her slim hips – 'boy's hips', Father called them – might prevent me from slipping out whole, or else squeeze me into horrid shapes. At night came the temporary relief of darkness, and all my energies came to the fore. I would kick and flail, testing my new subtlety of movement. It was then, overcome, she would weep silently into her pillow. She cursed me under her breath, then Father for his pleasure that had brought this about. She began to call on saints and whisper prayers, although she had no religion. Father would rise from his bed heavily, aware that he could not better the situation, and fumble for the border of his mosquito net. He would climb out and stand over Mother, who was wet with perspiration, not daring to lift her netting. 'Are you safe, Evelyn?' he would say. And, 'Is he coming now? Shall I call the doctor?' We were like enemies, Mother and I, joined, but in mutual loathing.

I was, I believe, an unreality to her. She tried to understand children and called for Ade.

'Play, Ade. I want to know about games.'

'I play outside.'

'You'll kindly adapt.'

Ade would visit her during the long, hot afternoons. He showed her how to fold a square of paper into a point, press a thumb along each edge, then snap one's fingers and transform the paper into a white aeroplane. He made telephones from empty cans and lengths of string. He broke bread into pieces and threw them from the window; all at once Hoopoe birds arrived and snatched the morsels from the air. It was learning about play that shifted her idea of me. She understood that soon I would be a presence on the outside. And when she understood this, she wanted rid of me. Until then we had been indissolubly tied to one another. I was nourished by her; equally, my mood and vigour or weaknesses affected her so finely that it changed her skin colour and textures and dictated her eating patterns as well as her body's shape. So we both understood that we were one thing and not a pair. But then, once I had reached the eighth month of my womb-term, and had manoeuvred into the birth position, Mother began to endow her swelling with the aspect of a recognizable form. And she wouldn't have me inside.

It was a crushingly hot morning in May. Father was at Ibadan for three days. Mother, dressed in a white wrapper, left the house with Ben – Ade's father and our cook and driver. They drove west along the Ikoyi Road, which ran between the golf course and the European cemetery, crossed the Macgregor Canal and on past the Brazilian quarter to the law courts. There, at Tinubu Square, Mother instructed Ben to let her out of the car. Walking through the dusty labyrinth of streets, she came to a lane where a clay hut lurched against a wall. She found them inside: mother, father and idiot son. They stood in the cluttered room, utterly remote from one another, their skin cracked and veined with mud. The man and the woman each held a teacup from England, the large, breakfast kind, flower-patterned like the cloth which covered the old woman's swollen hips. And the cups, which also lined the shelves, were cracked like their faces, with dirt also in the veins and without handles so that the pair – though not the son, who hadn't the grip to hold anything but the flowery rag he wrenched between the fingers of one hand – encircled them, tenderly, as if the cups themselves, and not their contents, were precious. Now and then a lorry passed by on the road outside, which caused the cups on the shelves to rattle and also the supply tins, cut in half and their tops discarded, which it seemed held the family's possessions – seeds, dried potatoes, gin, nails, nuts and bolts, clippings from *The Times*, resins, amulets, medicines, but also weirder things: shrunken monkey's heads, chameleon skins, white rooster feathers. The old woman shifted her cumbersome weight and gestured Mother to a corner of the room where tins of many-coloured liquids stood. Mother paid for a blue vial and pocketed it away.

I had not heard it at first, perhaps because of the whine of the traffic, but gradually, as I had become accustomed to the stillness of the room, not stillness but something weightier, viscous and blank-dark, I had started to hear a low yellow groan, a continuous whine voiced not out of conscious despair, nor anything thought-of, but simply to occupy the quiet. Later, when Mother was back at our house in Ikoyi, I understood that that strange groan had come from between the toothless gums of the idiot boy.

And it was that same unyielding naked moan that accompanied me during the following days, days in which every other sound was eclipsed, those shattered fighting days. Mother had swallowed the blue liquid and spent the next morning climbing stairs, and in the afternoon sweated hours in a hot bath. She went to bed after and shuddered, sobbed openly. The rainy season had begun, and I too was weeping, clamped limpet-like to the womb wall. At times Ben came in from the kitchen, bringing food and limewater. He said he was going to call the doctor, he knew what was coming, but Mother shooed him away, it was all right, he was not coming now, it was only a dress rehearsal. It felt like I was being forced by a vast sea, the indrifts came with pain, and I fought hard against Mother and her poison's will. But I knew I had won when her muscles relaxed and she cursed the old woman for giving her a weak drug.

When Father returned he found her in bed, still weeping. She shouldered him away and refused his touch lest he upset her and me inside. 'What have I done?' she whispered.

I do not know whether the poison was designed to finish me or simply to induce the birth. Whatever her intention by taking it, it made me more determined to stay put. Soon I had dwelt longer than nine months. Mother now lay motionless in the day, occasionally dozing. Father dared not leave her and spent much time chattering. His talk was different than before. Now I heard the Arthur Ransome stories, the adventures of the *Arabian Nights*. He read aloud portions of certain novels. I listened with puzzlement, although never with indifference. And the longer I delayed my birth, the keener my sense of hearing became.

Nevertheless, I began to conceive Father as a danger to me. He was, I told myself, an inverse Scheherazade: he told stories, true, yet they were intended not to preserve but arrest life – his purpose, I thought, was to prevent my birth. Could it be that as long as I listened to this nightly chatter I would be unable to emerge from the womb? I began to think it might be better on the outside. I knew that there was greater variety in the world than my father recognized. Had I not heard its miraculous cacophony? Might it not be my task to try to regain this lost possibility? Besides, I was tired of the dampened underwater sounds, of stories only ever half told. So I took the decision to be born.

By then, however, after the forty-sixth week of her pregnancy, the doctors had decided to have me induced. At the Children's Hospital midwives administered morphine and wet presses to my mother. Doctors swabbed below her belly button and readied their scalpels. They tried to cut me out. But no doctor ushered my arrival. I – myself only – timed my birth. On August the second at six o'clock, I began to initiate the contractions. In and out, in and out, I rocked the womb wall. There was tearing flesh. There was blood. And through her pain, mother whispered, 'Late, late. Stubborn as a splinter.'

Afterwards, Mother lay on the blooded sheets, empty and half-spent, blinking at me, unable to hold my weight. Father or one of the nurses would support me by the back and head and tilt me towards her. But she died after three days of this.

So the first ceremony I attended was my mother's funeral. I was not brought like every new-born to have holy water dowsed on my forehead. Instead, east we went, to St Saviour's Church on Ikoyi Island. As I lay quiet in my cot (and my mother in hers), the mourners' eyes flitted from cot to coffin, from coffin to cot, some sad for our family, others appalled, one pair of eyes, my father's, narrowed in shame.

I kept quiet. I shed no tears. And for the most part neither did my father. But – only I noticed – as the priest spoke his final lamentation, a single tear fell from my father's right eye. I see it now, inching down his cheek, slowly at first, then quickening, until it reaches the crest of his mouth; where it halts for a moment, caught between his closed lips; then, with their parting, Father's tear makes its way down to the tip of his chin; suspends; and falls, silently striking my forehead.

7

Transcribing My Mother's Diary

Sometimes I have the feeling that my memory is a mausoleum of broken sounds. I feel an almost unbearable sadness when I think of all I have heard, the little that I retain and everything that is gone, all those minute, unutterable tones which most faithfully encapsulate my history. I know that one day all the sounds will disappear. Occasionally they will drift towards me like ghosts and timorously make themselves known. But gradually they will be overwhelmed by the rising clamour in my ears, as stars are eclipsed by city lights. It will take a bit of time. To begin with there will be an intensifying of pitch and volume. Next, the higher registers will expire. Then all timbre will be lost. One by one the sounds will merge until my hearing is no more than a roar alternating with a terrible silence. All I will be left with are these words.

Arrived at Jebba on 17th November, reads the first entry in my mother's diary. It is a journal for the year 1945, leather-bound, measuring ten inches by five. It has been lying in Mother's trunk since her death, when Father packed her belongings away. Since I moved up to the attic I have read the diary many times; as, I imagine, did Father in the course of his top-floor retreat. Soon the mice will discover the journal. Like me, they will consume the words. And in the process they will destroy the paper on which they are written. I will, then, preserve, here on my computer, this record of my parents' tour. The diary continues: DO Niger met us at the station. We must have looked a couple of frights. Red dust matted my hair and Rex's eyebrows. The DO took us to the rest house.

The following day Mother writes: Up at dawn. Smell of the Niger upon waking. In the cheerful blueness of the sky I see a kite. It was white, like the djellabahs Moslems wear. Bright sunlight and the air fresh. We go down to the river, a broad, silvery expanse flowing slowly between low banks. Spiky acacias, tamarind, neem and I think mahogany trees of a great height. In one short avenue their branches intertwine, making arches. They call this place the Cathedral. – 20th November. We take an excursion in a dugout canoe, big enough for a half-a-dozen more besides Rex and myself. The water is the colour of polished steel and the clouds shine upwards from the surface. Rex is obsessed with shooting. We pass a Goliath Heron with a speckled breast. It is sitting on a log and Rex takes a shot at it, but the vibration of the boat makes him miss and it flies off the way we had come. – 25th November. From Jebba via Minna and Kaduna on the narrow-gauge railway and into Zaria province. The heat in the carriage is intolerable. Arrive Zaria late. Sick. This morning a fearsome racket. Sick again.

On the 28th of November Mother noted that her sickness was almost over. The following day, she writes: We have taken a truck north-west through flat farmland dotted with baobab trees. Villages frequent. After the first twenty miles the green country changes into arid scrub. In several places, bush fires rage close to the road. Rex restless after the long stay in Zaria. All are happy to be on our way again. The sun is large and orange and is very different to the sun in England. Dawn and dusk are the pleasantest hours. The sun peeps out over the horizon and then it seems to rise all at once. At dusk there is supposed to be a blue flash, which you can just see as the sun disappears and then it gets dark very quickly. Always we have a campfire. Then the mosquitoes arrive. You must have had your bath by then, or you'll be bitten. Next you get into your trousers and mosquito boots and a long-sleeved shirt and you sit by the campfire and have your drink of gin and bitter. The night closes around you and you are very aware of the stars.

The following day they reached Gusau. From here – writes Mother – we go by horseback. Rex excitable as he is keen to see the bush. Spends the whole day gathering porters. I wander through the town with the Resident, a General. Children follow us everywhere. At the market the noise is terrific. The General persuades a merchant to wave a spear in the air and, unbeknownst to him, takes his photograph. Decorated calabashes and spoons made from gourds. Food sellers. English cotton. We're followed everywhere by the rabble of inquisitive children and also disappointed traders. The General seemed very set on buying me some antimony. That evening at the club, without anyone asking, Rex said that the most remarkable thing he'd ever seen was a drawing of a pelican. She had a gash in her side, and her young fed boisterously from the wound.

– 3rd December. I knew that it was true because again this month it hasn't come. I feel neither gladness nor pain, only dazed.

– 4th December. At every village we approach now the district head arrives with a company of horsemen. He goes with us to our rest hut and exchanges greetings in Hausa. Sannu da ruwa, he says, which means, Welcome with the rain. And, Ranka ya dade, which means, May your life be long. One of the chief pleasures of touring is going for a walk between five and sunset. You stop and talk to people. Then someone might want to show you something. A bush with fragrant leaves, or a black and turquoise centipede, or their new baby. At night we hear voices calling and chatting and there is drumming. And wherever we go there is a dance laid on. The dancers wear magnificent head-dresses of sisal. Rex sits on his camp chair like a village Chief. Declares his approval, calling, Yâuwaa. And, Bàllee bàllee. At Maradun, a tiny outpost, with a police sergeant and no other Europeans, they were going to do us a dance called the Bòorii but they got so frightfully drunk they couldn't perform it. The sergeant left and came back with his men from the jail and all these jailbirds solemnly stripped in the moonlight and started to dance. The sergeant danced in the middle. I could see his bald head bobbing up and down. It reminded me of England. But that is another life. I can scarcely believe I am the same person, and in Africa.

It is clear from Mother's notes that they were travelling west. At times her handwriting is indecipherable, and pages are left entirely blank. The diary continues: Here the tiniest detail takes on enormous importance. One must establish a routine. After breakfast, if not travelling overland, a wash, a letter to be written, perhaps an entry in my diary, then a walk into the village. Rest during the hottest hours of the day, then a book, perhaps as yesterday a visit to the mosque, the evening glass of gin, dinner with the residents, bed. Equally the things one normally worries about seem quite trivial. This afternoon, for instance, we met a Scotsman, a small trader, and his son. Rex thought it was the 14th of December, the trader swore it was the 9th, and his son the 13th. We had lost the days of the week altogether. Haircut from Ben. Slept only for two hours, then lay awake imagining that the distant voices from the village meant danger.

– We have stopped in the forest town of W. Rex is gathering information about a group of ex-soldiers who are causing all manner of trouble in Sokoto province. Our house is no more than a hut. Of wattle and mud. It's round with a single room and mud floors. It is next to the village Mosque, which doubles as the courthouse. The coolness of the forest is welcome relief. And the silence is strange. It is not flat silence but everywhere the chirping of insects and the stirring of branches. This morning, Ben found a mongrel puppy and brought it to me. It was hurt. Rex said I should keep it and was terribly excited and went to fetch some meat. It was so afraid, it kept shivering away from my touch. When it had retreated a foot it would dip its head and weakly wag its tail. Eventually I shooed it away and Rex came in and said, Dammit, Eve, can't you give the little mite a chance, and I said nothing and walked out of the hut. Rex followed me and said, What's wrong? And suddenly I knew I hated him, standing there with healthy red cheeks, clear eyes. Every day they grow clearer.

— 14th December. It is remarkable how Ben manages to produce such delightful meals. He cooks with a debbie, a four-gallon paraffin tin with its top cut out and coals underneath. He mixes flour, yeast and water in the morning and has it carried in cloths. As soon as the fires are made in the evening out comes the dough, which he bakes at night in a hole in the ground, with cinders. Without our porters, eight in total, as well as Ben and Talle, it would be impossible to make headway in this terrain. One realizes the world is designed as one great work-pit so that certain people don't have to think about everyday affairs. What is done with our nightsoil, I wonder? Apart from suitcases, which contain our clothing, there are campbeds to be carried, tents, chairs and tables, the canvas bath, Lord's lamps, kerosene, cases of china, gas, cutlery, linen, even fireworks. And, of course, the chop box.

— 26th December. Everything suddenly changes. Woken in the afternoon to the sound of a sharp, persistent rattling on the roof. Like being in a tent during a downpour. The clouds, instead of disappearing after a while, as on previous days, all at once increased in size and advanced towards us, blotting out the sky. Ben and Talle appeared from nowhere and began to rush around the residence, pulling in curtains and shutting windows and banging doors. We were only just in time, for suddenly came a roaring wind. Then the dust. It battered violently against the window panes. Inside the house, the temperature dropped like a stone, and I found myself searching in my trunk for something warm to wear. The harmattan. It gusts in from the desert, lifting sand and insects and god knows what, then comes spinning south in a choking red cloud. I'm writing this from the house of the District Commissioner at Sokoto. The sun shines feebly through the window. It looks like an English fog, but instead of feeling clammy, it's harsh and stinging. Frequent applications of salve do not prevent our lips from cracking. This morning Rex left with Ben to check on the supplies. They returned, and for a terrible moment I thought they were coughing up blood. It was only the sand that had got through their scarves and into their mouths. We have been stuck indoors for three days. But we have only to wait until the wind passes. Then we'll press on.

Last night Rex, the Commissioner, Ben, Talle and I sat in the living room. The Commissioner told us about suicide among expats, a common phenomenon. But it is Ben's story I remember most clearly. He told us about the people of the Saharan desert and the tribes of the Sahel, who for centuries have practised a form of commerce known as silent trading. The inhabitants of the Sahara trade salt and receive gold in return. The salt is carried from the desert to the Niger River, where the transaction takes place. The Saharans leave a mound by the riverbank and then retreat. The Sahels deposit gold of equivalent value beside the mound. Once they have gone, the salt traders return. If they think the gold is sufficient, they take it, leaving the salt. If not, they take neither and retreat. The Sahels return and either increase the amount of gold or retrieve it. This process is repeated until both parties are satisfied and in this manner they conduct their commerce, never seeing one another and never speaking.

– And then, on the third evening of our confinement, the Commissioner stood up and raised his glass. Happy Christmas! he cried. We hadn't known! We sang carols. Played endless rounds of Bridge. Toasted George VI. Though not Talle, who doesn't recognize our King.

It is past twelve. I am writing this in near darkness, from the rest house where we are staying. I want to set down faithfully the events of the evening. We had been invited to the compound of Tanimu Usman. I had expected an official in his senior years. But the man who met us after the servant-boy had led us into the hall was young, in his early thirties, not much older than Rex. That was the first surprise. The second was that he was dressed in a sports suit, a Denman and Goddard, which, I learned, he had bought in Savile Row. His face was large and fine-boned, and his skin wonderfully reflective. He had round horn-rimmed spectacles, which he wore slightly tinted. Rex shook his hand and gave the traditional greeting. Tanimu Usman held his right hand up. Let us speak in English, he said. His voice was remarkably deep. I felt it in my stomach when he said, And this lovely lady must be your wife. He clasped my hands in his. He was not a big man, although his shoulders were very wide. I hope you like our country, he said. And he led us into the sitting room. There were several armchairs, a couch, a bookshelf and a handsome bureau, besides indigo cloths hanging on the walls. Standard lamps stood in three corners of the room. They gave off a warm yellow light.

Tanimu Usman opened a drinks cabinet and took out several bottles. He turned to Rex and poured a drink. I believe you are from Scotland, he said. I have been there. I travelled all over the United Kingdom after my studies. France and Belgium too. He paused. Since you are from Scotland you will understand something of our national aspirations. He poured a second drink and handed the glass to me. And you, he said, are from Oxford. I spent three happy years there as an undergraduate. Please, he said, gesturing to a side table, where a plate of gadgets lay. He himself didn't touch a morsel the entire evening. In the semi-darkness of the room Tanimu Usman got up from his chair and crossed to the bureau. I looked at his bookshelf, Marlowe, Orwell, Lincoln, Machiavelli, *The New History of Music*, as well as various mystery novels. Reading is my passion, he said when he returned. But I have another, even greater hobby. Music. I listen to music all the time. He held up a pile of records. There was a gramophone on a small table beside the couch. Tanimu Usman placed a record on the turntable and lowered the arm until we heard the speakers crackle. Then the sound of a piano. I knew the piece. It was Beethoven's *Les Adieux*. Strange! My favourite of the sonatas. Tanimu Usman unbuttoned his jacket. He offered Rex a cigar, and they walked to the bureau and began to smoke. I listened to the music. It was make believe. One couldn't listen to that melancholy piano in the middle of the bush without one's ideas of Africa being swept from under one. After some time the record came to an end. Tanimu Usman looked up from his conversation with Rex. He said, You can turn the record over. Or perhaps you would like to play another. I wanted to hear something other than piano music. But I turned the record and set down the needle. Rex said, Are you feeling all right? I said, Yes, and joined them beside the bureau. Tanimu Usman said, How do you like the music? I said, Very much. Tanimu Usman said, You know, every time I go to Europe I bring back some records. I have quite a collection. All the classics. But I also collect phonographs. I have nine in total. My prize piece is very old, one of, I believe, only seventeen still in existence. He pulled open a drawer on the bureau and revealed a wooden box, lifted its lid and brought out a pale, strangely expressionless doll. Her hair was blonde, almost white, as was her dress. She doesn't work any more, he said, but her mechanism is intact. She's an Edison talking doll. He turned her so that she was lying face down on the bureau. Then he unbuttoned her dress and exposed a metal torso. He lifted a panel on her back and carefully pulled from her chest a tiny piece of machinery. It looked like the mechanism of a simple clock. But it was in fact a phonograph. It consisted of several cylinders connected by springs, a handle and finally a horn from which, he explained, a voice reciting 'Mary Had a Little Lamb' once played. Isn't she beautiful, he said. There was a silence. We all looked at the doll. Tanimu Usman sat her on the edge of the bureau, buttoned her dress, put her back in the box and lay the mechanism at her feet. He shut the lid and closed her once again in the bureau. Then he said, Perhaps I seem uneasy to you. I confess to that. Just now, when we were looking at the Edison doll, I started to think that understanding between us, we Africans, you Europeans, might be an impossibility. I believe, he said, what has happened over the last one hundred years has been a great misunderstanding. Rex said, I don't believe it for one minute, Mr Usman. In time we will come to view Nigeria as a demonstration of great cooperation between two quite different breeds of men. Tanimu Usman smiled. Then he said, That universal restorer, time! Restoring us to ourselves. Revealing the truth of the past. But I find myself questioning this most pervasive of ideas. What have we learned from you? Have you really something to offer us? There was a pause. Rex said, We have helped hundreds of separate and hostile communities to live peacefully together. And this peace has allowed free movement for the first time, not only for commerce but also for ideas and men. Tanimu Usman tilted his head from side to side. He took his spectacles off, rubbed his eyes and gestured wearily towards the couch. It was then, as he turned away, and Rex and I sat on the couch, the thought came to me that had we not come into Africa, then this room, the house, would have been very different, no record player, no doll, only certain of the books, and, of course, Tanimu Usman himself would have been different, without his beautifully tailored suit, his horn-rimmed spectacles. The fabric of the couch rubbed uncomfortably against my legs. Rex shifted his weight and leaned into the stiff-sprung backrest. The music had come to an end, and Tanimu Usman placed a new record on to the turntable. Again, we heard the hum and crackle of the needle on the disk. Immediately a large orchestra began to play. I said, What is the music? Tanimu Usman said, Haydn's Symphony number 45. No one spoke. I concentrated on the music. It filled the room. I became very aware of myself, sitting next to Rex and in front of Tanimu Usman, who stood to the side of the couch, slightly back, so that he was out of sight. After some time Rex said, What concerns me are those boys in the bush. Tanimu Usman didn't hear him, or he chose not to answer, because from his position beside the couch he said, You know, five or six years ago I might have agreed with what you say. I thought that Empire was a necessary phase in my country's history, in spite of the indignity. But the war has changed every-thing. The boys you refer to fought in Burma. They became used to a regular income, martial respect and killing. They returned to the North and there's nothing here for them. Rex said, But you could stop them if you chose. Tanimu Usman said, Perhaps I could. Perhaps it would be impossible. But if I managed it they would only strike up again, or else another group would take their place. He paused. I don't think it's sufficiently understood how important it is to consider the larger picture. Rex straightened his back, then said, Once we have reined in those marauding boys I will consider the larger picture. No one spoke. The orchestra became quiet. The performance might have been recorded at a concert hall because I thought I heard a cough from a member of the audience. Now the violins sounded, high, fast notes, and the orchestra answered, fell quiet, answered again. Tanimu Usman lowered himself into the armchair opposite the couch. He said, The boys are unimportant. Or rather, the boys alone cannot trouble you greatly. What they are searching for is change. Those boys fought for the British Empire, for democracy. Instead they hear Churchill say the Atlantic Charter is a guide and not a rule, that it is not applicable to the colonies. This leads them, and many others in the country, I myself am no exception, to ponder whether we should not prepare our own blueprint for self-government. I can see no hope for a prosperous and contented Nigeria under the present rule. In the half-light of the room I felt very awake. No one spoke. The music was quiet. I heard an insect drumming against the window. Rex stood and began to look at the books on the shelf. Now only the lower string section played, then the rest of the orchestra joined in. Tanimu Usman had crossed his legs, leaned his head against the back of the armchair and closed his eyes. After some time he lowered the volume. He opened his eyes, and it seemed he was about to say something. But he only turned the volume up and closed his eyes again. At one point the white-jacketed boy came into the room. He said that a telegram had arrived, but

Tanimu Usman didn't stir. He was lost in the music. But only a little later he opened his eyes and said, This piece, the Haydn symphony. There is a story behind its composition. Rex looked up from his book. The year was 1772. Every summer Prince Nicolaus holidayed at his castle at Eszterháza, which was remote from the capital. His court, of which Haydn and his musicians formed a part, were forced to leave their families behind. One year, because of a strange sickness, marked by a bruise on his chest, which looked like a set of tiny teeth, the prince decided to stay on past summer. Haydn wanted to return to his family, and so he composed a symphony at the end of which, one by one, the instruments fell silent. The musicians were instructed to extinguish their lights as soon as their part had come to an end and leave with their instruments under their arms. The prince at once understood the point of the performance, and, despite his sickness, he prepared to leave. Tanimu Usman finished speaking and closed his eyes. I tried to concentrate on the music, which was growing steadily quieter. I became aware of the crackle of the needle on the disk. After some time, without opening his eyes, Tanimu Usman said, The reed instruments have stopped playing and are leaving the stage. A little later he said, The horn players are putting out their lights and departing. Rex had returned to looking at the book. The double bass fell silent. Now only two violins were left, sounding faintly. Then they too died. After a moment, Tanimu Usman said, I wish our evening could be longer, but unfortunately I must bring it to an end. He stood up. I have work to do. I was reminded of this as we listened to the music. It gave me an idea for a speech I am writing for a gathering of emirs. This speech has been troubling me for a while, and now I see what I must write. He began to move towards the door. He looked exhausted. He stopped and said, I am sorry that I wasn't able to help you. I see that you are disappointed. You must understand that, when one is attempting to do something new, something that has never been done before, it calls for a great singleness of mind. The European countries arrived at nationhood naturally, over many years, although there too was a great unleashing of violence. Perhaps this violence is necessary for the birth of a nation. Here, in Nigeria, as with all African nations, we have very many obstacles to overcome. One cannot create something new without destroying the old. The affirmation of the former requires the negation of that which came before. The emirs, for example, to whom I will speak tomorrow, have an interest in keeping Nigeria divided. But the process has begun. There is much anger and much enthusiasm among our people. It will take a bit of time. But independence will come. It must come. He ended abruptly, turned and left the room, leaving us in silence. – Later, walking to the rest house, with our backs to the small white moon, diffused by clouds, I slipped my hand into Rex's hand. He had said little since leaving the compound, and I knew he was very disappointed. We walked through the narrow streets. On either side were tall buildings, with white turrets. I squeezed Rex's hand. How are you feeling? I said. He didn't reply. Then he said, Did you notice Mr Usman didn't take his jacket off. When we were standing by the bureau I asked him to take it off, but he wouldn't. We walked a little more slowly. I heard a faint drumming sound. Rex said, I know why he refused. It was because his sleeves were dirty. I saw the dirt on his cuffs. He has dirty sleeves. I felt a tingling in my eyelids and when I closed them I saw bright lights. I took my hand back. In fact, Rex said, Mr Usman is in a spot of bother. He is well regarded in the South. But here, in the North, he has little power. He's one of only a handful of Northerners to have had a European education and is out of touch with the people. He takes orders from Nnamdi Azikiwe. But things in the South are happening very much quicker than here. Mr Usman will not accept this. And he is hated for it. We walked on through the still dark. Sometimes the clouds dispersed and we saw more clearly. We turned a corner and came across a young girl. She was standing in front of a latrine that served the adjoining compound, beating out a rhythm on an aluminium barrel. In spite of the drumming, I heard the agony and struggle of a man behind the latrine door. We walked on. The beating stopped. I heard the man in the latrine swallow painfully. Then the sound of pouring water and unhooking of the latch. I stopped walking, and Rex stopped beside me. I looked back, and a small boy emerged from the door. We walked on through the deep dark. In the middle of a square we saw two pigeons kicking up dust. The tips of their beaks were locked together. They were kissing or trying to bite one another or passing food from one to the other. Then one of the pigeons, the smaller, lighter one, hopped up on to the other's back and flurried her wings. After a spell of this she jumped to the ground and took flight. The other pigeon, startled, followed her up at a different angle but with an identical arc. Suddenly I felt faint. Let's stop a minute, I said. The clouds had cleared, and the light was very white. I looked up at Rex's face. It was pale, and I wanted to touch it. But I didn't feel able. Rex said, Are you feeling well? I said, Yes. And I was. I was feeling wonderfully light. I skipped forward five paces. Then I stopped. A large black cat became visible before us. It was crossing the road. Clasped between its jaws, and dragging on the road, was a hollow yellowy-white arrangement of bone. The cat reached the road's edge and stopped. Exhausted with the effort, it dropped its load and looked at me. It looked right at me. I lowered my eyes and saw a sheep's skull. When I looked up the cat, and its load, had disappeared. We forged on through the mostly dark. The buildings had become taller, cleaner, and the street broader. We came to our rest house. To enter we had to pass through a tall anteroom. I took Rex's hand and led him through. We arrived at a courtyard which rain had converted into a lake of mud. We tiptoed around the lake and walked through the hall. We entered the main room, which had vaulted ceilings. Barely visible at the end of the room was a metal stairway. The dome at its summit had become my sitting-place at night. I stood absolutely still in the middle of the room. My heart rose like a balloon. I cried out as deeply as I could, Heellooo. And again, this time in a high voice, Heelloooo. The words came back at me. Rex stared, I knew he thought me silly, but I didn't care. I twisted round and looked at him and I had crossed my eyes. I said, Where's dignity in feeding the ducks. I don't know why I said it. Those words echoed too. It was like a voice four rooms away in my head. I began to laugh. I couldn't stop, and I didn't want to. Suddenly I became scared. I closed my eyes. In the tallness of the room I felt very small, and the space felt enormous. Rex said, I've never seen you like this. I couldn't answer. Instead I turned to face him and laughed. Rex said, Why are you laughing? I didn't know. I was laughing for no reason. But I was laughing so hard I felt I had to sit down. I sat on the floor. It was cold, and I stopped laughing. Rex came and bent over me. His eyes were watery, pale blue in colour. I saw them widen, the lids blink, but he didn't say anything. He was a kind man, I always knew he was a kind man. He said, I'm not asking much, Eve, just tell me you are all right. I remember so clearly. He wanted to help me. But I didn't want him to touch me. I pushed him away. I was all right where I was. Then I said something under my breath. What did you say? Rex said. I didn't say anything, I said. You said something just now, Rex said. But

I didn't catch it. Catch? I said. You said something a moment ago, Rex said, I want to know what you said. I looked up at him. I said to you, I said. Louder, Rex said. I said that, I said. I can't hear you, Rex said. I said to you, I said, that you must tread softly. He brought his face close to mine. Tread softly for you tread on my dreams. When I opened my eyes Rex had taken a step back. – Later, in the silence of the night, I felt something stir in my belly. I lay still and thought of my mother, who had once carried me. I thought of her not as Julia but as Mother, who must also have faced this confusion in the night. Rex stirred from his sleep. Are you sleeping, Eve? he whispered. I didn't reply. I was thinking about the time in Oxford when we were watching a game of cricket. How Rex was trying to explain the difference between an off-break and a googly. How all at once I stopped listening to his explanation because I wanted to write something down. 'Tread softly for you tread on my dreams.' That is what I wanted to write. But at the time I didn't have a pencil, and it didn't occur to me to say it aloud. But then, there, lying in that bed in Africa, thinking about what I had wanted to write at the cricket match, and finally spoken in the room with the vaulted ceiling, and saying it again, this time to myself, I understood that I had got it wrong, that the line ought to have had ten syllables but the way I said it, it only had nine. I took out my diary because I wanted to note down this fact. I wrote, It is past twelve. I am writing this in near darkness, from the rest house where we are staying. I want to set down faithfully the events of the evening. And I have managed it, albeit it has taken several subsequent evenings to write. It has come to me that I ought not to keep this secret any longer. It is for Rex also. And he too had his pleasure that brought this about. It is settled. I'll tell him tomorrow. Yes. Tomorrow.

PART TWO

8

Mother's Silence

A doctor telephoned me this morning. She told me that Mr Rafferty was suffering one of his grey periods. He had fallen into a sort of neurasthenia, a lethargy from which nothing, it seemed, could rouse him. She thought it might help if he could spend some time outside the institution. I agreed; I would travel to Edinburgh and take him swimming. The doctor was waiting for me when I arrived. She wore a blush suit and vivid red bandeau. She shook my hand and brought me into her office.

'During his grey periods,' she said, glancing at a report, 'in between periods of exhausted silence, your grandfather generally becomes confused. It's a phase he returns to every so often. One knows he is about to enter this cycle when he insists he is hearing voices.' I knew this already, and I tried to tell the doctor, but she cut me off.

'The voices announce forceful and important thoughts, at least as far as your grandfather is concerned. They are sometimes reassuring, but more often menacing, commands or insults directed at him. *Someone has implanted a broadcasting device in me*, he will repeat. It is then he succumbs wholly to the voices. He literally does not know who he is and spends periods as a different person. One can never predict which personality he will choose, far less why he has chosen it. It is not that on certain days he *assumes* the persona of Thomas Mudge, watchmaker to George III; for him he *is* Thomas Mudge or Edward Dent or Taqî ad-Dîn or Ulysse Nardin or any number

97

of past clockmakers, with whom he shares significant characteristics.' The doctor picked up a book entitled *Antique Clocks and Their Makers* and turned to a fold-marked section. The verso page showed a gold pocket watch with black and gold hands; on the facing page a portrait of a man with a kind, energetic face.

'For example, one can deduce,' she said, pointing to the portrait, 'from the flat brow and protruding lower lip, the cheerful, childlike trusting gaze, that your grandfather has become Mr George Graham, known as "Honest George", who tramped to London in 1687 and became a leading watchmaker, but who never secured a monopoly on his inventions.' She closed the book. 'At other times it is impossible to know who your grandfather is, because he is wholly preoccupied and impenetrable.'

This morning the doctor told me she had been able to discover not only who Mr Rafferty had become, but also a significant event in this person's life. For the past six hours he'd been Abraham-Louis Breguet, one of his more frequent incarnations, and it was June 1780, the day Breguet's wife died.

'Indulge his fantasy,' she said. 'He may resent you if you attempt to set him straight.'

'Will he be all right?' I asked. We had been standing all this time, but now she invited me to sit. She offered me a cup of tea, which I declined, herself sat down, and told me the following story. – Some time ago she had been called to treat a twelve-year-old boy. He was typical in all aspects but one: since he was seven years old he had not spoken a single word. At first his parents thought he was merely brooding. Soon, however, his teachers expressed concern, and he was brought to a GP, who examined him but found nothing wrong. He was taken to a speech therapist, who decided that she too could be of no help, since the boy had once spoken fluently; the child, she said, simply had no desire to talk. There followed visits to various specialists, of whom she, the lady doctor, a psychiatric therapist, was the last. She told me she had asked the boy to draw and to note down his favourite actors. All of this he carried out willingly, in silence. She performed a Rorschach test, which demonstrated he had a critical side to his character, an unwillingness to cooperate with his peers, inclinations to purity, a sensual side outweighed by his facility for reasoning, a tendency to follow the crowd, to believe in his ambition, and to be both sensitive and untruthful; all of which was perfectly normal. She dismissed the case, recommending his silence be indulged, since she believed he would break it of his own free will. About a year later she received a letter from the boy's mother, who had decided to call in other specialists: Chinese herbalists, acousticologists, experts on whale song, yogis and clairaudients, none of whom had restored speech to him. Finally she contacted a famous hypnotist. The boy was instructed to lie on a kind of bed on stilts. The hypnotist stood on a wooden footstool from where he conducted the mesmerization. An hour later the parents were invited into the room; the boy looked just the same, but his speech had returned. That evening, over supper, he answered their excited questions. It seemed he wanted to unburden himself by relating certain episodes from his life; with great effort he spoke about his past. His words, however, were incoherent, disrupted by long pauses, and he repeated the same phrases again and again. His mother produced a jotter and invited him to note down the memories he was unable to voice. The boy went upstairs, brushed his teeth and climbed into bed. The next morning they found him hanging by the cord of his dressing-gown. The mother's letter went on to say that, before he died, her son had filled almost two-thirds of the jotter with tiny handwriting. The doctor had asked to see it; one passage in particular caught her attention. It related how, as a little boy, he had played a torch bearer at the fire festival on Beltane night. His mother, a keen dressmaker, sewed the pagan costume herself: the sable flowing robes, the black circlet, and she had daubed his skin with boot-black. His father made the torch from a broom handle topped with benzine-soaked rags. With solemn pride he carried his torch around the Calton Hill (wrote the boy), proceeding as one with the crowd in an upward spiral, under the fire arch, passing sprites representing the four elements, stopping in the hollow at the summit; where they were ambushed by the Red Man, who unleashed his wild and complex dance, before marrying the May Queen, so that blue aimless summer might begin.

I record here what I remember of the story, and what I remember of the story I do not remember word for word. It was at least twice as long. I have left out a passage concerning the boy's left-side right-side cerebral make-up, for instance. As soon as the doctor finished her narration she shook my hand and took me to see my grandfather. Perhaps she wanted to emphasize that she is not a magician, as I have heard her say before, that she cannot perform miracles for her patients. No doubt this is true. But I cannot help feeling that she spoke for my benefit.

I found my grandfather hunched at the low table, his fingers working rapidly and with delicacy on the air. He turned, and immediately I noticed a wild expression on his face, which he was struggling to hide. He got into bed. I saw that his eyes, heavily bagged, entirely filled by their black pupils, were shiny with tears that were still being shed, even after what must have been several hours. I remained in the doorway.

'I am not sure if you are able to receive visitors, Monsieur. I have . . . heard.'

Mr Rafferty peered uncertainly at me. Then his face creased in recognition. 'Thank you, Marat. It is Marat, isn't it? Yes, I knew it was you. I am inconsolable. But please, do come in. I welcome the distraction.'

I had no idea who Marat was. But, attentive to the doctor's advice, I decided to indulge his fantasy. I pulled the chair to his bedside and sat down, as if I were visiting an invalid in hospital. Then it occurred to me that this was, in fact, exactly what I was doing.

'I am . . . er . . . I am so sorry to have heard of your misfortune.' There was an awkward pause. Mr Rafferty placed his hand on top of mine, which was placed on my crossed knee.

'Dear Marat,' he said, 'you of all people will understand the enormity of my loss.' I lowered my head. I wanted him to release my hand, but he gripped harder. He was waiting for me to say something.

'Indeed . . .' I began. I could think of nothing else to say.

Suddenly Mr Rafferty shook his hand from mine and levered himself to a sitting position. 'We were married only five years.' He took a plastic tumbler filled with water and emptied it into his mouth. 'Tell me,' he gazed solemnly into my eyes. 'How will you remember her?'

I reached for the tumbler and filled it with water. Mr Rafferty emptied it again. There was a pause.

'Don't be shy, Marat.' I didn't say anything. He had a fleck of paper tissue stuck to his cheek. 'You are reluctant to talk about Cécile.' His eyes softened. 'You think I ought to put my mind to other things. Yet for the time being, I must reminisce. Tell me,' once again he had taken my hand in his, 'how will you remember her?' I looked up at the ceiling and cleared my throat.

'Her . . . happy gaze.' Mr Rafferty furrowed his brow. His tongue darted over his lower lip. Then he looked at me, astonished. 'How right you are! It was her eyes that first attracted me.' His own eyes were blurred with tears. 'Let us tell happy stories.'

I searched in my mind, but I could think of nothing to say.

'I never was much of a storyteller,' I said.

'What's come over you? I may be in mourning, but you mustn't treat me like a child!'

'Very well,' I said, 'let me see.' I filled the tumbler and took a large sip. I sat down and declared in a loud voice, 'There was a young man lost in a desert sandstorm . . .'

'I want to hear about *Cécile*.'

I stood. Mr Rafferty had begun to nod his head, waiting for me to speak, as though my words would stay his grief. Suddenly I wanted to leave his bedside. I had read about a gorilla at Edinburgh Zoo. A child had fallen into her enclosure, and had died from the impact. And yet for several minutes, until the zoo keeper arrived, the gorilla had cradled the child in her arms. I didn't move. Mr Rafferty must have sensed my uneasiness because he looked at the floor. He had been leaning against the metal bedstead, which had made a raw impression on his cheek. After a while he said, 'Nothing will cure my grief.'

'You've your work to be getting on with.'

'I'm distraught.'

'Your melancholy will pass.'

He didn't seem to hear me. 'When the doctor broke the news of her illness,' he said, 'I would not believe him . . . although Cécile knew. The afternoon we found out how advanced the malady was, we came here, to this sitting room, and we cried together.' Mr Rafferty closed his eyes and disappeared beneath the duvet. We were quiet for several minutes.

'Monsieur Breguet!' I said. 'Would you care for a walk?'

'Why not?' He was covered by the duvet. 'I will only sink further if I remain in this house that was yesterday brightened by Cécile's happy gaze.' I grabbed his swimming bag. He rose unsteadily and rubbed his eyes, which were circled with red.

Outside it was clear and cold and buildings stood out keenly against the sky. Unseen, through the sharp light, birds flitted and sang. We set off down Mankind Street. Mr Rafferty wore a long overcoat whose pockets sounded with loose change. Soft, squat, clock-faced, with busy hands, he shuffled over the paving stones. It took all my strength to guide him in a straight line. Soon we turned on to Morningside Road, with its row of shops and wide heath, and he became fearful of the cars. He tried to run off, but I managed to keep hold of him. We approached a homeless person with a bandaged face. Mr Rafferty came to a stop, produced a fistful of coins and placed them in her upturned cap. 'Alms for your plight,' he said. I wrapped my arm around his arm. We set off again, beneath the cloudless sky. At the Dominion we turned right and proceeded along Terrace Grange. To our backs rose Blackford Hill. Now he had begun to walk with confidence, and I thought he had forgotten Breguet. Of course I was relieved, for I was able to guide him without strain. Yet if I let go of his arm I knew he might begin to follow the cats, one of his favourite diversions. We proceeded down past the cemetery. Once or twice I attempted to start a conversation, but he didn't answer. We stopped beside a tramp sitting on an applecrate. Beside him lay his mongrel. Mr Rafferty sought the beggar's blessing and threw coins into his hat. We walked on. I intended to take him swimming, and now I suggested it. Mr Rafferty stopped, recoiled, thrust fists into his pockets. But I know how much he loves the water. Again I suggested it. He shook his head. People were beginning to stare.

I had an idea; I told him I would throw coins, that I would let them sink to the bottom of the pool, and that he could dive for them. He changed his mind, as I knew he would. The attendant at Warrender Baths knows us, and, since the men's changing room was empty, she allowed me to help him into his kit. We entered the swimming area, myself in my swimming suit, he in his large trunks and yellow goggles.

Immediately, in the open hall, I noticed a shift in the atmosphere. Every movement – the sweep of swimmers' arms, the nodding cork-lined rope, the attendant swaying on his high perch – seemed precise, lazy, stretched out, and every sound reverberated in the high space and dampness of the air. Mr Rafferty stepped down into the water. I stood to the side and wet my toes. Only a few bathers occupied the baths, all of them swimming lengths, and each, strangely, practising the back crawl. A trio of toddlers flapped their orange-banded arms. I stood listening to their cries – echoing – and the extractor fan – a low hum. Then, mid-pool, I dropped six penny-coins. Mr Rafferty swam back and forth for a few minutes, then sank below the surface. A few seconds later his head appeared, and his chest and arms; he was clutching a coin. I stepped down into the pool. Mr Rafferty glided to the edge and was beside me. His eyes shone. I swam for a while, then dived. I found a coin he had overlooked. Above me, I caught a flash of yellow from Mr Rafferty's goggles then heard a swifter resonance and saw bubbles rising from his mouth. I myself surfaced. Now he was standing. He pointed upwards. 'Look,' he said. The roof of Warrender Baths is made of glass, and the panes are framed by a domed latticework of iron. The building was enveloped in a blue haze, as if it were open to the air. And occasionally, as at that moment, a shaft of sunlight would stream through the glass and splinter on the water.

In the foyer everything seemed dark and sapped of colour. I bought Mr Rafferty a chocolate bar. I myself had a cup of tomato soup. Outside, I was surprised to find that it was still light. It was like coming out from watching a matinee performance. Mr Rafferty walked in silence, eating his chocolate bar and making a mess of his upper lip. I had forgotten to dry my hair and the cold air gnawed my scalp. We crossed the road on to the Meadows, over the humpy grass. By Jawbone Walk we sat on a bench. A fine rain had begun to fall. It made no sound. Mr Rafferty had sucked off the chocolate and was crunching the biscuit centre. It was some time before he spoke. 'Barbets have downed,' he said. I smiled in answer. There was a group of children in the distance; they were kicking a ball. 'What was Mother's star sign?' I said. He didn't seem to hear me. His eyes followed the movement of the ball. At that moment I wanted to throw my arms around him, although I knew it was impossible, because he doesn't like to be held. Without turning his gaze, he said, 'Who are you?' I didn't answer. We were quiet for a while. I looked across the Meadows, whose grass was silvered with rain. A little later I took him back to the institution.

The sky was starting to pink over and darken. Clouds, great zeppelins of amber and grey, crept across the horizon, as if, though lighter than the air, and floating in it, they were composed of a substance of great weight. Yet their edges were thinned and stirred, whisked almost. These clouds called up ponderous thoughts, but threw no shadow, and I had a notion it was not yet time to go home. So I took a diversion. I visited the zoo. Dusty from the evening's sweep-out, and aided by the rain – rain so fine it might have been a mist – the air smelled strongly, sweetly of truffles. I looked over the railing to the gorilla enclosure and saw a dark form among the knotted timber. I walked down into the monkey house and pressed my face to the glass. And there she was, sitting on a cement out-cropping, a mighty weight, perfectly balanced. As I approached she seemed to raise herself a little on her haunches, her black fingers husky, charred, her skin sparsely coated and patched with silver. Her eyes, a shade of deep red I have seen on a certain type of berry, stared coldly through the glass. Even colder was her indifference to my gaze, and the obvious might in her arms, with which she had held the child, but used now only to balance her movements and worry a welt on her thigh. I saw in her eyes, in their unconcern, something I did not wholly understand, but which linked, in my mind, the cement in her enclosure and the boy in the doctor's story and also the light of the swimming pool and my awareness of that light.

Travelling home, I looked through the window of the bus. The clouds had turned to ash, and ghosts of embers were scattered across the horizon. Below the sea and the tall-funnelled tanker with its row of lights slanting from masthead to bow, a string of beads, winking. The water was black; the wash inaudible. Not the engine of the bus. It throbbed in my chest. I turned my thoughts back to my history. I started to recall my mother's funeral. By the time I reached Gullane the clouds had disappeared, and a few stars were out. Now I am seated at my desk. The pocket watch ticks (from now on, unless I state otherwise, the pocket watch is always ticking); cars wash by outside; the mice are asleep in their holes. In the familiar quiet, I will press on with these stories of my past.

. . .

It was raining as the small group of mourners arrived at St Saviour's Church on Ikoyi Island. The priest was waiting below the pulpit. Thick-necked, with skin that had bled from his shaving, he stood with his arms spread before him, palms upturned. Pallbearers, Yoruba from the mission, set my mother's coffin to the priest's left; Ben, who bore my cot, placed me to his right. Mourners filed in, perspiring, occasionally coughing. Their footsteps clattered on the floor. Father approached last, worrying the scar on his chin and hauling his big frame with metre-strides. He thanked the men and took his place in the front pew. Lying on my back, I examined the ceiling. It was many-domed, of a dark wood that showed signs of swelling from the damp. I focused on a panel between two arched beams. As the priest began to speak, I kept looking – I could not move, the sheets cosseted me – and I saw that Christ was painted on the ceiling. His face was lean; the cheekbones high; his body wasted and pale; the ribs raised corrugations on his chest. No one attended him, not Mary his mother, nor St John, nor the captain Longinus, nor angels or thieves. A single bead fell from a wound in his right flank. Christ was dead, yet his eyes, an inordinate blue, were open. And for this reason, and the fact that the artist himself could not have set eyes on him, I felt that he was very beautiful. As I followed the play of brightness and shadow from the candles on the ceiling, Christ stared down at me, his face fading and rekindling by turns. I imagined what he would have seen from up there: the floor of black-and-white lozenge-shaped tiles, the rows of pews sparsely peopled, the apse depicting in stained glass his journey to Golgotha. But more vividly, I thought, he saw the two of us, my mother in her open coffin and me in my cot, lying side-by-side, directly in his line of vision; my mother's eyes closed, as if she had shut her lids to the warm light of the sun, the skin paler above her cheek bones, almost transparent; my eyes round, dry, wild amid my flushed and wrinkled face. And it struck me, as I listened to the priest, who spoke of the glory of the afterlife, that my mother could not have died in vain – to have perished so would have been an affront to Christ. The rain rattled on the roof. A candle hissed and was extinguished, and the priest told the story of the Passion, following the sequence from the Stations of the Cross to the Resurrection.

'Evelyn's untimely death,' he said, 'reflects Christ's own, for did he not, like Evelyn, who has given us a wonderful baby daughter, did he not also pass away in order to bring life into the world? Christ taught us that in nature every moment is new,' he said, 'that the coming is sacred.'

How right he was! It was then I hoped for a miracle. I willed my mother to wake, she who like me faced the painting of Christ. And if she would not enact a miracle, she might show a sign of forgiveness. Perhaps she would find a way to speak to me! I could not believe she had died for no reason. Even as I willed it, however, I sensed her lifeless form. The priest said, 'Let us pray.' I did not close my eyes or listen to his words. Instead I thought of my mother, urging her to speak. I felt there was something inside her that wanted to come out. But she did not speak; the stillness of her coffin, and the horrid heat in the church, and the dull responses of the mourners, only expressed the meaninglessness of her death. I closed my eyes and uttered my own prayer. From the grave comes life, I said to myself, from the coffin the cot, from death, birth. I itched under my sheets. Mother, I said, forgive me. Tell me you died for a reason. The rain continued to rattle on the roof. But my mother was silent.

When I opened my eyes Christ had disappeared; his chiaroscuro face eclipsed by Father's, equally shadowed. He had moved from the front pew and stood, head bowed, between the coffin and my cot. I saw his eyelids pulse, but his face was taut. As the tear slid from his cheek and struck my forehead, his expression did not change.

I turned, hot with fury. Why, I thought, did my mother have to die to bring me into the world? Where is the glory in death that the priest spoke of? Mother was not glorious. She was cold and mute and the heat in the church was putrefying her.

'Her soul is in heaven,' said the priest, 'filled with glory.' Mother is miserable, I thought, and she cannot say otherwise. The tear burned on my forehead. Mother's silence was something I could not fathom.

9

Unnamed

As a child I learned about the men who collect *unica*, a term which signifies objects that are the only one of their kind. Examples include: the stuffed corpse of Nipper, the Jack Russell depicted with his head cocked to the left, listening to the gramophone on the HMV record label; the tendrac Dasogale Fontoynanti, the sole specimen of which was caught in Madagascar in 1878; certain postage stamps, for instance a penny black printed with the queen's head upside-down; a disc featuring the singer Alessandro Moreschi, the last castrato, the only one of his kind to have had his voice recorded. Collectors of *unica* operate under the oddest of circumstances. Not only are the objects handled by gangs of unscrupulous agents, they are much sought after, and thus the collector, almost always an optimist, is often duped into buying a fake. These men, with their combination of passion and gullibility, fascinated me as a child: perhaps I saw in their vain but somehow necessary activity a symbol of my listener's art. It was because of those men that, as a child, I etched the word 'unica' on to the side of a biscuit tin. And in the tin, which sits before me now, I stored my favourite unique things. The tin measures twelve inches across and eight inches wide. Although the paint has faded one can make out a design of red-and-white arabesques in whose centre stands an elephant, her trunk gripping an identical tin which bears the same design of arabesques and elephant, tin in trunk, ad infinitum. Inside are some two-dozen items: my caul, my first tooth, a photograph of Father as a child holding tightly to a swing, a matchbox containing a pair of earplugs, a postcard entitled 'First Snow in Port Suez'. Of these – a gathering of objects unique to me, a positive companion to my history – I will speak later. The tin marked 'unica' also contains less tangible traces of the past, marked by their absence, a kind of negative impression of my life, like the brightness on a wall where a portrait formerly hung. I include them in my collection precisely because they ought to exist, unique because they are not there. The most conspicuous absence is my birth certificate.

. . .

Immediately after the funeral, Mother's coffin was burned. I was brought to our house in Ikoyi from where, the following day, Father left for England. He took a mailboat and buried her ashes in Botley cemetery, Oxford, to the right of the war dead. Before his departure, however, he overlooked one thing: he failed to name me.

I lay in my hot room at the back of the house. The sun fell between the shutters, describing a thin corridor of light from which I shrank. Why, I asked myself, had I not emerged after nine months? I had delighted in my gestation, in the sounds, diffuse and uncertain, that had filtered through into the womb. It was this same happiness, the happiness of the partially formed, that had fostered my unwillingness to be born and had killed my mother. Now – my thoughts continued – on the outside, I was assailed by a simultaneous spectacle of light, scent, flavour and noise. What disappointment! What fear and exhaustion! Having switched elements, mimicking the first creature to have crawled from sea to shore, I missed my spawning ground, that fecund soup out of which I had writhed and slithered and found myself breathing. I was, I thought bitterly, just like that Devonian creature: part fish and part creeping-thing, longing for water yet breathing air. I ached for the womb's familiar dark.

But I had emerged. And it was so.

I lay in my cot, wide-eyed and unmoving, like a stuffed animal. Every morning I heard the Lagos clock strike seven, accompanied by a siren that called workers from their beds (whilst simultaneously, across the city, night-workers were travelling home to pit and cellar, obscure quarters where they would sleep through the daylight hours to which they were no longer accustomed). Already at that hour, the air was stifling, smudged with insects. The town centre was teeming with traffic pushing upward dust, currents of heat and smoke. To reach our house in Ikoyi, the European quarter on the east island, the sound of the clock and the siren surged through the streets, together with the noise of the traffic. Like a tide the wind gathered the rising sounds of Lagos: the music of wireless sets, the cockerel's cry, trains heaving out of Iddo terminus and railworkers stamping their heavy boots; the noise travelling between brick walls and plywood, through the shanty town, where playing cards are slapped on crates and children play before the time of the greatest heat; the current of sound passes by way of the Jankara market, where hawkers' voices compete for attention, drawing with them the grating of a carpenter's saw, continuing east past the Saro quarter, the district of returned slaves, and proceeding over the Macgregor Canal and into Ikoyi; where by the roadside a sheet of newspaper flaps, its print bleeding on to the tarmac. The noise of the paper joins the morning chorus, which now flows past the racecourse, past Riley's Import Merchants and to the lagoon at the edge of our garden. – From the shore the lawn climbed towards a thicket of rose bush; there the ground levelled and extended as far as the rear veranda, strung with bougainvillea, that fierce vine whose leaves obscured the sun but could not stem the yellow tide of dawn.

I lay by the open window, pale and withdrawn, like an etching of myself. Now I had broken from the confines of the womb, I was struck by the different acoustical qualities. The new brightness of tone, as when a pianist takes her foot from the dampener pedal, interested me keenly. I noted in particular the higher registers, birdsong and the tinny melody of a radio. I attempted to locate myself in space. But since I had no name, and had few ways to distinguish my thoughts from the noise about me, they – my internal life and the life of the town – became confused. I began to bleed into my surroundings and my surroundings bled into me, like the sheet of newsprint flapping on the street. We – the town and I – took on aspects of one another.

Many years later I read about the beginnings of the city of my birth. Lagos had grown out of the water. At first the area was a swamp. Green mist veiled that boggy expanse, where insect-life prospered, little else. The mosquito and the tsetsefly, together with the heat and the shallow, hazardous passage from the sea, meant that few settlers managed to establish themselves. Over many centuries, however, different races arrived who learned how to survive and prosper. Each came by way of the sea; and each profited from it: Egba, who travelled east in search of fish and who built canoes and drew crawfish from the lagoon; Portuguese by way of their journey to India; slave brokers; merchants from North Africa and Europe; churchmen; returned slaves; the British. And each, in their individual way, reclaimed from the sea pieces of solid ground. Marshland was converted into mud huts. The veinings of creeks and inland channels were filled in or stitched with roads. Moles appeared at the harbour entrance, the channel was dredged, bridges built and canals cut, above which roads climbed and spiralled. Lagos spread outward, branching across the wetland, and as it spread, its centre was pressed upward, storey by storey, rising above the waves and spray. The water was tamed. But it was not wholly overcome.

Soft, dull, nodding, lit tremulously, hostile, refractive. – The water captured and bent the light, scattered and returned its rays; and one saw, laid out on its surface, a shining likeness of the streets. There was hardly a canal or lakeshore that did not have as much of the town in it as above. Vehicles, buildings, the gestures of passers-by, trees and their shaking leaves, all the hazy passages of sunshine and depths and tones of the sky – everything that happened or existed above ground was repeated upside down. And since the water was affected by the tide and ruffled by winds and crimped and eddied by a thousand unseen forces, Lagos, upturned, was transformed into a second town where order was mocked and rearranged. One saw the dark fabric of leaves, the reverse side of coins, creatures that live beneath eaves. Caught between the influences of concrete and water, Lagos softened, broke down the borders between dream life and reality; one felt as if the town had been constructed merely of gimcracks, and that the whole edifice would one day sink beneath the waves.

The duality of land and water marked the city of my childhood, and I too inherited the ability to live in more than a single world (so that, years later, when I went to live in the pits of the nightsoil workers, I felt quite at home). In appearance I was typical. Slightly large, due to my protracted gestation, yet slim-limbed and snub-nosed, I sported the appropriate number of toes and fingers. My skin was pale and downed softly. Without fuss I drank the milk formula my nursemaid mixed, released hiccups as required. And I slept, or rather did not stir, throughout the night. But my meekness belied the richness and turmoil of my inner life. Nothing in the way I looked could have suggested the complicated activity taking place in my head.

My ears were extraordinary. Crimson, membranous, graced with heavy lobes, they whorled their way into the hollow where ciliary movement stirred, absorbing the sounds. What else did I take in? A smell here and there that happened to find its way into my room, the sticky sweetness of milk formula. I filled my nappy whenever necessary but gave little else to the world. All my talent had gone into the development of my ears.

In those days I was tended by Taiwo, the nursemaid Father employed before he left for England. Previously she had hired herself out to scrub floors. On those unruly mornings when Lagos sang, Taiwo came into my room. The first thing she would do was close the window and throw open the shutters. The effect was to cut off the sounds and spill daylight into my room; with a hateful gesture she expelled both noise and shadows. Then she got me ready for the day. I was stripped and put into a robe. The tin bath rang out as she poured water into the tub, where she washed me vigorously, then towelled me down and clouded me with talcum. Finally she dressed me with equal spirit. It seemed that Taiwo, the former scullion, was simply doing what she knew best, had swapped mop and scourer for flannel and sponge, pumice and towel. I closed my eyes to her. She was a fat woman and sentimental. She had had a mission education and wore a pendant of the Cross. Some days she dressed in wide wraps of colourful cloth; on others her flesh was contained by a blouse. Her face was clove-black, and it was with cloves that she warmed the milk then pressed the teat between my lips. Once, as she bent to feed me, the pendant slipped from under her collar and struck me on the chest. Stung, I opened my eyes and noticed that her eyebrows were plucked. Taiwo called me 'Ikoko Omon', which in her language meant 'Newborn Child'. I did not know this at the time, and I did not know she referred to me with an impersonal pronoun. It was her people's custom to name a child one week after birth; and since I was now aged eight months, and still without a name, in her eyes I was not fully a person.

By the time Father returned to Lagos, I was nearly a year old. I hoped he would name me and make new arrangements for my care. He did neither; he only looked in on me now and then to check I was not sick. During the day Father disappeared into his work at the Executive Development Board. In the evenings he ate supper on the veranda, after which, bent over the table with his drink, he read his maps and papers. But he was not able to concentrate for long and fell to toying with his watch. Sometimes, after eating, he would call for Taiwo to bring me out to the veranda. He would stand up to hold my gaze in a strange, determined way, then open his mouth and look around helplessly, as if searching for something. He had loved Mother and ached on account of her absence. Her death had upset something fundamental in him.

There were times when my father spoke to me. His voice, heard in this intimate way across the veranda, was not deep, as one might have expected from someone so big and dishevelled, but low all the same, and sometimes it reached the higher registers. I had disliked its intonation when he talked during my gestation; and I disliked it still, its breathlessness, the barely distinguishable quality of the vowel-sounds.

'Daughter,' he said one evening on the veranda, 'there are times when I feel guilty that you have been left, not only motherless, but without a brother or sister, who might have distracted you from your loss. But, you know, after giving the matter some thought, I have to tell you that you're fortunate to be an only child. You will never know the resentment that will develop between siblings, the cruelty.' He lit a cigarette, which the wind smoked as he related the following story. – There was a shopkeeper who had two sons. He was so poor, he couldn't afford to feed them. So one day he told them they were old enough to make their own way in the world. He divided twenty pieces of bread and a chunk of mutton into two equal pack- ages, handed them to his sons, then waved them goodbye. The boys walked into the forest. After a while, the older brother, Sagoe, suggested they rest for a while and eat something. They should eat Little Brother's food first, said Sagoe, since he was smaller and weaker and would soon tire if he had to carry all that food. So they rested, and ate, then continued their journey. After several days of this, all of Little Brother's food had gone. When he became hungry, he asked for some of Sagoe's share. Sagoe refused! Little Brother reminded him that they'd agreed to share their bread and meat. Sagoe thought for a minute, then said, in a strange voice, I will give you some food, but only in return for an eye. Little Brother cried and pleaded, but in vain. Finally, he agreed to give up an eye. Sagoe tore out Little Brother's left eye, then gave him a piece of bread. They con- tinued their journey, Little Brother trembling with the pain. And he was still hungry! That piece of bread he'd received had scarcely made a dent in his appetite. When once again Sagoe stopped and sat down to eat, Little Brother could stand it no longer and pleaded for more food. Sagoe thought for a bit, then said he would give him more bread, but only in exchange for the other eye. What could Little Brother do? He pleaded for mercy, but Sagoe remained firm. Finally, Little Brother decided that it was better to be blind than to die of hunger. All right, he said, take my eye. So Sagoe tore out Little Brother's right, remaining, eye. Then, without the slightest bit of pity for Little Brother, who lay on the ground writhing in pain, he unpacked his bread and meat, took out a portion, left it beside Little Brother, and walked away. Hearing the twigs crack underfoot, and guessing what Sagoe had done, Little Brother begged him not to leave him alone there in the forest, weak and blind and without food, where he would surely die of hunger or be devoured by wild beasts. But Sagoe had gone.

I understood then that my father was lost. His wandering, decayed imagination, the imagination with which he had designed his world, and machined it, and bounded it, that same imagination was racked and transcended by my mother's death. His movements became furtive, difficult to interpret. He was not so much a presence, I thought, as a kind of silhouette, thrown like the wardrobe's shadow, around which, out of habit or superstition, Taiwo made sure to steal a wide berth. I did not feel lost on those evenings on the veranda, but rather invisible, like a dusty heirloom of uncertain origin. This did not trouble me greatly, because my mind, or rather my audile facilities, were keenly active and absorbed most of my attention.

So I lay and listened, and occasionally Father spoke to me on the veranda. My nursemaid fussed over my appearance. I felt empty, closed my eyes and drank from the teat. A year went by in this way. And then, one afternoon, whilst I was feeding, a thought came to me: how was it that each afternoon my window was open and the shutters closed? It was not Taiwo's doing – she who arrived each morning and poured light into my bedroom and spread silence – for she had no use for shadows. At some point in the afternoon, as I struggled in sleep, someone was correcting my nursemaid's hateful work. I knew because I would wake into shuttered darkness and vibrant sounds. For many weeks I was puzzled. Then, when I woke once before my usual time, I found a boy watching me – I knew it was he who had closed the shutters and opened the window. He was sitting on a stool beside my cot, pressing his face to the bars. We watched one another unblinkingly. His teeth were very white. I noticed that his hand picked at the hem of his shorts, his belly button, the knots of hair that were thickening on his head, and one leg persistently shook. I could feel the vibrations through my cot.

In the afternoon Taiwo sat in her room across the corridor, sewing angels for the Christmas fair. It was on account of her religion that she was sentimental. The firstborn of twins, the younger of whom had died, she said she knew what it was to lose family: and perhaps this was why she permitted the boy's presence in my room – I think she believed the companionship beneficial.

After our first encounter I woke often in the half-light to find the boy seated on the stool, watching me. His eyes seemed a kind of climate, wild and busy, with flecks of red spoking inward, each pupil merging into its dark iris, so dark I thought they were of the same black pigment. He looked. I looked. We looked at one another looking. And I began to feel that I was emerging from my emptiness. No longer did I wish to return to the womb. I could not deny it; I was beginning to like life better. Outside, a hot wind blew. The shutters stirred. I reached slowly through the bars to still the boy's trembling leg; I felt how bony his knee was and how soft the skin. For a moment the leg rested; when I withdrew my hand it resumed its shaking. He looked harder; he was interested in my fingers with their tiny pink nails. He knew I had done wrong, I think, which fascinated him; he got a strange satisfaction from it. Now and then the Lagos clock would strike, and he, who was always moving, but whose gaze rarely faltered, would look up for a moment or two.

Ade was four years my senior. He wore blue shorts and a jumper from which Iffe, his mother, had cut the sleeves. Mornings he spent with Iffe at Jankara market, where she traded onions. She brought him back in the afternoon, to their compound at the side of the house, where he was cared for by his father Ben, our cook. But he was spending longer and longer in my room and eventually started to return after his evening meal.

It was 1949. The rainy season had begun. I was nearly three years old and still did not have a name. If besotted, grieving, hard-working Father identified me with one, I did not know it. In semi-darkness Ade sat on his stool. Beside me, on a bedside table, stood a hurricane lamp, which threw a circle of light on to the wall. In this light the silhouettes of a thousand insects danced. The scene – accompanied by the rain, which beat a rapturous applause on the roof – absorbed us completely. At one point Ade raised his arm, and his hand, having moved in front of the lamp, was transformed into an enormous shadow on the wall. I laughed. Ade saw the effect, and his other hand joined the first; I watched the shadows: sometimes they came together and leaned, and leaned further and swayed, frequently they divided and spun, the movement effortless, dreamily pelagic. I stood up in my cot, fed my arm between its bars and thrust my hand in front of the lamp. We began to play, Ade tilting his hand to one side, me taking the opportunity to dip beneath them. It was then, I don't know why, as the insects circled, and our shadows danced, the thought came to me that had we not discovered this game, then we – Ade and I – might have quickly grown apart; but now we had made a surer connection.

For several evenings the shadows of our hands danced on the wall. Yet I found I missed our previous contact, face to face, on either side of the cot's bars. Something had changed in me. And something had changed and developed between us. And I knew this change was because of the game. Taiwo seldom noticed our animated wall; she dozed in her room or decorated herself or read spiritual pamphlets. Neither Ade nor I thought to fashion an object with our hands. Perhaps this was because the shadows themselves were imitations, and it did not occur to us to form an object – Pisces, a swan – and have it represented itself by a likeness. Or perhaps it was simply that we did not have time to develop the game, for not long after something happened to end it altogether.

The evening we played the game for the last time, Father returned early from work and invited a colleague for backgammon and drinks. His colleague laughed in shrill bursts that did not impart mirth, a mad laugh that unsettled me and kept us from our own game. My father lost badly that night. He was very low. The two argued. A glass was smashed. The colleague walked off. Father poured himself another drink, and for several minutes we heard his footsteps pacing the veranda floor. Ade and I returned to our game, the silhouettes of our hands danced on the wall. Soon we heard my father's footsteps growing louder. He entered the house and crossed the hallway. The footsteps grew louder still, stopped, my door drifted wide, and there stood Father. We withdrew our hands from the circle of light. Father's face was worn, the blond hair bound in crested tufts. Neither Ade nor I moved or spoke. At that moment Taiwo drifted or flowed into the room. She had painted her eyelids purple; I thought she looked magnificent. At that moment Father saw the crucifix hanging from her neck. He went to her and unhooked her necklace. He held the crucifix before his eyes, then walked to the lamp and let it fall in front of the shade. We all turned our eyes to the wall. There, framed by the circle of yellow light, hung the shadow of Christ, fixed to the cross. The shadows of insects swarmed all around him. No one spoke. We all looked at Christ and the insects. There was a silence. Then Father addressed us directly for the first time that evening.

'Here is Christ on the Cross,' he said. 'All kinds of insects are flying up to him, in order to torment him. When he sees them his spirit fails him. At the same time a moth is flying around Christ . . . *Kill him,* the insects shout to the moth. *Kill him for us!*' Father's voice became very quiet. '*That I cannot do*, says the moth, raising his wings above Christ, *that I cannot do, for he is of the house of David.*'

After the incident with Christ and the insects, Ade and I never again performed our shadow dance. Surprisingly, I did not suffer on account of the end of the game, although I regretted the change that came over the house, the dubious way Taiwo regarded Father, whom she seemed thereafter to consider idolatrous. And I too had found it strange, the story of Christ and the insects, could understand neither its origin nor meaning, and for many years believed it a symptom of his grief-cracked mind. But some three decades later, when we were living in Scotland, shortly before my father died, I came to understand, if not the significance of the incident, then at least its origin.

10

Taiwo Meets Her End

Tonight, the attic is quiet. Beyond my skylight the beech tree sways. It is late, cold, luminous. The sun falls or rotates, flames and dies. Whenever I finish a page of my history now I print out a fine white sheet with black type. It never ceases to thrill me, when the sheets fall from the printer on to the floor, echoing my words. Not my words: sounds – yes, those printed words are echoes of the sounds of my past. That is not right either. They are not echoes, but translations, mutations.

As I add the sheets to the stack in the wardrobe, where I keep the completed pages of my history, I ask myself: Who will read this? If someone were to look into the wardrobe, what would they think? Perhaps they would not read my history but wonder if I was preparing for a crisis. Stacked up on the back wall are my provisions: paper, napkins, bottles of water, tins of beans, etc. I have found it convenient to store them here since my meals now are more like snacks, taken at odd times; I never know when those will be. And these not being full meals, it is hard to justify a trip down to the kitchen. All that way for a spoonful of beans! Yes, it suits me to have a tin constantly to hand. It has come to me that my life or engagement with the world is diminishing with my needs. Sometimes I go three days and nights without leaving the house, the attic even. In a moment, then, I will take a walk on the beach, before I press on with my history.

. . .

After the incident with Christ and the insects the game ended and with it the first phase of my early life, the thrall and insouciant ties of infancy, the lovely mutual gaze. I was nearly three. The rainy season was over. The days were long, the sun large in the sky and hot.

There was an ebony tree on the flat of the lawn, and in one month of great heat in November Taiwo and I sat every morning in its shade. I started to take baths before going to bed, since Taiwo, who cherished warmth, but suffered in keener heat, would not miss morning in the garden. She woke me, and we dressed and she went to fetch fruit for breakfast. I would climb out of my window on to the smoking grass and fall beneath the shadow of the ebony tree. Taiwo's enormous underwear hung from the clothesline. My nursemaid came, and we ate. One morning, Taiwo introduced a new element to our routine. Along with our fruit that day, she had brought a *Children's Illustrated Bible*, saying, 'Mr Steppman asked me to begin your education.' I doubted the truth of this. And in her thick contralto she recited the story of the world's beginning, which was not the beginning of the world I recognized.

I had never liked Taiwo. From the start, when she appeared at my bedside and threw open the shutters, I figured her as an enemy. She expelled the shadows and my room became a void. How different it was when Ade entered that space! With his simple gesture, the pairing of the shutters, he reversed my nursemaid's work; or more precisely – for pitch-black is as empty as flat brilliance – Ade hung a delicate fabric on which the light could play: I remember the sense of coolness, the wet stillness, and I remember the frail sun-rays which served not so much to illuminate but to soften the darkness. And these rays, pierced with dancing lint, caught odd corners of objects, made the brass on the curtain rail glow, set Taiwo's gold ring smouldering. It was a mystery to me how in such gloom the gold drew light. In the dimness, when the shutters were wide, and light flooded my room, the metal merely sparkled and appeared gaudy. And Taiwo herself, with her painted face and jewellery and charms, seemed merely extravagant until Ade returned shadow to the room. Her beauty, I thought, was terrific in the darkness she sought to banish.

Taiwo was in her late twenties when she came to live with us. In addition to the plucked eyebrows, she had a shiny forehead, erratically powdered. She was breathless with full painted-red lips, and I never saw black skin blush so. Her hair she favoured bound tightly above her head. I thought it must have cost great pain to draw that kinked hair straight. Chairs would hardly contain her. Her back spilled out between the bars of the dining chair like a netted zeppelin, ground-strung. Her odour was rich. Cats adored her.

Although Taiwo was a scullion and nursemaid she believed neither in spotless floors nor well-tended children. She knew a great deal about cleanliness, was a friend of purity, and a Christian. But because of her great size, in her estimation she was not a true Christian. It was impossible for her to talk about religion without resorting to the language of gastronomy. 'I have fed my soul at the table of the Lord,' she would say. 'And He has blessed me for it.' Everything about Taiwo was overdone; she liked all that was bright and succulent. When she said 'religion' she meant eating; when she said 'eating' she meant a particular kind of self-loathing. The problem was her fondness for food. She liked food as much as religion and was tied to both. Taiwo hated her abundance, an excess that contradicted the teachings of the church.

So we lay in the shade of the ebony tree every morning while I listened (ears, unlike eyes, cannot be shut) to her spiritual instruction, the Creation story, Noah and the Flood, Christ's sojourn in the desert: *'You're hungry,'* read Taiwo, in her devil's voice. *'You have been fasting forty days. Look at these round stones. Don't they remind you of bread rolls?'* I had to feign interest, for if she caught me wandering in my mind, I was scolded, and the reading began over again. But when the passage was finished she asked to know my thoughts, since she was jealous of thoughts that were not on her. So I said I dreamed of her. To keep her happy I invented a catalogue of sins, phrased in child-talk, which she would take pleasure in admonishing, and forgive after, as if it were a game to release me from wrong, and that simple. Then she would go inside to fetch cakes and limewater.

On those mornings in the garden when she read from the Bible, she also advised me on hygiene: where to wash, and how often, and the special places a girl must tend to. 'Wash your cake,' she told me. 'Wash there with mild soap and water.' She warned me as well against fizzy drinks that Father occasionally brought home, the bottles were dirty from the shipping, she told me, the seamen filthy. And taps bred germs. It was past nine when the instruction finished and we ate our mid-morning snack. By then the heat of full day was approaching, and we would make for the house.

Outwardly, I obeyed Taiwo – what else could I do? Secretly, I yearned for change. I was powerless, physically, to alter my situation, and so I began to wish harm on Taiwo. If she were no longer in the world, I thought, Father would be forced to look after me himself. I admit it – there were days when I wished her dead. Other times my hopes for a different life focused on Ade. I had outgrown my cot, and in the afternoon when he returned from the market we were no longer separated by its bars. Undivided, a new intimacy developed between us. We began to talk, and I asked about his days at the market. I was happy, since human closeness was lacking in my life. More than this: I sensed Ade could help me to leave my stultifying nursemaid and do the only noble thing that lay in my power, which, I decided, was to escape into Lagos. Perhaps Ade would accompany me and teach me how to walk among crowds!

That was how it was when I was three years old. Whenever Ade was absent from my life, I suffered Taiwo's company or lay alone in my room. My days felt false and mundane. Father was distant as ever. Taiwo seemed keener in the pursuit of her religious attachment and appearance. I did not yet dare to ask Ade to help me leave the house. I was little nearer to becoming a full person with a proper name. The decade took flight and expired. I grew two inches.

That season, the first of the new decade, the 1950s, a decade which would close with independence for Nigeria and exile for Father and me, began under a cloud of boredom. I went through the motions of guilt, of anxiety and joy, of loneliness and pain with impressive though splenic energy. I was rehearsing the character that was expected of me, a girl-child of three and a half. Yet there were moments of respite. Although I was peculiar, and extraordinary in several ways, I was still a child, and I liked to play. Early afternoon I went out to the garden and found pleasure in games. I had an idea that a class of spirit lived inside every object, and I had only to brush against it, or stroke or tap it in a certain way, to draw forth that spirit. I was consciously touching things, and I burned in quiet bliss when the objects chimed or clattered or whispered. Absorbed in my game, I forgot mealtimes. Eating could wait, for I had made an important discovery: I had discovered how to wake the spirit that rests inside still and quiet things. I applied my new knowledge diligently. Any object whose sound I particularly liked, I would hide beneath my bed. My favourite was a length of twine which I stretched taut and passed my finger lightly across, and it produced a tremulous humming – not, I recognize now, unlike the Theremin. How dull all other objects seemed to me then!

At other times my play was more conventional. Behind the servants' compound (on whose lower floor stood the kitchen, on whose upper lived Ade, with Iffe and Ben, his parents), the garden began its decline to the lagoon. I would amble down to the lakeshore and from the crest of the lawn launch rocks, which rolled elliptically, then fell, with a heavy sucking of air, into the water – and for an instant there rose crystal beads containing the fantastic spectrum of rainbows. Sometimes, from his place at the kitchen window, I saw Ade toss scraps into the garden; into which immediately descended a volary of birds, a brilliant cloud of feathers. Once I saw Ade at his bedroom window directly above the kitchen. He was folding a rectangle of paper into a point. He pressed his thumb along each folded edge and held it to the light. Then he snapped his fingers, and the paper transformed into a white aeroplane! He held each wing carefully and, with one eye closed, peered along the point. Next he took a pencil and wrote something in the fold. He made several more. Then he piled the aeroplanes one into the next, drew back his arm and thrust them from his grip. I jumped to catch them, white darting flashes, as they streamed through the air, singly or in pairs. Catching three, I watched the rest flutter to the ground, like so many birds.

I took my catch up to Ade's bedroom, unfolded the aeroplanes and spread them on the floor.

********?

********?

********?

Ade had tried to communicate with me. But I could not read.

The rains arrived, and I was unable to play outside. I had been born during that same season four years previously, and now, amid the tumult, as when newly born, I felt exhausted once again. The rain beat down upon the roofs, on to the streets, the tangle of green, like so many exclamation marks puncturing the earth, thrumming up the water and effacing reflections.

Taiwo, for days now afflicted, like us all, with mindless boredom, sprawled in her armchair in an obscure and heavy trance. Occasionally she would wake, as if from hibernation, look around helplessly, then hunt for herself in the wardrobe mirror. But after a few minutes her eyelids would fall shut. And for days I had been confined to my room, with vacant Taiwo as my guard and keeper, with no more stimulus than the sodden scenery. Even the sounds of Lagos were crowded out by the beating of the rain, which afflicted everything, not only us, the human inhabitants of the house, but also the voiceless drunken animal life, the mice and the birds, who had disappeared at the first cloudburst, and most helplessly of all, the inanimate objects, the wardrobe, which pulped and swelled, Mother's trunk, the floorboards, which grew patches of white fur dotted with the blue eyes of mould.

Father, it seemed, was the only one among us untroubled by

the rain. He had become absorbed in his work at the Lagos Executive Development Board. In a large yellow mac he mounted his bicycle and left the house before dawn, no longer lunched at home and often returned after dark. Once I saw him pedalling furiously homeward, bent over his handlebars, his tailcoats flapping foolishly over the rear wheel. After he dried himself off he would sit on the veranda. Sometimes his colleague Mr Honeyman would stop by. There were blessed evenings when Father called me from my room, dismissing Taiwo for the night, evenings when, projected on a sheet hung at the far end of the veranda, I witnessed grainy, poorly shot photographs of Lagosians in fancy dress. Then, towards the end of the rainy season, Mr Honeyman produced a different kind of photograph, a bird's-eye view of Lagos. Father pointed to our house, which looked like a toy box. It was so tiny and inconsequential. And so near the centre! They were making plans to clear the slums, which were circled in red. They planned to install plumbing and a sewage system, evict people from their homes, which were to be replaced with hotels and office blocks, banks, parliament buildings and new roads. But what excited them most were skyscrapers.

'We will make ourselves comfortable among the clouds!' Mr Honeyman said, beneath the rattling veranda roof. 'We'll solve the problem of housing in Lagos, and overcome the spread of disease by elevation!'

While Father was absorbed in his city planner's dreams, I was making plans of my own. I knew I needed to leave the house and enter the town. Although I had resolved to take matters into my own hands, I did not know how to manage it. But then something quite unexpected happened.

It had been an afternoon of low cloud and relentless rain. That day I had sat with my elbows on the windowsill, gazing wall-eyed at the rain, in a stupidity of doubt, until Father called me, and at length we ate in the dining room. The meal was sombre but for the cutlery's chime and clatter. When I returned to my room I looked out of the window and found the world transformed! The sun had emerged, the wind had fallen to a soft breeze, which stirred the branches of the ebony tree. I climbed out through my bedroom window into the still-damp sun-bright garden, impossibly happy. I ran through grass, under the tree and around the kitchen compound to the lakeshore.

Taiwo was floating face-down in the water.

11

In Lagos

Came the great market days. The rains had flooded the town, filled the streets, overwhelmed our garden – but now grasses, tubers and flowers were everywhere springing up. Birds appeared, and the air vibrated with their wing beats. To think that only a week previously we had been besieged by that empty damp season, and in semi-darkness the world had shrunk to enclose us. But now, through cloudless skies, the sun shone brightly. A hot dry summer-season with far views across the lagoon. The lawn quickly became parched. The foundations of a swallow's nest appeared below the eaves. High-spirited in the new atmosphere, we rolled up our sleeves, and listened to the swallows, who rained down on us a living symphony, then took off, shrilling, to return with moss, twigs and rags.

It was during this season that I became acquainted for the first time with the market. Already a week had passed since Taiwo's death. Father had asked Iffe to take care of me until he found a new nursemaid (in fact he never found one). So here we were, Iffe, Ade and I, beneath the low sky, passing through the front garden on our way to Jankara market. We walked on the sandy road, by dew-damp lawns. Elephant grass waved its stalks far above my head. The shopkeeper Riley greeted us – 'Good morning!' – and the watchmen at the gate of the Honey-mans' did the same – 'E ku aro!' Beside us a cockerel was stirring up dust. He stopped, swelled his neck and summoned up a cry; the little thong-like tongue thrashed in the violent beak, and from deep in his throat he wished me well. We reached the street where buses ran amid clouds of dust. The yellow bus rounded a corner and, shuddering, pulled to a stop. We boarded, and the sky arched higher.

I thought, but not for long, of Taiwo. No one knew the exact manner of her death; there were no witnesses. Did she fall? Or had she taken her own life? I wondered if the church gave a full burial for suicides. The bus was picking up speed. On the seat beside Ade I leaned forward. Would Taiwo's family prepare her face – her last, set permanently – as she herself would have wished: scrubbed, hair pulled back from the wide forehead, painted lips and cheeks, eyebrows plucked? My feet in new leather shoes felt prickly. I heard a blend of bells and horns and turned to face the window. What, I asked myself, did thoughts of Taiwo matter now? Had I not wished my nursemaid dead? Happy or obedient fate had heard my plea! At that moment it simply stirred me that I had won my freedom, was seated presently on the tinny, but thunderous, bus looking through the dusty glass – we were crossing the Macgregor Canal. How my luck had changed!

The trading district came into view. We got off the bus and entered the market. Ade and I hung back and hurdled the bands of shade that spanned the walkway between stands – for no other reason than we wanted to – the rules of a game we had not discussed, and it made our progress slow. Every so often Iffe stopped, turned and clicked her tongue, which released us from the shadows' spell, and we came running to where, a moment earlier, she had been standing. The stalls rose hugely above me. We reached the section of fresh produce where each type of vegetable was stacked together: we walked among brown sticky roots, past oranges in tea chests, past tomatoes with their smell like sunshine, past masses of corncobs behind

Iffe to her stand. The morning was hot, damp, substantial, smelling of dust, and a warm sweet odour like caramelizing sugar.

At Iffe's instruction Ade and I stayed by the onion stand. We squatted beneath the table that held our wares, so my view was near-level to the ground, a view of stones, insects and straw, of sandals and bare feet with their movement of pendulums, of loose sack fibres, newspaper, a single crushed tomato, and with purple lizards darting between. Women – I quickly understood the market was a female realm – stopped beside us. Some bargained for onions, others exchanged greetings with Iffe, and each rested her gaze on mine. For many I was something new entirely and outside their reach of knowledge. Others bent, tight in their wrappers, to look more closely, to press my hand or grip me firmly, as though I was a robust and precious foodstuff, and called me beautiful and in admiration or with envy said I would attract customers, bring luck on Iffe. When they left I opened my hands to find I held gifts from their stalls, different kinds of fruit, which Ade and I ate. I recall particularly a guava, with its pink wet flesh, it was the first guava I had tasted, with a strange musty flavour I did not wholly like.

I took off my shoes. Ade and I huddled close, not speaking, and for some minutes we took in our ground-level view. A woman stopped who sold the morning's haul of lagoon-fruit. We pinched our noses. We stared into the dead eyes of fishes.

If I was a novelty, and attracted crowds, Iffe too was venerated among the traders. She was a significant woman, tall and uniformly wide from her shoulders to hips – and she had grace. Her movements were unhurried, stylish, difficult to interpret yet full of meaning, and I noticed a certain heaviness about her limbs, as though she bore or carried them through a thicker element. She wore sandals, a blue skirt and white blouse without sleeves, and looked wise, regal, with a blue headscarf sculpted on her head. I admired the flushed region of skin that dappled her upper arms.

But it was her voice that impressed me most and seeded a kind of devoted exhibitionism in me. When she called out the price and quality of her onions, the sound came from deep in her chest-cavity, and I had the impression her larynx was not a crude organ – not, like others', an instrument for telling lies – but cut and shaped like the sound-box of a cello; I judged there was freedom for such workmanship within her chest and neck. It wasn't merely that her voice was strong, although undeniably it was, but that when she spoke she seemed to cast out more than merely sound; she made the air vibrate and, yes, I felt she projected a kind of truth. I once caught the scent of cardamon on her breath but her words were not directed at me. I felt the drumming of my heart, I wanted her attention badly and caught my breath when I believed she glanced down.

Although Iffe's stand seemed modest with a single basket of onions, when one observed the small traders – there were several with sacking by the roadside which carried a dozen or fewer onions, surplus from their gardens, as well as roaming hawkers with their trays of cheap plastic wares, sea-sponges, matches, melon seeds, kola nuts, peanuts – seeing the hierarchy of sellers, I felt Iffe was a considerable woman. I learned this from one of her regular customers, the Honeymans' cook, who told me Iffe was in line to become an O-lo'ri Egbe – soon she would represent the interests of all the onion sellers in the market. I had noticed she was ready with advice and that she solved disputes and laughed and judged quantities and prices for others, as well as pursuing her own trading practice. So Iffe was in demand, and I remained unnoticed by her. But

But I listened for her voice with its rich, clear resonance emerging from between teeth that seemed to shine.

Our onions became fewer. The morning bloomed.

Some foods I knew, but several I had not encountered before. I had no need to ask, for Ade was being very attentive, in his man's vest and sun-blanched shorts. He seemed put out by the attention I was drawing, therefore proud to show his knowledge, and he pointed to one stall and then the next, identifying wares. 'Yam.' 'Cassava.' 'Okro.' And the vegetables, whose names Ade spoke aloud, and which I repeated, names that until now I had known only as sounds, acquired meaning: each became real to me. It did not escape me that I myself was still to find a proper name, yet in that moment I found no fault in this. It made me feel free. And it was fun to try each vegetable, newly labelled, to see how it suited. 'Okro,' I said aloud. 'O-k-r-o.' I thought it a pretty name, only I did not like the k's hard emphasis. 'C-a-s-s-a-v-a.' I liked it better, the middle fricative and the rhythm it made. But I was not a scaly root. I felt I had greater capacities.

With red-purple onions Iffe was filling the basin of the Honeymans' cook.

'When do we eat?' I asked.

'Soon,' Ade said. But business was good. Certainly I was bringing luck, for Iffe was already in conversation with the next buyer. Leaning forward on the table-edge was a fat man with tribal woundings. I drank some water. I felt a tingling in my eyelids and when I closed them I saw bright lights. I lay my back against Ade's. There was a sunburst in my head. Then momentary blackness. Until now, I thought, I had lived in small places: my knowledge was theoretical, principally aural. And just as, a fortnight ago, during the rainy season, I had dreamed of being in Lagos, so now, amid the heat and smells and peculiarity of the market, in the morning's white light, I dreamed of returning home.

Iffe bought soup and fufu and portioned our lunch into three. I ate happily, swallowing the meat, scooping the fufu into balls and dipping them into my soup. The food was wonderful, yet Ade refused to eat.

'Chop!' Iffe said, but Ade turned his head.

'Fufu makes me sick,' he said. Iffe put down her bowl.

'A disobedient chicken obeys in a pot of soup!' she said, and struck him sharply on his leg. Ade did not reply but stepped back among the onion sacks, and his eyes were bright as he bent his head to the bowl. He ate until the bowl was empty. Then, without warning, he jumped to his feet and fled from the stand.

'Trouble calls you!' Iffe said.

A cloud-shadow passed over the vegetable line. Traders returned to their stalls. I lay down beneath the table and for several minutes I did not move. Many stopped at our stand and many more passed by it. My feet pulsed. I felt I slept. The sky was vast, uncomplicated by cloud. My feet stopped hurting. I slept.

When I woke Ade was back by the onion stand. He knelt beside me. I saw that his shorts were torn, and his skin dusty, rank-smelling. He seemed as full of shame as of pride, and wretched in both. My instinct was to turn from him, for in Iffe's silence I sensed her anger, as she took down the table and began to gather the day's unsold onions into a heap. I too was disappointed with Ade, for though I liked him enough, he had abandoned me; my displeasure was not for being left alone but for the adventures he had had without me. For all this he was supporting my head, pillowing it in the crook of his arm, and, despite the sickly odour – he had vomited the soup, which had stained his vest – I smiled up at his face.

As we left the trading district I felt very aware of Iffe: when she walked, as when she stood at the onion stand, she seemed to inhabit a sovereign world – where, I thought, to be admitted would be the endorsement of my day. I ran to keep up with her; and when, on the yellow bus, she took a seat in the front row, and I saw the effort of our day's trading had raised a band of moisture across the bridge of her nose, I wanted to be beside her. But I followed Ade as he moved to the back of the bus. We motored quickly eastward. At one point during the journey Ade began to laugh.

We got off the bus.

'Why did you go there?' Iffe said, contemptuous.

'I didn't,' Ade said.

'I told you!' Iffe said. 'There will be trouble.'

What happened next, the trouble Iffe had spoken about, the rise and surfacing of that trouble, together with the atmosphere that evening in our house, has stayed with me. The events that came surprised me in both their force and their injustice, and with the casual ceremony with which they were enacted.

Immediately after entering the house, we were taken to the kitchen, where Iffe told us to wait. In the minutes she was gone there was desperate silence between myself and Ade, who avoided my looks, stared down at his feet. I felt my presence was troubling him. When Iffe returned she was with Ben, who appeared calm as, with a cold and hostile face, she told him of Ade's wickedness.

He asked Ade if it was true. Had he in fact gone to see Baba-tundi? Had he been into the garden of the idiot boy?

'Yes,' Ade breathed.

Who was Babatundi? What was in his garden?

'Bend over.'

I was frightened. Ade was shaking, his eyes wide, like a hare's. Ben held a cane. Iffe took my hand, attempting to lead me away, but I would not go. I stood by the kitchen door.

Ade tried once again.

'I didn't speak to him sef!' He was frantic, nearly hysterical in his fear.

'Water don pass garri,' Ben said.

Very slowly, Ade untied his shorts and pushed them below his ankles. His buttocks were so thin and smooth, and his nakedness so unexpected, so humbly revealed – I was repelled, ashamed, moved. Ade bent and gripped his ankles.

Crack! The stroke was like a rifle shot. For a few seconds I heard nothing. Then came the second crack.

I could not see Ben's face as he beat Ade, but I could hear from the way he was breathing that something had happened to him as he crossed the threshold into violence: he was seized with a kind of madness. Ade seemed to flinch a moment before each stroke of the cane, which was cutting into his buttocks. It was shocking to see the red-black wounds; they appeared so abruptly, as if painted by the cane. I counted six strokes and, after the last came down, my heart constricted with fear and pity. I wanted to go to Ade, since I knew a terrible injustice had been done. He pulled up his shorts and clutched his buttocks with both hands. He turned to leave the kitchen, and my feelings turned also; fear and pity joined with a third emotion, one that made me look at Ade anew. As he climbed the stairs to his room, I flushed with admiration. He had survived his beating in silence.

By seven o'clock, when Father returned from work and came

as usual to kiss me on the forehead, I was lying, exhausted, on my bed, but I could not sleep. My mind was wild with the thing I had seen, the casual violence, one person striking another, and that person the father, the action provoked by neither fever nor rage, but carried out formally, almost as a ritual. I lay in darkness but had no feeling of shelter. And heightening the injustice was the knowledge that Iffe, who was a queen to me, and someone with whom I felt a tie, had acceded to the violence. Although she had been a spectator to the beating, she had participated in it also. And it came to me, as I lay, that I had witnessed a kind of theatre, events that had prior meaning and in part existed for display. I was troubled by this thought, although I did not understand why. But I know now what I could not have known then: that to witness an event (and later to record it, as I am now, here in the attic, on my computer) is to take the decision not to intervene, and so to consider myself a spectator, as I did then, a bystander looking on, was to grant myself an innocence which that evening I ceased to have.

What could I have done? How might I have reacted in a different way? These are questions I ask myself now. I could have cried out or made myself faint. I might have disturbed events by sending dinner plates crashing to the floor. Yet I only watched. And if I did not understand the nature of my complicity at the time, if I did not feel that, like Iffe, I had acceded to the violence, nevertheless I could not sleep. I was filled with the atmosphere of the evening, of my fear and pity and admiration for Ade, and with the high colour that had appeared so suddenly on his skin, and I wandered in my thoughts for several hours, just as, for several hours, I turned in my sheets. And when, after the midnight chimes, I rose and climbed through my bedroom window and crossed the garden, black beneath the starless sky, to the compound and unlatched the door and

tiptoed up the stairs, uninvited, to let myself into Ade's bedroom, and behind the closed door took him in my arms, there
was no alteration from the atmosphere of the evening. He
accepted me without a sound. My hands moved over his back
and beneath his pyjama trousers, where I passed my fingers
over the welts. Ade stiffened and let out a soft high note, then
relaxed when I drew him to my chest.

Several days went by, curious memorable days, so short while
they lasted, and so long after, and already I was forgetting life
before the market – my period of confinement, as I thought of
it now. I tried to take in and appraise everything about me. And
I found myself passing through a threshold of understanding:
aspects of the market I had been unaware of, or confused by, or
careless towards, acquired meaning. For several weeks Lagos
vibrated in bright colours and tones. The town appeared avail-
able, well-ordered, fabulously precise.

I liked to be beside Iffe every hour of the day. With fierce
attention, unmoving, just as Riley's pointer would stand
beneath the swallow's nest with her head cocked, I studied Iffe.
In this way I was able to equip myself with a fixed point from
which to understand the market. I had always needed to create
order out of what confused me; even in the womb, on hearing
Father recite *Gray's Anatomy*, I had formed a crude taxonomy
of my body. Now, for the first time out of doors, I began to
understand the complex system of the market, its relationships, its rules of trade. A new world opened up to me.

Every morning Iffe brought out a table-top, cleaned its surface with a rag and propped it on two crates, on whose bleached
plywood sides was printed, as Ade read out, PEARS SOAP IS
THE BEST! The wholesale man arrived and filled her baskets,
and she formed the onions into piles. It was wonderful to see

the onions stacked this way – lovingly, in tiers like a ziggurat, and always the finest specimen, the ripest, most pinkly translucent onion at the summit.

I took my position beside Ade beneath the table. The sky, streaked with pale gold and a farther blue, spread itself towards the lagoon. The trading day had begun.

This was how the process went: the buyer approached, halted, greeted Iffe, then chose and paid for one of the piles; at which point, I supposed, she would pack up her onions and leave. But she would almost always remain by the table, for the most important part of the transaction was still to take place. The buyer would stand looking doubtfully at her pile. She was hoping to persuade Iffe to grant her a number of extra onions. This gift would vary – from a single onion to half-a-dozen, occasionally more – and was always contested.

There were a thousand techniques for obtaining a greater gift and a thousand small differences between each customer's technique. My impulse is to record them all, every ruse and procedure I observed. Yet I must press on with my history. So I will record here only the most common: there was the shaking of the head and the clicking of the tongue; there was the wry smile and placing of hands on hips; I witnessed buyers swaying from side-to-side while appearing to make complicated calculations; I heard suggestions that the pile might 'grow a little'; revelations of how little their husband earned, and what great appetites men possess; there were complaints about the meanness of their husband's elder wives; heartfelt flattery and crocodile tears, mocking laughter and veiled threats; pleading of great friendship and near-starvation; there was mention of heavy taxes and high-priced juju, of greedy uncles, outsize children, mute but hungry dependants with accusing eyes. And there were attempts to embarrass Iffe by refusing to leave until the gift had increased. Iffe countered each technique with arguments equal or greater in strength. Nevertheless, with reluctance, as if each concession amounted to an equivalent emptying of her belly, she would grant to each customer a few extra onions.

I noticed that, no matter how powerfully Iffe bargained, she always projected an image of friendship and generosity. To make each customer feel happy with her purchase, and return another day – that was her aim. And so Iffe introduced a kind of mock-intimacy at the onion stand, an air of human closeness mixed with spectacle; her gifts encouraged this, since the extra onions, wrapped at the end of the sale and quickly removed from view, could be assessed only by the one involved in the transaction; and since that person could not know the size of another's gift, she had no standard by which to judge her own, whose true value remained elusive.

Several times a week the Honeymans' cook came to buy onions. She was an old woman with dry skin, and her hair was wrapped in a white scarf, which indicated she had performed the hajj. Tall, yet hunched, grasping, shrewd, reptilian, she had very few of her teeth left. Often she chewed – but on what? And from between those dark gums came all her cunning, gossip and sour odours.

'Ku aro,' she said one afternoon, and put her empty basin on the ground. She chose a pile of onions and paid. There was a pause. The real bargaining was about to begin. The Honeymans' cook began to sway from side to side. She gathered her loose jaw into an attitude of firm (yet somehow benign) force, raised her black eyes to a point on the horizon and said, 'I think the world will soon end.'

'I cannot believe it,' Iffe replied.

'Buy a small pile for two pennies? Whasamatter?'

'I cannot believe the world will end because you don't get a pile for less than two pennies.'

'Can a porson chop if onions begin to cost money like that?' The Honeymans' cook gestured to a passer-by. 'Eh? Have you seen anything like it before?' But the woman continued down the vegetable line.

'This girl na *waya* o!' cried the Honeymans' cook. Then, imploringly, 'Drop on a little.'

'This is how I sell it.'

'Don't be a stronghead.'

Iffe said nothing.

'You think I'm an oyinbo?'

There was a pause.

'Or picken with a small belly?'

'I need to make profit,' Iffe said.

The Honeymans' cook remained silent. She passed a bead from hand to hand. Then, after several minutes, she bent as far as her hunched frame allowed and said, conspiratorially, her wide grey lips close to my ear, 'This is not the first time the price is so high.' She unbent herself and said loudly, 'Iffe, I think you can remember! That time of Hitla. There were very few onions in Eko. Five pennies couldn't buy a single pile. Ikoko Omon, can you imagine! People begin to use that onion powder. *Yekpe!*' The Honeymans' cook made a hacking sound that might have been laughter. 'Our trouble was more than. Iffe, can you remember?' Iffe nodded her head. 'So,' the Honeymans' cook bent to address me once again, 'I asked a few questions. And they said this Hitla is the man who is stopping onions from reaching Eko. I said this Hitla must be a nonsense foolish man. Does he want everybody to die? Ikoko Omon, do you hear! But it was not Hitla but the government. They were chopping onions for the soja! Ehen. Well, Iffe, she wouldn't allow her people to starve. Some woman. Not so? Ikoko Omon! Eh? So she said she must gather a protest because she wants her people to prosper. The reason is because she is a big honest woman.' The Honeymans' cook raised her hands above her head. Passers-by had stopped to listen. She coughed at length, then continued her story. 'Oh yes. I remember. Iffe went to the Alaga and said that she will join the onion sellers in a big protest. The Alaga began to look at Iffe, straight for her in face. "Iffe," she said. "Iffe, you are a good woman before." The next day now Iffe took the women to Government House. They were singing and dancing, up down, up down up. The noise of the women grew. But some they were getting scared. The government was trying to cut their heart. Some were forming fool. Some began to hala. So Iffe closed her eyes and said, "All those who are getting scared . . . go home." Not so?' Iffe smiled. The Honeymans' cook was enjoying her story, as was I, and the onlookers too. 'And Iffe kept her eyes closed. Well, so when she opened them no porson went. Very soon Iffe asked to see the governor. But he didn't agree to come out. So the women sang.' The Honeymans' cook gestured expansively. She sang for me.

> *Governor Richards!*
> *A big man with a big ulcer!*
> *Your behaviour is deplorable.*
> *Governor is a thief.*
> *Council members thief.*
> *Anyone who does not know Iffe*
> *trouble no dey ring bell.*
> *Oh you, vagina's head seeks vengeance.*
> *You men, vagina's head seeks vengeance.*

Ehen. Well, the Governor he didn't agree to Iffe's terms. So what did she do? She put stones in the onion sacks to make up the price! Ha! Iffe, God don butter your bread!'

It was a striking story. And yet what impressed me more than the account of the demonstration, more than the belligerence of the market women, was the excitement the Honeymans' cook had introduced to the bargaining process: the brilliant length of the tale, her bold flattery, the spectacular waving of her feeble arms. But even more striking was Iffe's response. She must have been aware of the charade, alert to the charming words whose purpose was self-gain. Nevertheless she granted a superior gift to the Honeymans' cook. Reward the deceiver? I was astonished. And I arrived at a fresh way of understanding the market: what I had thought was fuelled wholly by the need for profit was, I understood, reliant also on spectacle, on the ritual of display, so that she who bargained most creatively, or more skilfully and emotively than the other, or excited the other's pride, won the greater bargain. And I understood that to trade was, like other human endeavours, a form of theatre.

So there was play-acting involved in trading! This was a revelation to me. To have noticed drama at the market, and to have become aware of Iffe's place in that drama, might have been to shatter my admiration for her. It might have led me to feel I had caught her unawares, and had discovered the artlessness or inauthenticity beneath her charm. But it was the contrary. My eyes shone for her all over again. It was thrilling to recognize qualities in her that until now my observations of her had taught me to reject. Those gifts of presence and personality that had impressed me for their authenticity – the unhurried gestures which seemed always to call up from the well of human feelings a genuine response, the moisture on her nose indicating an honest day's work, her rich voice I thought the very embodiment of natural resonance – shifted meaning, became the contrary, for I now admired those gifts precisely for their theatricality.

By four o'clock, when the last of the onions had been packed away, we began our journey home. I paused before setting off, for I experienced a splendid joy in treading in the place Iffe's feet had landed only a moment before. I felt extraordinarily happy and light. On the bus, I recall the grey mass of cloud that hung over the sea. What else do I recall from that day? Stepping from the bus to discover the street-lamps had been newly electrified and the humming in and out as we walked between them. Coming round the corner to the first sight of home, where under the swallow's nest Riley's pointer sat waiting to gulp down what fell to her from that teeming pod. And yet the last thing I recall was the presence at my side of Iffe, who became more beautiful to me the longer I stayed in her company. And I knew I could no longer consider myself an autonomous being, and that I wanted to be like Iffe in every way, and would do everything in my power to assimilate her qualities, the moment when, walking through the front garden, she looked at me, raised her clammy fingers to her lips and yawned.

12

Babatundi the Idiot Boy or How I Acquired My Name

Near the beginning of my history, when I wrote, 'The only object that emits a sound is Father's pocket watch,' I was mistaken. There is a second object whose noise disrupts my work: a radio. Every evening at six it turns on automatically, and for half an hour, receiving a weak signal, hisses and pops; the volume of my tinnitus increases; I hear a kind of wandering, high-pitched tone, as well as certain voices, different in tone from the voices I normally hear – all of which ends abruptly after half an hour.

I suspect that, years ago, during his retreat in the attic, my father set the radio to switch itself on and off at these times. No doubt it has been sounding ever since, including these months when I myself have been living in the attic, writing these stories. Yet I only discovered the radio last week. Why? Perhaps because of my growing deafness. Perhaps because of my tinnitus. Or maybe because I have been concentrating so hard on interpreting the sounds of my past.

For a week now I have been trying to find the radio, in order to silence it. I wait for six o'clock, then attempt to follow the whispering and popping sounds to their source. I suspect the radio is hidden somewhere in the south-east corner of the attic, among debris and items of my father's – clothes, mouse droppings, discarded cups and plates, medals, mouldy cricket gear, boxes of maps and papers, dust-curtains that on windy nights swell and fug the room – but I cannot be sure, for the attic amplifies and distorts even the slightest sound. But this is only partly why I've failed to find it. The radio remains hidden chiefly because I confuse its noise with the noises in my head, which do not stem from a fixed point or source. They are not like other sounds – sounds which one can listen to at will and may silence by going away, stopping one's ears, or by refusing to listen – since not only do they fizz and thunder in my head, it is with my head, and not my ears, that I hear them.

It is half past six. I have just tried, and failed, to find the radio. Now I will return to my history. I must try to block out the sounds of the present and concentrate on those of my past, which I am trying to traduce into words, as the needle inscribes the wax disc. So then, I can reveal that some months after I started to accompany Iffe and Ade to the market, the harmattan season began.

· · ·

One could not see the harmattan when it came. One sensed its approach in the slightly cooler air, on hearing the sand-laden wind, in the grey clouds that began to outlast the day, but altogether more clearly in its effect on the animals. The watch-dogs and feral cats, the cart horses, lizards and birds – all grew quiet and recoiled from our human world. The swallows, who had appeared so riotously at the end of the rains, now sang mutedly, shot quickly from nest to garden and back again, cheerless in flight, and I noticed they shied from power cables, washing lines and radio masts and perched exclusively in trees. And Riley's pointer, normally so alert and friendly, with her heavy trembling head and giant's paws, she who with her enthusiasm sometimes knocked us over, now, upon seeing us pass, sadly lifted her muzzle, with drops of saliva hanging from it, then set it down on the kennel floor.

The harmattan, when it arrived in earnest, swept the streets clean. It left behind a red emptiness in our quarter of town. Only here and there a lonely man, with a beard of sand, bent horizontal by the force of the wind, could be seen clinging to the corner of a fence. The air was rich with the smell of desiccated earth, which pattered against the windows, blotting out the sounds.

I was not allowed out of doors. Father warned me that I might suffocate in the storm, and spoke about newspaper reports of an unfortunate child who had been discovered, many years after his disappearance, near Birnin Kebbi, his nostrils packed with sand. I pictured a body hauled up from the earth, shrivelled and grey, with a strange peaceful face. The boy continued to haunt me for several weeks. And yet my father's story, designed to prevent me from going outside, was unnecessary, not because I was afraid of the storm, but because I had little interest in it. I mocked the harmattan. It was so random and unrehearsed, nothing more than base elements picked up and blown south by the wind, the crude unthinking journey of sand. With my new-found esteem for the theatrical, I imputed to all natural phenomena a tired antiquity.

I had no desire to walk in that landscape swept of all colour but cinnamon, but I could not go with Iffe to the market. I became bored, and pestered Father to look after me. For several days he stayed at home, and he told me stories, and we played together, and I felt happy. Soon he was called back to work. To pacify my tears and rage, he let me take the radio to my room, and I listened to the BBC. I imagined the radio's interior as a tiny lounge where, at ten each morning, seated on a leather armchair, after having placed a record on his phonograph, the announcer spoke to me. I was ready to admit that in the radio – as in my dolls' house with its hinged façade, allowing me to manipulate its inhabitants' lives – there reigned a different scale of reality. But nothing was stranger than hearing the announcer's deep tone of voice, since I believed that little people spoke in small, high voices. This detail did not trouble me for long, since I reasoned that the radio, with its miraculous technology, transposed all voices into a lower key. I took great pleasure in listening to the BBC. I especially liked to hear the Bow Bells, with their sad and lovely descending peal, sounding just before the news.

Sometimes I would switch the radio off and try to pick out Iffe's voice from the uproar of the storm. I wished, by straining my powers, to absorb its rich timbres, as one slakes a thirst, experience them as she did, from deep within herself, from the great echo chamber of her chest. There was a patchwork quilt embroidered by my mother during the war, under which I tried to capture Iffe's lovely tones, so that I could study them in depth; in those thrilling moments when I thought I caught a word or two, I buried my head under the quilt. I had the sensation that somehow I inhabited Iffe and understood her from the inside out. By missing her, I sought to recreate her, summon her, by turning into her. How lucky I was to have her as my guide and teacher. If only she felt the same way about me. I wanted to believe she missed my presence at the market, and imagined her slumped over piles of unsold onions, tormented by the harmattan, cursing Father for preventing me from leaving the house.

It was strangely uplifting, then, when I discovered her in a bleak mood. One afternoon, on bringing home vegetables for our evening meal, she appeared quiet and sad, and spoke to Ade in undertones. She was short-tempered and, I noticed, eager for Ben's attention: very different from the person who until now had appeared so strong and sovereign. Did she miss me so much! I was not sure if I liked this new Iffe, however. She was distant and distracted; some of the playfulness had gone from her character, and with it, I felt, a little of her style. I noticed Ben addressed her with a strange new name, *Nne*. I do not know how long she suffered in that sombre mood. Nevertheless, the following morning, I noticed her presence was commanding once again. It was hard to imagine she had ever entered that melancholy region to which, out of vanity, I half-hoped she would return.

The pattern continued; on coming back from the market, Iffe, or Nne, as I had started to think of her after her return, spoke little and seemed afraid of being alone; each morning she shone anew. I had not known a person could hold within her such divided states. It was a thrilling discovery, and yet it posed a problem for me. I understood now I would have to assimilate not a single set of qualities, but two.

One evening towards the end of the harmattan I was sitting beneath the kitchen table, watching Ben prepare a chicken for our evening meal: he pulled apart its legs, first the left, then the right, then smashed down his knife to cleave them from its body. With what indifference Ben chopped that raw and pimpled flesh! There was no sign of grief in his eyes, not for the chicken (who, I knew, had spent its short life crowded into a dirty coop), nor for myself, who watched appalled. Ben cut the chicken into pieces and placed them into a pot of boiling water. He added chillies, onion, garlic and stockfish. After sprinkling salt and pepper into the pot, he covered it with a metal lid. Shortly after, Iffe or Nne came into the kitchen. Immediately the room dimmed, became dusted with a grimy atmosphere, and every sound seemed to fall an octave. We ate quickly and in silence. At one point during the meal Nne spoke. What she said was truly surprising to me, and helped me to understand the realm of high drama she moved in. Perhaps it was true; perhaps it was her way of demystifying the powers of her rival; or perhaps she was giving me a sign.

'The Honeymans' cook is a witch,' is what she said.

Ade and I gasped. We knew about witches; knew that they were mostly old women; knew that because of a mysterious object in their stomach, they needed only to wish evil and evil would happen. We had heard, enviously, that they could turn into any animal they chose, most often birds, in whose guise they did extraordinary things. And we had heard the stories about Mrs Honeyman, who had taken to her bed when her private parts had mysteriously caught fire.

The harmattan began to blow itself out. The animals returned. Lizards basked on the warm walls of our garden; for the first time in many weeks I heard the swallows, under whose nest, after dinner, I was allowed to sit. One evening as we were listening to the radio, Father said, 'Tomorrow you may go to the market.' Next morning my prospects swelled further; as we were walking to the bus stop, Ade whispered, 'Today you and I will visit Babatundi.'

In the weeks after the harmattan we went to visit Babatundi as often as we could. I remembered it was Babatundi Ade had visited on the day of his beating (which, of course, only added to my excitement). As we approached we always made sure that Sagoe, his older brother, was not around. Sagoe was greatly feared by the market children. It was said he had caused Babatundi's limp, having thrown him from the branches of a tree.

It was easy to slip from the onion stand to visit Babatundi: running north through the vegetable quarter; passing the meat section; skipping by cloth sellers and traders in bicycle parts where the market narrowed into uncovered lanes; hearing sounds of men and women calling and whispering; skirting the juju stalls to emerge into a wider space; running through the dusty labyrinth of streets; going by stalled trucks, porters with heavy loads; slowing to kick a fish head along the road; Ade shouting for me to hurry; running straight at houses, and between houses; and finally rounding a corner to a lane heaped with rubbish, sided by rows of flimsy huts with gaping doors – there, after checking that Sagoe was not around, we would come to a halt.

'Babatundi!'

We always found him guarding the lane which led to his garden. He stood on his gate with his feet between the bars, swinging back and forth. A thin boy, taller than Ade, his head was large. Somehow he appeared advanced in age, but I could not have said exactly why – perhaps it was his ashy skin, the corrugations below his eyes. He stood with bare feet on his gate. The sunlight showed the curious aspect of his baldness, his hair patched like continents on his skull. Later I saw beads of perspiration, which seemed threaded on his long lashes. And from beneath his lashes the eyes were wide, wet, slow-moving, and curiously grained.

'Babatundi!'

Ade sat on the kerb, cracked and mossy like Babatundi's feet, and threw stones at the rubbish heap. I joined him there. Babatundi wore military trousers torn at the knee, a filthy vest, a string of beads around his neck. Minutes passed before he seemed to notice us. There was a *patting* sound, a high jingle, and the gate swung, moaning at the hinge.

'Babatundi!'

His usual mood was one of indefinite sadness. But sometimes he threw out a look of violent force. Stepping off his gate, he would grip the bars with both hands and shake it ferociously.

Then he would thrust his head forward and let out an ugly bellow. I think it was rage born of anger at his own speechlessness. But the fit would leave him as suddenly as it arrived. He would step back on to his gate, pat the wall and start to swing back and forth, as if nothing out of the ordinary had occurred.

It was summer of 1953. I was six years old. At that time a delicious laziness invaded my whole being. Every afternoon Ade and I lay on the bank opposite Babatundi's gate, stretched out in the sun like lions, dozing, listening to the distant sound, like far-away crashing waves, of cars and trucks, and their bright horns, or else watching Babatundi swing back and forth on his gate. As the day grew late, we would pick ourselves up, brush the spores from our clothes, wave to Babatundi, and amble back to the market.

There was one afternoon when things happened differently, however; and it was on that afternoon I acquired my name. I remember very clearly. We were sitting on the bank. Hours passed, filled with heat and boredom. Babatundi quietly moaned, laughed to himself. Scorched thistles crackled on the rubbish heap, and the grass appeared to salivate with glistening sap. At one point in the afternoon Ade peeled himself from the grass and approached me, appearing serious. I sat up. He told me he had something to show me and took a playing card from his shorts' pocket. It was the Ace of Hearts. I gasped. It showed a nearly naked dancing girl. She was beautiful: blue-eyed, with dark hair clasped in a fountain above her head. Sitting on a baby elephant, with one leg stretched out in front of her, she wore nothing but a tiny blue skirt and tassels attached to her breasts. Ade pressed a finger to his lips. 'Shhh. I will show it to Babatundi. It is the way to reach his garden.' He walked slowly, earnestly up to the idiot boy with the card held before him. In a lightning movement, Babatundi jumped to his feet and started to run, limping down the alley leading to his garden, leaving his gate uncaptained.

'Come on!' Ade shouted. I let out a cry of delight and started to follow. As Babatundi moved futher off his legs became hidden from view – curious how he attained grace when just his upper half was visible. The slow climbing and falling, like the motion of a galloper on its carousel.

We ran to the end of the alley, and there it was: Babatundi's garden! A dusty yard scattered with patches of sour-smelling grass. In the middle was a tree whose trunk and lower limbs had been painted pale red. Broken mirrors hung from its branches by different lengths of cord, also cowrie shells, shining in the brightness, and little rounds of metal on which a strange script had been painted. The idiot boy was waiting for us under the tree. Solemnly, as if events had been rehearsed, Ade offered him the playing card, and Babatundi snatched it, turning his back on us. Emitting an obscene moan, he lowered himself heavily to the ground and started to rock back and forth with the card held close in front of his eyes. I was frightened and intrigued. I could tell Babatundi was enjoying himself because a certain softness had come into his movements. He seemed completely transformed and, as he leaned forward, dragging his bad leg behind him, and collapsed on his front, I became scared. I turned to leave, but Ade took hold of my arm. Putting a finger to his lips, he led me to the other side of the tree.

'Look,' Ade hissed. In front of us was some kind of barrow piled high with junk, through which Ade began to rummage. I was too excited to help, so I watched as Ade pulled out a collection of wonderful junk: cowries, pieces of broken pottery, feathers, flints, pages of books and magazines, stuffing into his pockets polished stones, badges marked with Babatundi's script, gutting the barrow of a shiny farthing, a postcard, a mouse's tail. I could not see Babatundi as Ade emptied the contents of the barrow, and at first I could not hear him, perhaps because of the whine of the traffic, or because he himself was quiet. But gradually I started to hear a low yellow groan that came and went and rose steadily in pitch.

Suddenly Ade pulled out a wooden box.

'What is it?' I asked. 'Open it!'

Inside were rows and rows of stamps representing letters of the alphabet. They were arranged in no order I could perceive, neither alphabetical nor, I suspected, into words. We sat on the ground with the printer's set open at our feet.

'Pick one,' Ade said, pointing to the letters.

'Which?'

'Your favourite.'

Forgetting Babatundi, I passed my fingers over the set, feeling the raised pattern of the letters. Unable to read, I knew them principally as shapes, and yet I had an idea of the sound they made. As I pointed to each letter, Ade voiced its sound. I paused over the *a*. There was something attractive about it. I felt it belonged wholly to my friend. I knew other words beginning with A, but I had come to think of these as steeped or tinted in his character, as a puddle takes on the colour of the sky.

'Choose one,' Ade said, and, laughing, I reached and took the *p*. It was surprisingly heavy. I held it up to the light. Then without warning Ade took it from me and stamped it on my arm. The ink made my skin tingle.

'Choose another,' Ade said, and I picked the *b*, because of the marvellous symmetry, and because I liked its curved belly, and because at that moment it seemed to me the greatest friend I could ever have. This time, aware of the game, I handed it to Ade, who stamped it on the same arm, higher up, just below my elbow. Again, my skin prickled and shivered.

Now it was Ade's turn to pick a letter. He chose the *A*. What was there to do but take it and stamp it on him? His arm quivered, and he raised it to the light. The ink was having an effect on him, penetrating his skin perhaps, giving him a pleasant feeling. He looked around to make sure Babatundi was still occupied with the dancing girl, and when he saw he was rubbing his loins back and forth on the ground, he picked another letter – *D* – which I took and stamped on him. One after another, we chose letters and stamped them all over our arms, laughing, setting our skins alight.

But now Babatundi's moaning grew in intensity, and I looked over and all at once I thought of the crackling thistles and the sap glistening on the grasses.

'We had better get back,' Ade said, and began to gather the stamps and put them back in their box.

I gazed at my arm; there they were, the small, dark letters, scattered from my elbow to my wrist. I shivered with delight.

'Wait,' I said and held up my arm. I let my finger run over the letters, and Ade named them: '*S . . . n . . . D . . . a . . . t . . . r . . . B . . . d . . . o . . . a . . . e . . . v.*'

I pointed to the final two letters again.

'*e,*' said Ade, '*v.*'

That is how I acquired my name.

13

Map of the World, 2: Massacre at Benin

Autumn has arrived. In my attic the air crackles with cold. Whenever the wind blows with extra force, the ceiling, long since rotten within, and yellowed by Father's tobacco smoke, rains down on me a kind of mustard dust or pollen. At the far end from where I sit, the roof has started to buckle, no doubt beginning to cave in. To the left, at knee-height, a crack has appeared in the boards. I have papered over it with sheets of old newspaper, but the wind blows them unstuck, and they flap violently against the wood. Sometimes, leaning my head against the wall, breathing deeply from tiredness, my hair a matted mass of curls, I think about how much of my history there is still to record. I think about my papers, which are scattered in the attic: novels, histories, reference books, magazines, reports, diaries, articles, letters and such like, most left by my father, some I brought here myself. I think about the times when each of them was new in the world: freshly printed, written, the ink still wet.

In the previous chapter I related how I acquired my name, an event that signals for me the end of my early childhood. I was six years old. My plan for this chapter was to focus on my life and adventures from then until my thirteenth year – my age at Nigerian independence, when I left Lagos with Father and moved here, to Gullane. For several hours I tried to make a start, in vain. I could barely compose a single sentence. What is more, the radio switched itself on, setting off a powerful ringing in my ears, dragging me further from my past. It seems

I cannot distinguish between the noise of the radio and the hubbub of my recalling. The hissing, rasping and popping, the irregular voices buzzing, that low asthmatic drawl, all this merges with the noises in my head.

Whenever the sounds become a meaningless clamour and I cannot concentrate on my past, I turn my attention to my present, to the objects that surround me in the attic, those still, meaningless, decrepit, mostly silent companions. It strikes me that I've hardly told a story unless it was about an object, or referred to an object, or else I would appropriate an object, borrow from it, by transcribing it, as illustrated by my mother's diary. The objects we think we know are shallow things, existing on a flat and insubstantial surface, because we value them only in terms of common use. Whenever I take up one of my objects, however, I spend a lot of time getting to know it. I seek out its various properties, smell, feel, taste, all of which I absorb readily and happily. Even to be near my objects is a pleasure for me, and I toy with the idea of naming my chapters in their honour: *Radio, Pocket Watch, Unica, Mother's Trunk*.

It is my intention now to focus on one object in particular: the mappa mundi. How shall I begin to describe it? The most striking feature is its dilapidation. The moths are feasting on the vellum, and the gaps and fissures grow larger and more numerous every month. Yes, that fantastical image of the world, with its lands and seas, its painted myths and imaginary beings, is disintegrating week by week, which at once pleases and saddens me. I have decided will do nothing to halt the course of its decay.

Whenever I examine the mappa mundi, my gaze is drawn to the monstrous races – Amyctyrae, Androgini, Astomi, Blemmyae, Cyclops and their sisters – depicted at the outer edges. They are my sisters too: I feel an affinity with those freakish souls, because of my monstrous late birth, perhaps.

Of all the living beings on the map, they are located farthest from Christ, who is shown nailed to the cross at the disc's centre. The monsters are cut off from the world by the Nile river, and from one another by the circumscribed frame in which each dwells, both graphic ornament and prison, ranked alongside one another and yet never touching.

Only two of the monsters are not enclosed in frames, and yet they are hardly free. The first, in Africa proper, west of the Nile, between Nubia and the Mountains of the Moon, is a member of the tribe Gorgades, the hairy women. She is running from a small army of Christian soldiers and is sweating what appears to be blood. A rubric to the right, entitled 'Letter of Alexander to Aristotle', comments on this scene: 'Then we saw women and men hairy in the manner of beasts, who, when we wished to approach nearer, fled towards a river and threw themselves into it.' Slightly to the left of the unfortunate Gorgad, dwelling in a kind of desert wasteland, is the second monster, a member of the Panotii tribe, with giant ears flapping frantically about her head in a pathetic attempt to take flight, but prevented from doing so by the ropes which bind her to a stake, held over the fire by a soldier with a forked stick.

If I have chosen to interrupt my history to focus on the mappa mundi, it is not only because the sounds in the attic and the din in my head distract me from my past. Nor is it only because I wish to fix the map in my mind, in words, before its deterioration is complete. Neither is it due solely to my feeling of kinship with those outlandish beings. No, I have chosen to speak about the mappa mundi because I wish to introduce a new character into my history. A man about whom I know little, despite my investigations, but whose writings mean a great deal to me. A man who, over the years, I have come to think of as both heir to, and modern-day chronicler of, the monstrous races, like myself. His name is Kemi Olabode, and his story will be the subject of the present chapter.

In 1956, during the months of June and July, colonial officers in Lagos received a series of pamphlets through the post. My father did not read them at the time. Nevertheless, he did not throw them out, whether deliberately or not, and the collection survived the end of Empire and found its way to Gullane. It was not until his final years that my father discovered the pamphlets among his papers. For a brief period he read them obsessively, and called me up to the attic to tell me about them. Collectively, the pamphlets tell the story of the first decades of Empire in Nigeria, from initial contact between British traders and West African chiefs, to the missionary movement, to the savage wars during which the chiefdoms fell to the British. It is a story which I have always associated with the mappa mundi (which, at the time of my father's obsession with the pamphlets, was barely touched by decay). Although the pamphlets concern events that took place several centuries after the mappa mundi was conceived, they tell of people whose fate mirrors that of the Gorgades, Panotii and their sisters.

I have the pamphlets before me now. There are five in total, printed on rough off-white paper, folded in half and stitched together with what looks like fishing wire. I wish to focus on one pamphlet in particular, entitled 'Massacre at Benin'. It concerns a particularly violent episode in the British colonization of Nigeria, depicting the brutalization and slaughter of the inhabitants of that ancient kingdom who tried to resist the forces of Empire.

The story set out in 'Massacre at Benin' begins in 1955, in a hut in Lagos. A frail old man is sitting at a table, before a wall of books, old volumes collectively entitled *The Complete History of Africa*. As the title suggests, the books concern the history of the entire continent, from the very first inhabitants to the Great War, and are authored by Kemi Olabode himself – who, we learn, is the very man sitting at the table. A strange odour rises from the volumes, writes Kemi Olabode, a strange and bitter, subtle-smelling odour, the odour of death. He goes on to describe how he locates then opens Volume IX, entitled 'The Savage Wars of Empire'; and, as he does so, writes Olabode, dust rises from the pages, obscuring the first sentences. He continues: I wrote those sentences over three decades ago. I was an ambitious youth, full of pride and rude health. I thought those sentences were a truthful account of my continent's past. I thought I was chronicling the birth of Nigeria. But, *Not everything that comes from the cow is butter*. Now, in my dotage, I see that those sentences are nothing but lies. Let me therefore get rid of them. Let me do away with those words, which, like the dust rising from the pages, serve only to conceal the past, which seems to surface from a veil of darkness and forgotten time. Instead I will rely entirely on my old man's memory. You see, dear reader, I am a Nigerian and I lived though the first years of the British Empire. Let me take you back to that time, a time of great hope, for me and my masters. Listen!

In those days I was travelling with the Protectorate. I was dealing with important business, and my job as a translator was carrying me far into the interior. I was assisting the British in signing treaties with the chiefs, whose lands they had acquired unlawfully at Berlin. 'In return for your forests,' I translated, 'we will protect you and make you rich!' And the chiefs signed. It was 1895. The Atlantic slave trade was over. Those greedy dupes who once sold their people to sugar barons in the West now gifted their land and rights, their laws and property, their dignity, their arts and their sovereignty, to the lords of Empire, who were the same hucksters as before, I came to realize, but they wore pith helmets instead of top hats. *A monkey broke the razor after shaving, not knowing that his hair would soon grow again.* With their bejewelled fingers the chiefs signed, some never having even held a pen until this moment. It did not matter. If they did not sign, they were made to sign. If they signed without understanding the true consequences of the pact, and objected, well, we unleashed our precision technology. We confounded them with bombs, we amazed them with bullets, we shelled them until they kissed our boots and begged to be allowed to sign all over again. 'Whatever happens, we have got / The Maxim gun, and they have not.'

Those savages were standing in the way of progress, of civilization, of commerce, obstructing all the forces working towards the great scheme of perfect happiness, and not only for the citizens of Europe, but for the entire population of the world as well, including (so I thought) my beautiful proto-nation of Nigeria. We (the British and educated Nigerians such as myself who assisted them in their work) took no account of incidental suffering, and our soldiers exterminated such brutes who stood in the way. We were alone in the forest. Who would talk, if we held our tongues?

So I translated, and the chiefs signed, and all the while I was harbouring a secret desire as ambitious as the British whose work I facilitated. I wanted to be the African Herodotus, the first to chronicle my continent's past, completely and exhaustively, studying every angle, cultural, economic, anthropological, diplomatic, social, geographical, intellectual, economic, martial, medical, political, psychological, etc., etc. For that, I required stories. The difficulty (which I hoped to turn to my advantage) was that Nigeria had no written record of her past.

It was stored between the ears of griots, fetid ancients whom I grabbed with my young man's fingers and grilled at every opportunity, even when they were in the line of fire, *especially* then, since I needed their stories before they were lost. Then, later in my tent, I transcribed their words into my India-paper jotter. I had a vision of our nation's history set down in ink, then printed and bound, and presented to the world, in a book! I was the Edison of History (so I thought), my pen like the needle of the phonograph, that sensitive point which scratches at the wax disc, translating sound and preserving it as signs.

Do not think I was unaware of the butchery going on in the name of Progress, or that I was ignorant of my part in this butchery. Regarding the suffering of my African brothers, well, I suffered along with them (so I imagined). Their pain stabbed me like a spear in the heart or a bayonet in the heart. That was the price I paid for electing to chronicle our history.

But let me return to the story at hand. I have told you that we visited many chiefs and used various methods of flattery, threats, bribery and violence to make them sign our treaties. In time, however, we encountered a chief who was wiser than the rest. Or prouder, richer, or less greedy, or more ignorant, or better armed, or else unable to understand my translation. This chief was the Oba of Benin, and he rejected the opportunity to gift his kingdom for illusory gains. *One who has been bitten by a snake lives in fear of worms* (as the prophets say). He not only defied the British, he banished them from his territory as well, killing over 200 of their men, including several whites!

This was in late December 1896. Soon news of the 'Benin Disaster' reached England. It was put about by the press that this Oba was a savage king. He had ambushed an innocent party who were trying to liberate the people of that territory, themselves exploited by their Oba. A cannibal, a great man for human sacrifice, men and women were being disembowelled on the orders of the fetish priests, and the Oba's palace was filled with human skulls. It was also agleam with gold, ivory, bronze, palm oil, valuable antiquities, etc., etc. The press named Benin the 'City of Blood' and demanded revenge.

Two weeks later the British had amassed a mighty force. The 'Benin Punitive Expedition' consisted of eight warships, 1,400 soldiers (armed with rifles, Maxim guns, rocket tubes, 7-pounders and mines), as well as 2,000 bearers, several doctors and 1 translator (myself). One morning in February 1897 we started up the Benin River. On either side of us rose steep walls of trees, millions of them, massive trees with rotting foliage, dripping thickets, hairy vegetation and provocative flowers clinging to their trunks. The river was narrow in places, and, as the ships steamed along, we could almost touch the trees (if we dared). I, however, stayed in the hold. Never without my notes and textbooks, I read, amassed knowledge and marshalled my arguments. At Warrigi we put ashore and set up camp.

It was later that evening (the moon was rising through a screen of crimson dust) when for the first time I set eyes on our leader, Rear-Admiral Harry Rawson. As he came out of his tent to detail the plan of attack, the night got darker, and the forest grew closer, and those who minutes before were chatting or smoking or cleaning their guns or eating or drinking or passing round pornographic playing cards, stopped. In the instant of seeing him, I knew him, without however knowing much about him. Let me mention, briefly, what I knew.

His eyes were like boiled eggs.

His lungs were like a diseased plant.

His fingers were like fufu squeezed inside pig-skin gloves.

When he spoke black rainbows came from his mouth.

His jokes were like wasps attacking a sick goat.

His stomach was like a barrel of maggots, and his arms were like legs.

His tongue was a hamper of soiled laundry left out in the sun.

His teeth were like gravestones.

His promises were like tsetse flies.

His orders were like being flogged with hippopotamus hide.

I should have mistrusted those orders. I should have thought: What do those orders mean? I should have asked myself which kind of man flogs you instead of telling you what to do. I should have consulted Herodotus for historical examples of fanatical leaders and I should have correctly identified the orders of Admiral Rawson as marking the beginning of my destruction.

But I did not, and that night went to my tent and fell asleep to the sound of witches feasting, whispering and copulating.

The following day the temperature reached 140 degrees. We could go no further by boat, and were forced to battle through the steaming bush. The column of scouts, Hausa soldiers, probed ahead, cutting through the foliage and searching out the enemy. Between the 10th and 12th our columns were engaged in sharp fighting. This removed any suspicion that the capture of Benin would be easy or that the people were cowardly or reluctant to fight, as the press had claimed.

Jungle warfare is a particularly harrowing and unnerving business. We had to move slowly through unmarked paths, and we were vulnerable to ambush at any time. So, every 500 yards we halted, set up our weaponry and astonished the bush with fire. The rocket tubes fizzed and crashed and the Maxims sputtered like handfuls of matches, sending swarms of angry bullets into the forest. The rifles grew hot, the Maxims exhausted all the water in their jackets, and the empty cartridge cases, tinkling to the ground, formed giant heaps round each man. And all the time our bullets were shearing through flesh, smashing and splintering bone. But the Benin army kept on coming, all day for many days, as we advanced towards the capital.

Dear reader, we took no chances. When we came to a village our soldiers fired volley after volley until the enemy was driven into the centre, which was then shelled remorselessly, rushed and captured. On arrival in a village Rawson would march in and call for the chief. I translated. He had a great idea that African chiefs should creep on all fours and kiss his left boot. Then we would plunder the supplies, throw fire into the huts and smash everything that would not burn. It was the same spectacle everywhere.

Did the British have no law against shooting at people they couldn't even see? It was an atrocity that ran contrary to the conventions of war in Europe, which forbade violence against those who were unable to defend themselves. Did such conventions not extend to Africa? Did the hearts of those officers not feel tainted by the slaughter they enacted? Were their souls not inwardly marked? Were they not cursed in later life, like myself? Did they not wake up exhausted with fevered dreams? The evidence points in the opposite direction. After the expedition, Rawson was knighted, and a Benin clasp was added to the General Africa Medal. Captains received CBs, Distinguished Service Orders, officers were promoted, etc., etc.

Alas, it was not the same for me. I trace the beginning of my destruction or mental unravelling to the following incident. At Ologbio, where we were resting before the final push, I was called before the Admiral. Perhaps I had mistranslated something, and one of the village chiefs had not kissed his left boot. I protested. But he was set on my punishment, and out came the hippopotamus whip. I was made to strip, kneel, and my hands were tied to a water cart. I am unable to recall what happened next. Therefore, I will quote from the diary of E. J. Grave, an English solider who witnessed such a flogging that same year: 'The *chicotte* of raw hippo hide,' Grave writes, 'especially a new one, trimmed like a corkscrew and with edges like knife blades, is a terrible weapon, and a few blows bring blood. Not more than twenty-five blows should be given unless the offence is very serious. Though we persuade ourselves that the African's skin is very tough, it needs an extraordinary constitution to withstand the terrible punishment of one hundred blows; generally the victim is in a state of insensibility after twenty-five or thirty blows. At the first blow, he yells abominably; then quiets down, and is a mere groaning, quivering body till the operation is over . . . I conscientiously believe that a man who receives one hundred blows is often nearly killed and has his spirit broken for life.'

The next thing I knew we were at Benin City. I was lying in a tent, gasping for air, writhing, nearly slayed, with a thousand rats scratching at my back and flies sucking at my wounds. I became delirious and remained that way for several weeks.

Terrible fate!

I returned to my village. My mother embraced me and put me to bed. I dreamed of my History. From between the covers of those (as yet incomplete) tomes came howls of anguish and hysterical laughter. I woke up trembling. After that I refused to leave my room. I lived as if in a dream. I was no longer able to walk or read or grasp a pen. Instead I listened into my thoughts. They scolded me in the harshest terms, mocked my life, my goals and ambitions. I did not eat for several weeks. And when I finally ate, at the bidding of my mother, nothing tasted as it had tasted before. Potatoes tasted like onions, and onions tasted like apples, and apples tasted like goat, and goat tasted like okro, and okro tasted like figs, and figs tasted like stew, and stew tasted like mud, and mud like bones left out in the sun and eaten out by rats, and these bones tasted like porridge, and porridge like vomit, and vomit like champagne, champagne on the king's table, which tasted like iron, and this iron like smoke in my mouth, which stung like smoke in my eyes.

What troubled me more than my malfunctioning taste buds were the howls and mad cries of my African brothers who had perished and who made a sound in my ears like forests falling, hideous cries like the sky in flames.

Who was torturing me?

I asked myself this question more than once.

In time I got better. I began to read. I told my mother to unpack my library and began to study. *With the end of the old rope we begin to weave the new.* For the next decade I lived in my mother's compound. I did nothing but write my long-planned History, and I forgot about the screams of my African brothers. I buried them between the covers of the tomes I was writing.

And here I am, today, an old man without the strength to leave my bed, or the courage to kill myself. The howls of my African brothers have returned to plague me. Now I make an effort to understand them, and they say to me, *The destruction of our African continent was not a unique event in the history of the world.* They say to me, *Honour, justice, compassion and freedom are ideas that have no converts.* They say to me, *There are only people who intoxicate themselves with words, shout them, imagining they believe them without believing in anything else but profit and personal advantage.* They say to me, *There is no document of civilization which is not at the same time a document of barbarism.*

14

'First Snow in Port Suez'

Today, I visited my maternal grandfather, Mr Rafferty. I had not intended to break from writing, but three nights ago, after finishing 'Massacre at Benin', I found myself unable to progress. I barely remember the process of transcribing the pamphlet; I worked without pause, hardly taking in the sense of the words – the relief of abandoning my own history and copying another's! It was not until the following day when I printed the chapter out and read it slowly, checking it against the original (two errors: 'smiled' for 'soiled', 'odours' for 'orders'), that I was stricken with fatigue and emptiness. I found myself in a bind. Far from calming me, as I had hoped, far from allowing time for the din of my past to quieten and become intelligible to me once again, the process of transcription stirred up clamours of a more disturbing kind – in me, but not of me. I was haunted by the swarms of bullets, the screams and hysterical laughter of the Benin army. It was as if the process or undertaking of these last months had been reversed: no longer was I traducing sounds of the past on to my computer, into words on the page; now words on the page – Kemi Olabode's words – were, as I copied them out, evoking ancient sounds.

I did not fully understand the source of those disturbing feelings, which were quite different – more painfully wretched, heavier – than the depression which sets in when confronted with barbarism, with evidence that all power is a form of violence exercised over men and women. I merely lay on my mattress, haunted by the sounds.

After seeing my grandfather this afternoon, however, I have a better understanding of my response. I had concentrated on 'Massacre at Benin' because I had wanted to take a break from writing my own history. But there was a second, more important reason: I realize I chose this text because Kemi Olabode's experience told me something about the country of my birth; something that was hidden from me during my childhood; something that, being unsavoury, and brutalizing, the British in Lagos did not talk about. Kemi Olabode sought to enlighten us; that is why he sent his pamphlets to every colonial officer, at his own expense. But he was mistaken; he had worked under the illusion that the British in Nigeria were ignorant, that they were unaware of the crimes of slaughter that had won them control of the colony. And perhaps some of us were genuinely ignorant. Perhaps there were people who, like the children of the colony, did not know how our home had been established and administered. But these were few. Most, like my father, knew enough. And so Kemi Olabode's writings were ignored. It was not knowledge the colonials lacked. What was missing was the courage to understand what they knew and to draw the right conclusions.

But I am getting ahead of myself. Before I understood this, I needed to dress myself, leave the attic, and the house, and travel to Edinburgh to visit Mr Rafferty.

. . .

The city was cold and dark. The pavements were damp, and people were walking with purpose. Orange streetlamps flickered on at some point; it can't have been much past two. I took my grandfather to the central library to choose some books, *Marine and Pocket Chronometers, English House Clocks*. As we left the library, walking along George IV Bridge, past empty cafés and slow-moving traffic, I said, for no reason in particular, 'When I take you back to the institution, perhaps I could stay on with you.'

Mr Rafferty cocked his head.

'Well,' I said as we stepped out into the road to pass a group of tourists. 'I feel as though I'm in need of a . . . rest.'

Mr Rafferty said nothing.

We continued on towards the Meadows. As we were crossing the fields, with their rows of cherry trees, bare in the chill air of winter, I stopped, and Mr Rafferty stopped beside me.

I said, 'What do you think?' Mr Rafferty said nothing. 'About me perhaps staying on as your neighbour?' I laughed. Mr Rafferty smiled, pointing to his mouth. Then he pressed his lips shut and placed a finger against them.

'I'm to be quiet?' He shook his head, pointing to himself. '*You* want to be quiet?' He nodded vigorously. I shrugged. I had heard from the doctor at the institution that he sometimes lapsed into episodes of speechlessness, but I had not yet encountered this myself.

I didn't know what to say, so I guided him to a bench, and we sat in silence for a while. To our right, in the near distance, rose the great mass of Arthur's Seat, concealed by low, drawn-out, unmoving banks of cloud. Here and there, moving in and out of the cloud, along the brown and black basalt crags and the vivid grass, I saw tiny figures, the last of the day's walkers, together with their dogs.

Eventually I said, 'Very well, there're too many words already.' I didn't know what I meant by that. The low sun hung over the muddy grass. The Meadows smelled of swamp. Groups of heavy boys butted against one another, while joggers made circuits of the park. Mr Rafferty seemed to enjoy the activity; his face was raised high, like a dog sniffing the wind.

I took a deep breath and said, 'My difficulty, Mr Rafferty, is this.' And I found myself explaining my troubles following the transcription of Kemi Olabode's pamphlet. Only then did I realize I hadn't yet not told him about my history. It is true, on previous visits, I'd asked him questions about my past, tried to gather information, but I'd never told him why. Now, as I explained my project in full, I became eager, almost excited, and I talker faster and faster.

Mr Rafferty's face was illuminated by an odd yellow light. It gave him a look of knowingness. I didn't know how much of what I'd said he'd understood, or even heard. I sighed.

'I'd better take you back . . .' Mr Rafferty said nothing. We rose and began to walk towards the institution. But I wasn't ready to leave him yet. I had an idea. 'Come,' I said and took his arm. 'There's a place I've been meaning to visit for a while.'

The bookshop had hardly changed. There was a time, in my twenties (during the lost years following the break-up of my first, and only, love affair), when I haunted its narrow shelves and rested on the trestle-tables piled with magazines: *Spare Rib, Living Marxism.* I would sit for hours on the wooden ladder, reading, or chatting to the owner of the shop. Now I hoped to find some literature about Benin. I sought out the 'Genocide' section and absorbed myself in the titles. Mr Rafferty shuffled through the shop, his book bag swinging like a pendulum from his wrist. He disappeared into the children's section.

Some time later I heard a loud crash, a yelp, a dog's bark. I looked to see Mr Rafferty kneeling on the floor, gathering fallen books, watched warily by the shop's dog, a wonderful black-and-tan creature which bore an injured expression. I rose and set Mr Rafferty upright. Still he didn't speak; he only looked at me with an expression not dissimilar to the dog's.

Walking home, I found I could not stop talking, an effect of my grandfather's silence. I told him about my childhood in Lagos and my friendship with Ade. Mr Rafferty said nothing. But when I told him of how I got my name – how, in fact, I had named myself – he squeezed my arm, and his lips curved into a smile.

We had reached the reception hall of the institution, and a nurse approached. Once again, Mr Rafferty squeezed my arm. He pointed to the ceiling. Immediately I understood.

'You would like me to come to your room with you?' He nodded. 'All right. But let's get some hot chocolate from the machine on the way.'

Mr Rafferty's room had been recently cleaned. The chair had been placed on the table and the floor shone, smelling of disinfectant. Mr Rafferty motioned for me to sit on the bed. I tried to hand him his chocolate, but he turned, took the chair down and climbed on to it.

'Mr Rafferty! Sit down!'

He was reaching for a shoebox on top of the wardrobe. Grasping it, he moved to step down from the chair; his foot wandered above the shining floor, feeling for the tiles, and I rose and helped him down. We sat together on the bed. Still ignoring his cup of chocolate, he put the box between us. Apparently it had once contained ladies' shoes. A picture of the model was pasted to its side: 'Nana'. It was a t-bar type shoe. This notion of giving shoe-styles ladies' names, like hurricanes! Mr Rafferty lifted the lid. Inside were piles of letters. He flicked through them until he found it: a postcard. He handed it to me. I looked briefly at the picture, then gasped in recognition. I turned it round and read the back: 'Dear Grandfather . . .'

15

The Snow Queen

It's a dog-eared black-and-white postcard, foxed heavily, especially around the sky. On the reverse is its title, 'First Snow in Port Suez', and the date of the snowfall, 12 January 1942. Below this is the message I wrote to Mr Rafferty:

Dear Grandfather, Today it has been decided by Her Majesty's Government that my country shall no longer be mine. I must come to Scotland, where I will see you. I am looking forward to meeting you and to hearing many new noises. Father says you are touched. Also, of hearing what the radio sounds like where you are. Your fond granddaughter, Evie.

I do not recall writing this message. I do recall the postcard, however, for there was a period when I would stare at it for hours. It interested me not so much because it connected me to Babatundi; nor because it found a natural place in my tin marked 'unica', whose contents I was always anxious to bolster. Its chief attraction was that it pictured a winter scene: a wide sky blurry with snow, under which flowed a street where people walked, past ice-spangled windows. It was 1956. I had lived only in Nigeria, where the seasons alternated between intense heat and torrential rain, a cycle broken only once a year, in November, by the harmattan. (Nearly five decades since leaving Nigeria I am still unused to northern winters.) So it was that, as a child, I associated snow with a kind of enchantment: with my father's stories of skating on frozen rivers; with ice-cream, that trace of winter, as dew is to spring, which I had tasted only once; and with Father Christmas circling over white-roofed cities. One of my greatest wishes at this time was to experience real snow. Since this was not yet possible, I concentrated my desire on the postcard.

It is a bright, shadowless street in Egypt. Children stand on the boulevard in the foreground, their faces turned up to the sky, arms outstretched to catch the swarming flakes. They are wearing hats. Hatted also, and in greatcoats, a dozen soldiers march off to the left, past the windows of the Grand Hotel Continental. Looking carefully, I can make out street signs in Arabic and English, half-hidden by the drifts. What interests me most of all, then as now, is a slight figure almost lost at the edge of the photograph, in pale bonnet and skirt, bent forward at the hips, thrusting out in front of her with a cane.

Although fixed forever in the photograph on that miraculous day in January 1942, I can see clearly – in her hunched shoulders and downward gaze, in the little spurt of snow pushed up by her dogged cane – that she longs to leave it. It is a sentiment I can now understand. Yet as a child this astonished me. I felt almost offended on behalf of the snow, to which I attributed a kind of sentience unique among the elements. It was my notion that clouds were not formed of dead matter, but were independent presences in the sky, one step higher in the chain of being from certain growths – sea-coral or bushes – with their ability to rise and drop at will. As for the storm, it was simply the clouds bidding to climb higher in the sky, so shedding their bulk in the form of snow, like a balloonist dropping ballast from her machine. I would imagine myself in 'First Snow in Port Suez', among the children, my face turned to the sky, my mouth open wide to gulp down the flakes of frozen cloud.

Previously I'd seen no value in photographs; their stillness, and their silencing effect on the past – separating sound from vision at the moment of the shutter's click – bred in me mistrust. Yet there must have been instances in my childhood when I'd overcome my scruples, because once or twice I had taken down the family album. I recall an image of my mother in her watch shop, one of Father on the swing, several of my parents' wedding, and one of a bagpiper with enormous cheeks. For several hours I had stared at the photographs. I was trying to imagine the sounds the camera had failed to capture. And as I tried – I was studying the inflated bagpipes and the player's puffed-out cheeks – I found I was able to hear the piercing drone of that animal-like instrument; and when, later, I examined the clock-faces in Mother's shop, I had heard, and even felt physically, the clamour of three o'clock. It was as if my eyes, in a process of miraculous traduction, were standing in for my powers of hearing. It was not unlike the process Riley's pointer undertook when, sitting on the veranda below the swallow's nest, some six feet above her big drooling jaws, she would savour with her eyes the chicklets' tender flesh.

Of course, 'First Snow in Port Suez' interested me for its content – the snowy scene. This was not its only charm. After all, I could have asked Father to tell me of winter in Scotland, or chosen as my bedtime story 'The Snow Queen', one of my favourites, with its illustrations by Edmund Dulac. No, the winter scene was not the sole or even chief source of my passion for the postcard. My absorption seeded from a union of its content and its form. A curious reversal had taken place: the very qualities that had once troubled me about the photographic method – the stillness, the silence – now drew me to it.

I was nine years old; at the market I had experienced much; I had learned new words, and a new language; I had become enamoured of Iffe; my relationship with Ade had taken a new turn; and only recently I had acquired a proper name. Is it any wonder I sought the stillness of the postcard? At every spare moment I held it before me. Eventually, when I felt the image had been imprinted on my mind, as bright light lingers on the retina long after we have closed our eyes, I would bury my head in my blanket and listen to 'First Snow in Port Suez'. What did I hear? At first very little. Curses from the bent woman. The faint crunching of the soldiers' boots. Of course, somewhere in the Grand Hotel the fire was hissing and crackling, but I was unable to hear it. This attenuation of sounds disturbed me. I felt as if the whole scene, in whose noise I wanted to delight, existed in a flat and insubstantial realm; my only awareness of it was what I could glean directly from my sense of vision. Nevertheless I continued to look – and, over time, I began to sense a quality that was not present in the scenes in our album, a muffled or stifling presence, a kind of quiescence dropping from the sky. I looked harder, and I became aware of something truly surprising: unlike my family photographs, whose noise I could discern, on that street in Port Suez there was a near-absence of sound; and I understood that the delicious silence of the snow, its slow thrilling descent, was the very thing seeding this effect. It seemed to me that the photographer, in an effect he could not have foreseen, had managed not only to capture a rare occurrence of snow in an African city, but to represent the absence or mutedness of sound caused by the snowfall.

During the Christmas period of 1956 I went with Iffe to St Saviour's Church on Ikoyi Island. Ade had been given a minor part in a production of *The Snow Queen*, a mission-school play of ill-timed entrances and stammered lines, with a zealous

pianist and shrieks from children in the audience. Nevertheless, I was greatly stirred, and not only because of my fascination with 'First Snow in Port Suez'.

I had admired drama at the market, and Iffe's place in that
drama. But here, in the church, before a white backdrop which
seemed imperceptibly to float, I was witnessing drama on a
formal stage for the first time, and I could not keep still. I
gasped and laughed out loud; my feet rattled the pew. I received
reproving glances from mothers in the audience, menacing
looks which, had my excitement stemmed from pleasure alone,
would have stopped my squirming. I was experiencing something far greater than pleasure, however. On that meagre platform where everything dull and ordinary appeared to shine I
became acquainted for the first time with theatre's power to
transform. The set was crude, the acting clownish. But I wanted
to believe in the reality of the performance, and my imagination supplied what the staging lacked. I could not deny that
the grubby wisps decorating the set were merely scraps of
cotton wool, and yet to my mind they were the embodiment
of snow, wet, fluffy and cold; and from my vantage beside Iffe
in the second row, the play took place not on a rough platform
made out of packing crates, not under pallid lights in a hot city,
but in a land of striking white vistas and strewn ice, peopled by
noble citizens in horse-drawn sleighs, with snowflakes as big
as hens!

Just as the elements of the set became greater than their
commonplace forms, so the child-actors, some of whom I
knew from the market – thin sun-baked children, dusty like
me, and who, like me, had the most fantastic concept of snow –
acquired a patina of dignity and grace. Inept with their lines,
stiff, bored, with shiny noses, and sweating in winter coats;
those same children (with whom days previously, by discarded

crates by the juju stalls, I had mixed a brew of chickens' feet, feathers, a dried lizard, spit, urine, sea water, sandal straps, stones and dust, bits of broken pottery, and some tobacco stolen from my father's pouch) seemed to me perfectly at home in Lapland.

All except Ade. His face was painted white, his cheeks rouged, and he was pretty, almost feminine in sandals and a long loose patchwork dress – I think he played a robber girl. He was so changed! And yet because I knew him well, and had made a study of his voice, and even his way of running was familiar to me, I could not forget I was watching my friend. Ade or the robber girl? The confusion between the two might have broken the illusion of the theatre. It might have exposed the base nature of those grubby wisps, which I refused to acknowledge. But from my earliest days, like all children per-haps, I had a need or capability to believe in more than a single world. It was not so much that I saw beyond the painted face to the boy I knew as that I found myself willing to believe simul-taneously in Ade and the robber girl, as if I was watching a kind of living emblem of the famous, double-ended caricature by W. E. Hill, which represents both a young and an old woman, the nose of the elder being the cheek of the younger. In one scene, when the robber girl stood still for a moment against a backdrop of white trees and briefly rested his eyes on me, I felt my heart lurch.

Towards the end of the play, as Gerda (absurdly played by Olu, the tallest of our friends, whose incipient moustache showed clearly under the spotlights) approached the Queen's palace, a storm came at us, an effect involving an electric fan and bagfuls of feathers. There was a brief spurt of applause; shrieks from the children in the audience echoed around the hall. I remained silent. I had to take home some of that snow.

It was my chance to step into 'First Snow in Port Suez', to become one of the children in the postcard. Leaping up on to my seat, I grabbed handfuls out of the air and stuffed them into my pockets. They were fluffy, wet and cold! I stood there with full pockets, ready to witness the finale. I was determined to believe in the illusion of winter. But seconds later the strange pretence was broken. A woman in the front row turned and gave me a look of such determined spite that I sat down and remained quiet for the rest of the play, which I could no longer believe in or follow. It was not so much a frown or glower as a kind of passionate demand – but for what? It appeared to take in the whole of the church, moving from the domed ceiling to the stage and on to the audience, and then it focused on me. *Careful*, that look said, *the theatre is a siren that can speak truths without possessing a hero's heart! You might convince yourself it is authentic, but you don't fool me!*

I did not know that the woman whose pale eyes had looked into my own was Mrs Honeyman. Nor could I guess that in the following months she was to have an influence over my life, that she would succeed (where others had failed) in bringing me into her realm, under the power of her ideas. Nevertheless, I sensed the challenge in that look. It was, I think now, both a recognition of a kindred spirit and an attempt to dominate that spirit in me. It saw my childish need to believe in the illusion of the theatre and wanted to expose, then crush, it. Later, when I knew her better, I recognized that look as forceful but not strong, like a powerful handshake that conceals the weak individual beyond the grip, and I found that she was jealous of many things, and that she acted strangely when she thought it would please me. Why, then, did I let myself be taken in by her, if even for a brief period? Now that I am here, recalling my history, I am seized by a suspicion: did I want her to rule me because I was tired of having no mother in my life?

After the play she approached our pew. She lit a cigarette and said to Iffe, 'I am glad you were able to come. Your boy made a wonderful little girl.' Iffe didn't reply but in her unhurried way only nodded her head. Then, addressing me, she said, 'Wait here,' and left to fetch Ade. I turned to examine Mrs Honeyman. She wore a raw silk dress and curious hat made out of black feathers. Part of her awkwardness came with her height; she held her long body very straight and seemed acutely aware of it, almost embarrassed by it. She watched until Iffe disappeared, then took off her hat, and her hair, like some wilting creeper, fell limply down the back of her neck. She said, 'Hello, Evie.' (How did she know my name?) 'I am Stephanie Honeyman.' Smiling, she said, 'I hope you liked the play, it was quite a triumph, don't you think?' She drew hungrily on her cigarette.

'I liked it very much,' I said truthfully. And since she did not immediately speak, I added, 'Especially the snow storm,' and looked at her with wide eyes.

'You liked my little trick with the feathers,' she said, through a mesh of blue smoke.

She sat down beside me on the pew and held her head very still. I said, 'I even got hold of some of the flakes and put them in my pocket. I wanted to take them home. But they've melted. And now my pockets are soaking wet.'

Mrs Honeyman opened her mouth. A kind of high, stifled laughter emerged from it. After several moments she composed herself and said, 'What a funny little girl!' and laughed again, which said to me, *If anyone heard you calling those feathers an instance of snow, what could she think but that you are out of your mind?*

She lit a cigarette. I felt she was daring me to speak. I said, 'Do you know, in 1942 it snowed in Port Suez?'

'I don't doubt you believe it,' she answered immediately. 'I dislike liars. I am drawn to storytellers, however. That is why I have taken an interest in you.'

Over the following weeks I got to know Mrs Honeyman. Ade, Ben and Iffe left to visit relatives for the Christmas period, and there was no one to cook for us. So at evening time the Honeymans came to our house; they brought supper, and the four of us ate on the veranda. The men talked, mostly about work, of their plans to clear the city's slums and the skyscrapers they wished to raise, after which they retired to Father's office. I was left alone with Mrs Honeyman. She would take out a cigarette from her silver case and with an excited gesture illuminate the tip. She sucked powerfully then exhaled with a look of keen pleasure, as if it tickled or amused her to smoke. Exhaling blue-grey clouds from her nose, she began to talk; as her cigarette spiced the air, her voice punctuated it.

I learned that she led an idle life, of no interest to anyone, and had cultivated a hatred of all action but the raising of the hand, with a cigarette in it, to the lips. Nevertheless I saw she attributed to the least of her sensations an extraordinary importance and was unable to keep them to herself. This might have led to tedious evenings on the veranda. Yet it was quite something what she made of her moods, from which she was apt to branch out to wider concerns (although she always returned to her ill-health or disequilibrium).

'Do you know,' she told me, 'last night I had the sensation I was floating above my bed. I must have been dreaming, although I was convinced I was awake. I think it had something to do with my body's quarrel with the fact of gravity.' And, later: 'It was very curious this morning when the cook came to bring me my replenishments. I could not help feeling that she was trying to poison me, as servants everywhere are wont to do. My great tiredness is no doubt linked to her cooking.' Another evening: 'Evie, do you hear the little catch in my throat when I pronounce the vowel *a*?' This she attributed to an apple pip that had got stuck in her throat, and she believed that by talking she would increase the blood flow to her neck, which in turn would increase the possibility of the pip being loosed, which, finally, would reduce the frequency of the fits of breathlessness and coughing from which she suffered.

Mrs Honeyman hinted that in her twenties she had been an actress, but since arriving in Nigeria five years earlier, in her mid-thirties, had spent nearly all of her days in bed, dozing and smoking. She hated the festive season because the mission-school play, which her husband and the priest pestered her to direct, forced her into activity. To 'over-extend' herself in this way was bad for her health. She even claimed that directing those hordes of 'niggers' (I noticed Mrs Honeyman took pride in using terms like 'nigger', 'savage', 'crowface' and 'cannibal') threatened her sanity. So much so that she maintained one could perceive in the Christmas play the mark of an unbalanced mind. (And, in fact, hearing this, I recalled something that hadn't struck me during the performance but which I now found odd: each of the boys had played female parts; and Dayo, the only girl, had been cast as Kai.)

'But perhaps you don't believe me,' she said (this on New Year's Eve, after Father and Mr Honeyman had left us at the table). 'Perhaps you think I am making the whole thing up. I knew it! You don't believe I am in any way responsible for the Christmas play!' I assured her that I believed her. 'That makes me very happy,' she said, breathing out a menthol cloud and bending double to cough. 'You see, I took great pains over its composition. It might seem to you that it was a small trifle of a thing. Getting those bandits to act was a labour in itself, because nigger children are forever joking around and telling lies. They don't know the difference between acting and real life! But, Evie, do you know that wasn't the hardest part. Not by any means. The adaptation of the Andersen tale cost me a great deal, to be honest with you.' She sighed and ran her fingers through her long, blonde, lifeless hair as if to emphasize the point. Then she made a claim that seemed to contradict what she had said only a moment before: 'Of course, it is all empty palaver,' and went on to disparage her efforts, saying the topic was too boring for a 'young *lady*' to have to endure. Nevertheless the following evening we picked the topic up again, analysed the speeches for false notes, talked about how she might have made the costumes more lifelike. I told her once again how much I had liked the simulated snowfall. 'Well now,' she said, 'I can't say what kind of peculiar serendipity led me to create that effect. Inspiration is a mysterious business, Evie, it can't be forced.'

For me these conversations were novel experiences and exciting. Not only was I lacking a mother figure in my life, the memory of *The Snow Queen* lived in me powerfully. I had been struck by the theatre's transformative powers, which had seemed to speak of my desire or will to shape my own personality. And yet it was Mrs Honeyman who had spoken – she whose pale eyes gave the colour of insincerity to everything she said!

Slender, angular, shrewd, washed out, gesticulating with her eyes which flashed and faded according to the quality of her mood, Mrs Honeyman attended to me, tried to please me even. She had the idea we were intimates, but the nature of the connection was unclear. Did she consider our relationship to be that of teacher to pupil, or nurse to troubled child, or guru to unbeliever, or seducer to victim, or even, as I briefly hoped, mother to daughter?

She had no children, and on hearing her talk about Mr Honeyman I could not believe she would ever conceive one. She called him, variously, 'sow', 'canned rhinoceros', 'blubber-lips', 'that spent parvenu'. 'You know,' she said once, towards the end of the Christmas holiday, 'the funny thing is that everyone considers my husband outstandingly clever. But, really, if you set it next to my own, his brain is like a raisin compared to the grape. I knew it when I married him. That is why I agreed to his proposal.' I laughed, and she turned violently round and said, 'I allow my husband great liberties. All I ask in return is that he stop spitting on the floor!'

That she should be so insulting to her husband, while being so well disposed towards males in general – almost girlish with laughter when I told her about my friendship with Ade – intrigued me; and this aspect of her character enabled me to forgive her sometimes heartless words.

'Wait until you find yourself in the arms of your man,' she said on one of our last evenings together. 'Evie . . . think of it. It will be twilight, the street-lamps will be flickering on the river, and he will stop joking – they do, you know, and that is because their blood-pressure alters – and he will take you like this – wait, there is no one to see us! – and press you like this, with his hands like so.' Clutching me, she said, 'I sometimes think that to be held tightly and kissed is the whole secret of life.' But a moment later she grew solemn. 'With your great ears and ill-proportioned face you will never attract Ade, or any man for that matter. That is probably a good thing, Evie, for children come out of women through tunnels of pain.'

'It can't be like that *really*,' I said.

'What do you know!' she said, stepping back. 'You are young. You should take advantage of your youth to learn one thing . . . refrain from expressing sentiments that are too natural not to be taken for granted. Oh, only a fool loves being alive!'

The following evening, the last before Iffe, Ben and Ade returned, Mrs Honeyman seemed distracted. She didn't eat. After supper she smoked in silence, then paced the veranda for a while. Standing behind my chair, with one hand resting gently on my shoulder, she whispered, 'I believe you have met my cook.' I straightened my back. Fear flashed through me. How could I have failed to link the Honeymans' cook, with her wizened face and keen bargaining and strange stories, with Mrs Honeyman? Before I could answer, Mrs Honeyman said, 'She is a remarkable creature in many ways. Very talkative and interesting . . . vindictive too. She leads what I call a quixotic life. Let me tell you something. The savage mind thinks very differently from mine and yours. It is not goaded by truth.' She came round to face me. 'My cook, for instance, will simply lie or tell stories if she thinks it will be of advantage to her.' Mrs Honeyman stroked the arm of my chair, and her voice became grave. 'To be honest with you, at this stage of your development you are not entirely unlike her. That is why I was not surprised when you insisted on calling those feathers an instance of snow. This has something to do with the fact of your being an exceptional late birth. I have seen it in your face, Evie, you are teetering on the precipice of barbarism.' She sat heavily in her chair. In her normal voice (soft, crumbling like ash from her cigarettes), she said, 'But where was I? Let me see. Ah, yes. Like all of her race, my cook does not know the difference between a lie and the truth. I will see that you learn that difference, because life punishes liars ruthlessly and indiscriminately. That is why the natives are so wretched.'

'What kind of lies does she tell?'

'She often pretends not to hear me when I call. Sometimes I find her in the backyard mixing herbs and powders. Once I witnessed her sacrificing a chicken. She really is a very original old creature. I sometimes wonder if she's not involved in juju. Anyway, she tells me everything.' She paused and looked into the distance. 'For instance, she has told me that your friendship with Ade is unnaturally close.' A look of quiet triumph illuminated her eyes. I felt heat rise to my face. (It was true: before Ade left for Christmas our relationship had taken a new turn, which I will talk about shortly.) 'Don't worry,' Mrs Honeyman said, 'we will put a stop to it.' Her eyes, grey once again, looked sternly into my own. 'Tomorrow Ade will return to Ikoyi. From now on I want you to treat him very differently. It is for his own good. Treat him as you would a stupid child, ceremoniously and with a slightly vexed indifference.' She rose from her chair. 'Take my advice, and I guarantee that very soon you will find him ugly.'

16

How I Developed My Powers of Listening

It was January 1957. The sun came early; there was a flash, and suddenly it was bright morning. Spilling on to our garden, the streets, roofs, windows and the lagoon's calm surface was the teeming yellow light. Everything flashed and burned. But a fetid odour like rotting leaves rose from the ground on which Ade and I were squatting, in the cool half-dark of an upturned fishing boat, playing our new game. We had known about the wreck for months, and before Christmas had visited it regularly: throwing stones at the clanging hull, climbing on to its bulbous tip, where gulls sat, scattering faeces, squabbling, eyeing the water. Only since Ade had returned from the Christmas break, however, had we found a way inside.

From the start, when we became acquainted from either side of the bars of my cot, I had admired certain qualities in my friend: his soft skin, his never keeping still, the scarred and always dirty knees. Added to this was his performance in *The Snow Queen*: just as, during the play, Ade's personality, voice and movements had marked the character of the robber girl, so the robber girl – with her painted face and squeaky voice and patchwork dress – had marked my friend. In my mind now he gave off a kind of feral elegance, a vibrating female charm, whose effect on me outlasted the performance. When I looked at him I could not fail to associate Ade with the spoiled and unmanageable bandit of the play, who had cried 'nanny goat!' as she tugged at her mother's beard.

This is how the game went: first I would lift my dress above my stomach, holding it to one side, and pull my knickers down until they stretched taut between my knees. Next I would squat and Ade would watch the stream of urine spill from between my legs and bounce off the broken shells and mix with the sea-scum on the ground. I would quickly pull my knickers up. Before the ground had absorbed my puddle, Ade would push his shorts down around his ankles and aim his okro at my pool. As I gazed in admiration, he would send a loud stream into its centre, where a virulent moss had started to grow, frothy like the tide-reach – we credited ourselves with its growth.

Now it was late, and we stood beneath the hull in the intimate dark, and the gulls raised hell above us. I had just pulled up my knickers under my righted dress. Ade lowered his shorts, giving off the sour smell of spoiled milk, and let his okro dangle above the ground. I stood opposite, watching. For several moments he remained still, staring with great concentration at the puddle I had made. As he drew in his stomach, I could see the outline of his ribs. He was straining hard, but nothing emerged. Turning his back, saying, 'Don't look!' he bent double, hands gripping his hips. I moved round to face him and saw his features tense and contort; with a furious internal energy he was trying to goad or force out the pee. 'Don't look!' he shouted. But I couldn't not look, because I had noticed something happening to his okro, something I knew was causing the drought – it was thickening and growing longer. I began to laugh, a high, nervous laughter that scared me and infuriated Ade. He winced, backing away. His okro seemed to be possessed of an independent life and a will contrary to his own, for now it began to rise like a pointing finger towards the hull. As I watched – amazed – Ade turned, pulled up his shorts and stumbled out through the gap.

After that encounter in the upturned boat, the mood between us changed. Ade began to ignore me. I felt shy in his company and stopped eating with him in the kitchen compound; instead I took supper on the veranda with my father. One evening I asked him about Mrs Honeyman.

'She's a writer,' he said, 'and a melancholic, and she keeps canaries.' I asked what a melancholic was, and Father thought for a while, then told me it was a person through whose head dark clouds frequently pass, and for whom the rainy season rages sometimes. He paused, then said, 'It's better to stay clear of Susan Honeyman, Evie, I won't invite her round again. One shouldn't believe a word she says.'

My father was right: Mrs Honeyman had told me I would find Ade ugly, but in the rusted chasm of the inverted hull, with its sour odours and spines of shifting light, he was more appealing to me than ever. But that did not stop our relationship from breaking apart. Now, at the market, I played alone; after which I went straight to my room and read or listened to the radio. And when, at the end of July, Ade started at the mission school, what was left of our friendship developed an antagonistic edge. Sometimes Ade mocked me openly. I felt we were on opposing sides – but of what? The more I felt scorned, the more anxious I was to be near him, and I started to watch him in secret. I noticed how bony he had become, and stronger-willed, deeper-voiced. He began to wear men's shoes with the laces taken out. Proud and unhurried, when he turned from his friends after grappling in play, I noticed he had acquired Iffe's grace in movement. In the evenings he padded to the bottom of the garden and skimmed stones on the surf. Sometimes I tried to follow, but he waved me away with the back of his hand.

It seemed inevitable to me that I should assume the responsibility of maintaining our relationship alone, in secret. In doing so I was aware of claiming more than my share of the shame our encounter had engendered. Perhaps it was recompense for my having witnessed his beating. Mrs Honeyman's belief that 'children come out of women through tunnels of pain' connected in my mind with my need to watch Ade, as well as my growing feeling that, to be an adult, a woman (though I was only ten), was to bear pain alone.

One evening after supper I watched Ade make his way across the lawn towards the lagoon. He was carrying some kind of package wrapped in newspaper. I followed him. He did not stop at the shore as usual, but turned and climbed over the fence, out of our garden. I waited until he had disappeared, then I too climbed the fence, entered the bush and fought my way through. On the other side, I stopped and parted the branches. Ade was walking across a thin stretch of wetland, towards an old wooden jetty, calling, 'Sagoe, Sagoe, I have it!'

Sagoe. Babatundi's elder brother! Like all the market children, Ade had feared him, his fabled cruelty; and together we'd worried he might appear on our visits to Babatundi. Now Ade was striding towards him, package held out almost in defence, it seemed to me, as one might offer meat to a vicious dog. I hid in the undergrowth. It was the first time I had seen Sagoe, who looked more like a feral cat, I thought, the kind that haunted the Apapa docks.

Sagoe was thin and tall and was smoking a cigarette. As he moved to take the package, he thrust his unfinished cigarette at Ade, who put it between his lips and began to smoke. Sagoe opened the package, tipped its contents out into his palm, then spat on it. He offered it to Ade, who did the same. Now Sagoe rolled it in his fingers. Then he took up a stick by his feet, a bamboo rod attached with a length of string, at the end of which gleamed a giant hook. So they were fishing! Sagoe fed the bait on to the hook then began to swing it around his head. He leaned back and launched the hook high over the water. Immediately a company of gulls swept down and began to snap at the bait as it fell through the air and then hit the water. Instead of letting the hook sink, as I expected, Sagoe hauled the line in as soon as it struck the surface. Four times Sagoe launched the hook into the air and hauled it in. On his fifth attempt a gull caught the bait in mid-air. There was a violent screech. Sagoe staggered on the jetty. Suddenly I understood Sagoe's project, and my heart sickened. The bird was flapping desperately, but its beak was caught in the hook. It was unable to make any headway through the air, and so it hovered above the water, fighting, dipping and rising. With a great effort of balance, his legs straining, back bent, Sagoe fought the gull. Ade was jumping up and down, in awe or excitement or, like myself, fear, I do not know. The gull let out a series of terrible cries. Its wings seemed to flap too slowly and it looked as if it would lose momentum and plummet to the water. Unable to bear the screams, I put my fingers in my ears. Sagoe and the gull fought for a very long time. Slowly, however, the bird grew tired; it dropped lower and lower, and Sagoe's arms slackened. I took my fingers from my ears. Sagoe called Ade. The bird, quiet now, fell and settled on the water, where it floated at an unnatural angle, its beak half-submerged. The two boys began to haul in the line. Now the gull was only several yards away from the jetty. Even from where I stood, in the undergrowth, some ten yards away, it looked enormous, bloody at its beak. As they dragged it out of the water, it began to shriek again. Ade took hold of the rod, and Sagoe picked up a stick and began to swing at the gull. He had trouble making contact, the bird was flapping and thrashing at the ground, but every so often he managed. Soon the bird became still, quiet, and Sagoe rained down on it a series of blows. At one point the head twisted and came free. That is when I cried out, and the boys turned and saw me.

Later, after Ade and Sagoe had gone, leaving me on the jetty, I lay on the boards until dusk. I could have washed the blood off in the lagoon. But I had not wanted to be near the gulls, who had not stopped swooping, hysterical; sensing, I knew, the unnatural death of one of their number. On hearing my cry, Sagoe had dragged me from the bushes and instructed Ade to hold me down on the jetty. He had picked up the gull's head and walked to where I lay, sobbing and twisting, and brushed its bloody neck across my face. 'Girls are bloody,' Sagoe had said, laughing.

After that I stopped spying on Ade. I withdrew into myself. Every morning on arriving at Jankara market with Iffe I crept beneath the onion table and sat there throughout the day, seized by a kind of enervating emptiness or hunger. The rainy season began. Every morning crowds of umbrellas sprung up like outlandish mushroom-growths. Now fewer customers came to the vegetable quarter; nevertheless, Iffe had no time for me, she was too much occupied with her plans to fight the slum clearances. Each day meetings were held. Lawyers came with scribes, and there was hardly a moment when she was not making a speech or dictating a letter or signing forms. I rarely saw her barter or even sell her wares – it seemed she was supported by donations from the other traders. I noticed a new meekness about her customers: few suggested the pile might grow a little; no longer did they attempt to embarrass her into giving a superior gift. She had become an O-lo'ri Egbe and represented the interests of the onion sellers. Sometimes I helped to pile onions on the table-top, and my arms ached. Or else I watched the sun drink up shadows on the street. Mostly, however, I sat beneath the onion stand, sucking on a stone, letting the world around me fade.

Several weeks went by in this way. I sat, bored, hardly moving, listening to the noise of the rain. But then something happened which marked the beginning of an important period of my life. This period did not last long (a couple of months at the most), and no one else knew about it (it occurred exclusively inside my head). What happened? I began not only to hear, but to *listen*, to take in the sounds, form distinctions and organize them into groups. For a time I forgot my loneliness. I forgot Ade and Iffe and my absent father. It was thrilling to discover I could shape raw noise into an intelligible order. In that period I was a kind of child-Linnaeus, charting not vegetative and animal matter, but the obscure life of the acoustic world. How boisterous and confusing Lagos had been until then! And myself, how ignorant! How innocent and forgetful!

It started with the sound of rain. One afternoon, pressing my ear against the underside of the onion table, I drew back sharply, for the vibrations thundered in my head; how violently the rain drummed on that hard surface! After that I began to listen *into* or *within* its grain, and soon I started to pick out its individual elements. I noted, for instance, the hissing as it fell through the elephant grass, and the slap and thud as it beat off roads, sounding like a team of barefoot runners sprinting over wet sand; also the high percussive noise as drops bounced off pots and pans; and when it passed through plants and foliage, the noise was more like a continuous sigh; which I set apart from the drops filtering through trees; or the brighter pop and loose tripping of the water falling and flowing in the gutter; or the violent clatter on corrugated iron, which sounded like prisoners banging tin cups against the bars of their cells. Sitting beneath the onion table, I found I was able to isolate the individual tones, set them apart and, as it were, spread them before me.

That is when I understood that raindrops themselves are silent, and in falling carry only the possibility of sound, just as the hammers of a piano, waiting silently above the strings until the pianist begins to play, hold in their matter a kind of latent music . . . except that the piano has a limited number of strings; but the rain – there was nothing on which it did not choose to drum! Each body on to which the droplets fell gave off its individual hum or resonance. I wondered what the rain might sound like if I was under the sea, or in a canyon, or on a cricket field, or else flying in an aeroplane. My favourite sound was also the hardest to make out: it was the hollow plash as the rain fell into puddles and the shallows and deeper waters of the lagoon.

And it was this same sense of delight in charting the hidden sounds of Lagos that coursed through me even after the wet season ended. The afternoon the rain stopped I recall the earth's sighs, accompanied by sheer blue light. Colour returned to Lagos, and Jankara market became bright with sound. As for myself, I remained quiet. Apart from the odd insect, I was rarely disturbed. At lunch Iffe continued to bring me soup, and every now and then she glanced down to make sure I was still there. Fortunately, I did not want company. I was happy to be alone, for I had discovered the most resonant spot, slightly to the right of the table's centre, squeezed between a pair of onion baskets. There I sat, cross-legged with my hands on my knees, my head cocked to the right, growing ever more solitary and reserved. Above me birds chattered. I made no noise. The sun shone fiercely. I closed my eyes to the sun. Nothing mattered to me so much as listening. The sounds arrived in torrents.

I developed a ritual to prepare myself to receive the city's sounds: on arriving at the market I would stand in the street, stretch my arms out and begin to spin, faster and faster, until the noise of Lagos rose up in a kind of liquid swell; then I would tumble beneath the onion stand and close my eyes; with the city still lurching, I would take deep breaths until my head began to clear; and, as the sounds composed themselves, I would begin to pick out each individual tone and timbre.

I heard corridors of cloth flapping in the textile section, the snap-snap of barbers' scissors, the awful sucking sound of the snail woman scooping snails from their shells, as well as the rattle of lizards circling their cages, also the furious buzzing of flies at the meat section, and the breathing – slow, heavy, guttural and irregular – of the homeless men on Broad Street. I listened to the footsteps of the delivery men: the tomato man had a heavy walk; the orange man walked with a limp and drew a wonky cart; as for the onion man, who was not a man but in fact a boy, he had a light tread, as of water trickling down steps, and he whistled Highlife tunes. Without moving, I liked to follow him on his rounds, up and down the onion line, and later, after his work was done, I would follow him to the north quarter of the market, where he visited the barber or scrounged palm wine and played cards.

Soon I had so thoroughly listened to Jankara market that, without stirring from my resonant cave, I could 'roam' the district, explore its every shack and alley, simply by picking out and following particular sources of sound. I began to expand my territory, first eastwards to Ikoyi, where I noted the wind fluting along the electricity wires, and the creaking of the weather vane on St Saviour's Church, and the whirr of bicycle wheels, and bells, and radios playing different kinds of music. Next I listened to the Brazilian quarter, with its narrow lanes of booming traffic, its thousand boisterous horns, and also the squeaking of a wheelbarrow. I heard hammering and sawing – much building work was taking place. I was drawn to one structure in particular, St Paul's Breadfruit Church on Broad Street; there every sound reflected off the cavernous walls, doubling, splitting, colliding, crashing. I was learning to make out the distinctive echoes of certain spaces. Next I travelled west, past Tinubu Square with its hissing waterfall, past the shore of the lagoon, where I noted the sounds of that day's catch, flapping and dying. After that, I travelled all over Lagos, listening to each district, each corner, each backyard and blind alley.

Meanwhile, the life of the market continued, unaware of the miracles happening between my ears. I was no longer a novelty for the traders, but merely strange, an oyinbo child sitting with closed eyes, saying nothing, needing nothing. Sometimes they brought their faces close to mine. I remember a large sweaty face with shining eyes asking, 'Wassamatter?' It was a tomato seller. She had became suspicious and suggested I was eavesdropping in order to tell my father about their plans to 'sit on a man'. (But she was mistaken; in this period I rarely listened for meaning; only raw sounds interested me, and if I heard the traders discussing their plan to *sit on a man* I was only dimly aware of the meaning of their words.) Mostly, however, the traders considered me harmless, a bored, solemn, remote little girl.

Had they observed me carefully, however, they might have seen signs of the complicated workings taking place inside my head. My ears, for instance . . . were they not a little too large in proportion to the rest of my features? And did I not feel them quiver, ever so slightly, as I struggled to hear the widest spectrum of sounds? I cannot be sure. What is certain is this: that while events took their course above the onion table; while

Nigerian statesmen called for self-government with increasing stridency; and my father continued to bury himself in his work at the Executive Board; while Iffe and the market leadership travelled to Government House to protest the slum clearances – while all this was going on in the world beyond the onion table, beneath it marvels were taking place.

Was it here, where I sat, that there existed a special property of sound? Had I chanced upon the city's acoustical hub, towards which all sounds were inexorably drawn, as in some cathedrals there exists a nook, designed by the architect, where one can hear the tiniest whisper? Or was I myself that hub? Perhaps, I thought, I was like the radio, which could gather sound waves from all over the world. Yes, from all over the city the sounds rushed to me, as if I, who until now had left their paths unchanged, had started to emit some principle of infinite attraction.

And yet, I thought, I was not exactly like the radio; I seemed to attract sounds, but I did not broadcast them, something I had no desire to do. What happened to a radio when it was turned off? I asked myself. I thought about this for a long time. What does a radio do with all the sounds when it is asleep? Perhaps it trembles internally, I thought. Perhaps its insides stir with the trapped energy of untransmitted sound. Yes, I thought, the radio must exist in a kind of tormented state when it is switched off, hounded by an internal din, like the drunks who wander the streets, arguing with invisible enemies.

It was at that point that I began to question my powers of listening. I began to feel that the richness of my audile faculties was a danger to me. Where did all these sounds go? I felt my insides quivering. The glittering noises of Lagos which came surging towards me, arriving at first in what had seemed like a necessary sequence, began to confuse me. Soon I was unable to decipher or name the individual tones. In time I even found I couldn't think properly. I mean I was unable to entertain ideas or sustain notions of a general sort. For instance, it became difficult for me to comprehend the word 'footstep'. I could not understand how one word was able to embrace so many unique treads, and it pained me that a footstep heard at midday on the market's gravel path should have the same name as the footstep heard at one o'clock on the asphalt pavement over Maloney Bridge. My own footsteps, my own voice, surprised me. I wanted to capture all these sounds, but I was condemned to listen to fragments.

In an attempt to contain the din in my head, I composed a catalogue of sounds. Now, all these years later, trying to recover this catalogue, I am plagued by doubts. I fear that, by committing it to writing, I will deaden what existed entirely in my head: the constantly shifting association of sounds. Displayed on my computer, my order will seem no order at all but an ugly, arbitrary act of preservation. What is more, it strikes me that the very act of preservation – the translation of sounds in my head to words on the page – signals the destruction of the very sounds I wish to save, just as for Linnaeus the only true subjects for contemplation were the specimens he collected and put to death, stifling life even as he tried to preserve it.

Nevertheless, I will transcribe my Universal Catalogue of Sounds (Lagos):

a) Sounds that come from me
b) Sounds that seem to rise from underground
c) Sounds that mimic other sounds
d) Sounds that I have never heard but which I will, one day

e) The sound that surrounds two people who'd like to speak but cannot

f) Sounds that only others can hear

g) Unearthly sounds

h) Sea-sounds

i) Sounds that cause my heart to beat faster

j) Sounds that have just caused a traffic accident

k) Sounds that seem commonplace but which become impressive when imitated by the human voice

l) Sounds that arouse a fond memory of the past

m) Wet-season sounds

n) Silence

o) Sounds that lose something each time they are repeated

p) Sounds that can be heard only in the month of January

q) Sounds that indicate the passage of time

r) Sounds that fall from the sky

s) Sounds that gain by being repeated

t) Insignificant sounds that become important on particular occasions

u) Outstandingly splendid sounds

v) Sounds that should only be heard by firelight

w) Sounds which I deliberately make, but which are not words

x) Sounds that come from inside me, involuntarily

y) Sounds with frightening names

z) Sounds that cannot be compared

17

How I Abandoned Ade

One evening after supper, when Father and I were listening to the news, there came a clattering from the garden path. Suddenly Riley's pointer was up beside us. Unable to decide who to greet first, she ran around the table, leaping and twisting like a salmon, until her tail caught the lead of the radio and sent it crashing to the floor. Father roared and struck out at her. But he missed and fell off his chair. Unable to understand his rage, Riley's pointer turned then loped back into the garden, leaving us in silence, looking at the battered radio.

The radio never worked properly again. Father took it apart, then screwed it back together, but it was no use. It would emit a broken whisper and we heard only fragments of the news. On fiddling with the tuning knob, it would stammer into life. No matter what the announcer spoke about – the Suez crisis, or the slaughter of the Mau Mau, or the latest dance craze in America – he spoke in the same deep, authoritative, almost indifferent voice, making it impossible to distinguish between the already scrambled news items. This did not bother me at all. What did I care for the news? I was more interested in the moments when the radio fell to static silence. Each time I felt the mood of the evening change. The temperature seemed to drop several degrees, and I would tremble with excitement. Mistaking my emotion for fear, Father would joke, saying, 'The radio must be tired tonight. Poor thing, it has fallen asleep.' I could not forget that noise which was also silence. I felt drawn to it. It spoke to me of another world.

One night I sneaked out on to the veranda to fetch the radio and bring it to my room. I sat it on my pillow and switched it on. There it was, the silence! I put my ear to the speaker – and withdrew, for it seemed to emit a kind of cold breath coming from a distant world. I held myself still, listening to that pool of shifting quiet, feeling it float about me, inside me. It was the most beautiful thing I had ever experienced.

Soon I could think of nothing else. A delicious pleasure had invaded me, isolated me, without my having any clear notion as to its source. It made everyday concerns seem trivial, and filled me with a kind of precious essence – acting in the same way as, years later, on meeting Damaris, I understood love to act. Where could it have come from, this powerful joy? It was connected to the radio silence, I knew, but went far beyond it. What did it mean? How could I grasp it?

Once after supper I followed Ade down to the bottom of the garden. I found him looking at a boxing magazine. That evening he didn't tell me to go away, so I sat down by the lake-shore, and we looked at photographs of the boxers. Ade told me about Hogan Bassey from Calabar, who was famous throughout Africa; he had become featherweight champion of the British Empire. At school they talked of nothing else, and there were bouts in the playground. The best boxer, Olu (he whose incipient moustache had showed under the spotlights during *The Snow Queen*), had bloodied another's nose.

'Well, but that's nothing,' Ade said. 'One day I will be as good as Hogan Bassey hisself. Remember that no person can escape his right hook. If he gets hit, O, he hits back twice as hard!' Ade stood up and started to swing his fists; jabbing, swiping, punching from all angles. When, finally, he stopped, he was breathing heavily, and there was a keen focus to his normally agitated eyes. Slowly and deliberately, he said, 'Hogan Bassey has beaten every *white* fighter put against him.' I recall the moment clearly, how he flashed his eyes then looked away, how he emphasized that word – white. I was stung. It was not the first time we had noted the colour difference. And yet until recently that difference had been a source of mutual interest. I thought: I hardly know Ade any more. He has a separate school-life, and separate friends, boxing one another, thinking of Hogan Bassey, and these friends knowing little or nothing of me, but hostile to me all the same.

'I have something to tell you,' I said.

'OK, but remember I'm going to be a champion boxer like Hogan Bassey.'

'OK,' I said. And I began to talk all about the instances of silence in my life; I wanted to communicate something important. I told him about the season in 1946 when the skies became quiet, and I was conceived; about my first weeks in the womb, when I had no ears to speak of, and the silence was in me; about Mother's funeral, her silence, which I could not grasp. I continued to speak, telling him about the period when I had lain in my cot, wide-eyed and unmoving. Without pause, halting Ade when he asked questions, I spoke of the cool quiet when he used to open the window and close the shutters of my room; of the silence dropping from the sky in 'First Snow in Port Suez'; about my admiration when he had survived his beating without uttering a cry.

Ade watched me with agitated eyes. Was he sceptical about my words? I could not be sure. The more he stayed quiet the more I wanted to talk. And it was with a sense of relief, almost, of wild hope or foolishness, that I told Ade next about my powers of listening, about how I could hear the tiniest sounds, unbelievable things, things no one else could hear. I asked him to go to the end of the garden and whisper something. When he came back I repeated exactly what I thought he had said. Inexplicably, I got it wrong. We tried again, and I got it wrong again. I asked Ade what he had whispered but he refused to say; he only repeated that I had got it wrong, and sat on the bank. He tilted his head to one side. There was scorn in his eyes, and I was stung once again. He brought a mouse's tail from his trouser pocket. It was then, as he began to twist the tail between his fingers, and the night darkened, and I felt his eyes watching me with a peculiar kind of focus, that I knew for certain that something between us had changed. That change, the challenge I saw in that moment, was affirmed and strengthened over the following weeks.

But I am getting ahead of myself. At the time, although I registered Ade's scorn, I was not prepared to believe it, and I did not allow it to stop me talking; now I had started, I did not want to stop. I said that the time had come for me to tell him something very important, something which no one else knew about and which would put our lives in danger.

'I have managed to make contact with another world.' I did not want our friendship to end. If I made myself extraordinary, perhaps Ade would pay me the attention I knew I deserved. He was unimpressed.

'It is an almost completely silent world,' I continued.

'What do you mean?'

'I mean somewhere not far from here is a place where people live in almost complete silence. My connection is very thin,' I said, looking at him directly, 'and it is only sometimes I can hear it.' I paused. Ade frowned and stared straight at me. I had the feeling, false I know now, that he believed me. Nevertheless, he was intrigued; his eyes became more active. I was unsure what I was going to say next. I said, 'Luckily for you, since you don't have my powers of listening, I have discovered another way to make contact with this world.' I was improvising. I ran to the house and fetched the radio. I switched it on, and Ade's eyes became wide – in fear or with mocking I do not know. I began to tell Ade all about the silent world; about how you could walk for days without your eyes settling on a single thing; how it was a bright empty land of raven skies alternating with flaming white light. I told him how in this world there were few objects, animals, and even fewer people; how on the few occasions when you did see something, you didn't really notice it, or rather you saw it but you didn't ask yourself what it was, because in this world without sound you just knew. I told him there were no names for things, because a footstep was just a footstep, a branch a branch, a stone a stone, and so on for everything, including people, because each thing was only what it was, and there were no echoes or reflections and nothing cast a shadow, I said.

That summer I spent an hour or two every day searching for the silent world. I would stand in an alley behind the onion line, stretch my arms out and start to spin, faster than I had ever done before, turning and turning until my head felt light. Sometimes the sun went black behind my eyes, and I would fall on the ground. Once or twice after school Ade found me; sometimes he even played along, saying, 'Have you found it yet?'

'Not yet,' I would say, lying there, waiting for the city's sounds to quieten, then compose themselves. I did not always manage to snare that pool of quiet (it was tiny, hardly noticeable, a slight disturbance of the air, and at first seemed to come from no place in particular), but whenever I did, I set off in pursuit. Sometimes, at weekends, when he had nothing better to do, Ade came along. Running south through the market against the flow of the crowd, between the high-backed stalls, coming out between the cloth sellers, entering the back streets of town, stopping for breath, chatting, drinking, setting off again, following no logical path, but moving instinctively, and always we found ourselves drawn south. Like Riley's pointer chasing a scent I was pulled along by something powerful which I could not see, a taut, quivering and irresistible force.

There were moments as we searched when we forgot our divide. Ade could be kind; for instance, when I fell on the ground he took my head in the crook of his arm. But there was also in all we did – not just in our search, but at the market also, and on the bus with Iffe – a touch of dishonesty. We did not acknowledge it; it was simply an omission, a silence we could not name. Many things had come between us – our ages and genders for instance – all of which contributed to this feeling of dishonesty. But what hurt me most, because it had come so suddenly, or I had become suddenly aware of it, was the race divide. Calls for independence were then ever-present in Lagos, and there was talk of 'sending the white man packing'. Until now I had been unaffected by this talk, for I had been living powerfully in the half-real region of sounds, and at the market I was treated no differently from the other children. Prior to that there had been Mrs Honeyman; she had made an absolute distinction between the European and African, had spoken of a gulf – of feeling, of intelligence, of dignity, of truth – separating black and white. For a while I had come under the influence of her ideas and had more than half-believed her.

After Ade's comment about Hogan Bassey, however, the divide was quite suddenly raised again. What is more, it became directly relevant to me. Ade seemed now to have his own way of talking about people and events, slightly alien or antagonistic to my own, and I thought his way seemed more in touch with the world than mine. How shut-away I had been all this time! It hurt me to think of it. What I had thought of as absolute – my right to consider Nigeria as home – others saw almost as an aberration. From Ade's small comments I sensed how he and his friends saw me – as well as Iffe and countless others I did not know. I sensed also how he worked to put me down. Even as we ran in search of the silent world I noticed his mocking eyes, which said to me: Perhaps I'll come along, but don't expect me to believe in your childish game.

Now it was late afternoon, and we were running past the slaughter district. I realized we had not brought any water. Turning back would be a waste of time, especially as it wasn't hot. In fact, I could feel waves of an unseasonally cool breeze. That afternoon the sky lay open, but big rust-coloured clouds came in from the lagoon, blocking the light – the harmattan season. It felt as if the sky was coming down to meet us.

I took Ade by the arm, saying, 'We're getting near. I can feel it.' I said this and yet I wondered how I would know when we arrived. We came to a square built up on three sides. On previous days, in other light, I had been here, when Ben or Father had sent me to buy provisions from Hardy's Euro-African Emporium. Now a row of houses had disappeared, and in their place modern buildings had sprung up, still half-built. At the far side a group of feral dogs was squabbling – the city was strangely full of them at the time. Elsewhere the space was wide and empty. The weather was cold, the air fuzzy, stale, bitter-tasting.

First the dust, then the cold drove us towards one of the new buildings. High above us rose a mass of girders, glass and steel sheeting, which merged into a tangle of vertical and diagonal lines. At the seventh or eighth floor the structure ended, and I saw a row of floating lights. Only then did I realize how dark it had become. Ade pointed to the lights, saying, 'The workmen.' And I noticed that the lights were attached to dark figures moving slowly over scaffolding. 'Let's go inside,' Ade said. We pulled back a wooden fence, entered, passed the foundations and started to climb. I took Ade's hand. He didn't pull away. We clambered over planks, then up staircases connecting partly finished floors. Now we reached the fourth floor. Here we were protected from the force of the wind, but not its noise, which boomed in my ears. How should I describe my feelings? Fear, thrill, uncertainty, tenderness?

After the market, after spinning around and around, after our running through the streets, and the empty square, after my thirst, and the dogs, and the hard climb to the fourth floor – after all this, a mood of exhilaration had come over me. Something inside me was straining towards Ade. I felt myself pulled physically, and walked towards him. He went to sit at the edge of the floor; his legs overhung the square. I sat down beside him, and he didn't move away. It was possible to hear, above or between the roar of the wind, a chiming sound, as of struck hollow pipes. I pointed into the darkness.

'What's over there?'

'The square,' Ade said

'And after that?'

'The sea.'

'And after that?'

'England.'

'And after that?'

'The silent world,' he said, and let out a nasty laugh.

I heard the clanging of the pipes, and the dogs, who had started barking, a restless, dangerous sound. Ade said, 'Over there is where Olu lives.' I got up. I no longer felt empty or light or lost, but enraged. I pressed my lips together and felt a knot of anger in my chest. I started to walk away. It was Ade's turn to follow.

'What's wrong?' he said. Now the dogs were laughing like hyenas. It was at that point that I should have left to go in search of the silent world. Instead, I got up and climbed some stairs. When I reached the final step I sat down and closed my eyes. The next thing I knew Ade was shaking me, saying, 'Quick.' I followed him up to the fifth floor. He had spotted the labourers coming down the stairs; it must have been the end of their working day. Soon we saw their lights, tiny flames encased in what looked like globes of glass, but that was all, we could see no other trace of the men. The lights winked at us from inside their tiny glass globes, and the globes moved also, but moved differently, swaying and jerking as if suspended on invisible strings. We watched until the last light vanished from the square.

I turned to Ade. 'I want to ask you something.'

'What?'

'What did you whisper that night after supper when I sent you to the other end of the garden?'

'Eh?'

'You know, when I was telling you about the silence.'

'I don't know what you are talking about.'

'You must remember,' I said. 'That evening when we were looking at *The Ring* magazine and you told me about Hogan Bassey and boxing at your school and Olu and all the rest.'

'Eh,' Ade said. 'When you told me you could hear *everything*, but you couldn't prove it.'

'Well,' I said, 'what did you whisper?'

'What does it matter?' Ade asked.

'Just tell me,' I said.

'Well. The first time I whispered, *Sammy McCarthy*. The second time, *Joe Lucy*.'

'Who are they?' I asked.

'They are the boxers Hogan Bassey defeated in Liverpool.'

I wanted to say, 'I bet Sagoe would crush you in a boxing match.' But I didn't. The dogs kept quiet too. Ade rose and found a stick, which he began to beat against the scaffolding.

What else do I recall from that evening? The cold, the air standing up against us like something solid, thoughts and feelings passing through me like a desert wind, my eyes running, my dry mouth. Huddling next to Ade under a sack, I thought about the night of his beating, how afterwards I had let myself into his bedroom and taken him in my arms, how I had moved my hand under his pyjama trousers then passed my fingers over the welts. And when I thought of this, I drew myself closer with one hand, and with the other I searched for the cord of his shorts. But the way he withdrew from my touch, not hurriedly but with a stony sort of dip of his head, I knew that this – my – privilege was gone. Once or twice in the night we heard a truck slipping along in the dark, and now and then its lights came sliding across our blind vista. I mention this only because light was the exception, it being pitch-dark and the harmattan.

It was somewhere towards morning when I opened my eyes. The sun was big and orange, its surface stained with black marks that appeared to spread like broken clouds of ink. Was it this that prompted us to try to leave the building? Was it as we climbed down the stairs that Ade fell over the edge? It was so sudden. I didn't even hear his cry. And I did not alter my course but carried on descending towards the square. As I walked via the foundations and peeled back the wooden fence, my thoughts darkened. What had happened to Ade? He had fallen. But where? How far? Later, I discovered that Ade had survived. In that moment, however, as I made my way out of the building, I neither knew nor cared. Hadn't he mocked me almost continually these past weeks? Hadn't he tried to ruin my self-belief? Yes, I thought, he had put himself on the right side of truth and wished me gone. I felt light. It was astonishing, the way I felt light, so suddenly. Out in the open I started to walk in the direction of the wind. Progress was difficult. I hardly thought of Ade, but when I did I thought how good it was that this had happened. I had come near to losing my confidence, and my faith in my powers of listening, also in the silent world. I started to run. It was all the same to me if Ade lay broken and dead, lost in the storm. My mind was black. My thoughts circled like ravens around a kill. I thought no more about going back. As I ran I told myself I would embrace darkness and silence, because that was what was in my nature, which was blacker than Ade's, and wicked, I thought; and love and friendship was not in my line. So I ran through the harmattan towards the silent world.

When the dust lifted next I had a glimpse of the water. Then the air thickened, and it was as if a red curtain had suddenly come down. I stopped to listen. The silent world was getting close. It was no longer a whisper but a swift wind or snow sliding, and my heart opened to its pull and storm-silence. The further I walked, the deeper it became, until, scrambling over rocks, I felt a force drawing in all the sounds, swallowing them towards its centre. I walked on, scared, more than half-willing, not caring, I thought, if I lived or died. I was tired. The thought of Ade was starting to weigh on my stomach. I pushed these thoughts away. Soon I found myself by the water's edge. The sky had lightened to a raw pink. I sensed a crack in the earth. I walked up to it and now I was standing before a chasm extending like a tram track to my left and right as far as I could see.

I stood shaking, doubting. Perhaps, I thought, Ade was lying in the foundations of the unfinished building, with broken bones. I half-turned, ready to retrace my steps to return to my friend. But the wind picked up, and I felt that charged whisper, and I left doubt behind.

I closed my eyes and stepped off the edge.

18

The Pit

I fell through the thick dark. I fell and fell. On hitting the ground I lost consciousness. When I woke my body felt hot and broken. I was in some kind of pit. Light of a kind came from I don't know where, a pale light unlike any I had seen or have seen since. Lying on my back I couldn't see beyond my knees, which gave me a thrill. I tried to lift my arm, but it was too stiff. The other was not so badly hurt and with great effort I managed to raise it in the air. Reaching up, I felt nothing, and I rejoiced. To my right and left were steep walls. They were damp and warm against my sides. Below the ground was more compact, but still warm, and it flaked off at the touch of my nails.

I had fallen into one of the city's open sewers, although I did not know this at the time, because I could see no further than half a yard. My body would barely move, I was in pain, and yet I felt terrifically happy. Strange! My whole being throbbed sweetly. After several hours of blissful rest I understood why. It was completely silent in this pit. I could hardly believe my good fortune. I listened hard, not wanting to hear, but trying desperately to hear, the tiniest sound. But there was none. I laughed and wept, celebrating my arrival in the silent world, until, exhausted, I fell asleep.

When I woke I felt thirsty. Using my one good arm I slid painfully forward, testing the ground for water. I started digging. It was slow work. After some time I scooped out a hollow, into which, very gradually, water seeped. It was not much, but I turned on to my stomach and lapped until the hollow was dry.

I paused. Soon the hollow became moist again, and I lapped, paused, then lapped again. I continued in this way until my thirst was quenched. After that I did nothing. I lay there like a grub in a dungheap, hearing nothing, seeing nothing, with my face pressed into the ground. My mind felt drugged and free from thought. Hours passed in joy and gladness. I did little else but lie in the murky light, turning from my stomach on to my back and vice versa. I was far from my thoughts. But there were moments when I did not seem so far, when for instance I became aware of my body, its stillness in that dark cramped space, its sweet aching. I became aware of my insides too, panting and ticking in spite of it all. And whenever I lapped from my hollow I felt a silver coolness running along my throat. The flavour of that water was the finest I had tasted or have tasted since. Its cloudy translucence, like sea-polished glass, made me feel calm; as I brought it into my mouth I felt as if the darkness around me was melting on my tongue.

Perhaps on lapping from my hollow I took nutrients from the earth, since I did not feel hungry. Maybe I chewed on certain kinds of fungus, gnarled growths surviving in the damp and dark, like those monstrous fish that haunt the lower depths. Or did I no longer need to eat? Perhaps time passed more slowly than I imagined. I had the idea I lay in that pit for several weeks – and yet it strikes me now the whole experience might have lasted no more than several hours. Nevertheless, I felt myself withdrawing into myself. I even had a notion that I was becoming thinner. Certainly, I grew more and more content. Every now and then my mind returned to Ade. I wondered what had happened to him after his fall. I thought he might have landed on something soft and was not hurt. I even fancied he would come to join me in my pit and grow to be my friend again, that we would be companions in silence and wickedness. I let these vain

hopes blossom in my chest, then I swept them away and surveyed the emptiness they had besmirched.

Absolute silence reigned in my pit; silence reigns in my attic
now. I am the only inhabitant of this tent-shaped space; in my
pit I dwelt alone. There are other parallels. A pale gloom
spreads from my computer screen, creating a kind of perpetual
dusk; so too in my pit twilight reigned – what little light there
was seemed to work its way up from the depths, serving not so
much to illuminate my pit as to draw shadows from the contours of its walls. I grew to love that light – less light, it seems
to me now, than a memory of light, a kind of wan reflected
sun, whose lack of clarity, far from disturbing me, perfectly
suited my condition. There are other correspondences. For
instance here in my attic with its deceptive feeling of freedom,
which makes dreamers of attic-dwellers, my thoughts turn
almost exclusively on myself; so too in my pit I mused on my
condition. Of what, concerning myself, did I think? Core
thoughts. Elemental broodings. In short, I wondered what I
had become. I questioned myself for a long time. I wondered
if I was not like some creature surviving from the azoic age.
Eventually I came up with the idea I was a kind of seed. That
was it! The pit in which I lay was the black enclosing husk, and
I was its naked white seed.

There within my husk I lived truly for the first time. I had
discovered an emptiness to rival the emptiness of the womb, a
sweet solitary void free from earthly limits and the rules of
men. My body felt weightless. I felt happier than at any other
time in my life. It had always been this way with me: right at
the beginning, when in the darkness of my mother's womb I
twisted and swam; before this even, before the tick-tock of the
pocket watch and the chimes of Lagos clock, before my father's

stories, before even the first stirrings of sound, when I had no ears to speak of, and the silence was in me – only then was I as happy and empty as I was in my pit. All this I understand now. At the time, however, every thought vanished from my mind, and my heart swelled with strange, nourishing energies. I drifted on an unseen volume of air or jet-black cloud, losing all purchase on myself. I wished nothing more than to lose awareness of the passage of time and lie there always thus entombed.

And perhaps, if things had happened differently, I would have done so. Perhaps I would have remained curled tightly like a partly germinated seed, half-grown but able to grow no more, rotting and disintegrating; perhaps my insides would have begun to fester and turn to mulch; perhaps my skin would have darkened like paper taking flame and I would have flaked or drifted away to settle as a layer of earth. Or maybe I would have taken seed; maybe my hair would have bedded itself into the ground and twisted with the root-work, my limbs atrophying, growing scaly, burrowing in the soil until I became just one more strangled growth surviving in the damp and dark. These dreams of dissolution I contemplate now. To have merged with my pit would have made me very happy. Of course I did not. I did not become earth or vegetable matter but remained myself, more or less; I grew into this woman who sits before her desk, listening to her past, attempting to make sense of its confusing din by typing these stories so that – finally, mercifully – she can become silent.

What prompted me to stir from my happy dissolution? Why was I unable to dwell forever in the midst of silence? Something shattered my peace. Listen!

It happened as I was turning from my stomach on to my back, having just drank from my hollow. Mid-revolution, as my ear passed over the ground, I heard a scratching sound, something like the scurrying of a mouse. I pressed my ear to the earth. The noise grew louder and more complicated; now a family of mice were scrabbling around inside my head. I had the painful feeling that by hearing it I was offending some kind of natural law. I squirmed until, eventually, I turned and flopped on my back.

I lay still and tried to forget what I had heard. I could not bear to think that silence, that perfect friend, had betrayed me. I said to myself, *So long as I remain on my back I will never hear that sound again.* But I was not able to remain lying on my back. And I did hear that sound again, because I became thirsty, and needed to turn back again on to my stomach to drink. As I neared the mid-point of my rotation my ear started to pass over the ground and I heard the scratching once again. Yet this time there was more to come from the earth; for soon I heard hissing and braying, sighs and sounds of lamentation. I even heard a kind of nasty cackle – yes, I thought, from its obscure depths the earth was having a good laugh at my expense. Parched, turning as fast as my benumbed body would allow, with my eyes shut to this disruption worse than thirst, I succumbed to the earth's dismal symphony: a strange, complicated, disharmonious music grinding blackly beneath my head, thundering against my skull, as if, deep underground, a medieval army was on the march. I heard creaking and groaning noises. Then, flaming as in some diabolical foundry, a series of sustained wailing notes. It was then – hearing the machinery of the turning earth, my eyes tight shut, trying desperately to turn on to my stomach and lap – I reached up and tore from the walls two clods of earth and stuffed them in my ears.

Nikolas, Leader of the Nightsoil Workers

The matchbox is almost four decades old. The cardboard has turned soft, and its lower right side is partially dissolved. I have discarded the matches and replaced them with one of my favourite objects, or rather a pair of objects, which I wish to preserve at all cost.

The matchbox is surprisingly intact. The strip of sandpaper remains rough to the touch, and the tray slides freely. On its age-stained label I can make out the legend, 'Paul & Virginie', beneath which is an etching of a man and woman, both very young. The young man is stripped to the waist, his trousers rolled up to his knees. He is standing on a rock in the middle of a swollen river, trying to cross it. On his back he carries the girl, who is clinging to him, arms around his neck, face half-buried in his hair. Over them looms a black mountain, at its foot banana trees whose serrated leaves appear to flap in the wind, the same wind which has whipped the river into a frenzy of white froth, the same wind which has unfurled the girl's hair from the scarf she has used to tie it back. The girl appears anxious, but the boy, smiling up at her, is happy to be carrying his load, which seems to give him the strength to carry on.

Only moments ago I fetched the matchbox from its hiding place: the tin marked 'unica' (which I keep in the wardrobe, behind the stack of papers printed with my history). Now it sits before me on my desk. Carefully, lovingly even, I blow from its surface the accumulated dust, which rises in a fizzing grey cloud. I blink several times, breathe deeply; then, taking the matchbox in my left palm, I slide it open, to reveal . . . a pair of earplugs. Happily I see they are still intact! Happily they remain a pair (being a pair, perhaps, they should not form part of my *unica* collection, but the tin is the best way to keep them safe from the mice and damp). The earplugs are not the common kind. Small – although too wide to fit into the average twelve-year-old ear – grey-black, friable, tapering to a blunt point, they look like a pair of goat's droppings. And yet I count them among my most treasured possessions. They are, of course, the very clods I gouged from the walls of my pit and stuffed in my ears. Not only do they sit mutely in their cotton-wool shroud, but their historical role was to restore silence. Thus they represent for me a goal attained, an example to every other object in the attic, the standard by which I judge them all.

How I would love to dwell longer on my earplugs. To note their weight and dimensions, to examine the material from which they are made. What a rest to speak of these broken objects from my past. And how instructional! But I must press on with these stories.

. . .

As soon as I stuffed my ears, the pits were restored to silence. But I continued to feel a faint trembling of the earth; which grew stronger and stronger, until it began to merge with the trembling of the shadows, which in turn resolved themselves into the form of a man. I looked up into a wide pair of eyes – trickster's eyes, handsome, dark, soporific – which were gazing down into my own. The eyes moved swiftly to and fro; in fact, the man's whole body seemed to be in motion, his hands and torso shook, and his naked skull bristled with night-static. I was too tired to move, and so I did not struggle as the man stooped and, with great care, lifted me in his arms. How had he found me? Had I cried out on hearing the dinning earth? Did he know I had fallen from a great height? He carried me along what I thought was a narrow corridor, then down stairs which must have been cut into the earth. We descended deeper underground, and the heat rose, and a sweet hot odour swelled my nostrils. We moved on, past closed cells and interior court-yards that resounded with his steps. Unspeaking, I clung tightly to his waist. The smell now was like a physical presence; it seemed to push at me with the force of a breeze. We entered a wider space and stopped. Slowly, as my eyes became accus-tomed to the dark, I saw that we had arrived in a large, sparsely furnished room. I made out a bed and two chairs and, rising from the ground, what looked like stalagmites on which candles burned. The man placed me gently on the bed. I slept at once.

Over the following days I lay on the bed in this dimly lit chamber. The smell was outrageous; sweet and fetid, it bloomed like a hothouse flower, and the temperature rose and rose. I did little but lie there, recovering. Sometimes I did not sleep for several nights. Sometimes I was overcome with laugh-ter. At others I forgot who I was. In time I felt restored and began to examine my surroundings. The light was dim, blue-black and spangled with pale yellow. The furniture seemed to rise seamlessly from the floor, as if cast in lava: black, organic table and chairs, a long, low bed without sheets where I lay, a high-backed armchair where the man with the bristling skull sat, watching me.

What follows is the story of my friendship with Nikolas, leader of the nightsoil workers, an eccentric tribe who were employed by night to clear the city's sewage and eject it into the lagoon; before dawn, the workers would descend to the pits, their home, into which I had fallen. The world of the nightsoil workers had evolved out of the city sewers. All this I learned from Nikolas in the first months of my stay.

In the beginning, he told me, Lagos' sewage system was little more than a network of shallow open channels into which the citizens threw their filth. But soon, as the city's population grew, they began to overflow, and the streets became filled with pools of stinking waste. With the streets overflowing, the council built a sanitary tramway. Every evening after dusk men in masks collected the nightsoil and shovelled it into the carriages. The line ran from Ikoyi Island, crossed the Macgregor Canal and tacked across the city centre, before turning south; when it reached Dejection Jetty on Victoria Island, its steaming cargo was loaded on to canoes and dumped in the lagoon.

Because of the tramway, Nikolas told me, the sewer system fell into disuse. That was when the nightsoil workers moved in; they went on to deepen the network, hollowing out a warren-matrix of rooms that spread slowly beneath the streets, an expanse made up of old nightsoil and every other kind of waste: rusty metal, sackcloth, planks, pipes, piles of tins, rags, old umbrellas, bottles, glass and broken metal. A second Lagos evolved, existing entirely underground, hidden from view, unknown to the majority, forgotten by those who walked the streets above it, a city made from all that was not wanted or had fallen into disuse. Nikolas delighted in showing me the ingenious uses to which the nightsoil workers had put the city's waste, pointing out a Guinness bottle used to roll pastry, a discarded stocking through which coffee could be strained, wrought-iron railings used as meat-skewers.

He was always in action, at every moment twitching and gesticulating, and he burned with a furious internal energy he was barely able to contain. As a child, I learned, he had fallen down a mine shaft and consequently his back was bent. In Ibadan, where he went to school, the missionaries had caned him repeatedly on his wrists. Now his hands wouldn't stop shaking. During the War he fought in Burma with the Frontier Force. His army-issue boots had been too small, and he lost the feeling in his toes. Because of this he limped. He held his tall frame loosely at odd angles, and his joints appeared twisted. In fact, thinking back, only once – later, towards the end of my stay in the pits, when I walked into his chamber and watched him sleep – do I recall seeing him completely still, and even then I could not help but be aware of a kind of slow combustion in his chest, an internal fire which recalled the legendary origin he claimed for himself, citing as its source the mythological coupling of a salamander and the Yoruban sky-god Sango.

At first, recovering in his chamber, I'd listened to Nikolas' talk in a sort of torpor. It had taken a considerable effort of will to wake from the enchantment of my twilit husk. Later, however, I found myself attempting to direct the flow of his speech, stopping him when he digressed and pressing him whenever his allusions intrigued me. One day, after he told me that he was not originally from Lagos, and frustrated by his elisions and ellipses, I asked for a fuller account.

'It was on the day I finished school that I came to Lagos,' he began. 'I had heard a man in my village say that its streets were paved in gold. But something must have arrived to spoil my mind, because I believed him . . . even though his advice was useless, less than useless even, because that town was to become the theatre for all my miseries to come. When I reached Lagos I was straight away robbed of all my belongings and forced to sleep inside a ditch. The next day I woke with no idea of what to do with myself. I was walking by an old clothes shop and

I saw a man with a broken head swap his vest for one or two pence. I caught the malady and was instantly relieved of my coat. I received in exchange seven pence. Now I was thinking only one thing to myself, and that was that I must have some food to chop, some drink to drink and a bed in which to sleep. Soup, some hot drink, and a cheap dosshouse was the first assault upon my seven pence. As for!

'Evie, believe me that night was a troublesome night indeed! I think you must remember what I told you about my life and maledictions. Well, many times my bedfellows spoke to me. *Are you asleep? Ehn? Are you asleep?* I was not in the mood to talk, and so I made no reply. To silence them completely I began to snore. *Zzzzz! Zzzzzz!* I began to snore very very loudly, and for some minutes everything that was not myself was very quiet. But soon one of my bedfellows got up and started to unlace my boots! Whoever said that poverty acquaints us with strange bedfellows was not telling a lie! Several times after I fell asleep this same fellow tried to unlace my boots, so I had to stay awake. After guarding my boots carefully throughout most of the night, I fell asleep just as day began to break. When I woke the sun was knocking on my skull. The sun knocks in the morning, Evie, that is a fact which has not been sufficiently observed. When I got up I found that my boots were not on my feet! And my pennies were not in my pocket. And not one of my bedfellows remained to wish me good morning.

'Are you following me?' Nikolas asked. I nodded. 'What do you make of that, eh?' He gave a peculiar kind of wise grin, as though I must now see what kind of legendary creature I was dealing with.

'After I left that dosshouse,' he continued, 'I strayed about town, looking for something to chop. I began to pray to God and I said to Him, *If You are thinking of me, and if You want me* to survive at all, *You must help me to find those golden streets*. I still believed the vulture who told me that the streets of Lagos were paved in gold. But it was not long before I discovered those words for what they were really worth . . . as much as the leaf which has been used to wipe somebody's backyard!

'So. I had to stop many times in order to lie down on the ground and pick the stones out of the bottom of my feet as well as rest my stiff leg. This was not an easy matter. And when I was occupied with lying on the ground, I was prey to everyone who wished to speak to me or accost me. I am not telling a lie if I say that I had plenty of strange encounters, and I acquainted myself with myself better than before, because what marks us bodily the mind cannot forget. And once during this period I even fell in love, but that is another matter entirely. On some days I received a penny or two. There were plenty of days when I received nothing at all, and I just lay there like *mumu*, not fit to pick myself up and begin to walk without falling on to the ground again.

'Once I was lying on the ground, and many wretched porsons came and sat down beside me. We discussed our terrible hunger. One of us thought we should go to the market and chop rotten oranges. I thought to myself that this was a very bad idea indeed. I accepted the invitation. At the market I filled my hat with oranges. I took a seat and chopped them all in one go. Every single one! And I am telling you they made a dirty supper. That night I slept with my belly full on a heap of stones. As day began to break I became sick. I experienced pains in my stomach and backyard. I vomited and shitted myself inside out. Day after day for many days I lay in the street and not one soul will come to help me. Even porsons will come to rob me and beat me with a mallet. That is when I knew for certain the truth of that wise man's saying, which is that man will be a beast to man. The next thing I remember is that I was up on my hands and knees. And I was very very thirsty. I crawled to the canal and drank plenty of water. It was after that I discovered that my hat was gone, and my vest and trousers were gone as well. And I discovered that I was bald, as if a bird had chopped all my hair. And inside my head was a kind of rumpus, as if a fly had flown through my earhole and was causing trouble, buzzing and dancing, conducting important business inside my head.

'I said to myself that a one-eared man does not thank God until he meets a deaf man at prayer. It was clear what was happening to me, but what could I do? Did I continue to have no sleep? Yes. Did I find my hat plus the rest of my clothes? No. Did I find a new pair of boots? No. Did my hair grow back? No. Was I at that time skinny like a reed, meaning a puff of wind will cause me to fall on to the ground? Yes. Had I lost every hope? Yes. Had I even lost the desire to better my condition as well? Yes. Did I learn a thing or two about trickery in order to chop? Yes. Did I drink plenty of hot drink? Yes. Did I respect female honour? No. Did my stiff leg get better? No. Did I frequently take refuge in the horizontal? Yes. Was God happy with me at all? No. Did I think the world was at its end? Yes.'

Nikolas paused. After I don't know how long, he said, mysteriously, 'If darkness on a visit is so dark, what does it look like in its own home?' I was close to tears. I shook my head. 'Evie, there are times in life when things are not themselves but stand for other things.'

'You are a philosopher,' I said.

'I just don't eat.'

But from his life of misfortune he had descended to a position of great power. I soothed him with this thought. I pointed to his gold bracelet, and his sleeveless jerkin brocaded with gold thread.

'Porsons nowadays,' he said, 'do not know a thing about gold. But we who live in the pits know one or two things. For instance, it is not so much gold's value or beauty which captivates us, but even its practical use as well. Look,' he held his bracelet up to the candle, 'see how the metal acts as a reflector? Perhaps you thought I was acting the big man, eh, Evie? But I was not acting the big man. I will not wear gold as a simple extravagance. We in the pits live in dimness, so we must put gold's reflective properties to use. This is why we value gold very highly.'

We were sitting in his chamber. The air was close, wet, pungent, stinging, and the warmth which rippled off the bare walls made me think of steam that rises from a horse's back. Nikolas said it was because we were closer to the earth's raging core, and I believed him. I believed everything he said. I had only recently recovered from my dissolution in my husk. I felt peculiarly vain and wicked, and sullen, proud, self-serving, even idealistic – I almost never thought of Ade and his fall. And yet there were moments when a great heat of kindness towards the world came over me. But the heat cooled easily, and my mind returned with base thoughts, blood-hate and destructive ill-will. I did not see the good in most. Those in whom I did, however, I abandoned myself to with child-like love. So it was with Nikolas. He had peculiar visceral ways and wanted to turn the world upside down, believing one learned more from suffering than from studying books, that darkness triumphed over light, and that nightsoil was not waste matter – not the ejected poisons of our human gut – but a precious resource; black gold he called it. Wasn't it nightsoil which caused flowers and vegetables to grow? Didn't that remarkable substance support the walls of certain houses and towns? And couldn't one use its dried-out cakes to fuel a fire that burns throughout the night?

'All this is true,' Nikolas told me. He was sitting on a black throne-like chair, myself on a stool by his feet. 'And believe me, it is no coincidence that when porsons sit on the toilet they come by many great ideas.' I started to laugh, but he silenced me with an upraised hand. 'Who is to say that nightsoil is unsavoury, eh, Evie?' His voice rose in anger. 'Europeans think the toilet is unclean and avoid mention of it at all. No doubt the toilet *is* unclean. But if the toilet is unclean so is their own backyard. I will never know why Europeans flush away their excrement but collect their nose-droppings in white little squares of cloth . . . what is it, a handkerchief!' His tone was facetious, and yet his nostrils flared, always a sign, I came to learn, that he spoke in earnest.

He continued, his voice growing brighter. 'Let me tell you something that is true. All of Africa has been plundered by Europeans who think our problems can be solved by exposing every speck of grime and eradicating it. This is why we nightsoil workers are such a denigrated race. Condemned to work by night. Cursed by God and the human race. Believe me, our only honour is precarious, our only liberty provisional and under-ground.'

It was 1959, or thereabouts. I was twelve years old and had been living with Nikolas for several months. At least that is what I believed at the time. I had fallen in with his routine, his strange talk and eccentric ways. The mood in his chamber was high-spirited, and I was infected by that mood. I felt hungry for kindness and knowledge and I was flattered that someone, finally, understood my worth – and that person a noble leader! And yet all this time I had barely left his chamber. Now, writing this history, it strikes me as odd that I did not yearn to discover the wider reaches of the pits. If the thought did not occur to me, I believe it was because I was overawed, and free and happy, simply, to be in Nikolas' company.

The heat in the pits was great, and yet Nikolas shook constantly. I thought his trembling came from violence-blighted youth; and also his agitated mind, which embraced a whole Westminster of plans, decrees, slanders, debates, advice, inventions, speeches and reforms. He had a theory about everything. He told me that most people would risk their lives over something they don't care a whole lot about.

'I am talking about a man's vest or his stone collection. But those things that are important to that very same porson,' Nikolas said, 'he will completely disregard. For reasons hardly imaginable he will build himself a house in a remote town with no running water, in some pit overgrown with thorns and which is scattered with stones.' Another time Nikolas advised on brushing my teeth. The common idea, he said, is to brush after breakfast. But this was a mistake. He told me I should brush my teeth as soon as I woke up, otherwise dirt accumulated during the night would be swallowed down with my first bite of the day.

He liked to keep up with the news and, I learned, had his men collect the papers from the bins outside Government House. Now I was fully recovered it became my job to read him the headlines, first the international headlines from *The Times*, then the national and local, most often from *The West African Pilot* and *The Daily Comet* – Lagos papers, Zik's papers. We read about the problem of hygiene at the shambles, and Nikolas said, 'The government is trying to shut the market butchers down even though they have been supplying the meat trade for many years. The government favour the great English firms.

They will grant plenty of licences to the English and even to some French. Never to a native butcher.' He mistrusted every colonial officer, as well as businessmen, politicians, priests, missionaries, military men, journalists, even nuns. 'Has it ever occurred to you that we might be confusing over politicians and thieves, eh, Evie? Lagos is built on stolen land, and the government is the biggest estate agent.' But Zik, for him, though a political man, the leader of the NCNC, in line even to become first President, was not wolf-like as were other politicians but honest, noble, a poet.

Nikolas now revealed that he acted as Zik's spiritual doctor. Apparently (though I never saw it) there was a tunnel leading from the pits straight to Zik's house. In twenty minutes, whenever he called (how? Was there a telephone in his chamber?), Nikolas could walk right into Zik's study, where he advised on cultural matters, war, diplomacy, love, the future soul of Nigeria. He also counselled Zik on his anxieties. Apparently the old politician's nerves were shot. He had a strange attachment to a mechanical doll that one of his deputies, Usman, had given him. He even thought of her as a living creature. He won't admit it in public, but to me he will come right out and say it, *'She's alive, she's alive, the little aje!'* Apparently he feared that the American doll with her white dress and plaits would escape and try to kill him.

Nikolas told countless such stories. From his perspective most of the population was nutty. Everybody in Lagos had some kind of loose bolt in her personality, a secret history or vice. A wife of one of the DOs liked to pretend she was the Austrian princess Sophia von Hohenberg. There was a government clerk from Hausaland who wrote perfect English and dealt with forestry and who claimed he had invented electricity. Everyone, said Nikolas, was like their reflection in the lagoon, turned face on face and scattered by the wind and tide.

'Maddest of all are the Europeans, the foolish, spiritless, cruel old colonials who will make the laws into an exquisite justification for plundering.' His voice rose half an octave. He was working himself into a fury. 'Nigeria,' he shouted, 'is nothing more than a cesspit for madmen and murderers.' He stretched himself higher, and his head struck the ceiling. 'Ow! . . . Look at this cave! Not a surface – not a cranny – that is clean. It stinks! It is a sewer! When a man is forced to dwell in shit, what does he care for beauty and truth?' Then he came over to my bed. Suddenly calm, he said, 'But you will understand all of this already, Evie . . . because if you are not yourself a nightsoil worker you must know that your soul speaks in fellowship with my own.'

Another evening he said, 'Evie, there are plenty of times when I wonder how different everything could be for us if we in Africa had developed our own Enlightenment. Our own science that will suit our African tempers better than as we find them today. Then we would not have been forced to adopt the European ways, and Africa might have opened up a world of technology entirely of its own.

'Let me give you an example that I have been thinking about for quite some time. Imagine if we Africans had not been taught to keep our history in books. Before the missionaries and that Crowther, do you think we could forget our history easily at all? Do you think our memories were very short? Not for one moment! Our memories were very very long. I am not saying that writing and books are completely at odds with what might be called a good idea. What I am saying is that, if books had been invented by Africans they would have been printed on something that will not dissolve in the rains and flake away in the dry season and give an honest man a paper cut. And let me mention as well that they would not have been so strictly ordered page by page as they are today, so that there is no changing them. And even they would somehow allow for – how shall I say it? – a kind of conversation inside them. If this had happened, English books would not be as popular as they are, and talk of throwing away our native languages would be less noisy. But more than that. Our thoughts might not be imitating Europe but might have pushed forward into territories quite of their own! Do you follow me, Evie?'

I suspected Nikolas spoke faultily, yet there was much originality in his ideas. Besides, his words were touching me in places where mere facts were unable to reach. I felt they did not circle round the true things of the world, but, like Iffe with her sonorous voice, strike to their very centre. The description of the African book had taken me by surprise, and I was silent for a while. I thought about Mrs Honeyman. She had believed absolutely in book-learning. She told me that if I did not study I would fall in with ignorance, with the natives – savages. No doubt she would have taken great pleasure in seeing me here, dressed in a loose frock of sackcloth. I let out a wicked burst of laughter. The pale deceiver was right, I had black blood running in my veins, and I had no use for the sun.

I looked up at Nikolas. 'I follow you,' I said.

He bent to examine me. 'What a beautiful face you have, Evie . . . you are a little bit vain, like myself! There will always be porsons who are stamped underfoot and hounded underground and these porsons must be honoured either with wonder or laughter.' He spread his mouth in a wide grin. 'As a matter of fact you have a fundamental character with plenty of creative talent. You will go on to achieve many significant things, and I even have a wish that one day you will inform the world of what is concealed in these pits.'

'But I have heard it already.'

And I told Nikolas what I had heard, as I lay in my hollow, before he rescued me.

– a gasping of machinery. Narrow conduits debouching on vast enclosed spaces, on subterranean halls high as cathedrals, their vaults clustered with chains, pulleys, cables, pipes, conduits, joists, with movable platforms attached to jacks bright with grease.

– and, lower, mine galleries with blind, ageing horses drawing carts filled with ore and slow processions of helmeted miners; and oozing passageways, reinforced with waterlogged timbers, that led down glistening steps to slapping blackish water; flint-bottomed boats, punts weighed with empty barrels sailing across a lightless lake.

– and, even lower, nearing the earth's centre, I heard a world of caverns whose walls were black with soot, a world of cesspools and sloughs, a world of grubs and beasts, of eyeless beings who drag animal carcasses behind them, of demoniacal monsters with bodies of birds, swine and fish, of dried-out corpses and yellow-skinned skeletons arrayed in attitudes of the living, of forges manned by dazed Cyclopes in black leather aprons, their single eyes shielded by metal-rimmed blue glass, hammering their brazen masses into dazzling shields.

Nikolas' eyes with their flickering rings gleamed kindly on me. 'You are feverish,' he said. 'Try to stay calm and quieten the raging in your head.' And he blew the candles out.

20

How I Found My Way Home

The fever broke this evening. For two days and nights I have been lying on my mattress in the middle of the attic, plagued by torrid dreams, dreams of the dinning earth – brought on, no doubt, by my recollection of the pits. A tempest blew through my head. My body became a mass of cramps. I felt my blood beating through my arteries, and angry drums played between my ears. I recognize this fever; it's come from inside me; I heard those same noises decades ago, when I lived with Nikolas in his kingdom underground.

Now, after washing and eating, I am back at my desk. The attic is almost completely dark. The noise in my head has subsided, but the blood is still beating at my temples. I must have knocked over my laptop computer in my delirium, since I found it on the floor. Lifting it on to the desk, I opened it up and saw it had been damaged; a crack runs diagonally across the length of the screen. My computer is old, as thick and heavy as a volume of the *Encyclopaedia*. It puffs and gasps like Mr Rafferty in his sleep. A moment ago I switched it on. Thankfully, it has survived its fall. I read over the last chapter. My words seem to dissolve rather than record my time in the pits, now sunk beneath a veil of marine light and rotten air. What was I thinking? *Blind, ageing horses. Helmeted miners. Cesspools and sloughs and Cyclopses in black leather aprons!* I don't remember writing any of these things. Did I really 'see' these strange visions? Or was it the raging in my head that led me to type out those false imaginings? I have no way of knowing, for I was quite out of my mind.

Forward!

. . .

It was 1960, let's say, when I emerged from the pits. The mist of morning stung my eyes. The sky, like every sky in Lagos before dawn, in the dry season, as I recalled it, rested darkly on the horizon of water. I stood and watched a canoe emerge from the gloom, and then, a little later, etched against the half-light of the sky, its fishing net. Presently the sun broke above the horizon, and I found myself drowning in white light. I covered my face with my hands. The sun shone . . . that is not the word. Sunlight poured down on me, spreading and contracting behind my closed lids, and I fell on the ground.

I dragged myself forward, feeling the ground with my hands, until I came to a stretch of elephant grass. Soon I was lying in its fronds. Happily they concealed the sun from me and me from the road, and I gained control of my breathing. How much time went by I do not know. My tongue felt dry, so I sucked dew from the elephant grass. At one point I heard footsteps on the road. Fearing discovery, I crawled through the fronds, away from the road, and came out at the water's edge. In time I was able to open my eyes. I saw the lagoon: clear and calm, it appeared no different from the days before the pits; it worked lazily against the shore, sighing as it rolled, and when I broke its surface with my hand, it felt soft and cold, and it distorted the image of my fingers, just as it had done before. I got on to my knees and washed my face. How different I looked! My features were thicker and longer, my nose sharper, and my skin appeared dark. The eyes I saw were not those I knew from childhood. I took off my rags, then walked into the water and began to wash. The filth of the pits came off me, first in small flakes, then in clods. I rubbed my skin, scooping water on to myself, and as I did I began to cry, great sobs of unhappiness and shame. When I was fully clean, I rose and stood in the shallows and watched the last traces of the pits disappear below the surface, carrying away from me what seemed the only thing that could have made me truly happy.

It was late afternoon when I stepped out on to the road. The sun had weakened, but the air was still hot, and the feel of it in my lungs heightened my desperate mood. I walked along the shore-road, disorientated. Eventually I found my way to the square where Ade and I had taken refuge during the harmattan. And it will give an indication of my confusion or wickedness if I say that I didn't think once of my friend and his fall. Perhaps it was because the square was greatly changed. High concrete buildings now lined three of its sides. Crowds of office workers, shoppers, hawkers, vagrants, people of every kind, swarmed the paved way. At least that is how I remember it. But perhaps I am confusing several different occasions, and different times. Was I in the pits long enough for so much change to have occurred? I do not think so. Perhaps, then, I came across the square at a later time. No matter, I will relate it as I remember, even though it seems unlikely, for I must press on with my story. I looked for a place to hide, but there was none. Squatting by the fountain in the middle of the square, I remembered a shop I once knew, Hardy's Euro-African Emporium. Ben had often sent Ade and me to buy rice or sugar, Ovaltine, dried fish or tins of hair oil. At other times Father would place in my outstretched palm a warm penny to fetch his tobacco, which Hardy spooned from outsized jars like ant-house colonies. I had smelled the variety of teas and the gummy smoke from

Hardy's pipe, lit always; and in the wet season, when the shop swelled and rain rattled the corrugated roof, the scent was of mushrooms. Now it was gone; in its place stood the glass heights of the Bank of Nigeria. But more than anything it was the square's acoustical qualities that made me understand how different Lagos had become. Here the clamour of the city was louder than ever; and yet it was not so much the volume of noise that spoke of change, but rather the way the traffic suggested by its boom that air could be perforated. And just as, years previously, the return of the swallows had signalled the end of the rains, suggesting to me a new life at the market, so now it was the lack of birdsong, and indeed any of the sounds of nature, that made me feel my old life had come to an end.

I returned to Ikoyi. I don't know how I got there. I recall passing through alleyways, backyards, gardens, crossing roads and footbridges, avoiding people as much as possible. I remember the sun sparking on the lagoon. And its rays beating down upon me. I remember the aching of my body. And my dizziness. For long stretches I knew neither where I was, nor where I was going, nor how I arrived at this place, which seemed like another world. At night I slept in boats moored by the shore and suffered appalling dreams. It was in this way I found my way to Ikoyi. It took a long time. I even got there without knowing it. 'Evie!' a voice cried one day. That is how I remember it. It was my father. His chest was heaving, his breath hot, and he lifted me up and carried me to the house that I could no longer consider home.

In the weeks after I returned to Ikoyi, I fell sick. I had emerged from underground and the sun-shafts had worked on me. I felt limp, breathless, crushed, unable to endure light. Every voice cut into my head. Every touch was rough. Days passed before

I could take in food. I felt hot, yet did not sweat. In time my breathing eased. The fever broke. And I became aware that my father had cared for me during the sickness; it was he who had pressed wet cottons to my forehead and offered water through a straw and peeled fruit to feed the pulp between my lips, which were broken. I did not see Ade in my periods of waking and I feared he had died from the impact of his fall. Later, when I had recovered from my fever, I learned he'd survived, but that he was no longer living with us. There had been trouble between my father and Iffe over Ade's accident and my disappearance. Now Iffe, Ben and Ade lived in the new township of Suru Lere on the outskirts of Lagos.

With the breaking of the fever my father began to question me about where I had been. I tried to tell him about the pits, about Nikolas and the nightsoil workers, but he would not believe me. He thought my sickness had affected my mind and claimed I'd been absent for no more than several days! If my father himself had been more complete in the mind, I might have trusted his judgement. But I noticed something tragic and false about him. Although he still worked for the Lagos Development Board, although the slum clearances had begun and every day he went to oversee the demolition work, although the last years of Empire seemed to have inspired in him a kind of manic confidence – despite all this, I saw that the lines on his forehead had deepened, and his long figure seemed curved inward at the middle, and his pale eyes expressed continually less sense. So I did not believe him when he told me I had lost my sense of time. Even today, when I ask myself how long I lived with Nikolas in the pits, I defy my father's judgement and estimate it to be something like nine months. Of course, the figure satisfies something in me.

At that time the British were preparing to leave Nigeria:

Independence was approaching; Nigeria had her first prime minister, Alhaji Abubakar Tafawa Balewa, and in December 1959 federal elections had been held. In the European quarter of Ikoyi several houses were already boarded up. During the day I sat in the garden and watched the light creep up my leg, or listened to the silence, which rose like vapour from the lagoon. The air was still, hot, thick, and light cloud-columns split the sky. Everything felt deadened, not least my feeling for time, which seemed both to slow down and to change rhythm. Although the calendar above my bed continued to count the days, it counted days that lacked new occurrences. Father told me I would start school once we arrived in Scotland. The prospect neither disturbed me nor made me especially excited.

Conscientiously, if somewhat morosely, I sought silence, and I plugged my ears with clods from the walls of my pit, the only trace of that underground kingdom I had managed to keep. When I had lain alone in my hollow I had delighted in the emptiness and silence; now, that same emptiness and silence left me feeling lost. The world and its energies seemed far removed; and the more distant they seemed, the more my thoughts reached out to them.

I tried to persuade Father to take me with him into town, but he would not be moved, the demolition work was too dangerous, he said. To keep me company he gave me a radio of my own, a shiny portable device with a sky-blue case and concealed speaker, which emitted a beautiful deep, crisp sound. I listened to it obsessively, and for a while I forgot my loneliness. Of course, I no longer believed that the announcer lived inside the radio. My father had explained that he lived in England, and the broadcast came all the way from Bush House, in London's Strand. The announcer's voice, Father said, was carried through the medium of air, and sounded in all the radios of

the world at once. The idea that it did not stop at the edge
of the city, and that it jumped rivers, mountains and seas, amazed
me. To think that a voice could hop continents. And that it was
able to bring so many people simultaneously under its spell!

It was strange to think that people in Britain, fellow citizens
of the announcer, might be strolling down the Strand at the
very moment he began broadcasting the news and by chance
might look up at the sky, where, invisible but apparent, pleat-
ing the air with its waves, his voice would be floating above
their heads. I had lost forever the belief that the announcer
lived in our radio. And yet I'd gained a new feeling of sanctu-
ary: now I knew there was a community of listeners on ver-
andas all around the world. I liked to think that my grandfather,
Mr Rafferty (who I'd never met, but whom Father had told me
about – I was to meet him when we got to Scotland), might be
tuning in at the same time every evening, hearing the same
words spoken with the same voice. Like Father, I learned, Mr
Rafferty was a cricket fan, so I took an interest in the test match
reports, broadcast after the main items. My thoughts reached
out to Mr Rafferty; they travelled up from our garden, so I
imagined, and over the Atlantic Ocean, describing a parallel
path to the radio waves, but in the opposite direction, until
they found their way into his ear.

One evening after supper Father poured me a glass of lemonade and asked me to bring the radio out on to the veranda.
He was nervous and excited. I knew this because he worried
the scar on his chin.

'Lagos will be on the radio tonight,' he said, and laughed.
'Switch it on!'

Soon the Bow Bells chimed out over the dark garden. I recall
only one item from that evening, the story of a signal worker at
Euston Station who had been run over by a train. When, finally,

the news broadcast ended, the announcer said, *Now for a special report from Lagos, capital of the British territory of Nigeria . . .* How strange to hear the name of our home town broadcast on the radio! *Tomorrow in Lagos a special building will be opened. Independence House. For years the British administration has been building a wonderful capital city for Nigeria, which will soon take over the reins of self-governance. Independence House, symbol of all that the British have given to this once-impoverished country, will be opened by the Governor, Sir James Wilson Robertson . . .* The announcer continued to speak in his lulling and authoritative voice, in 'BBC English', whose intonation seemed to draw out the vowel-sounds, and I had the impression that Lagos had been held for a moment in his mouth, exposed, freed from the daily concerns of us, its inhabitants, in order to reveal its pure form. *We are witnessing the awakening of national consciousness in a people who have for centuries lived in the dependence of some other power. A wind of change is blowing through Nigeria, and Lagos, its glittering capital, is the centre of the change.*

21

Exile

The crowd came from all over the town: people poured out of lanes, out of houses and backyards and made their way to Broad Street to join the celebrations. Before the glass façade of Independence House stood a makeshift stage, painted black, with a microphone, and chairs for the dignitaries. It was three o'clock. The Governor stepped out from the motionless shade of Independence House, on to the bright stage. Then came the architect, accompanied by Tafawa Balewa, the Prime Minister, in his white robes. For ten minutes, possibly more, the civic leadership emerged, followed by the members of the Lagos Executive Development Board, including my father and Mr Honeyman. A boy worked a fan to keep the flies from the Governor's face. There was a pause. The crowd made a peculiar high-pitched noise. Drums sounded, there was a collective gasp as a pair of wooden poles were raised above the stage; unseen hands drew the poles apart to reveal a banner painted with the words: 'MAY GOD GRANT PROSPERITY TO THE NEW NIGERIA'.

I stood to the side of the stage, with the children of the dignitaries, my hands resting on the edge. Young men perched in trees all along the street. Hawkers stopped, put down their wares; they too stared at the spectacle. Independence House, twenty storeys high, its windows flashing in the sun, shone brilliantly out above the crowd.

The Governor held his hand up for silence; uplifted, his sleeve fell below the elbow, and the drums became quiet. Presently we saw, stepping up to the microphone, a tall, pale man in a grey suit, with a powerful moustache. He put his spectacles on and said, 'Welcome, friends of Nigeria. It is an honour to be opening this splendid building, the tallest Nigeria has ever seen. Independence House is much more than a mere architectural triumph, however. As its name suggests, it is a symbol of the great strides Nigeria is taking towards nationhood.' The Governor paused and surveyed the crowd. 'However,' he continued, 'there is much work still to be done. For instance, we must encourage the northern territories to participate more enthusiastically in democratic Nigeria. Hausa, Yoruba and Ibo must learn to put their own narrow interests aside . . .'

Suddenly I heard a rattling sound.

'Ikoko Omon,' said a familiar voice, a voice crackling like flaming leaves. 'Ikoko Omon! Is that you?' I turned, and gasped. Fighting her way through the children was the Honeymans' cook: arms frail, wrapper hardly bulking out a withered crone's frame, loose skin gathered below the chin, hanging like a lizard's dewlap.

'What have you been chopping, eh, Ikoko Omon? You are growing faster than a bamboo!' I moved through the children to greet her. But she grabbed my hand and turned to face the stage, saying, 'Not now. Listen. What a stupid man, with big big grammar. Look! Ikoko Omon. He begins to sweat for his pink face!'

'Permit me to use an analogy,' the Governor was saying. 'If the wealth of Nigeria may be likened to a great communal pot of soup, then Lagos, this thriving city, is the ladle which serves the soup.' He paused. 'If the ladle does not serve the soup, then there will simply be no soup for the people. Nobody would be able to eat. Therefore, the ladle is important to everyone, to the soup, and to the whole country.' He looked up from his notes. 'Suppose,' he said, mysteriously, 'if there was no ladle to serve the soup, what would happen then?'

'This question *na war oh*,' cried the Honeymans' cook. Several of the children turned their heads towards her. 'Ikoko Omon! Not everything that comes from a cow is butter.'

The Honeymans' cook, peering between creased lids, turned from me to hurl a silent curse at the Governor. I shifted my weight. The Governor dropped his papers and bent to gather the loose sheets. Upright, he took his spectacles off and wiped his eyes. The Honeymans' cook began to speak under her breath; chewing, spitting, formulating, with vitriol, arguments to undermine the dignitaries. She passed from curse to mockery, from mockery to incantation, as the Governor, returning the spectacles to the bridge of his nose, addressed us once again. Now he spoke of the darkness of Africa many years past, at the time of the Berlin conference, of the forces of evil, bad faith, cruelty and oppression, the intolerance, prejudice and poverty, the ignorance and superstition that had entombed the territory. 'Empire has spanned a fine period in the transition of Nigeria,' he said. 'And the architects of Independence House have, in their own small way, contributed to that change. Thank you,' he said, raising his arms and stepping back to take his seat.

Drums sounded, hands were flung in the air, faces glared with heat. But the awe that shone in every face seemed to cast a cloud on the Honeymans' cook.

'This big big grammar oh, he is a useless man,' she said. 'Can't he shut his mouth? He will have sunstroke for his tongue. Talking this nonsense . . .'

Suddenly there was a shrieking sound. I reached for the Honeymans' cook. Amid a great general roar, I saw a stream of women running down Broad Street towards the stage, leaping and screaming in a sort of frenzy. I saw that the women wore crowns of ferns and they had tied leaves around their waists, and they brandished sticks. The Governor and the dignitaries were hurrying from the stage, and voices were calling for we children to withdraw. But the Honeymans' cook led me into the street, into the mass of bodies, and I didn't stop her. I wanted to be there among the women. Perhaps I would come across Iffe! I raised my voice to ask after Iffe, but it was lost in the noise. It was exhilarating to see the women jerking left then right, answering unseen drums, kicking up their knees and thrashing their sticks.

What was happening?

As the crowd parted to let the women approach the stage, a voice rang out:

> *Whiteness is the beauty of the teeth.*
> *Length is the beauty of the neck.*
> *Full breasts are the beauty of a woman,*
> *Whose nipples poke into mens' eyes.*

The women were flourishing their sticks. I stood some ten yards back, keeping close to the Honeymans' cook.

The same voice cried out again: 'All right, Balewa, it is four o'clock and we go come for you. Governor Mr Robertson don't fear we will teach you a lesson with our sticks! Where is he who is called Robertson? Something very bad will happen to you!'

The street was white and hot, the sun directly overhead, and the women shouted and spoiled for trouble. To our right I heard a high wailing; it grew louder, higher and seemed to come deep from within the mourner's chest. The Honeymans' cook pointed out a young woman surrounded by onlookers, some of whom were trying to calm her stricken movements. Her grief could not be checked. Her body convulsed, tears slid freely from her face; her despair was palpable, open. Suddenly I felt light. I closed my eyes. The mourner continued to wail but her cries came to me now from a great distance. I leaned against the Honeymans' cook, who whispered to me. Apparently the grieving woman's husband had been killed in the slum clearances. He had refused to leave his house, and the bulldozers had knocked it down with him inside.

Suddenly there was a sharp crashing sound, and birds fled upward from the trees. In place of the dignitaries, soldiers had come on to the stage. They were shooting their rifles in the air. They stopped shooting, and a small dark man pushed through to the front of the stage. His voice was remarkably deep. I felt it in my stomach when he spoke into the microphone, 'Quiet! Quiet please. Listen!' He signalled to the soldiers, who shot into the air once more, several quick deafening shots.

'Listen to me,' the speaker said, 'I have something to tell you. Do not worry yourselves. You will be compensated by the Executive Board. Every one of you. That is a promise. Remember, God can turn a poor man today into a rich man tomorrow!'

There was more shouting, a tremendous noise. I was thrown violently forward. Then the voice which had sung out several minutes previously called out to the speaker on the stage. The voice demanded that his promises should be typewritten, stamped and put into registered envelopes.

'That can be done,' said the speaker, despatching a soldier, before stepping to the microphone again. Now he told the women that their former homes had been fever dens where diseases such as pneumonia, dysentery and malaria thrived, not to mention crime, drunkenness, prostitution, social unrest, vice, feckless poverty and mental pathology.

'It is imperative for us to demonstrate that Nigeria can survive as a viable nation on her own,' he said. 'Your government will provide roads, water, electricity, a piped sewage system and drains!'

'Mothers cannot chop. Picken cannot chop sef!' someone shouted.

The Honeymans' cook bent to speak in my ear. 'It is true what the people are saying, because the land which he has told the people will be theirs to build their houses on again is being given to big men in the government.'

'Friends,' the speaker said. 'Perhaps you think you are still living your village lives. But you are mistaken. You are living in a city, a modern city, the domain of reason. Hence your problems must be solved by the exercise of reason alone. It is a question of finding the right road system,' he said, 'safe housing, the correct proportion of green space, and so forth.'

'I can no longer support my family,' someone shouted.

'From time to time it becomes necessary to eat the onion,' the speaker said, 'no matter how bitter, and sometimes in the interest of the well-being of your nation.'

'What nation?' someone asked.

'The great nation of Nigeria. You may not find it easy at first to accept without question or reservation what I have to say,' he continued, 'but finally you will reconcile yourselves to it. It will take a bit of time. But modernization will come. You will have to accept it. Otherwise there will be no place for you in the new Nigeria.'

I had heard these same words years ago, when Mr Honeyman came to our veranda and showed us the bird's-eye view of Lagos, with the sites penned for destruction circled in red. He had spoken of sanitation and green space and skyscrapers, and I had thought these ideas mere dreams. Now his ideas had been adopted by the leaders of Nigeria. Land had been cleared, and the people of the market district had been forced from their homes. The speaker had brought along his own map, a hand-drawn view of central Lagos, and he had the soldiers scatter copies from the stage. The women reached to catch them as they fell through the air. I picked one up from the ground and put it in my pocket.

'I have nowhere to sell my oranges!' someone cried. But she was hushed by other members of the crowd, for the speaker had changed his argument. He was speaking of the benefits modernization would bring; soon, he said, the people of Lagos would be able to afford proper homes, filled with furniture of modern durable design, 'metal tables, oak chests, china plate, booth seating, Bokhara rugs, lacquered cabinets, night stands, bubble lamps, glass sconces, telephones, coloured-glass coasters, as well as exotic foods, jam, hams, apples, sacks of almonds, walnuts, pistachios, raisins and sultanas, *patisseries*, candied fruits from France, everything a man can eat, everything a man can drink, all laid out before you on your metal tables. You will drown in plenty,' he told the astonished crowd. 'Have you ever tasted hare?' he asked. 'Or quail, or spit-roast pig? I do not think you have. Soon you will dine like the Gauls! You will see shopping centres rising from the ashes of old Lagos,' he said, 'skyscrapers climbing one hundred storeys high!'

'Do not listen to that man!' shouted the voice. 'He wishes the food we chop to be insect wey we find on the street. The government is using us like goat.' The crowd roared and surged forward, jeering, urging, indignant, crying, and I shouted my support. I was happy and dizzy in this hothouse of screaming and white light. And that was the thrilling thing, I thought, to be here, among the bodies, hearing the street rumbling with the weight of thousands and the cries of anger and sorrow.

Now the women started to beat the stage with their sticks, and the speaker shouted for calm, and for the women to withdraw, but they took no notice and flocked forward. It was then I saw the soldiers lower their rifles. This time they did not fire over our heads, but right into us, into the crowd. I was stunned. We began to scatter. I held on to the Honeymans' cook. We took a street to the side of Independence House, and emerged at the rear of the building. Amid the fleeing bodies and confusion and dust I lost hold of the Honeymans' cook. I ran on, further from the site of the shooting, until, eventually, unable to run any more, I came to a stop. I heard drumming and I watched streams of women, some still running, others dragging themselves along the street, weeping and screaming. I searched for the Honeymans' cook, and still full of the mood of the violence, not ready to turn and try to find my way back to my father, I managed to pick her out. She was walking slowly, supporting a wounded trader I recognized from the onion line. And there, right beside her, was Iffe! They came to a halt. I gazed at Iffe: now she was standing quite still among the wounded, set apart in the shade of an uprooted tree, her expression fixed in an attitude of profound grief. I jumped up, crying, 'Iffe, Iffe!'

It was not until I was beside her that she noticed me. Her gaze fell on me for a brief moment, then with her unhurried grace of movement, she turned her back on me.

'Go away,' she said with her back still turned. Those words astonished me. All the years I had known Iffe, she had been indifferent to my presence. At the onion stand, travelling home on the bus, sitting at the kitchen table eating our evening meal – she had seldom paid me any attention. Now she had addressed me directly and, what is more, she had demonstrated high feeling. And yet what she said sent a pain through my limbs, for with those words, spoken with her back turned, she no longer expressed indifference, but contempt.

I walked away half stunned, half afraid, my feet hurting. I made my way further from the site of the shooting, dragging myself out of sight of Iffe and the wounded women. I stumbled and fell in a heap on the ground, weeping from sheer exhaustion.

The place I had come to was almost unrecognizable. Shattered stalls and enormous upturned coils of corrugated iron poked out of the debris. I sat on a basket and looked out at the grey vista between two broken shacks opening on to the wreckage beyond. I could see no people, only squashed fruits, bright colours staining the ground. I had entered the former market district, which had been razed to the ground. I looked about me, seeing what was left of the trading lines, which could only tentatively be called lines, since all things appeared alike on the levelled land. To my right was a highway in the process of construction, and beyond this other new roads, lined with banks of trees, symmetrically spaced, and tall buildings forming street-canyons that reflected sounds, doubling them, making them collide, overlap and shooting them upward towards the high roofs, invisible in evening light.

On the other side of the new thoroughfare I saw that fires had blackened the streets, and in places still burned. The smoking earth was dotted with irregular pale-red flares. I came across a trestle table shorn of its feet, propped against an upturned cart, and the pair formed a crooked tent-shaped space, into which I crawled. I told myself that I had come across the remains of the onion table, the very table under which I had spent so many hours, listening, and this made me happy and bitter. By my feet a few embers still lingered on the scorched earth, and I saw that the fire that had razed the market district had exposed a cluster of new shoots; those untouched by the flames shone the freshest green. I settled under my shelter, and my thoughts were sad and fearful, many-branched, thoughts that turned, first on Iffe, then on Ade, and finally on the pits, to which I longed to return. I had been drawn to that underground kingdom because I believed it would bring me darkness and silence. I had believed I would remain for ever in my husk. I had thought that I would live as truly as I had lived in the womb. And yet from that desperate kind of quest, from that heady feeling of having been able to make out a silent world, nothing now remained.

It was early morning when I woke. I sat up, shivering. Drawing my blouse close, I found a piece of paper in my pocket. I unfolded it and spread it flat on the ground. It was the bird's-eye view of central Lagos, one of the hand-drawn maps from the demonstration, which I had collected when the speaker with the deep voice had had his soldiers scatter them from the stage. As the sun rose I examined the map. And there I saw, laid flat before my eyes, the island on which I had spent my whole life; and at its centre I could pick out the nearly complete rect-angle of Tinubu Square, the grey lines indicating the principal streets, with black dots representing the palm trees, as well as the lighter, more intricate paths of the market district, where the occasional forked outline marked the artist's impression of a passer-by. And later, when I rose and ducked under my shelter and walked beneath the highway, over rubble which in places still smoked, I was myself standing on the grey streets lined with palm trees. I was myself the pale outline on the market path, a tiny blot on the wasted land. I looked around at the high buildings quivering in the new day's light. And I felt crushed.

PART THREE

22

The Hothouse

This afternoon I travelled to Edinburgh to visit Mr Rafferty. Stepping from the bus on to his street, I heard the church clock strike three. It was starting to get dark. A chill wind blew across my legs. By the churchyard gates I stopped to remove my earplugs: ever since I finished the chapter on the pits of the nightsoil workers, when the noise of the earth blighted my dreams, my tinnitus has become louder and louder – my head is filled with all kinds of whizzing, popping and hissing noises. I'm finding it harder and harder to press on with this history. Every now and then, if I am lucky, I manage to write for an hour or two. But it's slow work.

On the street I stopped to listen to a group of children running from school. Above the shapeless hubbub now and then I heard a cry – perhaps of joy, or of fear. A trio of cyclists coasted past. Did one of them ring her bell? I couldn't say. I stood shivering, listening to the sounds. This occupied me for a while. Finally, the green man's pips started up, and I crossed the road and entered the hospital grounds. It was getting colder. Nevertheless the December sun shone richly on the twisted grass.

The door to my grandfather's room was open, and I entered without knocking. He was waiting for me, dressed in his greatcoat and hat.

'Hello, Evie,' he said and kissed me on the forehead. Happily he knew me this afternoon. Happily he seemed to know himself too. This was a good sign, for I had come to ask him about 1961, the year I arrived in Scotland, of which I recall very little.

I *do* remember my first visit to Mr Rafferty. Even then, his needs were minimal, like my own today. He no longer travelled, rarely left the institution, and his main pastime was restoring clockwork. Now the staff have confiscated his tools, but then my father and I would bring him watches from the junk shops on Cockburn Street. We would look on as he squinted at the silver cogs and loosely sprung coils, picking them apart. Then, hunched over the hands restored behind glass, he would wind the mainspring and wait for the miracle.

Now Mr Rafferty was struggling with his laces. He had shaved off his moustache (I felt before I saw it) and grazed his upper lip. It was difficult to connect this pale old man with the masterly watchmaker he had once been. I looked away. The whining in my ears climbed in pitch, and for several minutes I sat on the bed.

'Shall we get going?' I said. I was keen to leave the institution. My grandfather is more likely to engage in conversation outside the building.

As we left the institution I saw he was in a happy, helpful mood. He led me through the hospital grounds, saying, 'I want to show you something.' The late sun fell on his face, which seemed naked and embarrassed without his moustache. We walked along a ridge by the perimeter wall, then joined a walkway cut between rose thickets. Mr Rafferty said, 'It's brisk out,' and his breath rose visibly. This seemed to please him. I took his arm to stop him slipping on the flagstones, and after a while he led me to a clearing. In front of us stood a hothouse. Lately I have noticed that when I stop still after walking I hear a deep sound in my head, like a funeral chord. I heard it now. Perhaps that is why I let Mr Rafferty pause outside the glass doors: the bass notes made me forget my purpose.

The hothouse is a big, square building with arched windows

set in pillars of stone. A sweep of glass forms the roof. Mr Rafferty said, 'Let's go inside.' I wanted to leave the institution and get to the park, where I planned to question him about our first meeting, and about my father's state of mind in those days. But now the funeral chord shifted several keys higher, acquired dissonance, distracting me. Mr Rafferty was tugging at my sleeve.

'Hold on,' I said, 'look!' As the sun sank lower in the sky the clear arches with their glistening panes flamed with colour, and smoke rose from the roof. I looked through the windows at the fire and gasped, then pointed, and Mr Rafferty laughed, then I understood: the fire was not fire, but the sun reflecting off the panes; the smoke, not smoke, but vapour rising where the hot glass met the outside air. Mr Rafferty took my arm and led me through the doors.

'The building is never so beautiful as at this hour,' he said.

Inside, the air was wet. We wandered among the rotting plant life, brushed ferns with our hands, smelled the stink flower and mounted a narrow gantry spanning the north wall. Large climbers grew on the trunks of the banana trees, and blue moisture dripped from the ceiling. The drops hit, then slid along the serrated leaves, then fell; and the whole canopy seemed slowly to dip and rise.

Mr Rafferty peeled off his greatcoat and loosened his shirt. Sweat-beads had formed on his upper lip, clinging to the graze, and his temples were dark and flushed. I mopped his face and neck and retied his laces. On entering the building the shift in temperature had been sudden, and I had welcomed it. Yet I saw that Mr Rafferty was suffering. And I myself was feeling restless and fatigued, although not on account of the heat. It was rather because of the swollen, almost meaty quality of the leaves, and the unreal greenish colour of the light. Breathing deeply, my grandfather stepped back down on to the hothouse floor. I followed him along the pathway, and we came to a pond with a mechanical waterfall, buzzing and whispering. It was cooler here, where spume from the falls sugared our faces, and we sat to take a rest. A coin fell from his pocket and rolled into the pond, but he didn't notice.

'May I ask you something?' I said. He didn't answer. His eyes were following a movement in the foliage.

'Well, isn't that Perry?' he said. An old man in a motor-powered wheelchair was steering clumsily towards us. 'I think he ought to stop driving that chair. His hands are too shaky.'

Perry did not advance smoothly. He kept veering from the pathway, cursing the undergrowth.

'There's not a day passes without his baking himself in the hothouse,' Mr Rafferty said. 'It's the only thing keeping him alive.' The old cripple lurched forward then puttered to a stand-still. For a moment he adjusted the vehicle and then he raised his face to us – pale, with a bony nose, powerfully hooked, and thick grizzled eyebrows. It was the only hair left on his entire head. In spite of the heat, his shoulders were wrapped in a blanket. He squinted up at me. Mr Rafferty said, 'Old Perry, he's virtually a tropical plant himself,' which made perfect sense, as all at once I took in the waxy skin, the thick, blighted fingers, his corpse-like smell.

Perry beckoned me with a trembling hand. In a rasping voice he commanded, 'Take me tae the carnivorous plants.'

'Me –?'

Mr Rafferty spoke quietly. 'He can't make it past the African palm.'

'We don't have the time,' I said, 'I've got something important to talk to you about.'

'Don't refuse the old veteran. Go ahead.'

'Take me,' said the cripple.

Annoyed, I put my hand on the armrest. 'Perhaps another time,' I said. But Perry had shuddered into motion, saying, 'Dinnay let the fronds get in my road.'

I strode in front. 'The plants, they're a worry,' he said. 'I used tae cut them back. But since this –' he kicked feebly at the metal frame, 'you might as well no bother.'

'A shame,' I said. 'Which way is it?'

'Round tae the left. Behind the great palm . . . Hang up.' The chair swerved off the pathway and collided with an iron pillar. As I righted him, Perry said, 'What a beauty!' We were before the palm, which reached massively upwards, its trunk rising column-like almost to the roof.

The cripple said, 'It's older than you.'

'Come, where are we going?'

'Hang up a minute.' He wanted to talk. 'If I dinnay bring out the tree surgeon soon, it'll die like the rest. Christ almighty. Look.' The palm pushed its fronds vigorously against the roof; and yet on examining the ribbed and flaking trunk, I saw it was lesioned in many places and supported by iron bars. Its growth had been carefully manipulated by the hothouse gardeners.

'Old Mister Sandor –'

'Let's get on.'

I parted a thick leaf-curtain. On the other side we came to a bank of flowers with gaping pink mouths. They appeared ravenous. Perry took out a matchbox and slid open the lid. For a moment I mistook its contents for sultanas, then I recoiled – the box was filled with dead flies.

'They destroy themselves on the window panes in my room,' he said and emptied the box into his palm. Taking one after another delicately by its wings, he began to drop them into the long-lashed flytraps, which closed lazily around their prey. I watched amazed for several minutes as, swaying gently from side to side, with a kind of fierce pleasure, or so it seemed, the cripple's plants set about digesting the flies.

'How do you like that?' he asked.

'I must be getting back,' I said, parting the leaf-curtain.

As we made our way along the path, Perry muttered to himself, coughed, jerked to and fro in his battery-powered machine, cursed the hospital management. 'It wasn't like that in Mister Sandor's day,' he breathed.

'Watch the stones,' I said.

Perry talked on, and my sense of hearing started to leave me. His voice seemed very far away. In a few minutes every sound was deep and unclear, like noises underwater. No doubt because of this my eyes were active. I was looking at the chaos of fetid undergrowth, which restricted the chair's movements. It had not always been this way. At one time the flora had been ordered and cut back, regulated by the great steam heaters, the sprinkler system, the complicated mass of blinds and pulleys. Now it was overgrown, prehistoric. It smelled of decay.

By the time I got back to the pond Perry was no longer with me; he must have taken a different path. I noticed Mr Rafferty had fallen asleep. Bubbles formed between his slightly open lips. I wanted to wake him; it was getting late and I didn't want him to grow tired, in which case he would surely refuse to answer my questions. Nevertheless I let him rest for a while longer. I was thinking of the venus flytraps, as I had left them a moment ago, potent and gorged, and the funeral chord sounded again, stronger than before. Could my grandfather hear it in his sleep? Could Perry, wherever he was? I didn't think so. Every other sound had disappeared. My sense of vision loomed enormously. I sat there gazing at the falls. I began to study its appearance, as though I'd never seen a waterfall before, its thousand glistening surfaces, the spray or mist rising where it struck the pond. The chord became gradually quieter, and I grew more and more content. Everything appeared dense and still, in particular the falls, which looped down now in a continuous silent flood and seemed made not of water, but, impossibly, of ice.

Some time later my hearing returned. I leaned over and whispered in my grandfather's ear. There was a hatching of froth on his chin. Had he been dribbling? It was likely. To wake him seemed cruel, but I shook him anyway. He didn't stir. I thought about what I would do if my hearing deteriorated again. I shook him violently. His gaze roamed upwards, then his eyes fell on me and glazed over. I saw a dark patch at the end of his shoe, where he had let it dip into the pond.

'Did you have a good nap?' I said, finally. He told me that he was too hot. My grandfather's answers are often beside the point. 'Listen,' I said. 'There are certain things I'd like to talk to you about, things which are important to me, which only you can help with.' He stared at me in astonishment. Perhaps he wasn't yet fully awake. I waited several minutes then asked if he knew who I was. After a short pause he spoke my name.

'Good,' I said. 'Shall we go to the park?' I was trying to be clear. I asked him if he understood. He did not look like he understood. After several minutes, he said, 'My toe is wet.' He hadn't understood a thing. Or perhaps he was being difficult because I had disturbed his sleep.

'OK,' I said. 'We don't have to go anywhere, if you don't want to. Let's chat here.' I paused. Then I said, 'Tell me, do you remember when we first met, when I came to visit you, here in the hospital? Do you remember how I was in those days? And Father, what kind of state of mind was he in?' I asked several more questions. Mr Rafferty waited for me to finish. Then he opened his mouth and spoke. But I couldn't hear him clearly.

I looked up at the roof. It had started to snow. I saw shadows flitting across the glass, projected by the streetlamps.

After some time I said, 'Mr Rafferty?'

I won't narrate this duet in full. Suffice to say there were further misunderstandings. Perhaps my grandfather answered my questions, but I think not. I think he was being deliberately obtuse, since at one point he took his yellow goggles from his pocket and began to fiddle with the elastic. Did he think I was going to take him swimming? It must not be forgotten that all this time my ears were of more or less value as sense organs. And my mind kept returning to the flytraps. It was odd to think of vegetative matter eating insect-life. And it was even odder when one thought of Perry feeding them with sweepings from the window panes of his room. Could the old cripple's plants not fend for themselves? Perhaps the air in the hothouse was not fit to sustain flies, and the plants, like zoo animals unable to hunt their prey, relied on human offerings.

Outside, in the hospital grounds, snow was falling silently. In each band of orange lamplight the flakes sifted gently down. We walked along the path by the perimeter wall. I had given up my quest to have Mr Rafferty help me with my history. He was intent on stepping in the snow, which was starting to settle. Now both his feet were wet. I put my hands in my skirt pockets. But for the noise of the traffic and the crunching underfoot, all was quiet. The graze on my grandfather's upper lip had turned crimson. As we approached the front door, he stopped and said, 'Is it both ears?'

'Sorry?'

'Are you deaf in both ears?'

I nodded, taken aback.

'How long has it been going on?'

'Well, it's happened several times before.'

'Have you seen a doctor?'

'Not yet, no. Besides, I'm not deaf,' I said sharply. 'I have a very keen sense of hearing. It's only that it is erratic . . . Bwha, it's cold.'

'Does it worry you?' he asked.

In truth I was wretched, wandering in my thoughts, but I didn't reply.

By the time we got to the front door of the institution the snow had started to fall in clusters of feathery flakes. Deepening blue drifts lay all over the grass. We stood with our backs to the door. I rubbed my hands together, and we huddled close. Mr Rafferty wanted to talk some more, but I wouldn't allow it.

23

Father's Madness and Death

It's been over a week since my visit to Mr Rafferty. In that time I've done very little. Finally, however, I feel able to press on. What happened in the interim?

The snow continued to fall. In between periods of silence, the funeral chord continued to sound, and I was unable to recall my first months and years in Scotland. I wrapped myself in my patchwork blanket and lay on my mattress, which had been my father's, but which I now think of as my own, staring at the skylight. Some mornings the condensation on the glass turned to ice, and my breath rose visibly. I cut the tips from a pair of gloves; together with a scarf from Mother's trunk, they helped against the cold. As far as I could tell my hearing had not become worse. It had not grown more sensitive either. I was having trouble sleeping, the days seemed long, so I busied myself as best I could: I swept the floor, thought about tidying the attic, about throwing some of the clutter away. I went into Gullane and bought a supply of beans.

The nights seemed even longer than the days. I missed my grandfather. Now that I wore the fingerless gloves, my hands were warmer, and I managed to write a little. I was trying to recount my afternoon at the hothouse, but it was slow progress. One evening, sitting at my desk facing the screen, which was misted over, but which nevertheless smouldered a pale blue, I read over my work, then closed my computer. Progress? It was the contrary. In five days I'd succeeded in blackening only two pages. What is more, I could hardly connect what I'd written to my ordeal in the hothouse. My words seemed to describe another experience entirely.

That was last week. This morning when I got up, crossed to the skylight, with its smattering of snow and looked up at the sky, I saw the night was fine and clear and I saw the flakes pawing the glass. All was quiet, even the gulls; perhaps they'd fled to inland roosts. I climbed over the heap of junk to the wardrobe, where I keep the completed pages of my history, printed on sheets of unbound paper. I took them out and glanced over the first chapters. It was a mistake. Not even at the outset, when I'd asked myself some questions, and answered with deceit, was my history credible. I read on, past the questions and into the following chapters. I encountered the half-truths, elisions and embellishments. I threw down the pages in disgust. They scattered over the floor.

It was starting to get light. I wanted to sleep, but I was unable. I began to march over the strewn pages of my history, experiencing an immediate feeling of triumph, and I even chuckled to myself as my shoes dirtied the already blemished sheets. The sun was bright; no doubt reflecting off the snow, it produced a glare from the skylight. I gathered several handfuls of my history in order to tape them over the glass. Three or four layers and the glare was sufficiently diminished to resemble twilight. I bent down and picked up the remaining sheets, which I had forgotten to number, and stacked them haphazardly together. Scrabbling in the half-dark, I came across the pocket watch. I hadn't even known I had lost it! Its glass front was cracked, the chain missing; added to the scratch on its underside, a series of marks obscured yet more of the inscription, which I read in the light on my computer:

> *Could not _____ move _____ this _____,*
> *Not _____ passion _____ by spleen.*

And _____ *power,*
By _____ *acts* _____

I held it to my ear. Not a sound. I put the watch into my pocket and finished collecting the sheets. Finally I rose, returned my history to the wardrobe and sat at my desk. I glanced about the attic, saw nothing but the usual clutter of objects. I took a deep breath, rubbed my hands together, focused my mind on my ordeal in the hothouse and, all in a rush, managed to set it down on my computer.

That was a moment ago. Now I will turn my mind back to my first years in Scotland.

. . .

The dark two-storey house in Gullane was full of neglected rooms, vast sofas and cheap artificial plants. The noise of the sea was ever-present, as was the overbearingly loud ticking of the grandfather clock in the hall. Already, when we arrived from Nigeria, the house was in a state of neglect: rotten wood, threadbare curtains, carpets scuffed to brown matting, and everything covered in a dim greasy flour. The chairs with their green hide felt cold against my bottom, the leather torn, cracked, blackened. Also avian-soiled, since birds found their way into the house. With no one to chase them away, they acquired free reign of the space, flying like darts from room to room, perching on beams and pelmets and often, frighteningly, stunning themselves on the window panes.

All of this owing to the indolence of my father. I barely recall him in those first years in Gullane. He slept most of the day. Having inherited the house from his parents, as well as a small allowance, he had no need to work. Tall, with uncombed hair, his limbs were thin, and as the years passed they knotted in a horrible contraction of all his muscles – one can never observe the passage of time but only its effects. He quickly became quiet and confused. Like an old mirror his skin developed brown spots. If time marked his outward appearance, however, turning that powerful figure into a discoloured old man, inwardly it had a paradoxical effect. For a brief period the spirit of childhood entered him, his energies revived, and his mood and mobility improved. He began to ride his bicycle around the living room, laughing uncontrollably whenever he knocked over a plant. Once I caught sight of him lying on the carpet, legs tangled in the frame, ringing the bell and shouting, 'Out of my way,' over and over again.

When his legs healed he began to explore the house on foot. He discovered the room where we'd stored our possessions on returning from Lagos. Some he threw away, some he gave to the charity shop on Main Street. Most he carried up to the attic. He tipped their contents into a heap and began to sort through them, working hard, even frantically, but without method or conviction. The mouldy cricket gear, the pocket watch he had broken so many times but which continued to tick, the mappa mundi, the bronze pendant from Benin, letters, papers, the endless stubs of cigarettes and piles of ash, the moth-eaten books, the trunk in which Mother's clothes lay, as well as old photographs, medals, pencils, lamps with torn shades – all these things made him seem detached and apart from life. As the years passed – and I grew into a monstrous solitary teenager, and in my fourteenth year left for boarding school in Edinburgh, about which the less said the better – I barely thought about him. Sometimes I arrived home for the weekend to discover that my father was missing. I would wander all over the house, calling his name and knocking on walls, until he emerged from under a table or bed; only to scurry back up to his perch beneath the eaves. I asked him why he spent so much time in the attic. Apparently he was more comfortable when closer to the clouds.

Enough! I am tired of this chapter. Thinking back to those years in Scotland, trying to relate the circumstances of my father's madness and death, I can barely recover the memories. With the greatest effort I have managed to set something down. And yet I can't help feeling that the process of remembering has hidden something, and that something the most important part. What is more, I'm exhausted by the labour, and in between writing I have lain on my mattress, immobile.

In the past, when I have been unable to go on, I would pick up one of the books – histories, pamphlets, novels, treatises, letters, the *Encyclopaedia Britannica* – from the pile in the attic and seek inspiration in its pages. I would find a sentence I liked and transcribe it on to my computer; even, at times, whole paragraphs. Or else I would copy out a description – a gesture, a landscape, more often an object – perhaps substituting a word here and there for one of my own, in order to smooth over false notes. Yes, that is something I have frequently resorted to, in the course of writing this history. At other times I was happy to exaggerate details of my past, details that were plausible, perhaps, but not indisputably true. I was like the unknown cartographer of the mappa mundi, he who when ignorant of lakes and towns sketched savage beasts and elephants, and in place of contour lines created improbable realms . . . and what kind of lunatic would use such a map to find her way? In short, I have been happy to tell stories. No longer. Now I would rather stay silent than risk telling a lie.

Forward.

. . .

Boarding school. What is there to say? I was unhappy and confused. I recall the cherry blossoms on the front lawn, and Mrs Ling, my English teacher, an unconscious whistler. I recall being made to run through a field of nettles, a collective punishment. I recall the stationery cupboard in which I hid during PE lessons. I had few friends, was alienated from the other girls, who figured me as a freak. My ears had begun to grow at an extraordinary rate. Already large when I left Nigeria at the age of fourteen, by my fifteenth birthday they had begun to develop thick veins and pendulous lobes, and felt far too heavy for my head. Those organs of hearing which I had once prized, and put all my energies into developing, now felt alien, ineffectual, crude, a pair of outsize fungal-growths sprouting from my head.

It was during this period that my fascination with the mappa mundi began. When I returned for the holidays my father would sometimes call me up to the attic to sit with him, although he did not sit but paced in a state of constant agitation, shedding ash from his cigarettes (I felt that those flakes were shedding from *him*, and that with each cigarette, he was gradually diminishing). One afternoon, his pacing making me dizzy, I tried to fix my attention on to a point of stillness in the room. The mappa mundi. I came to study it more closely on subsequent visits. I felt an affinity with the monstrous races depicted on the map. I knew I was one of them.

When my schooling finished I took a job ushering in a theatre in Edinburgh. It was summer, the city was hot, loud, dense, vivid, carnal, and I became deeply involved in the life of the theatre. I worked hard. I listened to music. I felt free for the first time since leaving Nigeria. I even fell in love – with Damaris, an actress, a thin, beautiful creature who occupied all my thoughts and just about toppled my soul.

Damaris wanted to know all about my father, his life, my relationship with him, and even his work in Nigeria, which I had figured as a cause of his madness. I told her what I knew: he was a broken man who had lost a great many illusions. What were these? He'd helped to build Lagos into a modern city; he'd brought to a peasant population the gift of city planning; he'd played a small part of the great enterprise of the British Empire. But really, I told her, he had done nothing more than project his own perverse fantasies on to Nigeria. All his life he'd believed in a kind of progress for humankind, and his work in Nigeria had been based on this idea. He believed Africa existed in a backward state of time, a wild and immature childhood which Empire would bring into the present age. It was a complete idea, I told her, blinding him to any other. But this idea of his hadn't worked out the way he'd hoped, and he – *we* – were forced to leave. Now he found himself without desires or energy. He'd lost his faith in Progress, I told her. (But I was wrong; my father had lost faith in Progress years before that, with my mother's death and the birth of a daughter and not a son.) In Lagos, I told her, he had been able to escape into dreams of town planning, so that he did not have to know his malaise. Now he fled in the face of it up to the attic, like birds flocking to the tree tops before a storm.

'He repulses me,' I told her.

'Why?' she said, horrified.

'He is a broken man. He brought it on himself with his bad faith in Empire.'

'You're a monster, Evie Steppman,' she said.

But Damaris was not satisfied and set me a task. I was to find out one thing about my father's life, something I didn't know, a story. She gave me a tape recorder for my birthday and instructed me to record him.

. . .

I found him in the attic. His hair was no longer blond but silvery, and sallow from tobacco smoke.

'Hello, Evie,' he said and backed into the corner. I felt a kind of effusive kinship towards him. Not filial, I don't want to suggest that. And yet it was a type of fondness, and for a moment I wanted to hold him in my arms. I shook out a rug, then laid it on a patch of floor and sat opposite him. We were silent for a while. Then I began to ask him questions about his past, his childhood. I knew that my father had been born in another country and had moved to Scotland as a child. But either sensing his own reticence, or from lack of interest, I had never asked more. Now, as I did, he started to speak, very softly, relating the events which saw him and his family undergo a change of nation, a change of name – in short, a turning away from his family's past. I put the headphones over my ears, switched the tape recorder on and held the microphone close to his mouth. His voice, heard in this intimate way through the headphones, was not weak as I had expected from someone so thin and dishevelled, but low, cracked, oddly powerful. I had disliked its intonation when he talked during my gestation, and I disliked it still, the bass pitch, the barely distinguishable quality of the vowel-sounds. Nevertheless, that evening I captured the story my father told, which I will transcribe in the following chapter.

The next time I saw him, he was terrible to contemplate. Pale, wearing the purple dressing-gown, he sat rocking on his mattress, a glazed look in his eyes. His face seemed to lack coordination, the wet mouth undisciplined. I approached. He didn't seem to see me. I remember very clearly. His inability to master his lips had spread to the whole of his face. After that he made almost no mark on the world, occasional moth-light footsteps perhaps, now and then a little noise, low nocturnal murmur-ings, whispers and interrupted cries, the sound of pacing and coaxing. He had withdrawn completely from practical affairs, and I felt that the objects in the midst of which he dwelt had taken the place of his personality, had come to represent him more truthfully than his presence in space. From that day on I gave my father up for lost. What still remained of him – the small shroud of his body and the handful of nonsensical oddities – would finally disappear one day, as unremarked as the grey heaps of ash beside his armchair, waiting to be blown away on the next windy day.

24

Jesus the Jew or How My
Father Acquired His Name

In a moment I will transcribe my father's story. The thought pleases me enormously. Not so much because I wish to reveal what my father told me that evening shortly before he died. No, my history is already overburdened with stories. It is the process that counts, the labour of transcribing his words. It is not a difficult process, although it is time-consuming, since the tape is damaged in places and, although my father talked at length, he didn't always make sense. Nevertheless, I hope, with repeated listening, to make a coherent story. What a happy prospect to stop writing my own history and make use of another's words!

I lean over, place the cassette into the tape recorder, close the lid, put my headphones on, take a deep breath and press play. The reels turn, the tape shuttles through the mechanism, I hear the hiss of warm static, that pool of shifting quiet which is one of the most beautiful sounds I have ever heard. Then, breaking the silence, as if coming to me from a great distance, I hear the sound of my father's voice.

. . .

When I was five years old I left with my family for Scotland. It was the summer of 1923, and we travelled to Lublin on the banks of the River Vistula, about four hundred miles from our home town.

That is how the tape begins. From what I can gather from the tape my father's father had been a doctor in a small town somewhere in North Poland. Because he was Jewish, he had been dismissed from his job and was unable to find work. Apparently in 1923 the government had passed a decree making it impossible for Jews to practise medicine. My father, bizarrely, and without saying how or why, says his parents had been promised the sale of a jam factory in Dundee, and took the decision to travel west, across Europe to Scotland.

The tape continues: There were three of us in the group that sat for three days and nights in a first-class carriage to Vienna, then Munich, Strasbourg and finally Calais, from where we took the boat to Dover. It was a strange route our broker had arranged. At the time I had no idea why we were moving to a different country. Nor do I remember much about the journey itself, only small glimpses snatched from the train window: the faces of peasants selling hot chestnuts, a team of horses which ran for a short while alongside our carriage, and the dawn, which I watched stealing across the panes of a station with an arched glass roof. It seems that, more vividly than the specific events of the journey, my father recalled the travelling itself. We were always moving, he says, if not overland or sea, then in our beds at station-side hotels, or else my hands were fidgeting in my pockets. In addition to the movement, he remembers this mood during the journey, which was of great anticipation, and strangely he wasn't afraid. But even these memories shift in his mind, he says; which strikes me as entirely appropriate, for he was constantly moving, and what seemed half-erased to him in adulthood, was then too: the packed trains, the blurred scenery, the sleep that was always broken.

The tape continues: When we got to Dover the officer asked to see our papers. We had two or three surnames and, what is more, the official did not recognize my parents' marriage certificate, so he wasn't prepared to let us enter the country. My parents must have carried bribes, since we were allowed to enter. On our new papers our surnames had been cut short and changed, I have forgotten from what. And in fact it felt as if we had left our old life behind at the station in Lublin. It wasn't until several years later, after an incident which altered the course of my life irrevocably, an incident which, though in the general sense was minor and insignificant, meant so extraordinarily much to me that even now, some fifty years later, I still burn with the memory of it, the shame and the sudden intrusion into my life that impelled me to renounce not only my parents, but also our religion.

We settled in a village called Newport, my father continues, which overlooks the Tay estuary. I still remember the view we had of the river, and of the railway bridge, which was the second on that site, since I learned that the first had collapsed in 1879, only two years after it had been built. I remember the sunsets, which were so dramatic one felt a pain as the red light died. My father bought the jam factory and put what was left of his life into the business. I seldom saw either him or my mother, both because they worked long hours and, since I was often unwell, and attended school only now and then, I was sent to a home for sick children, Comerton House, just a few miles outside Newport. By that time I was speaking English fluently, which even as a small child in Poland had come easily to me, and already I spoke it without an accent. The children at the home found it difficult to pronounce my name, Rechavam, so I became known, simply, as Rex.

I remember, my father says, my days at Comerton House more keenly than almost any other time in my life. There was a large garden which ran alongside the road and was separated from it by a wall. The garden itself was divided into two sections. In the fore-section, the smaller part nearest the house, the janitor, Mr Welsh, grew our vegetables. Further back, concealed from the house, was the larger, always slightly wild section. Nettles grew abundantly in summer, and, although Mr Welsh cut them back, they seemed to spring up all the taller. There were playthings in this back section, a set of swings, a crooked seesaw which gave you splinters and a roundabout on which we were not allowed to play. But best of all was a strange contraption called a Witch's Hat. It was shaped just like that, a conical structure of metal rods with a wooden bench that ran around the lip. The whole thing was raised a yard or so off the ground by a central pole crowned by a ball bearing. This simple device allowed the Witch's Hat to rotate from its tip. We sat on the bench and with our feet drove it around and around, and all of us, the thin, pale children, most of whom had ginger hair, liked it better than anything else at Comerton House. I remember the nights too, which I dreaded. In the library, a large pine-panelled room which was used also as the assembly hall, the gym in winter and for staging the Christmas play, there, among the poorly stocked shelves, was a book of ghost stories. I knew it would terrify me to look at it, but I couldn't help myself. I always regretted looking at that book, and I regretted my curiosity, and that the other children brought it out, others who, unlike me, seemed to enjoy their fear, and for whom darkness held a weird appeal.

I dreaded the nights in Comerton House. By dinner time, two hours before curfew, I would start to shake and involuntarily wave my spoon. Eating had always been difficult for me, and fear of the approaching night intensified my distaste for food, especially meat, which I have always associated with murder, and it was during that period, the time of the great fear, that I became a vegetarian. At night I would wake into a foreign land. My shoulders shook uncontrollably, and I would draw my blankets over my head. I believed that unless every part of me was covered the banshee would be able to take me away, to where I did not know. There were two of us in the dorm who experienced acute fear at night. We had an agreement that if one needed to go to the bathroom we could wake the other. We would hold hands and advance half-running along the hall, all the while chanting, as loudly as we dared, *We're getting married, We're getting married*, not stopping as we passed water but only when we were back beneath the blankets. In fact the whole of Comerton House was filled with noise at night, for sick children away from home tend not to sleep, and when they do they almost always have nightmares. I've since learned that the home is now privately owned, and I often imagine the present occupants must be aware of the noise that by night filled Comerton House. For where have all those cries gone?

At this point on the tape my father starts to ramble. I hear the fizz of matches as he lights his cigarettes. He goes on to talk more about his daily life at Comerton House, the lessons, fears, rituals, punishments and so on. But I am unable to arrange them into any kind of coherent order. No matter. For long stretches as I worked my father's voice flowed effortlessly from the tape to my ears, from my ears to my fingers, from my fingers to the keyboard, and from there on to the screen.

What a relief to forget my history and copy someone else's words!

The tape continues: What I remember best of all is my dearest friend at the home. His name was Nicholas. Let me tell you how we met. Once after lunch Nicholas approached me in the corridor and said he had a secret to tell me, he said it was a serious matter which no one else knew about and would put both our lives in danger. I was to meet him at the Witch's Hat later that afternoon. He was there when I arrived and invited me to sit. He looked me sternly in the eyes and told me that he was the son of the Devil. I believed him instantly. But to prove it he pulled up his shirt and showed me a birthmark on the left side of his chest. It seemed no more than a faint web of veins showing beneath the skin, but he told me to look harder and I saw it resembled a medallion, a small circle that enclosed a tiny crenulated shape, like a rose. *Have you ever seen anything like it?* Nicholas asked. Of course I had not. He said the secret of his ancestry had plagued him all his life, that he had never been at home in this world, and had felt condemned to wander. But since he had told me, Nicholas continued, he felt much better both about his sinister paternity and about things in general. He asked if I had any sweets, which I did, since my mother had only recently sent a package, and I offered to share them with him. But he told me he must have them all. He opened his large eyes very wide, and I gave him my sweets. On another occasion he stole my wooden train, I knew it was him, although I was unable to prove it. Nonetheless, we became friends. I learned that in fact he wasn't the son of the Devil but of a widower. Shortly after this, Nicholas and I became inseparable. We did everything together. I remember we made declarations of love by the Witch's Hat, and one evening cut small lesions in our wrists and mixed the blood. Yet there was a spiteful side to our relationship. I forgave him for tricking me into giving up my sweets, but I never forgot what he told me, and I think there lived in me an impression that he was somehow connected to dark forces. He was in my mind a golem, or a child-moloch to whom my love was sacrificed. There were times when I was afraid of him, when he looked at me intensely with those large dark-brown eyes, or when he told me he had been in contact with a banshee and had instructed her to take me away.

When I was ten and Nicholas eleven something happened, which at the time seemed relatively insignificant, but which now I see was an important point in a friendship that was soon to fall apart. You see, we both had beautiful singing voices. And for each of the three years I stayed at Comerton House the children put on a Christmas play, a rendition of the nativity. There was a tradition at the home whereby one member of the class was given the part of Balthazar, the leader of the wise men, whose role was to sing a eulogy to the Lord. The lucky child was he whose voice was judged sweetest by the home staff. We each chose a verse from 'In the Bleak Midwinter' and stood in the assembly hall to deliver our recital. This was one month before Christmas. On the night of the performance the winner would sing the entire carol in front of the parents. It is hard to convey the importance of this role to the children of Comerton House. I think that most of us, though each from a prosperous family, were not used to feeling at all special, except that each of us was damaged in some particular way. Several months before the day of the competition we began to practise our chosen verse. We compared voices and judged our closest rivals. Nicholas had a very pure and natural singing voice and without effort reached the highest notes. I had a more roughly cadenced voice, although I felt I was able to inspire deeper emotion. In each of the previous years we had been overlooked, but in the third year of my stay at Comerton House I was given the part of Balthazar. Nicholas was deeply affected by my victory. I think he felt it as an insult. I was thrilled to be playing the part, yet I was careful to hide my happiness, and although I felt I concealed it well, I suppose it showed on my face and gestures and in my whole person.

If the sole effect of my winning the part of Balthazar had been the cooling of our friendship, says my father, then the event would not have lodged so firmly in my memory. But it had a second and, I now know, more destructive and significant effect on my life, an effect that, in addition to harming the friendship between myself and Nicholas, cut me irrevocably from my parents; not physically, for I was still too young to leave their care, but in my heart, which from that day on turned both from them and the Jewish faith. On the night of the performance, held in the large pine-panelled hall at the back of Comerton House, my parents arrived early. I had not told them anything about the performance, only that I would be singing a solo. They sat in the audience as we, the children, each dressed in his costume, gathered behind the makeshift stage. The performance was proceeding well, the baby Jesus had appeared among the animals. I came on to the stage and, together with my two associates, moved beside the manger. The piano began to play. I held my breath for the duration of the introductory bars. Then I started to sing. I kept my eyes focused on the bookshelf at the far end of the hall. I saw a spider on a thick volume. There was a fly caught in its web. The stage was brightly lit. Soon after the second chorus I became aware of a movement in the audience. It was my father. He had risen from his chair. People turned to look. I was singing the third verse.

He walked quickly out of the hall and into the dark garden. The door slammed behind him. My eyes followed him as he walked down the garden path, and I faltered for what seemed like an inordinately long time. The piano played on without me, and when I tried to sing again, I had forgotten the words. I stood there in front of the crowd, paralysed. Later, back at our house, my father called me into his study and told me that I was no longer allowed to go to school at Comerton House. Then he said something which I have never been able to forget. He told me that Jesus was a Jew, that Matthew was a Jew, that so were Mark and John, and that Luke too was a Jew, although he had been born a Gentile. The following summer I was taken from Comerton House, and I never went back; the period of my sickness had long since ended. But I felt a sickness in my heart, which over time became a feeling of emptiness that has returned every so often.

Here, said my father, this is me in the garden at Comerton House.

That is when he handed me the photograph. I must have glanced at it at the time, even taken it to show Damaris, but I don't remember. Sometime later I must have stored it with the tape recorder, because that is where I found it. I am holding it now, before my computer; the light from the screen reveals a small boy no more than nine years old, sitting on a swing. In the picture, taken many years before I was born, and which I look at now some three decades after my father's death, I see him in a curious grey-blue light. He is looking fixedly at the camera. Behind him rises a stone wall partially covered with ivy. The boy has small white hands that grip the twine of the swing. He is wearing winter clothes: knitted cap, house slippers, ribbed woollen socks, kilt, tweed waistcoat beneath an open blazer. His eyes seem to stare back at me with great anxi-ety. The way he holds himself – stiff-necked, eyes focused intensely on the lens – expresses great worry, as if he felt like an intruder in the garden, as if he feared that at any moment someone would come to turn him out, as if the swing, the ivy, the vegetables, the paths and all the lovely things had been intended for another boy entirely, and that his enjoyment of them was eclipsed by the knowledge that at any moment now this error would be discovered, and that he would be obliged to give up what was the only truly happy period of his life.

25

Transcribing Damaris' Diary: Britain

The night my father told his stories, the wind blew strongly. I can hear it whistling and moaning in the background of the tape. It got through the walls, stirred the air, raised dust and ash from my father's spent cigarettes and made him cough. Today in my attic the wind is blowing strongly too. All kinds of eerie, whining noises float up through the floor. The sheets of my history, which cover the skylight, flutter in the breeze, like outsized moths. It took me two nights to transcribe my father's story. I worked for hours without pause. Sitting at my desk, headphones over my ears, listening, copying, stopping the tape, rewinding, watching the numbers tick on the counter, noting where the relevant details lay, going over them again, pausing, copying, beginning again – such happiness I have not known in years! As soon as I finished the transcription I printed it out, twice by mistake, which gave me a thrilling sensation. I even laughed as the printer coughed up the sheets and delivered them out on to the floor. I didn't pick them up or read them but just left them right where they lay. When my laughter stopped I felt quiet and calm. I sat on my mattress and closed my eyes, thinking of nothing in particular. I felt terrifically happy. Apart from the moaning of the wind, the attic was quiet. Every now and then there was a gust, fluttering my sheets. Sometime later I stood and began to busy myself with domestic tasks. I swept the floor. I emptied my bucket. I went down to the pantry and renewed my supply of beans. I had a sudden urge to take a walk. Strange. I had not left the house in quite some time. I got dressed and brushed my teeth. I stuffed my ears with cotton wool. It was late morning. Quite a breeze. I stood for a while letting the wind play with my hair. On the way to the beach I had a scuffle with a cat. I dusted myself off then walked on the sand. I watched the dogs, many different breeds, chasing the surf. Their owners I noted too. The Lindsay twins. Mrs Ewan.

Now I am back at my desk. Before me is the diary that belonged to Damaris. There was a time in my history when I would have paused to describe it at length, noting its appearance, its size, make, the image on its cover, as well as the condition of the paper, its general state of decay and so on. I might have related how Damaris left her diary behind when she left me. Perhaps I would have talked of the difficulties of deciphering her handwriting, how she never used 'and' but a sign which looks like an inverted 'y'. No longer. All I can say at this late stage is that I brought the diary from the wardrobe and opened it somewhere near the beginning.

28 May 1972

Night falls and so do I. The terrors. Always on tour and in cities like this. What's his word again? Spectral? Edinburgh, he said, is like a pen-and-ink drawing left out in the rain. Rehearsals going well. The most beautiful drowner he's ever seen, he said.

Silent terrors, and they silence me too when I'm awake because I can't describe them. They turn me to stone. Ironic really, is what I think whenever I sneak off in between rehearsals to go stand frozen on the Royal Mile, acting the statue. He'd go mad if he knew.

1 June

Today is his birthday. Champagne after rehearsals in the theatre bar, this far out little cellar dive with red-check tablecloths and candles in old wine bottles. One by one the rest of them leave until it's just him and me. Then he went to the toilet, and I left. Walking out the door, I saw the barmaid give me this look. I've seen her before. She works as an usher here. Strange bird.

2 June

This morning at rehearsal I winked at him. He ignored me. He won't have liked being left like that. As though I'd just let him pounce! He looked more annoyed than usual during the lost in the forest scene when Jack has to carry me across the river. Me and Jack had a laugh about that, wondering which of us he was more jealous of. We open in six days. I'm out of money. So tomorrow after rehearsal I'll spend the evening as I'll have doubtless spent the night, dead still, dead silent. A living statue.

It's not just the money. I like being looked at. And it's different, in the street, in the middle of the crowd. When you're on stage, the audience can't touch you, even if they want to. Out in the street, they could but they don't. They know the rules. I like that. You pick your spot, lay down your crate, put out your tin, step on to the crate, assume a pose. They flip a coin into the tin and I shudder into motion, then halt, only moving again when they drop in more coins. Mostly it's kids and couples, tourists. But sometimes it's men on their own. With them it's different. To them I'm an object. How could I not be, a statue! They stare openly, rudely, crudely, knowing I can't stare back.

They walk round me, farmers inspecting cattle at auction, knowing I can't turn to follow their gaze. My costume, black leotard and tights, a shadow made solid with my face painted out a ghostly white. They stare, then, having established they're masters of the situation, drop money into the tin, allowing me a few seconds of freedom. Turns me on a bit, I think.

4 June

That bargirl from the other night. She came up to me today, as I was playing the statue. Girl I say but more like a young man with her cricketer's stride, hands in trouser pockets. That's how she approaches, and then she stands in front of me, never minding that a couple of young boys are there, about to make me move. She elbows them to one side then stares so hard at me she freaks them and they skedaddle. Meanwhile I'm still standing there, still. Usually, I can't look over the person looking me over – being looked at makes it impossible to do any looking yourself. Like being onstage when the footlights blind you to the individual members of the audience. But this bird spends so long in front of me, drops so many coins into my tin, that with each move I'm able to take in a bit more, until I get a sense of the whole of her. Which is, strong and determined like a Channel swimmer. One from the 1920s. Tall, flat-chested, severe bob. And those ears! A boat with its oars out, I thought. Something paddle-ish

Paddle-ish!

Something paddle-ish about her shape too. Something Edwardian about her. But she's young, my age. And so the young Edwardian man-woman

Man-woman!

the young Edwardian woman stands in front of me for quite a while, giving me this funny look. Different funny to the other night, but still funny. Head to one side, smile lopsided like it's about to slip off her face altogether, looking for all the world like she's expecting something, like she's waiting for me to do something she's known all along I was about to do. That annoyed me, and I wanted to wrongfoot her. So I gave her the Seven Deadly Sins. When she dropped in her change, I moved into a different position. More coins. Again, I moved position. I gave her several versions of Lust. The one where I look like a gargoyle. The ones from the convent I used to commune with during mass. She didn't seem impressed. Or unimpressed. It was as if she was expecting me to assume a particular pose, and, when I didn't, felt the need to keep paying up until I moved into the exact position that would satisfy her. What this position was, I never knew, cos after an hour or so of this, I saw her pat her pockets and look at me sadly. I knew from her gestures and sorry expression that she'd run out of money, and I knew too she'd come back. And it was funny, I realized as she walked away, never looking back as she loped off in that way of hers, how she'd communicated all this to me without a single word.

5 June

Yesterday she came back. I gave her Pride every time. Hand on hip, chin tilted, and, as I turned my cheek, I thought I saw the wardrobe girl, Tamara, passing through the crowd. I hope not. She's having a thing with Jack and doesn't like me. She's bound to tell on me.

6 June

That strange girl came back this morning. But this time, she just put down a crate of her own, painted white in contrast to mine, positioned herself in front of me, in my direct line of sight, face a foot from my face, and stood still as a statue herself. Copying my exact pose. For the full twenty-seven minutes she was there – according to the clock tower – passers-by just kept passing by, staring, to be sure, but at her, instead of me. No one stopped to put money in my tin. Don't know if they found the whole scene too strange or too intimate – it felt both – they just walked straight past me and my odd, inverse shadow. She was dressed all in white, gauzy white fabric like paper with the light shining through it. And her face all smeared in black boot polish! Between us, this channel of silence, despite the mad noise of the crowd all around. But though we stood in identical poses, and though I now had a clear image of her, I still felt like it was her looking at me, because, I suppose, the rules of our game meant that she could, if she chose, move any time she liked. But also, there was something – what's that word from the Commandments – covetous? – something about her stare, trying to claim me, her look pinning me as though she was a butterfly collector and me a brittle and unwieldy specimen. There was a kind of effort in her stare. Then, abruptly, she broke out of her position, stepped down, picked up her crate and strode briskly off. And it really was like she'd pinned me in place, because I realized, after she had left my line of vision, that I would have run after her, had I been able. And this bothered me. Me, who never runs after anyone.

What a joy to transcribe from Damaris' diary!

8 June

Fuck fuck fuck. He only caught me! Didn't see him till it was too late. I was looking out for her. When he came out of nowhere I really did fucking freeze. His face went as white as mine in mime. We open tonight, he says, You'll need your rest, and sends me back to the b'n'b telling me, We will talk about this later. So I'm lying here now picking at the bobbly bedspread, supposedly resting up for tonight, half of me wondering what the fuck he's going to do about all this – if he gets me kicked off the American tour! – while the other half wonders if she came back to find me this afternoon.

9 June

We opened last night. Full house. We went down well but we won't know what's what till the papers tomorrow, if there's even any mention of us. He was completely satisfied with my performance. And I don't mean by that that I was satisfactory, more that everything he was hoping for, I did. I felt that even on stage, but he could hardly look me in the face when he told me as much afterwards. Not after running into me in the street like that. I have betrayed him. Made a fool of him for the second time in two weeks. Afterwards, we had drinks in the theatre bar. I looked for her, but she was not there. Instead this Orcadian chick with those faraway fisherman's eyes some have. I asked about her colleague, a bit embarrassed when describing her, and she says, Oh you mean Evie. She's away looking after her da. She wasn't able to tell me any more. So I invited her to come and have drinks with us. But she was shy of me as pretty girls often are, and said she couldn't, she was working. D came down later, said how much he'd loved the show. I noticed the kinds of looks he attracted, and the look he gave in response. Acknowledging their acknowledgement of his fame, as though it was he who had recognized them. And it made me think of her. Evie. That look she gave me that first night. As though she knew me.

10 *June*

So this is how he's getting his revenge. He's using the reviews as an excuse. Some are cautious, some are catty, some are raving. And one was smutty. I didn't look virginal enough to play the title role, ha!

Ha!

He thinks what the reviews are saying is that something is missing. He wants to freak 'em all out, he says. So this is what he's done: in the mornings, we're rehearsing the whole show again, with me as the boy and Jack as the girl. I have to forget my part and learn Jack's and vice versa. Everyone else has to play to me where they played to Jack and vice versa. Unlearn in order to create he says, with a foxy smile, aimed straight at me. The cheese weasel. We both know what this is about.

16 *June*

Exhausted. Sleep walked through rehearsals. He says I'm miming being a mime. Ha. Ha.

17 *June*

Today in rehearsals, when me and Jack were tripping up on bits of our old roles that remain like debris in our memories, he said again, Unlearn to create! Unlearn to create! No, I screamed. DESTROY! I screamed louder, DESTROY TO CREATE. Then I kicked a jug of water across the stage which smashed hysterically, and I walked out.

18 *June*

Last night was our last night and the opening of the reversed version. We all felt something. It felt right. And knowing this, we felt exhausted. After a few drinks, we said our goodbyes until Oxford next week and slipped off separately into the night. A hot night in Edinburgh, damp heat off bare skin and the smell of sweat mixing in with reefer and patchouli. Got a bit stirred up by all that and found myself wandering down a cobbled side-street when someone grips my elbow.

It's her. That bird. Evie.

You're better as the boy, she said. When she smiled it threw me a bit. A real freak when she smiles. Nothing wrong with the smile itself except it doesn't belong to her face. It's like one of those children's flip-books where the pages are cut into top, middle and bottom sections which you match randomly. The top half of her face does not go with the bottom half.

I've been to every one of your shows, she said. This did not surprise me.

We ducked into a bar, to a tiny table in the corner where the walls were all pasted over with playbills and covering those a slight sheen of condensation from the heat of the summer bodies pressed in together, and we ordered some red wine, and I said, How's your Dad? Mad, she says, and we both laugh, surprised. That's where you get it from then, I say, and she doesn't smile at this but says, What do you mean? And I chuck her under the chin. Last time I saw you you were more of a statue than I was myself! An experiment, she mumbles. I don't know if the mumbling is her being embarrassed about admitting this or because I just touched her face. Both, I realize. What kind of experiment? An experiment in (mumbles). In what? I cup my ear, miming, Pardon? I still can't hear. I lean closer. She can see down my shirt. No bra as usual. She jumps back like she's been burned. An experiment in what? SILENCE she says, louder than she meant. Asked her to explain. The essence of mime is silence. She says this quietly. The essence of mime is imitation, I say. And I tell her where the word comes from. It's how we learn. How we learn to do anything. By copying. And then I notice that we are both in the same pose, elbows up on the table, chin in hands, and when she clocks that I've clocked this I look straight at her. She drops her gaze. You are a vessel of silence. She is mumbling again. I am a mirror, I say. What you see is what you see. So I tell her what he said in our first ever rehearsal, in his little speech about mime (a contradiction in terms): 'The fire which I see flames in me. I can know that fire only when I identify with it, and play at being fire. I give my fire to the fire.'

I reach out my fingers as though to stroke her face. Again, she jumps back, fearing to be burned. I reach for my cigarettes instead. After the wine came whisky. She asked me about the statue thing. Why I did it. So I told her. I like being looked at. I'd imagine you get looked at anyway. It's very zen, I said, just emptying yourself out like that.

I told her a joke. This couple, two statues in Hyde Park, are granted a wish by a fairy who feels sorry for them. They wish to be human for the day. They spend it touring London, seeing the sights, going to a fancy restaurant and so on. At midnight the fairy comes back to meet them in Hyde Park to reverse the spell, as agreed, but the statues are not there. Then the fairy hears rustling in the bushes and goes to investigate. The fairy finds one of the statues clutching a pigeon, while the other one says, Quick, hold him still while I shit on his head.

Then Evie told me the story of the Happy Prince. Who wasn't really, in the end. The whole time she tells the story, she's not looking at me. She's smoothing over the same patch of wax which has dripped from the candle on to the table. She smooths away at it and tells me the story of a young prince who has all that he desires, and lives a decadent, pampered life until he dies. Once he is dead, he is turned into a statue. A statue as beautiful as he was in real life, Evie says, with skin made of pure gold, and eyes of sapphires. His statue is set up high over the city, where he can see all the misery that was hidden from him during his life of luxury. The poor seamstress with the feverish child who cries for oranges she cannot afford. The young writer, freezing in his garret, unable to complete his work of genius for he is too cold. The prince sees all this, Evie says, now scratching at the wax with her little finger. And it kills him. As a statue, he is powerless. He can't move. It's only now, as I'm writing, that I realize what a sweet, sad story this is. One day, Evie says, a swallow comes to shelter under the statue of the prince, on his way to join his friends in Egypt for the winter. The prince asks the swallow to delay his journey by a day, and to deliver the jewels in his scabbard to the poor people he sees. The swallow obliges and delays his journey to help the prince. The next day, the prince makes a similar request, asking the swallow to delay his departure by another day to deliver valuable bits of himself – gold leaf from his skin, sapphires from his eyes – to the poor. And now that the prince has given away the jewels in his eyes, he is blind. So the swallow stays with him, and tells him stories of the misery he sees, stripping the rest of the gold leaf from the prince at his direction and distributing it to all these unfortunates. In the end the swallow decides to abandon his journey to Egypt and stay with the prince, because he loves him. The swallow dies from the cold. The prince's lead heart cracks. And the prince – now stripped of his jewels and his gold leaf – is considered shabby and unsightly by the town councillors so he is taken down from his pedestal and scrapped.

When Evie reaches the end of her story she is crying. And then she says, Do you know why the swallow fell behind his friends on their way to Egypt, why he delayed his journey in the first place? No, I said. You must read the story then, Evie said. Oscar Wilde.

We must have been pretty drunk by the time we left the bar cos she had one of my smokes and she doesn't. She snatched it out of the pack as we were leaving the bar, and when I went to light it for her she grabbed my wrist to look at the matchbox. It was a souvenir one from the play. She asked to keep it.

19 *June*

A strange and sad and funny day. Woke this morning to a note left by Evie. She'd obviously stayed the night. Don't remember her being there. Would you meet me today at 3 p.m. by the cemetery gates?

Which fucking cemetery? Too hungover to think of how I might start asking so I leave it to chance and walk around the b'n'b in circles – bigger and bigger circles – till I hit one. It's after 3 p.m. She's not there. That's how I know it's the wrong one. I continue circling. I hit another one. It's 4 p.m.-ish. She's not there either. I carry on. A third – Edinburgh's full of cemeteries! – a fourth, and she's there, waiting. I asked if she wanted to show me a grave. Said she was taking me to visit Mr Rafferty. Her grandfather. He was quite mad, and we would be visiting him at the institution where he lived.

To someone else it might have looked liked a country house. Walked into the building and felt small with something sad and familiar. That smell. The convent came back in a rush. Evie warned me that Mr Rafferty might mistake me for someone else and if so, would I mind playing along? Of course, I make my living doing just that!

He's in his seventies with a face like a soft felt hat, one that has been sat on, with its hollows and bulges. Hair a deep blue black and obviously dyed, giving him a sort of surprised look. Gave me the most delighted smile, Evie's smile. But on his face, it fit.

Called me Julia and gave me a big hug, crying into my hair. Glowered at Evie as though she were intruding. Called her Rex. Who were these people he had taken us for? He swept us into the room. Quite bare. Just a bed, desk and chair, and wardrobe. The chair was set askew, the desk cluttered. I saw that he'd made some strange little object out of what looked like tiddlywinks sellotaped together. He grabbed it, then presented it to me with a sort of bow. Thank you, I said. He'd been working on it for months, apparently. I made appreciative noises. Evie peered over at it, and, addressing me as Julia, asked if I had ever seen such a beautiful timepiece! No, I murmured, choking back the urge to laugh. Mr Rafferty said it was his wedding gift to me. He looked into my eyes and squeezed my hands. His gaze made me think of the near-human look you see in pictures of chimpanzees sometimes.

After, me and Evie went to the pub. She told me she planned to travel to Easdale, a tiny island off the West Coast of Scotland, for a few days, to stay in a friend's cottage. Asked me to join her.

So I said, Why not?

It's only now, writing this, that I'm wondering why I said

yes. Sometimes I don't know what I think until I write about it in my diary. Like that reed. Oh! Now I remember. Something from our night together. Early in the morning, asking Evie, pestering Evie, to tell me about the swallow from the story, why he had delayed his journey. Eventually she mumbles, Fell in love. I pester some more then she says, Reed. The swallow fell in love with a reed. This silent, graceful thing just blown about in the wind. It never even noticed him. And now something that Evie said in the bar that night comes back to me. A vessel of silence. More emptiness, I think. There's got to be a link between that and keeping this diary. There's got to be a link between that and saying yes to invitations made by near-strangers.

20 June

We drove here in a single night. I don't know why she wanted to drive at night, but she did, and that was the plan, and I was just bumming a ride so what could I say? The others were already on their way to Oxford when she pulled up in her dad's Morris Minor. Dusk had just fallen, the sky was that fairytale blue. A few stars starting to poke through. I slung my bag in the back and myself in the front. I was bad driving company, just dozing off in the front seat and twitching awake at intervals to fiddle about with the radio. It made her wince. She is sensitive to sound. Vibrates a bit like a violin string depending on what's playing. Rock got her all taut like she was overstrung. I left on some jazz until the lights of a combine harvester flashing across us woke me up. And I thought harvesting was daylight work, such a city girl am I! I found something beautiful and classical, and she seemed to slacken, and her eyes went dreamy and a little less, well, pebbly looking. We listened together to this sad noble music which I thought was Mozart, but the only Mozart I knew was jolly stuff. This got quieter and quieter, or rather, fewer and fewer instruments played, until there was only this lonely violin. Towards the end, Evie lifted a hand from the wheel and then brought it down, as if wielding a conductor's baton, in time with the final note. But there was no final note. Or rather, the note she was anticipating was not played. She had got it wrong. We both laughed. But of course I didn't really miss that last note, she said. What do you mean? Well, everyone thinks that music begins and ends with the first and last notes. And it doesn't? No. Music begins and ends with silence, she said.

The radio announcer was explaining how Haydn had come to write the symphony. Evie was about to speak. I told her to shush cos I wanted to listen and she gives me this funny look. You like stories, don't you? she said. Who doesn't?

Woke up to Oban at sunrise. Drove up to Ellanbeich where Evie turned off the engine and slumped over the wheel like we'd crashed. Exhaustion. Slept for a couple of hours then stood on the dock by our bags, waiting for the first ferry, drinking bitter black coffee from styrofoam cups. Just the smell of it when you're wrung out with tiredness! And the smell mixing in with old fish and wet rope and the slapping waves . . . We're at the cottage now. My room is right at the top, under the eaves. Ha! So why come here? To get away from him, from the others, to be taken somewhere I've never been before? We'll sleep a little and then explore.

21 June

Not writing so much as dragging my pen across the page. Out here the salt air comes at you from everywhere, this being an island and a tiny one at that. It leaches your energy and turns your blood to porridge. Eyelids at halfmast. All I want to do is sleep. But I have to write about today. After the tour, it's no surprise I'm exhausted. But this air! By the time we came back this afternoon we were sleepwalking. Maybe the air made us mad. Maybe we were dreaming. I would pinch myself but there are scratch marks from the bushes. And the light! So late here and so light. It won't leave us alone. Maddening and magical and not like daylight but like night with the darkness leached out of it.

We started off fresh enough. A clear morning, like a kid's crayon drawing, green lawn, blue sky, white cottage, red roof, yellow gorse. We ran outside, down the springy grass to the path. Two dogs came, a sheepdog and a black labrador. Dogs sometimes look like they feel an excess of joy, so much it confuses them and they almost seem in pain with it. The sheepdog and the lab bounded on ahead, looking back every now and then to make sure we were following, as though they'd arranged to take us on a tour. We let them. They took us through tangles of wildflowers, over hillocks and hummocks and down to the rocks, where the air became damper and saltier as we approached the sea, turning, eventually, to seaspray. Then we could get no closer as the waves got high and snatched at the rocks and whatever might be on them and we shouted and laughed and scrabbled back to a safe distance as fast as we could. She is clumsy, I've noticed, and looks like a puppet when she runs. Not a puppet, no, one of those Victorian children's toys, paper figures with jointed limbs that swivel stiffly. The dogs wandered off, and with them went Evie's energy. Before, with the dogs, she had run with me, not saying much, just laughing, almost hysterically, harder and harder, as if her laugh was something funny which made her laugh even more. But now she was quiet. With the dogs gone she seemed to feel more alone with me. We came inland a little, into the open, where there was nothing else to focus on except each other. Whenever I made some comment, she only mumbled. When I looked at her, she turned her eyes away, seemed to struggle not to turn her *head* away. She's the shyest person I've ever met. There was something about her nervousness which provoked me. We came to an abandoned quarry which had been flooded. We stood on the edge and looked down. Sunbeams reaching right into the water. Up went my dress, down went my knickers, off came my shoes. Come on! I said to Evie. She couldn't look at me. She shuffled around, trying to unhook her bra under her t-shirt and slip off her knickers under her skirt. I leaped out over the edge. Water so cold, it stung. She asked me what the water was like. Refreshing! (teeth chattering). In she jumped and up she came, gasping and laughing. We swam. The ruins of a roman bath. Water slate blue, smooth, calm, shadowy. The walls sheer rock flecked with gold. When I got tired of swimming I started on Evie. She's easy to tease. I ducked down underwater and she started thrashing around, trying to cover herself up. She needn't have bothered, all I saw was a greenish white glow. I grabbed for her feet, she kicked out, I came up, pretended she'd hit me in the face, she swam up to me all concerned then I splashed her. It was fun. When we got tired of that we thought about going back. And then she realized. How are we supposed to get out? I pointed to some rocks and laughed when I saw her realize we would have to climb them naked and walk all the way round to fetch our clothes.

The sun was bright but we were cold. The best thing to do was run out quick and warm yourself like a lizard on one of the rocks higher up which got the sun. That's what I did. When

I looked down to find Evie she looked so funny I had to ask her what the fuck she was doing. What do you mean? She was cross. You look like some creature crawling out of the primordial soup. It was true. She was crawling over the rocks on her belly but with arse and legs tucked under. Trying to show as little of herself as possible. So I stood high up on my rock and stretched my beautiful arms out to the sun and lifted my breasts to the sun and turned up my beautiful face to the sun and said, Here, this is what a woman looks like, and she looked up at me from the rocks below. That is what *you* look like. And what do you look like? I said. She slowly stood up from her horizontal crouch. Long, white feet, strong white legs, flat hips, a fluffy, tea-coloured bush, concave belly, long waist, small low breasts with large pink nipples, wide shoulders. I can't say she has a body I want, but I've had people with bodies I wanted less. And I cannot say I wanted *her* because she was nothing I wanted, not sassy or cute or strong or sly or ironic or teasing or searching or dangerous or pure or delightful or feral or any of the other things that have made me look past a body I don't want to the force of the person within. She is clumsy, awkward, bizarre, self-absorbed. But I like the way she looks at me. And there is always one thing. One thing to want about someone. Her sides, her long waist and flanks, like a boy's, I liked, I decided. And so I reached out my hand, and she climbed up the rocks, upright this time, and took it.

We must have looked like a painting to him, the young guy out walking his dog who saw us in the distance, me and Evie holding hands. Another woman would have squealed instead of the sound Evie actually made, a kind of surprised bark like a seal. Before I knew it she had shoved me into a bush and fallen in on top of me.

I was held in suspension. It hurt to move.

When the knowledge of the branches became old I became aware of Evie's weight on my back, her breasts pressing into me, and a softness, her bush, on my arse. And close to this, suddenly, barking – the dog. Honey! Away home! A smile in the guy's voice. The dog yelped with disappointment as her master dragged her off, whistling. We stayed there a while. Evie's breath in my ear, first a sound, then a warmth. Then, very slowly, she started to move on me. The branches needling but she didn't care. Slowly, I felt her getting wet, slippery, faster, her breath hot in my ear, her lips not quite touching me, and me suddenly wanting to feel a kiss and what I got then was a lick, she was licking my ear and she was grinding, pressing me into the needles, and then that sealbark again and she was still.

What a joy! To copy Damaris' diary, to type out words no longer my own, leaves me feeling calm. My whole being throbs sweetly. Every now and then I pause to gaze around the attic, at my skylight, which gives off a white luminousness, and then at the piles of papers, of which Damaris' diary is just one among many, barely distinguishable from my other objects. And yet those papers, which until recently I have thought of as just another kind of object, decaying in the moist air, like the rest, seem to take on an enormous importance. They seem to emit a special kind of radiance. I can think of nothing better than to take them in my hands, spread them out on my desk and rifle their precious contents – not so much because of what they say, but because they contain thousands of words to transcribe.

We got our clothes back. We dressed without speaking. On the way home, she was quiet again, but not self-conscious at all this time. No, self-absorbed, dreamy. This made me angry. When we got into the cottage, I felt like punishing her. I brought her into the front room. Evie, I said. What you did in that bush. She smiled. You hurt me, I said. I sat on the edge of the couch. I slipped off my knickers and pulled up my dress. I lay back and opened my legs. You need to soothe me, I said. And she kneeled down before me, and I took her head in my hands and I guided her mouth to my cunt.

Later this evening. She's a terrible cook. She thinks adding lots of cream to the dish (a mixture of chicken, red wine and orange juice) will improve it. It hasn't. But it could have been my being in the kitchen. She seemed clumsy. Horribly shy. My glance was caustic to her. When she poured in the cream, she dropped the tub and it went everywhere. I got up and took her hand and licked it off. Then in between her fingers, slowly.

When you are drunk and you fall it doesn't hurt, not until the drink's worn off. Then you feel tender and offended at gravity. You feel more mortal than you did before. And so it was with this salt air, and Evie, I think. It made her drunk. And drunk on that she'd touched me all over in the branches and only now was she starting to really feel me. With my creamy lips, my creamy tongue, I kissed her. I knew from this great feeling she gave off of . . . What was it? Relief? Gratitude? I knew then that no one had touched her like that before. I could feel how much she was feeling. And the more she felt, the more I realized I had never felt anything like that myself, starting so young and so casually. And that no matter how good it was with someone, it always felt rehearsed. I'd never had my touch received like this before. And to be felt like that was to feel like that myself – too much. I broke off, told her the colour of the food looked wrong, I didn't want to eat it, and went up to bed, and locked my door.

23 June

The salt-air and too much fucking.
  What day is this anyway?

24 June

Our last night. Too full up on each other to touch. We fall on
talk as something new. We talk about the island. I said how this
would be a bleak place in winter. Exposed to wild winds with
the great heaps of slate piled everywhere grey and unforgiving
with no sun to pick out the metallic sheen. The wind *would* be
wild, wouldn't it? She sounded almost envious. You would like
that? When we walk inland, in the quieter places, I feel anxious, she said. About seeing people? (We had seen that same
guy with his dog that afternoon.) No, she said. The quiet. I
thought you worshipped quiet. In others, I envy it. But quiet
for me is torture. Why? I can hear myself. Your thoughts, you
mean? The sound of me. I like it best by the sea or in the wind,
where I can't hear myself. Most people feel anxious when they
can't hear themselves. 'I can't hear myself think.' Then I told
her about D's brother. He heard voices. It was bad in the wind
or by the sea. Noises outside turned to voices inside. He goes
mad with the sound of other people in his head. And you go
mad with the sound of yourself!
  Evie told me about the castrati then. Those boys who had
their balls cut off to keep their voices sweet and high. When
they sang they did not sound like boys, and they did not sound
like women. It was an eerie sound, Evie said. The practice had
been banned by the Vatican in the nineteenth century, but
she had heard a recording, made during the earliest days of
recording technology, when the last castrato was still alive and

singing in the Sistine Chapel. A moment in time, she said, when the sound could be captured for ever. What were her words? Beautiful synchronicity. But think! (she clapped a hand over her mouth). Think of all the sounds we will never hear! And what about the sounds that are facing extinction, she said. Sounds that future generations will never hear!

Like certain rare songbirds, I said. Or the din of yourself.

The castrati! I have not thought of the castrati in decades. There was a period in my teenage years, before I met Damaris, when I thought about almost nothing else. One day in Edinburgh, in a charity shop, I came across a recording of Alessandro Moreschi, the last castrato, who died in . . . I forget the year, I will have to consult the *Encyclopaedia*. What *do* I recall of Alessandro's entry, read all those years ago, after I returned from the charity shop? That as a child he had a beautiful singing voice (needless to say). That at the age of nine he was placed in a warm bath, drugged with opium and castrated. That he sang in the Sistine Chapel choir. That he was the only castrati to have made a recording. As soon as I returned from the charity shop – this, shortly after I left boarding school – I went to my room and listened to the recording of his voice. I became obsessed by Alessandro Moreschi, as well as by the strange race of which he was a last member: emasculated giants whose voices did not change with puberty, but whose limbs and ribcages, lacking testosterone, developed abnormally: long and heavy for the limbs; thick-boned and swollen for the ribcages. By the time Alessandro reached maturity, I read, his chest was cavernous, his lungs enormously powerful, and he could sustain a high c, no, d for over a minute. More than this I cannot recall. Once again I am forced to consult my *Encyclopaedia*. That is something I have often found myself doing, while writing this history. It has never been easy. The set is in constant use, although not the use for which it is intended. The volumes of my *Encyclopaedia* are not so much repositories of information as elements of furniture, since they comprise the legs of my desk, four pillars supporting the wardrobe door. Let me (briefly) describe the *Encyclopaedia*. Bound in blue leather, each volume measures approximately ten by seven inches. The pages are yellowed and in places eaten away by the moths and damp. Pasted on the inside front cover of Volume 1 is an advert cut from a magazine.

WHEN IN DOUBT – 'LOOK IT UP' IN The Encyclopaedia Britannica, THE SUM OF HUMAN KNOWLEDGE, 32 volumes, 31,150 pages, 48,000,000 words of text. Printed on thin, but strong opaque India paper. A COMPLETE and MODERN exposition of THOUGHT, LEARNING and ACHIEVEMENT, a vivid representation of the WORLD'S PROGRESS, embodying everything that can possibly interest or concern a civilized people, all reduced to an A B C simplicity of arrangement.

So much for the *Encyclopaedia*. Let me describe how I constructed my desk. Having decided to use the wardrobe door as a surface, I searched for the volumes of the *Encyclopaedia*, which were scattered about the attic, mixed in with other books. When the set was complete (except for Volume 13, which I could not find), I arranged it into alpha-numerical order. Then I made four pillars out of the volumes: Volumes 1 to 8 for the front-left leg of my desk; 9 to 16 the back-left; 17 to 24 the back-right (replacing the missing volume with a book of similar thickness); Volumes 25 to 32 formed the front-right leg. Now the pillars were in place, I placed the wardrobe door on them.

That is how I constructed my desk. The problem was that now, whenever I wanted to consult the *Encyclopaedia,* I had to take my desk apart! Let me demonstrate the difficulty. Say, as now, I wish to read about Alessandro Moreschi, I must carry out the following steps:

- Take the computer off my desk and hold it in my hands
- Kneel down before the legs of my desk
- By the light of the computer locate the relevant leg (in this instance the back-right) and, within that leg, the relevant volume (MEDAL–MUMPS)
- Place my computer on the floor with the screen facing the relevant leg
- Stand up, remove the various items that have accumulated on my desk – cups, pencils, rubber bands, books, the tape recorder, Damaris' diary, paperclips, keys, a hair slide, a lamp, a vase, some stones – and place them on the floor
- Lift the wardrobe door and lean it against the attic wall
- Take the topmost volume of the relevant leg (Vol. 24, back-right) and place it on the floor
- Take the next volume (23) and place it on top of the first (24)
- Repeat the process with the succeeding volumes (22 on 23, 21, on 22, and so on), until the volume I wish to consult (18) is exposed
- Take that volume and, by the light of the computer, locate and read the relevant entry (MORESCHI, Alessandro)
- Enough!

26 June

Oxford. A golden crust, hot from the oven. Me and Evie wander the city, hot and golden ourselves. My skin, her hair (lemon juice, like I told her) in love, why not, and, in a week's time, with nothing to do for the rest of the summer. She's coming to London with me. She follows me everywhere. She came to our show last night. *He* was not surprised to see her. He made a bitchy comment. A chick this time? Too quietly for her to hear. But then, this afternoon, she mentions it. Comes to meet me after rehearsal and we go down to the river. Lying on the grass, my head on her belly as usual. She has a horror of lying on mine, sensitive as she is to the sound of me. Her fingers twining the roots of my hair, as though her fingers themselves were trying to take root in my scalp. Lightly she says, So the last one was a boy? I say, Yeah he was, the boy in the play. Or the chick now. She said he was handsome and what was it like with a boy. Told her me and Jack would show her sometime. I asked if she was jealous (seems that's always a rhetorical question). No, she says, just curious. I ask if she gets jealous when I'm on stage. What with everyone watching me. She said, No. Then she gives me this big speech, not really looking at me. About how when I'm miming, the audience, strangers to her, to me, to each other, all of them, and her, are looking at me. She says, We forget ourselves. We forget ourselves, and one another. Only you exist. And you? she says, You are oblivious to everyone except yourself. I imagine you to be moving in a different element, a heavy silence, the kind one might experience after a loud and sudden explosion, in the seconds before one's ears begin to ring. Or some such scat. Then, to herself, Hiroshima after the bomb, what were the first sounds made after that? She went on. She couldn't say she was jealous at these times cos I was trapped. Trapped in my own silence, or my illusion of it, up there on the stage, with everyone looking at me. She said that at those times she felt nothing but pity for me. For me! That made me angry and I pulled her fingers out of my hair so roughly it hurt, and still hurts. Can't say exactly why I was angry, but as I write now, I think perhaps it was fear, fear that she was right. Fear of the loneliness that gets me sometimes. I went apeshit on her. Pity for me? You pity me? Look at yourself! You're trying to dress like me, you follow my hairstyling advice, you've started to put on make-up now to make yourself more attractive to me, but you look like a monkey in a wedding dress! You know nothing about life, modern or otherwise, you don't know what's hip, you've got no sense of humour, no *idea* how to speak to people, how to behave, how to move or even how to fucking *fuck* for fuck's sake! And YOU pity ME?

Here was the silence after the loud explosion. She sat staring at her hands with her pebbly eyes wide open, shining with tears that she would not allow herself to shed. I had no idea, she says. If I am so . . . pitiful (electric blue mascara now starting to run), why are you . . . with me?

I thought about the poor swallow and wondered why anyone loved anyone. Because I realized then that I loved her. I was in love with her. I just wanted to take the poor lost freak in my arms and kiss her and that is what I did and as I did I said, Why Evie Steppman, can't you see, it's *because* I pity you. She made a good job of trying to laugh then. Later that night, after we'd fucked she said, puzzled, No sense of humour? How could you say that? I am always laughing. Yeah, Evie, but at things no one else can dig.

27 June

Today we went to Botley cemetery to visit Evie's mother's grave. She has never been before. Her mother was from Oxford, she told me this morning when she announced the trip. I invited myself along. To protect you from your sentimental excesses, I said. She told me I was rude but she said it like it was a compliment. The chapel was one of these buildings that look like a toy-sized building built to human scale. It was squared off by cherry trees. After we had found the gravestone I left Evie crouching by it and wandered the grounds. As I did I felt as though I were looking for something, but wasn't quite sure what until I came across the grave of a woman named Virginie, born in the same year as me. I realized then that I was looking for some sign of myself. Damaris X. Born 1950–Died 5 Minutes Ago. All this time I was breathing in the ashes of the dead, since the crematorium next door was in use. Those great ostrich plumes of smoke seemed extravagantly Art Nouveau and gave me an idea. I ran back to where Evie was kneeling, tugging up weeds, dandelions which looked rather pretty, I thought. So now a flowerbed, as well as a deathbed (and to the French, Piss-in-Bed). Oh Evie, you are a sentimental old boot, I said, pulling her up to her feet, just how she was pulling up the weeds, How can you cry for a mother you never knew! I never knew my parents. Do you see me weep for them? No. They should weep for the loss of me. Besides, it's too hot for manual labour today. I know somewhere lovely and cool.

And that is how we came to visit the Pitt Rivers museum. To be wandering in that dusty Victorian half-gloom on a hot summer's day – what a treat! We walked around together until I got impatient cos she lingered too long by each case. Me, I was keen to see as much as I could, moving on quickly from whatever didn't interest me. Stayed until the guard announced the museum was closing and we were reunited outside. On the walk back to the boarding house, through the long slants of light and the lengthening shadows, I counted off all the things I had seen. Let me try to remember:

A cabinet of benevolent charms entitled, Sympathetic Magic.

A cabinet of objects occurring in nature which had been collected because they look like something else in nature (a seed pod which looked like a snake; a rock which looked like a monkey's head, etc.).

A cabinet called Treatment of Dead Enemies, which included a skull that looked like it had sharpened pencils sticking out of its nose.

A huge, swishy-looking Hawaiian ceremonial cape in a striking black, yellow and red pattern that looked as though it were made of fur, but when you looked closer you realized it was made up of feathers, thousands and thousands of hummingbirds' feathers.

A charm with a label written in tiny, tiny writing which stated matter-of-factly how / where it should be displayed (I forget) its particular powers (I forget), and its ingredients, some of which I remember. They included:

Earth from the grave of a man who has killed a tiger.

Earth from the grave of a woman who has died in childbirth (except I misread the label and saw, at first, Earth from the grave of a man who has killed a tiger that has died in childbirth).

A letter in some ancient Eastern pictographic language on a very long strip of palm leaf that looked like silvery skin which had been rolled into a tight neat coil.

A display on the West African communication system based on the exchange of those tiny cowrie shells that look like Sugar Puffs. A single shell sent to someone conveyed the message: I consider you less than nothing and have no wish to ever see you.

A foetus in a jar. It must have been about four months old. Its little ears had been pierced and it was wearing a necklace.

An odd-looking fifteen-year-old girl with thick glasses shouting, 'Paula! I've found the shrunken heads!'

The shrunken heads. Like withered apples.

And you, Evie? What did you see? Just the Benin Bronzes. But that's where I left you! What's so interesting about them? I asked her, annoyed. Just a load of bronze masks. Look, I said as we passed a couple of beautiful young guys with perfectly symmetrical golden features, See their faces in the sun! They make more beautiful bronzed masks. E shakes her arm out of mine and tells me I don't understand, more sad than angry.

28 June

E didn't turn up to meet me after rehearsals today. After waiting fifteen minutes, I went back to the boarding house, but she was not there. I waited there until it was time to leave for the show but she didn't turn up. After the show I waited backstage for her. She didn't come. When I got back to the boarding house she was there in her bed, asleep. I got into my bed, and turned my back to her. I left the room in the morning and when I got back after rehearsals she was still there, in bed. I asked if she was ill and she said no. She hasn't said a word more all afternoon. I'm in bed now, writing this. I'm due to leave for the theatre in twenty minutes and she's still here. I don't know where she was yesterday, or what she did. A moment ago I put my face close to hers, to see if she really was sleeping. I saw a small tear, like a bead, lodged in the corner of her eye.

29 June

Evie has spent the last two days, Alice-like, swimming in circles in her own tears. What can I do? I kept saying. As though I were at fault for not being able to dispel this, this I want to say blizzard, or fog, or downpour. Why is it we reach for meteorological metaphors to talk about our moods? Our many weathers. If anything, it is like the sandstorm in Nigeria that Evie has told me about, the kind that blinds and chokes. Is it your mother? I ask. Is it the Benin Bronzes? She shakes her head and laughs at me, a laugh which causes her some pain.

30 June

I wonder about those Bronzes. I wonder if they carry some curse. I wonder if E has been cursed by them. Objects are not mute. That cape from the museum. My guess is that you couldn't fail to sense a thousand heartbeats, the thrum of a thousand tiny pairs of wings, if you swished about in it, knowing what it is made of. And perhaps that bestows some power on the wearer. To be able to stand in a cape like that you'd quell compassion, conscience. And that would make you more ruthless, more powerful.

Today Evie, exhausted with crying, was able to sit up in bed and eat a little soup, after refusing food these past days. She told me she periodically experiences such episodes. Calls such attacks the Faulty. Believes the Faulty was passed on to her by a woman she knew as a child, some blonde who smoked a lot and believed in Voodoo! When I ask her what causes them, she says, The din of myself, and laughs.

1 July

I've not slept all night. Last night, Evie began to talk, after four days of silence. It came out in a flood. She told me all about her bedroom in Lagos, about all the sounds she could hear from it. She told me stories about her mother and father, stories from her childhood. Stories her father told her when she was a child. And in the womb?!? One nasty little story about a medieval mapmaker who arranged the mass abduction of women from Nubia then basically raped them. She told me that story in raptures, not hearing what she was saying. And the opposite happened with me. I could not speak as she told me those stories, such stories. A story about a kind of spirit-child called Sagoe. Stories about the people she'd known in Lagos. Most of it lies. No doubt as a child she believed this stuff really did happen. But when she tells me now, is she relating what she believed as a child, or what she believes now? If she believes it now, that would make her mad.

2 July

Last night was the last show. Evie came along. When we got back to the boarding house, I slipped into her bed, hoping we could fuck since the last time had been just after our row, and that had felt disconnected. She felt far away again. The gratitude, the relief, have gone. I wonder if she feels like we're just rehearsing now.

10 July, London

E is a blind person to be guided. No. She sees too much. She can't screen out the distractions you need to ignore to make safe/efficient progress down a London street. Head in the air, looking up, around, never ahead. Or swivelling with each beautiful freak who walks past, ignoring her. Evie's feeling free, giddy with it, no longer a freak of the first rank.

Now Jack has moved in with Tamara, I've moved us into his room. The best room, the attic, where I am now, Evie making supper in the kitchen, down in the basement, full of green light from the garden down there, feels like it runs on for miles, getting wilder. The attic covers the whole house. You come up through a hole in the floor. Like camping, Evie says, laughing, and it's true, the room is tent-shaped and we've draped fabric on the wall behind our mattress which Evie has christened Bedouin. As in, Let's go to Bedouin now.

Orange walls. Two huge dusty skylights at either end we've covered in chiffon scarves – one seaweed green, one red – underwater or perpetual sunset depending on which end of the room you're in. It's hot in here, but we can't leave the skylights open or pigeons gatecrash. We hear them constantly. So loud and close it feels like we're eavesdropping. Our first day we left the skylights open to air the place. We came back, via the florist's with armfuls of lilies I stole from outside the shop, to find a pigeon sitting on Bedouin. A terrible thing to chase it out, flapping and shitting everywhere. Evie dropped a wastepaper bin over it. I slid an LP (Harvest – sorry, Neil) underneath. The bin was openwork raffia. We could see it panic, trying to peck us through the holes as we bundled it out of the skylight.

There's a broken piano in a corner of the room. Evie tries to play it sometimes. In another a stack of half-finished canvases. Impossible to guess what they were meant to be. All that's left of the original ideas are pencil marks and vague brushstrokes. The room encourages laziness. Mostly we lie on Bedouin in the stifling heat, smoking pot and fucking, the room like a hothouse, the lilies shedding mustard dust on the floorboards.

Feel a bit lost. I wanted that tour. His doing, of course.

12 July

E loves the squat. A house full of young people after that big old place on her own with a madman in the attic. Today, we all sat in the kitchen, shelling peas from the garden (eating them sweet and raw from the pod as we did). Evie told the joke about the statues in Hyde Park and everyone laughed. She looked so pleased I could have kissed her.

15 July

Last night at dinner we were talking about star signs, and the others found out it's E's birthday soon. Michael suggested a house birthday dinner. Evie, I thought, would hate the fuss. I'd planned on serving her a special meal in Bedouin, Birgitte already cast as waitress (her first role in months). But no, Evie puffed up like a pigeon at the idea. I found this too funny. I think we're her first real friends.

20 July

We wake up, and Bedouin feels like a womb. Today we are born, I say. Let's go out into the world. We spend the whole day out in the garden, sunbathing naked.

25 July

The Faulty. E lying in Bedouin, naked and sweating as though knocked out by some tropical disease, eyes closed. No, not closed, screwed shut, as if what little light there is in here pains her. I apply more chiffon scarves to the window, wipe her body with damp flannels.

I put a record on and she says, Take it off, like she is choking.

I make her pink lemonade. She waves it away. I ask her, What is it? What is it, Evie, dear? She shakes her head slowly as though it hurts to move. A small tear is squeezed out, like the last drops of juice from the lemons.

26 July

Day two of the Faulty and she is lying now with her back to the room, face to the wall, staring at it, though there is nothing to see, no interesting cracks or whorls in the paintwork that might be turned into new planets and escaped to.

So I take an old postcard I saw in a pile of books downstairs, one showing a snowstorm in an Egyptian city, and I pin it to the wall, just in front of her. I couldn't bear for her to stare at nothing like that. But she does not blink or focus on it or acknowledge my presence. This devastates me. I cannot stand to be ignored.

28 July

E beginning to walk and talk again. She doesn't say much, but at least she is able to read. After three days without attention, barely existing for her, I am jealous of her books, as I am jealous of her staring into nothing and of her silence and of her sleep and of her dreams and yes, even of her Faulty.

That is, jealous of any time she is removed from me. Perhaps not jealous. Fearful, maybe. I don't know what I am without her attention.

Growing times. In knowing Evie, and learning how Evie is beginning to know me, I begin to know myself. And so I am beginning to realize the extent of my jealousy. What a bitch! My need to be noticed. In between shows, I barely exist. Keep thinking about that tour I've missed out on. And now that Evie has been accepted by the others, I feel I exist a little less. She's no longer the freak who needs me. Not here, at least.

Michael and Birgitte upset tonight since Finn cooked lamb in the vegetarian casserole dish. Delicious!

30 July

I found Evie's birthday present today. No, like the best presents, it found me.

This is how. I wake up, and she's not there. I can smell something cooking so I lie waiting for my breakfast until I realize she isn't coming up. Find her in the kitchen with Michael. Eating food I don't recognize, something Michael has made. Look! Eyes shining, spearing what looks like a slice of fried banana on her fork. Plantain! I haven't had plantain since I was a girl! Taste it.

Ashamed to say I pull a face. Say Yuk, as though it's disgusting. It wasn't. It wasn't anything really. Just tasted of fried oil.

Michael says they're celebrating. That cat has this habit of never giving you quite enough information, so that you have almost to ask for it, and he makes you feel you've begged it off him. So I don't ask what they're celebrating and leave them to it. I go looking for Evie's birthday present. No money. And I don't want to lift it. Go down Trafalgar Square – a couple of hours' statue-ing. Walk up Charing Cross Road and into all the second-hand bookshops. I want something big and antique with beautiful engravings. I find an edition of *Paul et Virginie*! One lovely engraving of them both, the same one from the box of matches. Paul stripped to the waist, trousers rolled up to his knees. Standing on a rock in the middle of a swollen river, trying to cross it, Virginie on his back. But I hadn't enough money. Too late to earn more, so I walked until I hit Bloomsbury. That dusty part of the city left me feeling thirsty so I walked up

Rosebery Avenue to Angel, then all the way along Upper Street, heading, I realized when I got there, for the William Camden. Had half a bitter I lingered over, exchanging humid glances with the boy (all eyes and lips) behind the bar. He came out to collect empties and as he leaned over to wipe my table I told him to follow me out back. A good cock, thick and hard. Nice surprise and all the hotter from someone so slight and pretty. I sat on a bin and sucked him, not off though. Brought him close – brought me close – then stood up, hitched up my dress. He slid my panties down then stayed there, licking. The sweetest tongue. Then we fucked, kissing. I came quick on that cock, quicker than I wanted, he held off for as long as he could but I saw it in his eyes when he just couldn't any longer, and it was during his sharp last reflexive shudders, almost piercing, that I saw it, in a cardboard box full of junk by the bins. The tape recorder. After we had finished and he'd gone back inside, I picked up the tape recorder and put it in my bag.

When I got back, Michael and Evie were out. I just had time to check it worked (it does!) then hide it when Evie came in. She told me they'd been to the British Museum, to see more, different, Benin Bronzes. What? The museum in Oxford, she said. Suddenly I remembered. Just before her first attack of the Faulty. I am livid with Michael for having taken her there, and her not long past that last attack.

Right now E is lying next to me on Bedouin, reading. *The Walk* by Robert Walser. I have hidden the tape recorder inside the broken piano. She has no idea.

2 Aug

Evie's birthday, mid-morning. We're in the kitchen. The others wander in and out and kiss her, saying Happy Birthday. I tell her she'll have to wait until tonight for her present from me. Birgitte takes pity on her, Ach Evie you should hev one gift to open, and gives her a bundle wrapped up in some pages from *The Stage*. A rose-printed shawl. What is Birgitte thinking of? Evie delighted with it but yes, I will say it again, looking like a monkey in fancy dress when she threw it around her. I would dress Evie in nothing but shifts. Plain madhouse garments of hemp. What is odd in her and freakish becomes gaunt and beautiful if you look hard enough. Like those Depression-era photos of raw-boned lank-haired women tired and tragic in floral prints, but heroic in denim. What do you think, says Evie, looking down at herself in the shawl. I am spared from either insulting her or being forced to lie when Finn announces I have a visitor. And in *he* walks. I am stunned. What is he doing here? I take a look at his expression, shit-eating, bit pissed off, and I know it means he is resentful of having to give me some good news. And I'm right. I'm in! Felicity twisted her ankle and I'm needed for the Rainbow Theatre gig. Which means I get the US tour too!! So I'm whooping round the kitchen, and Evie asks what's up, and I tell her: a show with one of the hottest, hippest, coolest cats in rock history. Then a two-month tour round America. And then I look at E, hunched up in her shawl, and the scraps of *The Stage* on the table where she tore the paper open so excited was she to get this gift. And suddenly I wonder. When was it that anyone last remembered E's birthday?

Before I know it, I throw my arms around her. Evie! Evie! We're going to America! And I realize now I must give her the present, that it is somehow linked to our trip around America. So I drag her upstairs, push her down on Bedouin, take the shawl from her shoulders and throw it over her head. As though she were a parrot. The tape recorder feels satisfyingly bulky, all wrapped in newspaper. When I place it in her hands she tears off the shawl, then the paper. You will record America, I say, hugging her from behind with my arms and legs. She just sat there, turning the thing over in her hands and half-pressing the buttons a little cautiously. Lost sounds, she mumbles. When I ask what she means she says she can record the sounds of America which will soon be lost for ever. Tears in her eyes. You can record the sound of wind through bluegrass, I tell her, kissing the back of her neck. The alien corn.

25 Aug

Tonight, three weeks before we are due to leave for America, he told me that none of us will be going after all. It's too costly a project. D will make do with just the band.

I have not yet told Evie. She has been working hard on her plans for the archive. Every day she goes to the British Museum reading room, where she fills ledgers full of notes. She has not had an attack of the Faulty since before her birthday. She barely notices the others.

I have written to D asking if we might accompany him anyway. He liked my style at the gig. Said I'd pay our way by assisting somehow. Told him about Evie's project. The entourage is planning to travel by bus. He can spare two seats, I'm sure. And there is always money to be made making myself into an object.

26

Transcribing Damaris' Diary: America

The attic is almost completely dark. The only light comes from my electric heater and the insipid blue seeping from my computer screen, which gives me a feeling of emptiness and peace. I have always been drawn to darkness, which I associate with silence. That is why, whenever I sense a trace of the sun, I paste another page over the skylight, or else cover one of the blades of light that slice through the gaps in the walls or roof, even the floorboards. The attic is covered with printed sheets. How happy to think my history is not idle! Just yesterday I pasted up my transcription of Damaris' dairy. This happy period – one of the few in my adulthood – stares down on me now. That is as it should be.

Forward.

17 Sept 1972

We packed up Bedouin. Joined this caravan of freaks. Heading down the highway to Cleveland, first show of the tour. D's trying tricks out on his guitar, the starts of songs, an almost chorus. White heat as the sun streams in. Me and Evie up front, quiet, on our own. E's got the window seat, leaning on the glass, hypnotized by the long cars and the road-signs sliding past – there goes Nanticoke! – still thinking of New York.

We got in two days ago. Flew. Our first time! Though we didn't need that plane, still high on being together after two weeks apart. E went to Edinburgh to get her passport. Also to see her dad. He won't be here when I get back, she said. The day I left her at Kings Cross I noticed the freckles. Mustard dust. How you've come out of yourself, I thought. She kissed me goodbye without caring who saw, then loped off down the platform not glancing back. I am always the one who leaves. I do not like this, being left.

And oh I enjoy remembering how much I missed her, now she's sitting curled up on the bus seat beside me. The pleasure of gently testing a new bruise. When she was away, each minute took its time. That dumb ache! Just how I've heard boys describe getting kicked in the balls. One night we speak on the phone for the first time. Standing in that phonebox she rushed in at me. Her smell of Rich Tea biscuits. Her hands, too heavy for her wrists. Overblown flowers. Something ridiculous, like chrysanthemums.

Flying's heavy. You feel the plane butting its head against gravity. You fly despite it. To spite it. E's fingers twisting round mine as the plane lumbers along (me scared, saying stupid shit, I love you, I've always loved you, I'll always love you), then it stampedes . . . a run-up at the sky and we're in the air. This great beast hauling itself up, and Evie takes her fingers from mine to stick them in her ears, screaming with laughter, with disbelief, over the noise of the engines. Clouds hang below us. Unmoving. Sculpted. Weighty. Evie puts her hand back in mine as the air hostess passes (bright hair, red lips). She smiles. Welcome to America!

And then it was my turn to laugh, out of shock, as we drive into Manhattan. Like I'd always known it, the way I would my own mother if I ever met her. A stranger looking strangely familiar, someone you have always known, without knowing. Like seeing a mythical beast for real, but then we get out and we hear it. New York Fucking City.

Later we leave our room to find food, Evie wearing the

beaded headband I bought her from Carnaby Street. The turquoise a nice surprise against her unwashed hair. Evie entranced, following trails of sounds like a dog on the scent, changing tack when she picks up a new one . . . clanks and hisses and taxi brakes and stand-up rows in the street . . . I chase her this way and that. New York, she says, sounds like prisoners banging tin cups on the bars of their cells.

23 Sept

On the bus. Can't take in much. Way too twitchy, too horny . . . feeling pretty high from last night, and then there's this local kind of high I've got, right between the legs . . . Oh Mama! We opened last night. Saw some of the show from the wings but mostly heard it from backstage. Wardrobe duties. D'd rush in, shrug into whatever alien kimono we held out for him, then rush out. A couple of times he got the chance to smoke a fag, too hyped to sit, leaning back instead against the dressing table with one leg folded under him like a long white locust. But Evie. Evie was out there in the audience. I caught the end from the wings, saw the guys take their applause like soldiers home from battle, sweaty and victorious, bloodied almost in the lights, the rest of us standing around like handmaidens. When they came off I caught a look in D's eyes that made me flinch. The emptiness you get. Hung around backstage as long as I could, waiting for E. She never showed. Went with the others to the aftershow party. I'm getting drunk fast on the champagne and the mood, stumbling around looking for her. Then I spot her. She's under the piano. Sitting cross-legged, palms on knees guru-style. She smiles up at me then takes tissue paper out of her ears. She's had it in most of the night. The gig was too loud. But not at first: she dug the idea of this whole alter ego thing, the band stepping out on stage as characters. But then at its peak, during the anthem, staring in wonder at this beautiful alien come to Earth to save the kids with rock 'n' roll, she catches the eye of a woman in the front row who gave her such a look – 'she could see I was believing a lie and despised me for it' – and that was when she had torn up some tissue paper and stuffed it into her ears –

Scribus interruptus. Evie read the first line over my shoulder. Gave me a kiss that nearly made me come, then took matters into her own . . . fingers. Slipped them into my jeans and into me and fingered me right there under cover of my denim jacket. Wow. Wow. Wow.

24 Sept

Another hotel. E asleep, hair the colour of damp sand. Our things less ours with each new room we move to. On the cabinet between our beds (but we only sleep in one), E's beaded headband has the look of an object left behind by someone else. Is this true of people too? No. In an unfamiliar room, crammed together in a single bed, we're more each other's than ever. No sign of the night terrors. She's my amulet.

Last night, in bed, after a languorous fuck, stretching our limbs most extravagantly (the luxury of a bed!), I told E about Elvis, since we *are* in Memphis. She'd only just about heard of him. Such a square! So I held her tenderly in my arms and sang 'Love Me Tender'. Then I taught her the words. We sang it together, and she recorded it. Like most people with terrible voices, she sings with great enthusiasm.

25 Sept

Travelling to New York. Night. Lying in Evie's lap, eyes closed, a sleep that itself feels in transit, Evie stroking my hair, me vaguely aware of E and Zed, the make-up artist, talking in low voices over me. Far away and in my head as voices sound when you're half asleep. E telling Zed about her project. About how, in Memphis, she'd gone to a barber's to record the sound of a wet shave, the stropping of razor on leather, the slapping-on of foam, the razor rasping skin. Then she'd recorded the sound of the barber ringing up payment in his old-fashioned cash register. That's when she realized that any sound she chose to record would, at the point of her hearing it, become in some way extinct: she would never again hear the sounds she was hearing right there, right then, in that way.

Evie gently shakes me awake, into that close, womb-like dark that settles over you when you're driving at night. Look! she says, pointing at the moon. Huge, champagne-coloured, low in the sky. You could reach out and touch it and as I think that, she puts her fingers to the glass. Makes me glad and sad at once to think we've reached a point of remembering when she says, Reminds me of the night we drove to Easdale.

28 Sept, New York

They got me doing the statue thing out front for all the freaks coming in. Evie a no-show. Drinking after. Went to sit on what I thought was a chair but turned out to be a cunning arrangement of shadows – a strong grip on my wrist. I was caught in time. Zed. A gymnast's body and the kind of rolling bowlegged walk of a cowboy. Zed asked about me being painted up like a mime, and I told her my story. She gave me some shit – 'This'll make you feel like you're on stage.' We spent the whole night talking. Me mostly, about Evie. Her old-fashioned face and tissue paper in her ears and the recording project and the din of herself. Zed told me about anechoic chambers – dead rooms – where all sound is absorbed and all you hear is the blood in your head.

– Evie has just come in and jumped into bed all excited about having recorded some girls singing skipping rhymes in a part of town we were told to stay away from but Evie, she's an angel who walks unthinking of the harm that melts to let her pass. They just dig her here. Didn't mention the anechoic chamber.

29 Sept

Monster America! Riding the back of it. An endless spine of road that rolls through rocks and crags and mountains, dark banks of trees as far as forever. The wide, blue jeans sky. We flash by gas stations, small towns, low-roofed barns. We glimpse horses, wind ruffling the pastures and making warm pelts of them. Now and then goods trains run alongside. Different from English trains – more resolved with their long blunt noses. Bull-headed. Evie loves the sound of their horns blaring.

Two hours from Washington we get out at a truck stop and order pancakes. Evie chats to a big-shouldered man on his way to a cattle auction. Asks if she can record him. They go outside into the parking lot. I see her point up at the sky. A single cloud. Can't hear but I can tell. Auction that, she's saying. He fixes his eyes on the cloud. Inhales deeply. Launches into a spiel without stopping. A controlled kind of babbling. He looks possessed, eyes rolled up at the sky like that. Evie stands amazed, holding out her mic. He's finished. For a moment, Evie's static with shock, then she launches into gestures of amazement.

She played it to us now on the bus. Like nothing I've ever heard before. A foreign language. A kind of yodelling. Like the same two strings on a banjo twanged again and again, a rhythm to his babble, and remembering how he looked possessed, I think of speaking in tongues. And then it occurs to me. What Evie is doing with her project. She is divorcing sound from gesture. Opposite to me.

3 Oct (I think)

New York again. Shitty hotel in xx. Our room looks out on to a blackened wall. 5 a.m. and I've been lying here since I got in, an hour ago, staring at that wall. Evie not back yet from wherever she went tonight: said she'd go out and record. I had no gig tonight but she didn't ask me to come. Went out nightclubbing with Zed. Quite a scene here. Everyone a star but me a black one, a collapsed one. Invisible somehow. Afterwards, walking back to the hotel, everything still leaking neon in the early hours of the morning, I had that feeling you get on tour sometimes, of forgetting where you are, your centre. I feel very far away. But from what?

Evie just in. Couldn't stop talking, then crashed. She rode the subway. She met a group of young guys. They were going to paint the subway trains – graffiti artists. They took her to an underground yard where the trains are parked when they stop running for the night. They made a strange noise, Evie says, like a mechanical panting, a melancholy, musical clanking, the heat of their bodies cooling. She recorded that and the sound of the boys climbing the trains, calling out to one another, the rattle and spray of their cans, the hiss of the paint on hot metal.

That faraway feeling has not gone even with Evie near, sleeping. A mime is used to being silent. But not invisible. Not *backstage*. Writing helps.

11 Oct, Kansas City

Coming down with something like the Faulty. After last night's gig – 11,000-seater stadium and only 180 people show up – they got me out front. Zed makes me up to look like D in character, lightning-slash cheekbones, refrigerated lips, hair cut and dyed burned orange and spiked like his. Stand outside all day, a statue of him, to draw in the kids. And they come. And they all look like me, or rather, me dressed as him, and not really him, but him on stage. Me an idol of their idol. I watch the show. The kids, all dressed like him, screaming at him. Him smiling back. I get scared. Leave. Evie wasn't back. When she came in early this morning – out recording, an anti-war rally – she found me with my head over the sink, streaks of what looked like ink running into the plughole. 'Sorcière', it says on the bottle.

Pasted underneath this entry, without comment, is the following paragraph, carefully cut out from the page of a book.

You see, Oz is a great Wizard, and can take on any form he wishes. So that some say he looks like a bird; and some say he looks like an elephant; and some say he looks like a cat. To others he appears as a beautiful fairy, or a brownie, or in any other form that pleases him. But who the real Oz is, when he is in his own form, no living person can tell.

26 Oct, San Francisco

We got to LA and I freaked out. *I don't know where I am I don't where I am I don't know where I am.* Evie runs in to borrow a map from Jerry-The-Driver. Spreads it out for me. This is where we are, my heart, this is where we are. But so folded over, so used, that where she's pointing there's nothing but a deep crease and I bellow in fear.

We went on ahead, to San Francisco, to a b'n'b in an odd part of town with ice-cream coloured houses and steep, winding lanes. Beautiful girls and boys wandering the streets hand-in-hand. Girls with girls, boys with boys. We never felt so free. I write this lying here in bed with E, watching the light from that island prison sweep our walls, in counterpoint to Evie's stroking of my thigh.

27 Oct, San Francisco

Yesterday. We're given the most beautiful gift. Evie and I are passing a florist's. The owner comes out, a flower painted on his face, presents Evie with a bunch of tropical-looking flowers. She charms them, these Americans. I only merit a glance. This glance, taking in my looks, looks no further. But with Evie they look and look. They realize she doesn't know what she is, and this intrigues them. These Americans, so open, confident of what they are, find people like her a puzzle, those who are a mystery to them-selves and are unaware of it. She's that peculiarly English thing, to them: an eccentric. It's in her face. Me, I'm invisible.

We chat with the florist. Evie tells him about her recording. He's fascinated. And what about sounds you wouldn't nor-mally hear? The sound, he says, touching the flowers, of these birds of paradise singing? Oh, if I could hear sounds like that! And the florist says, You will. He gives us each a tab, and, Alice-like, we swallow.

We talked for a while until, from the corner of my eye, I saw the birds of paradise began to twitch. To preen, poised. Poison-ous. Possessed. In their burned orange crests I saw D's hair. The birds of paradise began to sing. His song. The florist gave us acid, Evie! Stick out your tongue and say Ahhhhhhhhhhhh-hhhhhhhh . . . Haaaaaaaaaaaaaah, Evie! What fun we had! We thanked the florist and left him smiling, by his singing flowers. We wandered the streets till we reached the water. Water running in different directions, we stood staring, looking at this rush of water, in such a rush, where is it rushing to? we wondered. And then we see him. The dog. A ginger dog, lost. Tail hovering (how are you feeling? Oh so-so). You say, How do you know it's lost, and I say, Cos it's alone: dogs on their own are always lost. But what about cats? Cats are different, I said. But why? and I said, Because.

The dog nosed around our legs, sniffed our feet. We could keep it, maybe, you squat down, throw your arms around his neck, kiss his flat, greasy head. No, I feel deep in his bristly ruff for a collar. Look. A bronze disk. 'Brumby'. That's his name. He lives at this address. He must have been gone from home a while. He's lost weight: look how loose his collar is. Brumby lifts his eyes from the pavement, they shift from me to you. His brown eyes have an orange glow. Like amber. No like yours, you say. Then, Who's Amber?

Brumby licked the pavement. Do you think he's hungry? Yeah, probably, But we don't have any money. We should just get him back to his home and then he can eat. Before I realize what you're doing you run up to a man in the street. You point to Brumby and look at the man, who digs in his pocket and hands you change. Then you run into a shop and run up to me, ripping the wrapper off a Hershey Bar. Brumby swipes his bit off the palm of your hand with his bacon rasher tongue then looks hopeful while we eat ours. We have trouble. This chunk of Hershey Bar is getting BIGGER in my mouth you want to say, but I can't hear you cos the chunk of Hershey Bar is too big in your mouth and all I hear is grwmmmmgnnn and I say, Same here but all you hear is grwmmmmgnnn. You hold out sticky hands to Brumby saying, All gone, all gone. So Brumby licks your fingers and you melt. Try it, you tell me, Let him lick your fingers. We stand there a while, letting Brumby lick our fingers. It feels like he's sculpting us with his tongue, like you do ice-cream in a cone. I am an ice-cream statue you say, Let me stand very still until I melt away. But the idea of statues freaks me out right now, Let's take him back, I say. Let's claim the reward. Will there be a reward? Oh yes, a big reward, he is a rare and valuable breed, and we snigger, poor Brumby looking up, trying to get the joke. We walk along the water, Brumby trotting at our heels or stopping to bury his nose into god knows what or just standing dead at the waterside looking deep into it. Sour, green. Can you taste that water? Yes, gooseberries. We screw our faces with the tartness. Brumby, what are you staring at? I drag him back by the collar. Fish, you say. There's no fish in there. Later, we walk down an avenue of tall slim trees with smooth white bark and leaves that snap in the wind. Large leaves, red, white and blue

The entry is incomplete, and there follows several pages with doodles of flowers, giant tropical flowers that often look like birds.

Dania, Atlanta, Nashville

In Dania, or Atlanta, or Nashville, we saw a bus close its doors in the face of a young black girl. Plaits, yellow ribbons, Sunday shoes. She ran a good way down the road, shouting. Evie wanted to get out and record her.

In Dania, or Atlanta, or Nashville, I was spat on by a middle-aged black woman who walked past me and Evie. We were not holding hands.

In Dania, or Atlanta, or Nashville, I picked up a young white boy who was hanging out at the stage door, hoping to see D. He was dressed like D. I took him round the corner and fucked him. Later, in the washroom of a bar, I saw that some of his make-up had come off against my cheek. That same night, in that same bar, in that same city, I got punched by a cowboy.

Before that, long days and short nights in the desert. Crickets, fire, the skitter of lizards. And in the distance, coyotes. Evie records them all. Nothing of me on the tapes. I barely speak. Deserts have a silencing effect.

22 November, New Orleans

Swamp fever. Something weirdly familiar about this city. Feels rotten, tropical. Spoiled. It's in the air. Easdale! The air draws life from you. I wander like a zombie down antique streets rich with stink. People more variously coloured here. Last night I saw a man stabbed. Wandered out late to buy some cigarettes from a shack. Two winos are pushing and shoving one another, both of them grasping a bottle in a brown paper bag. They seem evenly matched in weight and strength – the pushing and shoving metronomical but then one of the men takes an extra step back – staggers, in fact – and as he does I see a dark spray of blood shoot from his neck in an arc like water from the mouth of an ornamental cherub. I run back to the hotel room. Evie out recording. Evie always out fucking recording.

23 Nov

She came in early this morning. Slept a couple of hours and crept out again. I did not get the chance to tell her about the stabbing. And so it lives in my head and somehow stains my thoughts, the way a drop of ink can tint a glass of water. Sorcière.

The following entries do not have dates, just place names, if anything.

X cities in X days and X nights of the terrors. Not sure if I am awake or asleep or if what I see I have seen before. All these cities, these small towns we pass through, this stuff that unspools outside our windows, this scenery – the furze and the pine and the rocks and the people look painted in.

When she's lying next to me, or when we fuck, she's elsewhere, listening to her recordings. I've lost the will. Every city we get to she wants to be alone. With that tape recorder. I hear better when you're not with me. Closest times are on the bus. There's nowhere else for her to go. Nowhere else for her head to fall when she sleeps, except on my shoulder.

E mummifies herself in tape. Splitting sound from gesture. Me from her. Every time I speak all she hears is a ringing. She winces. Stops listening.

Philadelphia

He looked like a Mormon but I met him in a bar. Weirdly lit. Him, I mean. That's what they're like, the Mormons I've seen. He worked for the National Association for Standards and Testing. We decide the standards, he said and when I asked, For what?, he said, Everything. We talked about testing. He told me about the extreme conditions under which things had to be tested. He mentioned sound.

I promised him a fuck with us if he'd do it. I was asking a lot, I knew. A high state of security exists around such places. I myself in a high state of insecurity. In a room where she'd hear no sound but herself, what else could she do but turn to me?

I asked about her plans. Out recording, she said. Told her she should forget about recording for today. Said I wanted to conduct an experiment on her. An experiment in sound. In listening. She smiled. A proper smile. First time in weeks. She let me blindfold her. And here was Evie. Evie who fell in love with me. Needing me to guide her.

He meets us at the security gate. Flashes his pass at the guard, climbs into the cab with us. Has Evie turn her head away so the guard can't see she's blindfolded. We drive to a fire door round the back of the building. An almost anonymous flat-roofed concrete building surrounded by barbed wire. The door's unlocked. We walk quickly along a corridor with rubberized flooring, Evie mute, having to be steered, giving herself up to the guidance of me on one side, him on the other. Then he pulls open with all his strength a huge black door and pushes us through it.

I should have realized the effect it would have on her. So happy losing herself in this rich new world of sounds. In that room, the atmosphere pressing more heavily than gravity, when I turned to her (still blindfolded) and said, I love you, all nuance, all tone, all resonance, dead on my tongue.

I like this hotel room. White walls, gauzy curtains. Sunlight sifting through the fine mesh. Like that dress of hers. Our things look shabby, travelworn, in this clean, white space. I haven't seen her beaded headband in a while.

Evie has not spoken since.

New York

Strange shadows. An old factory. What did they make here? The silent machines give off a metal stink in the heat. We live in one small corner, a mattress where Evie lies twisted up in the sheets, asleep. Last night, a terrible scene. Evie sobbing, rocking, racked. Her first real words since. The gist of it: Mother's womb – an echo chamber. In it she was alive to all sound, 'and all sound alive to me. And then this dead room you lead me into, this – this – slaughterhouse with its hostile air, enemy to all sound! Yes! (screaming now) the very air seeks out sound, seizes it, crushes it. I heard your heartbeat and I heard it stifled, all at once. When I collapsed you carried me from that anti-womb, stillborn.'

What have I done?

Something exhausted about this city. The neighbourhood. The derelict buildings and everywhere rubbish and the people subdued or enraged. I take her out for a walk. Alleys and back-streets and boarded-up shops. The air so muggy, it feels quilted. We see a crowd of people gathered in an abandoned lot. Some guy with a chainsaw slicing into this old clapboard building, cutting out a section from it. The delicacy and precision of this action – instead of a wrecking-ball, say – makes it a particularly intimate, painful kind of destruction. Almost loving. Evie makes no mention of recording.

Today we had news of her father's death. Evie unmoved, it seems. A growing sense of terror in me. Because of her lack of emotion, I think, which is monstrous. She wasn't close enough to him for this to be shock. Nor does it seem as though she's pre-feeling: on the edge of feeling *something*, just trying to work out what. She doesn't care. She's gonna leave.

Evie asleep. It's airless. I take her for a walk. When we return, we lie on the mattress, drained. I wake when I feel her fingers lightly brushing my belly. Her first real contact with me since the dead room, since before that. She made love to me. Kept saying my name, kept whispering to me. Tears in my eyes which didn't spill cos I couldn't move. I just lay there and let her wander all over me, and I couldn't tell you what I was feeling except it just built and built until I thought I would choke, and then the tears did slide off my face. I moved my head, and that's when I saw it. A red light, half-hidden under a heap of clothes at the foot of the mattress. She was recording us. These are my last words. I will leave this for her. I'm leaving.

27

Tinnitus

Spring has arrived in my attic. The gulls bicker. The trees are budding and all day rap knuckles against my roof. Small creatures nest in their hiding places under the floor. Inside my head the old familiar rumpus. It's been several weeks since I completed the transcription of Damaris' diary. Since then, I've written little, and that little has been lost in false starts and evasions. I was trying to recount the days and weeks after she left me in the hotel room in New York, but I was unable to remember anything I could set down in words. My powers of listening weaken daily; and so the gaps in my history grow wider, and the silences more frequent with every page.

This morning the sun arrived in earnest. It fell obliquely on the roof, filtered through my skylight, via the sheets printed with my history, those same sheets I taped over the glass and which at one time functioned like a shade, snuffing out the sun. Now the sun has bleached the paper, erased the ink, and the attic gleams with spidered light. I woke earlier than usual. It was early afternoon. My habit is to sleep during the day and work – if I am able to work – by night. I remained there on my mattress, hoping to doze off, to rest until dusk. But the light, together with the trees knocking on the roof, as well as the gulls, not to mention the ringing in my ears, made sleep impossible. I lay with my eyes closed, wondering if today I would manage to write, until I felt the first poison of a headache coming on. I got up and performed my waking rituals. Then I sat down at my desk and opened my computer. It was no use, the sun fell down on me like a shower of coins, and I found myself unable to compose a single sentence. I said to myself, *Perhaps, if I can shut out the sun, I will be able to work*. I climbed over the heap of junk to my wardrobe, grabbed a sheaf of papers, climbed back, then on to my chair. In a kind of animal frenzy, like some nocturnal creature woken in the day, I taped them up, darkening with those black lies the confusing light of the sun. I continued to travel back and forth between my wardrobe and chair, pasting layer upon layer, and not only over the skylight, for now I noticed cracks of light between the wooden boards of the roof. I taped my history over these too, avoiding the mappa mundi, which imperfectly covers one-third of the south-facing wall. As I did I found that my anguish began to fade, and the ringing in my ears became faint, light and remote, and my head stopped hurting, and I began to laugh, first under my breath, then louder and louder.

I did not know if it was day or night. Even now I am not certain. The attic was dark, as now, and quiet, as if it had sunk to the bottom of the sea. I stopped taping, went over to my computer and woke it from its own kind of sleep. Without any preparation – no deep breaths or questions – I started to type, and in no time I had related the foregoing. 'Yes!' I cried, happy at last. That was a moment ago. Now I am waiting for the sounds of my past to declare themselves . . . and here they come, in fragments it is true, and yet the important thing is that they arrive, now in wretched torn shreds, now musical and precise, now as a kind of unconscious ringing in my head. And all is quiet outside my head. And the sun does not shine in my attic. From now on, whenever I grow frustrated with my history, whenever I curse these words perhaps better left unwritten, I shall comfort myself with the thought that each page I turn out will give me an opportunity to subdue the sun. That more words mean less light.

. . .

After Damaris left I took the plane to Scotland. My father had died while I was in America, and on returning to Gullane I found the house boarded up. The birds had taken over. The walls and furniture, everything, was covered in their filth. The attic was the only room they had not managed to enter. I climbed the ladder, opened the trap door and lay there at the top of the house, eyes closed, trying to ignore their screeching. After a while even the birds didn't bother me. My mind was on Damaris. I thought a great deal about what she had whispered to me on the bus leaving Nashville: that I did not have a remarkable sense of hearing, that I was just a freak with large ears.

After that, every morning for a week I smashed bottles on the beach, then returned to my retreat at the top of the house and ate beans with my coffee. In time I came down from the attic. I threw open the windows and doors and chased the birds away with a broom. I should have got a cat, but I couldn't bear the sight of one. I sat on the sofa and stared at the wall. For weeks I hardly left the sofa. I felt empty, an emptiness which left me feeling totally inert, or furious, or helplessly bored, a sickening kind of refined boredom which provoked in me the desire to destroy things, all things, objects, texts, animals, friendships, property.

Instead, I fought with Damaris in my mind. If, I reasoned, she had loved me she would have stayed with me in spite of my distractedness, my obsessions. I knew she had suffered because of my plan to record the sounds. Perhaps she had amused herself with Zed, the make-up girl? Perhaps, like me with the sounds, she had found pleasure in other things. Yes, I thought – sure of it now – she was already with Zed, and if not Zed then certainly another. Hadn't she told me that she couldn't bear to be alone? And when I thought this, and imagined her touching someone else in the places she had touched me, and her wandering naked in front of that person, who would lean over to kiss her on the mouth, wild with tenderness, I felt like I was splitting in two. I packed a bag and rushed to Edinburgh airport. As soon as I arrived, however, my thoughts turned, and I wouldn't board the flight. If Damaris had loved me, I reasoned now, why had she tried to hurt or destroy me? She had blindfolded me and taken me to the anechoic chamber, that graveyard of sounds.

I have often spoken of the noises in my head. It was in that terrifying chamber I became aware of them for the first time. I recall the powerful heat, and the air – the weight of it – which did not transmit sound, and I felt like I was suffocating. I took my blindfold off. Damaris was watching me intensely. I fell back into her arms, frightened. She was studying me, smiling, but without the least bit of humour in her face. She spoke, and her words sank or perhaps rose – they seemed to do both – and were swallowed up in that strange, heavy air. I leaned back, my head in her lap, and it was then I heard it: a kind of slow sighing that came and went. I thought, which is to say listened, for a while, and then I understood: the sighing was not the sound of Damaris breathing, as I had believed, but – how shall I say? – the noise of myself. It grew louder and deeper, and I sat upright. Soon I heard fluting and whistling noises, and a soft kind of whirring busyness, together with a low thunder, and smacking little clicks, uneven and stabbing, and burbling as of water falling and flowing in the gutter. I sat there listening to the humming of the little world of my own body. Its wild resonance disgusted me.

We returned to our hotel and that uneven, braying, coruscating tone continued to haunt me. I had the bitter revelation it was not entirely new; I had heard it before, in the pits, immediately after the accident involving my left ear. Then the noise had gone as quickly as it had arrived. Now it – *I* – continued . . . dinning through my final days with Damaris, rising in pitch after she left me in the hotel, unchangingly loud as I packed my bag and travelled to the airport in New York, terrorizing me on the plane, maddening me when I reached Gullane – and really, ever since, no matter how hard I have tried to block it out, it has never ceased.

Yes, my experience in that room has affected everything in my life. I have told no one about it; perhaps because I myself do not understand its essential aspects, perhaps out of a sense of embarrassment at being so unnerved by something so ordinary, by hearing what doctors hear every day and for which there is a dedicated instrument, the stethoscope. What I heard in the anechoic chamber was merely the healthy functioning of my body: the air passing through my lungs, my heartbeat, the rush of my blood, the creaking and trickling of my empty stomach. Later, in my forties, I would read about a composer's own experience in an anechoic chamber; he noted two sounds: a low thunder, which was his blood in circulation, and a high-pitched humming, which was his nervous system in operation. Later still, through my research, I would understand that silence may achieve significance only in relation to what it denies, displaces or disavows, just as there is no up without down, or left without right. And even later, when I began to write these stories, in the process of attempting to speak about silence, the true subject of my history, I would realize that one may do so only by breaking it. At the time, however, in that room without echo, I merely held my stomach and wept. I felt sickened, appalled. I felt too the stirrings of a kind of resignation or shame to which I could not give a name, but which would continue to haunt me to this very day. What was so disturbing for me that afternoon in 1972? Quite simply I realized that to be alive is to emit sound. The sensation marked me so deeply that I wonder if it does not in fact expose a more disturbing revelation: not fear of the noise of myself, but the loss of the silence it for ever crowded out. Yes, in the anechoic chamber I understood for the first time that silence does not exist.

My father was dead. I'd inherited the house and his allowance. I did not work. How did I spend those years? I took walks on the beach. I visited Mr Rafferty. I spent more and more time in the attic, attempting to clear out my father's things. More often than not I would become distracted by the objects. Selecting one from the heap, I'd take it in my hands, open it up, take it apart, all the while attempting to tease out the stories it could never tell. I would tap, stroke and shake it, noting its particular sound. Then I would imagine its past life in sound. Once I even detached the needle from the phonograph and tried to 'play' an old plate of my mother's, thinking its grooves might reveal buried signals from the past. Then there was the period when I stared for hours at the photographs in our family album, imagining – *hearing* – the sounds the camera had failed to capture. It was as if my eyes, in a process of miraculous traduction, were standing in for my powers of hearing.

I tried to distract myself with certain projects. I listened to the tapes I had made in America and attempted to categorize the sounds. I had an idea I'd fly to America exactly a decade after my first visit; I'd return to where I'd recorded the sounds, and in those exact same places, ten years later, at exactly the same hour, I would make a new series of recordings. I failed to leave the country. After that I spent a lot of time in the public library in Edinburgh, reading, novels mostly. I'd found a wonderful passage in *The Adventures of Huckleberry Finn*, at that time my favourite book. Jim and Huckleberry are drifting on the Mississippi, chatting and smoking, with the whole river to themselves. 'Next you'd see a raft sliding by, away off younder, and maybe a galoot on it chopping, because they're most always doing it on the raft; you'd see the axe flash, and come down – you don't hear nothing; you see that axe go up again, and by the time it's above the man's head, then you hear the *k'chunk!* – it had took all that time to come over the water. So we would put in the day, lazing around, listening to the stillness. Once there was a fog, and the rafts and things that went by was beating tin pans so the steamboats wouldn't run over them. A scow or a raft went by so close we could hear them talking and cussing and laughing – heard them plain; but we couldn't see no sign of them; it made you feel crawly, it was like spirits carrying on that way in the air.' I started to work my way through the novels in the library, from A to Z, in order to create an Encyclopaedia of Novelistic Sounds. I barely got started.

Then one day in 1997 I received a letter. It was from Ade. He had found my address on an old envelope addressed to my father, among Iffe's possessions. He was married and living in the outskirts of Lagos. Having been a corporal in the Nigerian army, he was now a taxi driver. We corresponded for several months. One of Ade's letters, his last, made the most vivid impression on me. It concerns a terrible incident in 1966, a massacre, in which both he and Sagoe – Babatundi's older brother, the one with whom I had witnessed Ade fish for seagulls – were involved. In a moment I will proceed to transcribe this letter on to my computer; not only because in Ade's story I recognize a thread that runs through this history, via Edrisi's story and the massacre at Benin, the thread of violence, which I have come to associate with the mappa mundi; not only because I wish to cease writing in my own words and continue to transcribe from my papers; but because I regard Ade's letter as signalling the end of the period in my life of which I have just been speaking, the period set off by my visit to the anechoic chamber – the lost decades, as I think of them – and the beginning of the next, which would culminate in my beginning to write my history.

Enough! I am speaking in my own words when, in order to stop speaking, I should be transcribing from my papers.

28

Map of the World, 3: Ade's Story

The mappa mundi. A few brief words about the mappa mundi. In the years I have been writing this history, the moths have not stopped feasting on that ancient fake. Every now and then I rise from my desk and, in the light of my computer, take note of the ever-advancing decay: today, the map's destruction is almost complete; all that is left is a network of frayed channels connecting some two-dozen holes. Where once I could gaze on seas, continents and fantastic events – Noah and his ark, the pelican feeding her young from a wound in her side, the amorphous, disproportionately large landmass of Britain – now all I can make out are larger or smaller holes, exposing the wooden wall. Gone too are the monstrous races, those men and women who once crowded the east bank of the Nile River, Amyctyrae with her giant lip, Androgini the man-woman, Blemmyae whose head grew beneath her shoulders, not to mention Panotii with her ears that reached the ground and served as blankets. Yes, that eccentric tribe who've kept me company for so long have been almost completely wiped out.

Only a single trace of the monsters remain, not a portrait but a text. Inscribed on a scrap of vellum, located in what must have been the earth's upper right-hand corner, is a short paragraph designed to elucidate the drawings themselves. The paragraph tells the story of how the monstrous races came into the world. One day Noah fell asleep naked on the ground. He was mocked by his son Ham and, on waking, cursed him, saying, 'A servant shall you be all your life.' Noah asked God to stain Ham's children black. And that, so the rubric says, is how there sprung into the world all the dark and savage creatures, the ill-shaped forms and specious, corrupt personalities, condemned to grovel and serve mankind as a warning of the sins of pride and disobedience. Less than fully human, the paragraph continues, but human nonetheless, they have been punished by divine decree, some with heads like dogs, some with mouths on their breasts, others with eyes on their shoulders, still more with a massive single foot, which, ironically, impedes their progress, and all so hideous that they make even the Devil scared.

Dear Evie,

I am very happy to be corresponding with you and I pray this letter finds you well. My mother is content that you asked about her health, and she is surprised to hear that you are not married at all. Do you know, Evie, I myself was surprised that you do not remember many of the things I wrote to you about in my last letter. I am especially surprised that you forgot Babatundi, he was your favourite. Your little b! I will tell you about him in another letter.

For now since you asked I will tell you what happened when I joined the army. They were terrible things, so terrible I think they will give you bad dreams. I am talking about what I witnessed in October 1966, when I was twenty-four years old, not long before the war in Biafra began. Some of the people who took part are still alive and living as free men of Nigeria, so please do not repeat this letter to anyone. Promise me that, Evie! Myself, I have told only one other person. My wife, Sue. When my nightmares arrive it is Sue who wakes me up. Then we go to the kitchen and drink some whisky. But sometimes my nightmares arrive too often during the night, and she says to me, 'Try to stay calm, and do not shout too loudly, because our son will know that you have trouble.' 'Yes, Sue,' I tell her, 'I will try to stay calm.' I will try to stay calm in this letter as well, even though I must recall a troop of ravenous wild men.

It began when the Ibos arrived at Kano airport. There were many of them, men with their wives and children, and their luggage too, all standing on the runway in a group. They wanted to escape from Kano, but they had no luck, because we in the 5th Battalion had been ordered to surround the plane. Twice that morning they had tried to board, and twice we had made them go back.

Evie, what happened next I saw with my bare eyes. Suddenly a Land Rover drove on to the runway. It was carrying soldiers, and they were shooting their rifles in the air, shouting, 'Ina nyammari.' When the Ibos heard this, they began to run, and the soldiers jumped out and started shooting. *Ka-Ka-Ka*. The Ibos were running helter-skelter all over the runway and getting shot down before they could escape. When the other soldiers saw that their brothers from the Land Rover were shooting, they started shooting too, in the direction of the Ibos, flinging their rifles up and down.

Myself, I just stood there on the spot. What grievance did I have against the Ibos? I was very surprised because even though I knew there would be trouble, no one had told me that killing was going to happen at Kano airport. A battalion leader called Mai Karfi, a Hausa, came to me and shouted. He said that since I was a Southerner and a Yoruba if I did not want to shoot I must go to the airport office and cut the telephone wire. I did this and returned to the runway. Now there were no more Ibos running. Some had bullets in their stomach, some were gasping, some were screaming, and blood was rushing everywhere, from their nose and legs and arms, everywhere. What I saw was a massacre, and if you see me trembling you will know what a massacre is.

Mai Karfi ordered the soldiers to stand at ease. Mai Karfi means The Most Powerful Man. His Lieutenant was Mai Yanka. Mai Yanka means Great Killer of Human Beings. Mai Karfi was thirty-three and he had helped to torture General Ironsi in the July coup. He had been promoted after that. Mai Yanka was twenty-two. He was very ugly. He was thin and looked like a starving cat. His favourite film was *Gone with the Wind* and he had seen it seven times. Evie, do you know who this Mai Yanka was? He was Sagoe. You must remember Sagoe! Babatundi's brother! But we did not call him Sagoe anymore. In fact he is a completely different person to the person you and I were afraid of when we were children in Lagos. And some of the things I saw Mai Yanka do, before the time in the airport that I am telling you about now, as well as what he did at the airport, as you will soon see, and also what he did to other humans later during the war, well, Evie, all this means that I cannot think of Mai Yanka as Sagoe, and I cannot think of Sagoe the child we both knew as Mai Yanka, and I will advise you to do the same.

Mai Karfi reloaded his rifle and approached the plane. During the commotion some of the Ibos had run up the steps to enter the plane, a VC10, and they had kicked the steps down. There was screaming coming from inside, and I saw faces looking out from the windows of the plane as well. Me, I was very aware of the bodies lying all over the runway, some of which were moving and groaning. But Mai Karfi did not seem aware at all. He ordered us to attach the steps back to the plane. But we couldn't lift them up straight. Mai Karfi told us to stand at ease. He cursed the Ibos and lit a cigarette, one for himself, and he gave one to Mai Yanka too.

Mai Yanka had this clever way of starting his cigarettes, of putting them into his mouth. I had admired it plenty of times.

What he did was this, first he lit the cigarette, but not in the usual way of sucking with his mouth. He held the cigarette in his hand and put the flame to the tip until it was alight, then he flipped the cigarette up into the air. It jumped up from his finger, tumbled around, then he jerked his head forward. He caught the cigarette between his teeth. It happened very quickly. After that Mai Yanka always looked proud and he smoked his cigarette in silence until it was completely smoked.

But there was one time when he made a mistake. It happened in the yard at Kano barracks. All the soldiers saw it, and what we saw amazed us. What happened was that Mai Yanka lit his cigarette as usual in his hands. He flicked it up, but just then a breeze came, and that cigarette tumbled too far, so what Mai Yanka caught between his teeth was not the filter end but the fire end, which jammed quite far inside his mouth! He shuddered, and a small whimper came from his throat. Maybe the fire was burning his throat. Very slowly he took the cigarette out of his mouth and held it in front of his face. Next he did a strange thing. Evie, he put the cigarette back between his teeth again, the fire end, and closed his mouth around it!

Only a small part of the filter end was poking out from his mouth. I could not believe my eyes. Mai Yanka looked at all the soldiers with a sly look, as if he were daring us to speak. He shuddered again and a small puff of cloud came out from his mouth. Not one person said a single word. Mai Yanka is a famous man. He has done things to human beings that no human being can ever do to a fellow human. Now plenty of smoke was coming from Mai Yanka's mouth, and now smoke started to come out of his nose as well, and smoke was pouring from his whole face. Evie, he looked like a kettle boiling on a stove.

Do you know what Mai Yanka did next? He started to smile. Now you know that this Mai Yanka is a famous man. As he smiled the smoke rose into the air above his head, and it was snatched by the breeze, and suddenly I saw it form into strange shapes before my eyes, snakes and arms and fists and smashed faces and women's breasts and the Devil's horns and broken teeth and penises and old men's beards. I asked myself what would happen if that cigarette wasn't finished soon. Would Mai Yanka catch fire? Would he melt? Would he ever be the same man after that fire inside his brain? Mai Yanka grinned back at us as if he was enjoying that cigarette more than any other cigarette he had ever smoked in his whole life. When it was finished his face was very dark. He spat the butt on to the drill yard, then pulled his boots and socks off one by one. He took his shirt off as well, and then he started to pace back and forth across the drill yard, very quickly, back and forth and to and fro, swinging his arms. Mai Yanka was cooling off.

Now it is late at night. Evie, it has taken me longer than I thought to write this letter. I am tired and in one minute I will put my pen down and go to the kitchen and drink some whisky with Sue. Then perhaps I will come back and continue to write this letter. Or perhaps I will go to sleep and continue to write tomorrow evening when I get back from work.

So, it is the next evening after I wrote those words about Mai Yanka and the mistake he made with his cigarette. Evie, I know I am taking a lot of your time with this letter. Please have patience! I will not waste any more time. I will get straight to the point of what I am trying to tell you, which is more terrible than the things I have thus far related.

I was telling you about the Ibos and how some of them had managed to escape up on to the plane. Well, now Mai Yanka looked up at the plane and shouted, 'Ibos off!' I don't know how the Ibos could come down without steps. He shouted again, 'If you do not come down, know that things will be very bad for you.' More faces appeared at the windows of the plane. But the Ibos did not come down. Now it was Mai Karfi's turn to shout. He said, 'Perhaps you do not understand what my colleague is telling you. I will speak plainly. If you do not come down now, we will crucify you.' The Ibos did not come down. Mai Karfi said, 'OK. I will leave you to think about what I have just said.'

Someone was sent to get some hot drink. We passed the bottles around between the soldiers. When we finished, Mai Karfi went up to the plane and shouted at the Ibos. He said that it was their last chance to come down. They did not come down. He said, 'Bring me a rocket gun.' Some soldiers went to the Land Rover and brought out the rocket gun. All the time it was being built Mai Karfi cursed the Ibos. He called them stupid goat and nyamiri and he told them that Ironsi was nyamiri, and that many Ibos had been killed and now it was the turn of the Hausas to rule. When the rocket gun was built Mai Karfi pointed it at the belly of the plane. I could see the faces of the Ibos in the windows. Their eyes were very wide. But they did not come down. Mai Karfi thought for several minutes. He talked to Mai Yanka. I think that he was afraid to rocket the plane. The reason is because it belongs to a European. After some time Mai Karfi shouted at the Ibos. He said, 'OK. Listen to me. You cannot stay on that plane for ever. We are patient. We will wait. Perhaps we will find another set of steps. Perhaps we will open fire with our rifles. Perhaps you will die of thirst. Perhaps I will rocket the plane. But whatever happens you will all die. Listen to me. Listen to what I propose. If you come down from the plane now, not all of you will die. Do you understand? If you come down now only the men will die, not your women or children. That is all I have to say.' Mai Karfi paused. Then he said, 'My colleague and I will smoke a cigarette and when we have finished you will give me an answer.'

I do not know what the atmosphere was like on that plane as Mai Karfi and Mai Yanka smoked their cigarettes. When they were completely smoked the door of the plane opened and an Ibo man was standing in the doorway. He looked very small. All the soldiers pointed their rifles at his heart, myself included. The Ibo man said, 'We will come down.' His voice was stony. 'How will we come down?' That was a question every soldier was asking himself. I was no exception. The sun was very bright. One of the soldiers suggested that we should make them jump and smash into the ground. Everyone laughed, even Mai Yanka. The Ibos in the plane were no longer looking out of the windows. They had become quiet. Mai Karfi thought for a bit then ordered us to form a line of twenty soldiers, ten on one side and ten on the other side, standing face to face. We had to hold hands with the soldier opposite to us, with our arms crossed over very tightly to form a hammock on to which the Ibos would jump.

The Ibo man watched from the door of the plane. He didn't jump but instead said, in the same stony voice as before, 'What are you going to do with us?' 'Shoot you,' Mai Karfi said. 'When?' 'Now,' Mai Karfi said. 'Where?' the Ibo man said. 'Here,' Mai Karfi said. 'On the runway. Against the wall.' 'And you will not shoot the women and children?' 'No,' Mai Karfi said, 'that is what I have said.' 'What will you do with the women and children?' the Ibo man said. 'We will send them to the hospital at Enugu. Now, jump! I will count to three.'

That is what the Ibos did, they jumped, the women, the children, and the men. There were nine of them, three men, four women and two children. The children were two girls who were gripping their mother's breasts. Most of them were bleeding. It was a terrible sight. I had to look. But I could not say a thing. One of the women could not stand up because her foot was shot off, and her daughter just stood beside her and held on to her hand. A Land Rover came, and the women and children got in, and the Land Rover drove away to Enugu hospital.

Now it was the three men who were left. Mai Karfi lined them up. No one spoke for quite a bit of time. Two of the men were bleeding, one from his arm and one from his head and leg as well. Mai Karfi said, 'Has anyone anything to say?' No one replied. He asked again. One of the Ibo men said that he had something to say, the one who was bleeding from his head and leg. Mai Karfi asked why he had kept quiet at first. The Ibo man said he had only just thought of something that he wanted to say. 'Say,' said Mai Karfi. 'What have I done?' the man said. 'Do you want to know what you have done?' Mai Karfi shouted. 'Do you remember January 15th?' The man replied that he remembered January 15th but even before January 15th he had been in the Police Force and that he was neither a politician nor a soldier. Mai Karfi shouted, 'Nonsense. The point is that you are an Ibo man.' Mai Yanka dragged that Ibo man to the wall. The Ibo man started to struggle and shout, but Mai Yanka is very strong. Mai Yanka is thin like a hungry cat, but he is very strong. The Ibo man struggled harder, and Mai Yanka hit him on the head with his gun. A hole appeared in the Ibo man's head, and blood poured from it. He still struggled, but now he was twitching as well, and Mai Yanka kicked him on to the ground and dragged him against the the wall and shot him in the head.

Mai Karfi spoke to the two Ibos who were still alive. He said, 'Has anyone got anything to say?' The second Ibo man, who was an old man with bullet wounds in his arms, said, 'May God forgive the Hausas for they do not know what they are doing. May God bring unity to Nigeria.' This made the soldiers laugh again. Mai Karfi laughed loudly too, and then Mai Yanka took the old man to the wall and made him kneel on the ground with his face against the wall, and he did that quietly, and then we heard him praying to God, and Mai Yanka shot him in the head. He fell down on top of his dead brother with his head in his dead brother's lap, right where his blokkus were, and when the soldiers saw this they let out plenty of cheers and laughter, and more hot drink was passed around. Myself, I did not want to cheer, because although the Ibos were not my brothers, even so they were not my enemy. But I could not do a single thing. Evie, I could do nothing at all, because I was not Hausa and I had to prove to the Hausas that I wanted the Ibos out of the North. That was what I had to do if I did not want to die.

When the drinking and laughing finished we turned to the last Ibo man, who was still alive. He was a young man with a handsome face. If Mai Yanka is ugly this man was handsome to the same degree that Mai Yanka is not. Mai Karfi said to him, 'Have you anything to say?' He looked at Mai Karfi in his eye but did not say anything. Mai Karfi stood looking at him in the eye and taking puffs of his cigarette. The Ibo man smiled to himself and then spat on the feet of Mai Karfi. Mai Karfi did not flinch. Very slowly he said, 'I see we will have to shut up your foolish mouth.' The Ibo man smiled again. Even though he was very handsome when he smiled his face became even more handsome than before. He smiled and then he spat on the feet of Mai Karfi. This time Mai Karfi flinched. He said, 'Take that shege and hold him tight.' Two solders took his arms and twisted them behind his back. Mai Karfi said, 'Get me some hot drink.' We drank from the bottles of hot drink, and the soldiers mocked the Ibo man. They told him things were very bad for him and that he was not going to live many more minutes, and that the minutes he had left in this life would be the most terrible time for him.

When all the soldiers had drunk plenty of hot drink, Mai

Karfi made us quiet and took a big swig from the bottle and with the bottle still in his hand he said to the Ibo man, 'Let me tell you a story.' All the soldiers looked at Mai Karfi with wide eyes. We knew what this meant. So now he was telling this Ibo man a story. Well, it was not going to be a happy afternoon for the Ibo man. The Ibo man did not seem interested at all. He just went on smiling and staring. Mai Karfi said, 'Once there was a boy called Mai Yanka.' I had heard the story one time before. 'One day Mai Yanka saw a sheep's head in a butcher's window,' Mai Karfi said. 'He told his father about the sheep. His father said, "Go and buy me the sheep's head!" Mai Yanka went to the butcher and bought the sheep's head,' said Mai Karfi, 'but on the way home he ate the meat and returned to his father with the skull in his hand. "What have you brought me?" his father said. "A sheep's head," Mai Yanka replied. "Where are the eyes?" his father said. "The sheep was blind," Mai Yanka replied. "Where is the tongue?" his father said. "The sheep was dumb," Mai Yanka replied. "Where are the ears?" his father said. "The sheep was deaf," Mai Yanka replied.'

When Mai Karfi finished telling the story no one spoke for a long time. The Ibo man did not change his expression or even seem to hear at all. I could hear the insects in the grass. It was late in the afternoon but the sun was still bright. After a few minutes Mai Karfi looked at the Ibo man. He said, 'How do you like the story?' The Ibo man did not say anything. Mai Karfi said, 'I must tell you something about my colleague. Stand forward.' Mai Yanka stood forward. 'This is Mai Yanka. Do you know what Mai Yanka means?' The Ibo man didn't move or make a noise. Mai Yanka stood still and watched the Ibo man for a minute, then he took a knife out from his trousers. The Ibo man did not change his expression in any way that I could see. Mai Karfi said, 'You know, nyamiri, humans are very like animals. There is really only a small difference between an animal and a human being, especially an Ibo brute like you. You refuse to speak. But we will make you scream.'

Evie, what happened next happened very quickly. Mai Yanka stepped up to the Ibo man with his knife in his hand and stuck it into the left side of the Ibo man's face and then into the right side, and his face burst open and blood poured from it, and when Mai Yanka stepped back he was holding the Ibo man's eyes in his hand. What was strange was that the Ibo man did not make a sound. He was shaking and falling on the soldiers, but he did not make a noise. This made Mai Karfi angry. He said, 'So, even now you do not speak.' Mai Yanka threw the eyes on the runway and flipped a cigarette into his mouth and approached the Ibo man. He held his ear in his left hand and sliced it off his head. It came off just like that. Some of the soldiers were not laughing any more. When Mai Yanka sliced his right ear off I began to vomit. The next time I looked it was when two soldiers were holding his mouth open and Mai Yanka was putting his hand inside his mouth. Mai Yanka pulled out his tongue with his fingers. Evie, that tongue came out further than I knew a person's tongue could come out of his mouth. I have never seen something so terrible as that tongue on that face with no ears and no eyes and blood pouring from it. It was just as Mai Yanka was pulling out his tongue that the Ibo man began to scream. I vomited again. When I looked the Ibo man was lying on the ground and the soldiers were beating him with their rifles. Now his face was completely gone. I did not beat him with my rifle. I just stood on that runway watching. Do you understand what I am saying? I just stood and watched them beat that Ibo man. I knew I was condemning myself for all eternity, but I just watched.

29

Last Visit to Mr Rafferty

I visited Mr Rafferty today. We had arranged to meet outside the institution, by the churchyard gates, but when I arrived he wasn't there. The air was mild but damp. The sun nowhere to be seen. Yes, the sun could be seen, I don't want to mistake any facts, there was a tiny trace of it, a leaden spoke of sunlight basking on the cemetery lawn. I stood watching the light on the unkempt grass, wet from the early rain. It wasn't green but a hazy dun colour, like everything else that day. It was because of the dark glasses I was wearing, I realize now. The glasses are large and rectangular. The lenses extend around my ears, covering my temples, the kind partially sighted people wear, or the very old; and it was from my neighbour, the blind old woman who says *Pff* instead of good morning, that I stole them.

There I stood by the churchyard gates. Everything was dim and quiet. It was Sunday, and the street was remarkably bare. Nobody seemed to have any business in town. I turned and pressed my face between the bars of the gate. I watched the trees lining the cemetery path, saw their boughs swaying in the wind, displaying the first shoots of spring. I don't know how much time went by. I said to myself, *Perhaps Mr Rafferty has forgotten our arrangement*, and felt a sliding sensation, since I'd been looking forward to this visit. Did I miss my grandfather? I think rather it was because of a hope. Three weeks ago I completed my transcription of Ade's letter. Since then I've been barely able to write. In the attic all is quiet. The sounds of my past are muted too. The only unceasing noise is the ringing in my ears, now nearer, now further, now filling my head. It seems to grow louder as the other sounds fall quiet. I write 'ringing', but it is also a hissing, roaring, buzzing, humming, fizzing, and any number of maddening sounds. Sometimes they are soft and merely annoying. At other times they are so persistently loud as to torment me. And so, frustrated by my internal clamours, I've been unable to concentrate on my past. Sometimes I think I should stop writing my history altogether.

When, previously, I turned to my papers – transcribing Mother's diary, as well as Kemi Olabode's pamphlet relating the Benin massacre, and Ade's letter – I felt calm, a kind of happy emptiness, despite the appalling content of the stories. Copying, I was able to work for hours without pause. I forgot all noises, internal and external, past and present. No doubt they continued to sound, but I no longer heard them. It was as if a mesh of silence had fallen and enveloped me, as if the radio silence I loved as a child had invaded me once again. To cease writing in my own words and simply copy and copy and copy – that is something I would like to do. But first let me try to relate my trip to Edinburgh. Perhaps, by writing about the present, I will be able to block out its noise and finish with these stories of my past, complete my history before it is lost.

Forward.

I felt a presence behind me, turned and saw my grandfather. He was dressed in a raincoat and hat and, with his round un-evenly shaved face, he looked ancient and lovely in the tawny light. I saw immediately he was in one of his restless moods. He'd dressed hurriedly. His trousers were somebody else's, and he'd mixed up his coat buttons. At that moment every sad thought vanished from my mind. He clutched me to his chest.

He gave off a pungent, earthy scent, a smell of damp wool and rotten leaves (Perry had died, and Mr Rafferty had taken over the hothouse). Then he spoke – but no sound came from his mouth. 'Sorry,' I said. My earplugs! If I was to communicate with him it was necessary for me to unblock my ears. I removed the cotton wool and put it in my coat pocket. I had expected, the instant of removing the plugs, the light, the full sunlight of sound, to intrude blindingly into my day. But the world was silent as before. I looked at the ground, astonished. Had I become completely deaf to the outside world? It is true that sometimes I hear little for hours on end, but I had thought this was because the attic had fallen silent. For the first time I was out of doors without my earplugs – and on the street all was quiet. Mr Rafferty's lips continued to move. I linked my arm in his, and we set off down Mankind Street.

The question was to examine this new silence. It had a disturbing empty quality (accentuated by the dark glasses), very different from the attic, that echo chamber of whispers and faint rustlings. And this quiet on the street was different too from when I stuffed my ears with cotton wool. Then I heard, more clearly than ever, the din of myself. We turned on to a busier street then joined a path that wound over a rolling grass heath. I looked at Mr Rafferty, whose lips were moving. He was talking. But to whom? Did he know I could not hear a single word? That's not quite right. Did he know I could *scarcely* hear a single word? I caught, here and there, a murmur corresponding to the motions of his lips. In truth I was not completely deaf. But it strikes me that I would be better off if I were completely deaf, since I heard enough to be distracted by the sound of his words, although too little to make sense of them.

What am I saying?

Where was I? On the street. With my grandfather. We walked beside a rise of black rock and sick-looking weeds. At the top of the hill we stopped. That's when I noticed the passers-by, looking at me, not at my face but right into me. With my dark glasses and uneven gait it seemed they thought I couldn't see. They stared brazenly, amusement on their faces. I was almost totally deaf, and the passers-by looked at me in the mistaken belief that I was blind! It began to rain. I guided Mr Rafferty to a bus shelter, and we sat on the red plastic bench. The passers-by were no longer staring but running for cover. Under the low grey sky, on the black, narrow street of few sounds, I watched them flee. After a while my grandfather said, 'It's getting dark.' This I heard – I hear things a little more clearly when sitting – but not immediately. His words seemed to expire as soon as they left his mouth, before they made sense. It was like hearing a complex piece of music for the first time. I asked him to repeat. He did, a little louder. I shook my head, asked him to repeat himself once more. Finally he brought his lips up to my ear and shouted. My head rang. And yet I understood him. *It's getting dark*. It had taken nearly ten minutes for him to convey the simple fact that the afternoon was drawing to a close!

How strange the human heart is! My condition was dismal. I was wet, cold, deaf, mistaken for blind, sitting at a bus stop sheltering from the rain, with a man who is not complete in the mind, myself of late having been feeling strange, bodily, and spiritless also, resigned to the knowledge that things are changing and ending – and yet my joy was limitless.

I asked my grandfather to lean forward and speak into my better, right ear. I held up my hand for him to stop, so that I might take in what he had said. And yet this time all I heard was a series of consonant-sounds and vowel-sounds, scattered, dissipated, each one isolated from the rest. They carried less significance than a sneeze, since I was absorbing only the physical or tonal quality of his words. I asked him to repeat himself once again, and, as he did, at certain moments, without being able to give the sequence any clear sense, I managed to collect, hold and finally reproduce, in my head, the sound of individual words; from these I managed to piece together a kind of meaning.

'Yes!' I cried, beside myself with joy. It was as if, after listening to the complex piece a number of times, I began to pick out a phrase or harmony. I wanted to be certain I had understood correctly, so I repeated what I thought he had said. Mr Rafferty stood up and began to wring his hands, a new development. What was he trying to convey?

'Sorry?' I said. He repeated. We repeated the process just described. Finally I understood that I had been shouting.

'Ah,' I said, as quietly as I could. And yet it was hard for me to judge the volume of my voice. In this the loss of hearing is like the loss of smell. The person who cannot smell may give off a strong unpleasant odour, and so it is with deafness; unable to hear the fullness of my own voice, I am prone to shout.

'Now we have established I need to speak quietly,' I said or shouted, 'let's go back to what you were trying to say *originally*.' I repeated what I thought he'd originally said. Mr Rafferty concentrated hard, trying to string my words together, then smiled and nodded his head. Apparently my meaning matched his meaning. What a bother to understand the most basic things! It had taken ten minutes to establish that the afternoon was ending. A further ten for me to understand I had been shouting. Night was drawing in. The longer we talked the darker it became. Nevertheless, we proceeded. Word by word. Sentence by sentence. No syntax to speak of. Here is a part of our conversation.

Mr Rafferty: It's getting dark.
Me: Let's get along.
Mr Rafferty: Where to?
Me: Back home.
Mr Rafferty: . . .
Me: Sorry?
Mr Rafferty: . . .
Me: I can't hear you.
Mr Rafferty: You're shouting!
Me: I'll try to speak quieter.
Mr Rafferty: Sorry?
Me: I said I'll speak quietly.
Mr Rafferty: Night is drawing in.
Me: The longer we talk the darker it becomes.
Mr Rafferty: Where are we?
Me: I don't understand.
Mr Rafferty: Who are you?

Between my grandfather's words and my replies a greater or lesser interval passed. The problem was that in the interval he grew impatient, and often spoke again, so my replies did not always connect to what had gone immediately before. What is more, I tended to respond without taking the necessary time to make sense of his words, acting on what I believed he *might* have said, rather than what I thought he *had* said. And when I paused so he could absorb my response, we encountered further problems, for once he had strung together from my words the sentence I had pieced together from his, as far as I understood it, the original meaning was more or less changed, or altogether lost, according to I don't know what principle. We were like deaf-mutes, signing in the dark. And indeed, as we talked, I saw pools of streetlight sparkling on the wet road.

Dusk had turned to night. Soon after, we came to a halt. Not a conclusion, nothing so satisfying. Mr Rafferty stood, turned and in exasperation leaned his forehead against the bus shelter. I took my glasses off and rubbed my temples. His breath was steaming up the perspex. The little round of fog grew with each exhalation. I stepped forward and brought my right cheek close to his left cheek. I wanted to get a better look. He didn't seem to notice me, so I leaned my forehead against the shelter. For a moment our breaths mingled on the perspex. There was no one else on the street. We remained side by side without moving. Now and then a drop of moisture, slipping down the perspex, cut a channel through the fog. We tried to converse again, this time with me talking and him tracing words in the fog, but without success, for it seemed that with each word we spoke we understood less, and the more we talked the darker it became.

30

Auto da Fé

Let me do away with my papers. I do not want to see them again. I will burn them, my personal papers I mean. The others I will keep. The *Encyclopaedia Britannica*? It will remain in the attic to help me with my work. As legs for my desk. As printed matter to transcribe. What else? Novels, histories, newspapers, books of poems and essays, testimonies, labels, handbooks, posters, timetables. These papers will also be saved from the fire. My objects? It is long past the time when I should have cleared out the attic.

In a moment I will carry my objects to the garden. I will descend the ladder with a succession of loads and assemble them into a heap by the marram grass. No, not a heap. By nature I have always been meticulous. So then. I will categorize them, according to their degree of inflammability. I will start with my own papers, Damaris' diary, and my mother's, and Ade's letters, all those I have copied on to my computer. I will also burn the personal papers I have not transcribed. Yes, on to that pile I will throw Aunt Phoene's letters, tickets from Damaris' shows, 'First Snow in Port Suez', Taiwo's Gideon Bible, my father's magazines, as well as the mimeographed sheet depicting the bird's-eye view of Lagos (whose street-names I had planned to type out). The sheets of my history? They ought to be the first of my papers into the flames; for, having been dried out by the sun, they are highly flammable. What is more, they are the most personal of all my papers. And yet I have decided to spare them, even though it pains me to corrupt my order, since I wish to continue to block the light. *Objects to be spared*. That is a category all of its own. It will include – let me see – the wardrobe door, my computer, printer, blank paper, heater, my supply of beans. What else? I will keep the hand-painted miniatures Mr Rafferty gave my mother (every now and then, as I work on my transcriptions, I may want to gaze on them, as others gaze on a view, you never know): the littoral with full tide and crab, the warship setting sail from an Eastern city, Scheherazade kneeling beside King Shahrayar, who is wrapped in the bejewelled blankets of his divan. Once my personal papers have been separated from the heap, I will set them alight. Then I will cast my collection of photographs into the fire. One by one will go pictures of Damaris – naked in Easdale, asleep on Route 61 – as well as group photos of Ben, Iffe, Ade and myself standing awkwardly on the lawn in Ikoyi, also the portrait of Hogan Bassey, glistening with sweat and holding aloft his champion's belt, torn from the boxing magazine, and Father on his swing, and the drop spilling upward from the bowl of milk, together with the family album, Mother in her watch shop, the bagpiper with enormous cheeks, and all the rest. Next, I will feed the fire with the fabrics I own, including all my clothes (except my pyjamas and dressing-gown, which I am wearing): the patchwork quilt, the Indian dhurri, the seaweed-green chiffon scarf, the white dress I wore on the Royal Mile to mimic Damaris in mime. Next, animal matter: an elephant tusk, a fishing eagle Father shot during his tour with Mother, also the mouse's tail, my whale-tooth necklace, a twist of hair from Riley's pointer, and my collection of feathers, including those I kept from *The Snow Queen*, as well as the mappa mundi, I must not forget the mappa mundi, since it is made of vellum.

Now I have mentioned it, let me pause to say a few words

about that decrepit map, before returning to the matter of the pyre. Throughout this history I have noted its dissolution, mostly on account of the moths. What I have not realized until now is the ingenious effect the process of destruction has brought about. A moment ago I got up, unhooked the mappa mundi and threw it on the floor, with the other animal matter to be burned. And there on the wall, in the space where the map had hung, I noticed a series of patches – light, roughly circular shapes, set off against the darkness of the wood. I stepped back. I stared at the pattern on the wall, then understood. The moths had eaten holes in the mappa mundi, exposing the wooden boards beneath. Where the holes appeared, the sun (this, before I covered the skylight) had blanched the wood. And so the mappa mundi, that fantastic counterfeit which my father bought in 1963, has left a kind of negative impression of its decayed state, a series of brightnesses, like smaller continents themselves, joined by darker connecting lines. All that is left of the map is a record of the moths' hunger, a static, lucent accumulation of all the seas, nations and races they have devoured, a disturbing image of dissolution that has reduced the original (if I may say this of a forgery) to a few faint patches on the attic wall. As I continue to gaze at the wall, I realize that this second map is not so much a negative impression, but rather a reinterpretation of the first. Of course, the moths did not honour national boundaries or geographical facts, but diverted rivers, joined states, parted continents, creating fresh rifts, new gulfs; they flattened mountain ranges and worked landmasses into disparate shapes. The process of creative destruction was arbitrary; or rather, the process was dictated entirely by the hunger of the moths. And yet it strikes me now that the map engendered by the moths is every bit as real or valid a representation of the world as the mappa mundi itself.

Where was I? The fire. After animal I will throw in all those objects made of vegetable matter: elephant grass, melon seeds, the length of twine which I stretched taut and passed my finger lightly across to produce a tremulous humming, as well as mother's trunk itself. What next? Technology: the pocket watch, the tape recorder, the telephone from empty cans and lengths of string, not to mention Father's bike, and the phonograph with its great horn. But how will I know if they will burn less readily than certain items of animal matter? It is not so easy to order my objects strictly in terms of inflammability.

Perhaps I should begin again, using a different method. Maybe I should burn my objects chronologically, according to their date of arrival in the world. No, this method would not be an easy thing to determine either. To judge the age of the elephant tusk, say, I would need to know the age of the elephant. And how to judge the age of the elephant in comparison to the chameleon, or the slate from Easdale, or the mappa mundi? (A further complication: should the impression of the map now be classed as an object? If so, how would I burn it without destroying my attic? And into what category would it fall? Animal? Vegetable? *Unica*?). Impossible!

What I would like is to link each of my objects in a particular way, before throwing them into the fire. For instance, by common function: the feathers, pencils and printer's set (systems of writing); the railway timetable, the elephant tusk, Father's bike and the boat setting sail from an Eastern city (transport). Or else I would like to group them by relationships based not on similarity but on opposition, or by some tangential association, the gauzy dress followed by the chameleon skin, fireworks followed by candles and Father's cigarettes, the machete followed by the mappa mundi, the feathers by the LP Damaris gave me when we lived in Bedouin. It would not be hard to burn my objects according to this system, but it would be nearly useless, for if I leave my objects unsorted and take a pair at random, I can be sure they will have at least three things in common. And does it matter what order I choose? In the end they will all be burned. And isn't it precisely to do away with order that I have decided to burn my objects?

Forward.

So then, I will simply start a fire and throw everything into it, all the objects I have mentioned, and all those I have not. And if I find the radio I will throw that into the fire too. It will be a happy day. I will think about my history for a final time. I will shake with laughter, an indecent, shameful, helpless laughter. I have lived among this clutter for too long. I shall not put up with it any more. A superb day. A thousand useless possessions – the frightful prodigality of objects – which, undisturbed, might have survived for decades, will be destroyed in a single afternoon.

Will they make a noise as they burn? A great noise! They will burst, hissing and snapping, cracking like crinoline, like sticks, like flags. – And I note here the day in America, with Damaris, in San Francisco, the afternoon we found a ginger dog, and walked it back along the avenue with flags snapping in the wind, an incident Damaris started to relate in her diary, on 26 October 1972, but which she did not finish and whose conclusion I now recall: how when we got to his master's door we knocked, and an old young man or a young old man with a white quiff answered; how we both began to laugh, as he cried, 'Brumby!'; how Brumby cowered, and the man came out on to the porch and grabbed the dog by the collar to drag him into the house; how, as he did, we could see the hairs on the man's arms turning into vines; how I wanted to grab Brumby but I couldn't, so I clung to the railings; how Damaris clung to me; how the man said, 'Damn dog's always running away'; how, as he closed the door, Damaris said, 'Can we have our reward?'; how the man stopped and looked at us, then stared and smiled, seeing the goodness in us, between us; how he went away, leaving the door open; how Brumby followed him tail down; how, as we stood there, we saw vines trailing from the wallpaper, choking the doorway; how the man suddenly materialized, parting the vines, plucking from them two glowing balls; how he said, 'Here you go, girls'; how he closed the door; how we weighed the oranges in our hands; how I said, 'Should we throw them away?'; and how Damaris said, 'They are our reward'; how we noticed that they were the colour of Brumby's eyes; how Damaris said, 'We can't throw them away'; how we heard the man shouting; how Brumby yelped; how I cried, 'Brumby! Damaris! Do something!'; how Damaris said, 'I can't, he doesn't belong to us'; how she threw her orange hard and we watched it burst and dribble down the man's door; how I threw my orange, and it fell short and rolled back down the steps towards us, following us; how we backed away and looked at each other and grabbed hands and ran.

Forward.

The attic. On my return it will be nearly empty. The acoustics will be different, but that will not matter. There will be very little left. My computer, printer, wardrobe door, the volumes, and so on. That is all. That will be all. It is a moment I have been working towards for months. I will rebuild my desk. I will open my computer. I will choose one of my papers and begin to copy. Every now and then, as I work, I will print my transcriptions out and tape them over the skylight. And at the sight of those words which I will look at without knowing what they mean, I will feel happy, happier than I have done in years. A fresh start. I will live in my attic. I will never go out. I will take my supply of beans by delivery. I will sleep on my mattress, unless I decide to burn that too. In that case I will sleep on the floor, under my desk, my heater beside me. Perhaps, on occasion, a few faint sounds will break the calm, a little cry perhaps, a clock ticking. I will hear them. But I will not let them affect my work. The din of myself? It has not gone away, although it has lessened, now that I have begun to transcribe. That is not to say it will always be so. It will come and go, as it has always done. I am still terrified of it. Perhaps I will get to know it better, to understand what it wants. I will feel calm. Happy. Sometimes I will think of the silence. Knowing there is no such thing, I will think of it. I will listen. I will not hear. I will listen. I will listen into the silence, into its centre. That absence too will have to be imagined. There have been times in writing this history when I have asked myself what the first thing was that I ever heard. Once, when I was lying in the elephant grass, I tried to imagine the world before it was made. I was unable. I am no closer now. I will continue to try. I will continue to try to imagine the world as it was before the great noise which formed it, this world which could not have known such a noise because it existed – if that is the word – in silence.

Postscript

This book contains passages, all of them slightly altered, from the following works:

Charles Allen, *Tales from the Dark Continent*, part of the trilogy, *Plain Tales from the British Empire*, Little, Brown, 1998.

Isaac Babel, *Red Cavalry*, trans. David McDuff, Penguin, 2005.

Günter Grass, *The Tin Drum*, trans. Ralph Manheim, Vintage, 2004.

George Perec, *Life A User's Manual*, trans. David Bellos, Harvill, 1996.

Bruno Schulz, *The Street of Crocodiles*, trans. Celina Wieniewska, Penguin, 1992.

Joan Sharwood-Smith *Diary of a Colonial Wife: An African Experience*, Radcliffe Press, 1992.

Robert Louis Stevenson, 'From a Railway Carriage'.

Acknowledgements

My first debt goes to Natasha Soobramanien. I couldn't have written this book without her – literally. She was my first reader throughout and consequently knew the book, and Evie, better than anyone else bar me. It seemed natural, then, and wholly in keeping with her contribution thus far, when, on completing the second part, I asked her to write Damaris' diary. I gave her some dates and a few sketchy plot lines; other than this, she conceived and wrote what turned out to be chapters twenty-five and twenty-six entirely without my meddling.

Enormous thanks must also go to my family, Glenna, Derek, Hilery, Martin, Saul and Thea.

Tracy Bohan at the Wylie Agency was amazing: enthusiastic, encouraging, patient and a great reader.

Thanks also to my editors at Hamish Hamilton: Simon Prosser, Juliette Mitchell and Anna Kelly.

I am grateful to the Arts Council East and the Charles Pick Fellowship for their generous financial support of this project.

Many others helped in the process of writing, each in their individual ways. Thanks to you all:

Sara De Bondt, Fiona Bowden, Lawrence Bradby, Jon Cook,

Andrew Cowan, Owen Dudley Edwards, Oliver Emanuel, Alex Graves, Sara Heitlinger, Sophie Logan, Robert McGill, Richard Misek, Sam Mungall, Paul Nugent, Martin Pick, Chris Power, Max Schaefer, Michal Shavit, Ali Smith, Lucy Steeds, Mada Vicassiau, Yair Wallach and Josh Warren.